HEART OF VENOM

HEART OF VENOM

THE VALLEY OF SCALES SAGA

SYDNEY WILDER

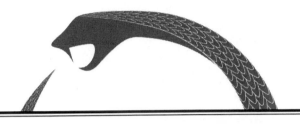

To my parents, Betsy and Wayne.

You've always been so supportive,
from giving me my first computer at age six
to buying the first physical copy of my books.
I love you both.

Table of Contents

Prologue

*C*ASSANDRA COULDN'T HEAR THEM.

But she knew that they weren't far behind.

She couldn't run, so she pressed on at an ambling jog, stopping every few minutes to catch her breath. Everything from her navel down was on fire, her body screaming at her to go back to the shack and get some rest. To abandon the bundle in her arms out here alone, in the woods, and forget all about this surreal mess.

She leaned against a tree branch, her shaky legs barely able to hold her weight. Above them, her belly was still swollen, puffy and sagging like a partially deflated balloon. She couldn't see her own clothes in the rapidly fading sunlight, her body too cast in shadows to make out her features. But she could feel it, damp and incriminating, staining the cloth of her dress just below her hips.

Blood.

She was far from healed down there. In her weak, vulnerable state, she felt like her body was being torn apart for a second time. And this journey, sneaking through the woods all the way from Live Oak to Vale, would only exacerbate her pain. She was beginning to doubt if she'd ever make it there at all.

She peered down at the bundle in her arms. The living creature within cooed, a strangely human action for a being almost entirely covered in scales.

Yet when the baby opened her mouth, Cassandra could clearly see them. Long, narrow, needle-like teeth, one on each side of her lips.

Fangs. An irrefutable trait of her half-Naga heritage.

Cassandra suppressed the shudder trickling down her spine and kept walking. Thankfully, the baby was calm, satiated by her meal from earlier. Cassandra was relieved that she'd taken to eating reptilian food; those venom-filled fangs would make breastfeeding impossible.

She still didn't know how those at her destination would react to the baby. Sure, she was covered in scales, but she was still a child, wasn't she? She was still half-human. She deserved a chance.

The baby's mouth gaped open, and Cassandra knew she was about to let out a cry. She soothed the baby with a gentle shush.

I'm so sorry, she sighed, locking eyes with the little infant. Despite the child's serpentine features, she still had one trait that was distinctly Cassandra's – those vibrant blue eyes.

I can't raise you. But I'm going to give you the best chance I can.

A faint rumble in the distance caused Cassandra to jolt, taking off at a slow jog. She had to be close. Although it was hard to tell - the rapidly darkening forest was incredibly disorienting. Taking the main road wasn't an option. Not only would she be easily spotted, but she wouldn't be able to hear them coming.

Because she was almost completely deaf.

Therefore, she had to rely on the shroud of the nighttime foliage to keep her safe. To keep her hidden. The woods were an endless maze that was easy to get lost in, which she hoped would keep her pursuers from finding her.

But she was beginning to get lost herself.

Veer to the right... no, left... I swear the main road shouldn't be too far from here...

Just... keep... walking...

Cassandra's knees buckled, and she fumbled to the ground, her legs folding in on themselves until she was in a squatting position. She pulled the infant closer to her chest, desperate to prevent it from crying.

Wait... is that... a light?

Cassandra struggled to her feet. Up on the top of a small hill, she could just barely make out the outline of a building. An old estate, its features barely visible under the orange glow of oil lamps.

The Thorburn Estate.

She knew that Lucy was long gone, and that Jonas had been in poor health for the past year. She knew that she couldn't let anyone there see her face or know who she was. And most importantly, she had no idea if the family would accept this half-reptilian baby.

But she had few options, and to her, this was the best one.

She had to give this child a chance.

Even if it wasn't with her own parents.

The uphill walk felt like an eternity, and by the end, Cassandra was nearly crawling on all fours. But she made it. The sconces outside the pillared entrance bathed her in a warm orange glow as she approached.

Cassandra placed the baby on the doorstep, an action that caused her a great deal of emotional turmoil. She couldn't raise her. She had her own family, her own life, one that she couldn't cast away to live in seclusion with a child that shouldn't even exist. She knew it was a selfish decision, but it was one that she wasn't willing to reconsider.

And on top of everything else, she was barely an adult herself.

She left one more item on the doorstep – a neatly folded note. One that she'd frantically scrawled before escaping the shack. Part explanation, part plea – Cassandra hoped it would help persuade them to not turn the infant away.

She took a deep breath, accepting her decision as final, and rang the doorbell.

She couldn't hear it go off, but she fled as soon as she released her finger from the button.

She didn't want to know what the answer was. Whether they'd accept her or not. All she wanted was to bolt, all the way back to Live Oak, and try to move on with her life. To try with every fiber of her being to forget this disaster ever happened.

Chapter 1

‹**My Father!?**›
Marissa didn't mean for her shout to echo throughout the entire hut, but as soon as the Naga's words hit her ears, her shock and bewilderment spilled out like a tidal wave. This was the moment she never thought would happen. Out of the thousands of Naga in the Valley of Scales, *this* was the one responsible for her existence. The one that they'd scoured the entire valley for, the one that bit a human and burned down a mining camp.

The one that plotted to destroy Brennan.

She kept her gaze locked on the slit-eyed snake as he towered above her. Her reptilian nostrils flared, and her chest shook with every breath. Upon seeing her reaction, Ezrinth's face fell, his scaled hands loosening their grasp on the idol pieces. Marissa could feel her frantic thoughts tangling and writhing like a pit full of snakes. *All my life... wondering... waiting... trying to forget... I never thought I would find you.*

As the initial torrent of emotion wore off and Ezrinth's despondent gaze softened her frustration, Marissa managed to pull her spiraling mind together. <I'm sorry, I just... I don't understand. You're really my father? Where have you been all this time?>

<I can't imagine how difficult it's been for you.> Ezrinth's eyes dropped to the ground. He solemnly placed the idol pieces back on the pedestal and slithered into a chair, gesturing for Marissa to do the same. <My dear, I wish it was easier to explain. I've wanted to see you for so long. You were just a hatchling the last time I laid eyes on you...>

Ezrinth's thoughts trailed off, his words engulfed in sorrow. Marissa shifted in her seat, her scales quivering as she pondered the circumstances surrounding her birth. When she was a young child, she spent many nights contemplating her heritage, wondering where her mother and father might be. What it would be like to meet them, talk to them, touch them. In her dreams, she saw then as warm, loving beings, longing to raise her but torn apart by their vastly different origins. But the reality that they'd abandoned her always lurked in the back of her mind, and it cause a deep bubble of resentment to cloud her fond visions of them. The older she became, the more she pushed her parents out of her mind.

But Ezrinth was looking for me. He scoured the Valley of Scales, breaking into countless villages... but why did it take him eighteen years to find me?

Marissa's throat tightened as she realized Ezrinth was only half of the story.

\<My mother...>

\<Your mother was my best friend.> Ezrinth sighed. \<And I loved her dearly. We grew up together, visiting each other in secret for years. We were so happy together. All I wanted was to be with her... but she was always being pulled away by the human world.>

\<But where is she now?>

\<I don't know.> Ezrinth shook his head. \<She ran off with you shortly after you were born. I'm assuming she dropped you off at that horrid orphanage and fled for the kingdom. That was the last time I saw either of you. But-> Ezrinth's sorrows hardened, and his scaled face was steely with determination. \<Now that I have you back, my beloved child, I am determined to track her down and reunite this family. Your mother has been brainwashed by those humans, and I want to bring her back here, where she belongs.>

Marissa gulped as she caught a glimpse of the pedestal, just a few feet to the right of the giant, wistful Naga seated in the chair next to her. Ezrinth's remorseful tenderness mixed with the reality of his vile plans made Marissa's stomach swirl with too many emotions for her to comprehend.

\<But at what cost?>

Ezrinth's serpentine face hardened at Marissa's words, and he stood up straighter.

\<You're really going through with this?> Marissa continued, struggling to keep her tone from being accusatory. \<You're really going to destroy Brennan and kill thousands

of people? How does that make you any less terrible than the humans that made me live in a storeroom? Or the humans you claim brainwashed my mother?>

<I don't understand.> Ezrinth's thoughts were soft, but with a hint of a growl. <I saw where you were living. The humans treated you as a monster, didn't they?>

Monster. The same nefarious word that always snaked its way through Marissa's existence. She remembered the times when Arthur told her that she wasn't one... and then a horrible revelation about Ezrinth's plan made her stomach drop. *A week ago, before I met Arthur, before all this happened... I might have agreed to it.* The thought soured her throat, but she couldn't deny her previous reality. *Outcast, homeless, hated by humans...* but through it all, ever since she first bumped into Arthur at The Menagerie, she had seen glimpses of human compassion. Glimpses she refused to forget.

<You're right. Humans did hate me.> Marissa stated firmly, rising from her chair. <They did treat me as a monster. But if I help you, it will truly make me one. It will make me the villain the humans always believed me to be. So no, I won't agree to this.>

Ezrinth's nostrils flared. Marissa's stomach tightened as the warm paternal glow in his eyes faded and was replaced by fury at his daughter's indignance.

<Marissa, you- >

<Ezrinth, sir.> A sudden thought interrupted their minds. A tense-faced Varan guard popped into the room, his hesitant tone indicating his apologies for interrupting them.

<What is it?> Ezrinth huffed, his long body rising from his chair in slithering coils.

<My sincerest apologies, but at the entrance...>

<Let the guards deal with it.> Ezrinth hissed, turning back toward Marissa. <I'm busy.>

<But sir, it's a human. It's here alone and is carrying a strange object. Should we just kill it?>

<Yes, and- >

<Wait!!> Marissa shot out of her seat. Ezrinth and the Varan guard stared at her, their reptilian faces bewildered. She turned toward the guard. <What did the human look like?>

<Uh, it was a tall thin one, short hair the color of sandy dirt, had some of those wiry glass circles on its eyes...>

Marissa didn't hear another word. She dove out of the hut, her scaled legs pumping as she wove between wandering Varan and charged for the entrance to Komodo. As she ran, the faint shouting thoughts of Ezrinth and the Varan guard trickled through her mind as they chased after her. But she would worry about them later.

Right now, she had to find Arthur.

12 Hours Earlier

THERE WAS A SINISTER CHILL IN THE AIR AS Arthur charged through the maze of Silverkeep late into the night, jolting every time he heard footsteps in the distance. He didn't dare go home and change out of his fancy clothes – he needed to flee Brennan as quickly as possible. And as he did so, the reality that he and Marissa were now wanted fugitives sank to the bottom of his stomach like a rock.

Relief flooded his body as he reached the southern gates and approached the carriage house. The establishment was closed – the cashier's window was shuttered, and a long row of horses slumbered in their stalls. Arthur eyed a small slit where the shutters didn't quite reach the counter, and he discreetly slid two silver coins underneath the barrier. *It's not stealing if I paid them... right?* He swallowed heavily and spun around, cautious of potential onlookers. He knew how suspicious he looked - finely dressed young men didn't generally pilfer carts and ride off into the outer villages well past midnight. He smoothed his rumpled suit and ran a hand through his disheveled hair, trying not to appear as distraught as he felt.

Thankfully, the square was empty. His only company was the eerie orange glow of the streetlamps lining the road. He scampered into the stables, thankful that his black suit blended in with the inky darkness, and hitched the calmest horse to the nearest cart. His hands trembled as he fumbled with the harness, tacking up as quickly as possible while making sure every strap was secure. Within a few minutes, he perched himself in the front seat of the cart and emerged from the shadowy stables, the clip-clop of his horse's hooves ringing like gongs in his worried eardrums.

Arthur tilted his head up as he approached the southern gates, realizing that the indigo sky was so dark that he couldn't make out the spikes that lined the top of the massive iron barrier. He felt his breath hang in his chest as he caught a glimpse of the guards lining either side of the gates – the towering structures were attended to twenty-four hours a day. He exhaled, terrified that they would stop and question him. But the carriage house had been far enough away from the gates for him to steal a cart unnoticed, and the guards didn't seem perturbed. In a few swift motions, they hauled the heavy gates open, and Arthur passed through.

Maybe it's the clothes. He peered down at his wrinkled yet very expensive suit. He held his head up high as his horse trotted past the guards, emitting a facade of confidence. As much as he detested the fact, he knew that even just the appearance of wealth opened all sorts of doors. *Or in this case, gates.*

But it was all an illusion. He, Arthur Brennan, once a member of the royal family, was now a wanted man. He knew it wouldn't be long before word of his crimes crept through the rest of the kingdom. And by that time, he needed to be as far away from it as possible.

The journey was dark and quiet, which gave Arthur's mind the opportunity to haunt him with memories of the past few days. As his horse clip-clopped down the road, leaves crunching under its feet, all he could think about was Marissa. His face flushed with warmth as he pretended that she was sitting in the cart next to him - a dark-haired, pale-skinned woman with a scarf pressed against her face, her brilliant blue eyes burning with a mixture of fascination and fear. He took a deep sigh and reminisced on the two of them swimming through the stream, her bare scales glittering under the lacey bits of sunlight peeking through the trees. *Her voice, her laugh, her smile...* it sent a warm, burning sensation through his chest, like he'd had one too many glasses of mead.

But his sweet memories of her were entwined with pain and worry. He knew Marissa was on her way to Varan territory, and he had no idea how the reptilians would react to her presence. As desperate as he was to stay positive, he couldn't help but fear the worst, and he repeatedly shoved images of the reptilians slaying Marissa out of his mind.

But while he feared for Marissa, he also feared for his brother. The way Ramsey confronted him in the storage room at the Castellas' estate, his weary body leaning against the door frame. *His exhausted face, his frantic demeanor... what has he been through?* Ramsey was clearly much closer to King Gabriel than Arthur had realized, and it made him worry. Ramsey had always been stubbornly obedient, and Arthur feared that whatever the king had promised his brother was just a ruse to manipulate him.

He was so lost in thought that he hadn't realized that the winding dirt path was coming to an end; he was just a few miles from Varan territory. It was dawn, and a warm, orange glow was creeping up the indigo sky. He pulled the cart to a halt, his horse huffing and stomping its foot. In the still silence, Arthur noticed that the wind had picked up, carrying small brown oak leaves past the cart and bristling Arthur's suit jacket. *The weather really has been strange lately.*

The silence also made Arthur realize how exhausted he was. Realization overtook him, and he sighed. If he was going to trudge through reptilian territory and risk being killed on sight, he at least needed to be well-rested. He parked the cart behind a large oak tree and settled into the bed of the cart, covering his eyes with his maroon bow tie.

The one I spent twenty minutes digging out of storage to match Marissa's dress...

He took a deep breath and closed his eyes. Eventually, his fear and anxiety melted with his fading consciousness, and he fell asleep as the wind whistled around him.

AFTER MANY HOURS OF TRAVEL, BEING FORCED TO abandon his cart, and trudging through the thick Varan jungle with bulky armor slung over his shoulder, Arthur had finally made it.

It was now early afternoon, and he'd been dragging himself through the swampland for hours. As he stumbled wearily down the sandy path to Komodo, his dress shoes scuffed and his suit pants fraying at the hem, his harrowing journey through reptilian territory engulfed his mind.

The first and scariest obstacle was the human guards. As soon as he saw them earlier that day, patrolling the border between human and reptilian territory, he yanked back so forcefully on the reins that his horse jerked its head upwards. Not only were the guards a hindrance to Arthur's journey, but they were a frightening reminder of the escalating war. Arthur knew that it wouldn't be long before more guards joined them.

He had no choice but to abandon his horse and cart. *It really counts as stealing if I don't return them*, he grumbled as he snuck through the brush, keeping his eye on the guards in the distance. He knew from his university studies that the Varan capital wasn't too far away, but the trip would feel a lot longer in muggy clothes with the scaled armor set on his back.

Not to mention, if I encounter any Varan out hunting, they'll kill me on sight.

But he'd made it. The noonday sun was high in the sky, and just a few hundred feet beyond him was the entrance to the largest of the Varan settlements. *Marissa must be here.* As he trudged onward, the reality of how dangerous this plan was crept up his throat like bile. Not only was he praying Marissa was here, but also that she was unharmed. *What if she was rejected and turned away, or taken prisoner, or worse...*

He stopped. Three tall, gangly Varan, bare-chested but with their arms and legs adorned in bright strips of cloth, had caught sight of him up ahead. *I haven't seen a reptilian in years...* He stumbled backwards as fear gripped his stomach. One Varan ran back toward the settlement while the other two charged him, sharp hisses echoing from their throats. Arthur attempted to flee, but the Varan quickly tackled him, pinning his arms back with frightening strength. The armor set fell from his hands, thudding onto the sandy dirt at his feet.

Soft hisses echoed from one Varan to the other, and Arthur knew from the way they eyed each other that they were communicating. One of the Varan stepped behind Arthur and plucked the armor set off the ground. As it ran a crescent-shaped claw over the scales, its face contorted into a mixture of fear and horror. Arthur noticed its lower jaw tremble as its eyes crept from the remains of the slain reptilian back to the human who brought it there.

Arthur opened his mouth, but nothing came out. He had no way of communicating with them, and a scream would only alert the rest of the village. As the Varan glowered at him, hatred burning in their eyes, a deep, nauseating dread made his legs unsteady. *This is it. In my fear for Marissa and my anger over what the kingdom has done, I made the stupidest mistake of my life. These Varan blame me for this, and they're going to kill me. I just wish-*

"Arthur!!"

Is that...?

As he caught sight of her, running down the village path with a slithering Naga in tow, all Arthur wanted to do was leap past the stunned guards and hug her. Not only was she safe, but her sudden presence had saved him from certain death.

His eyes sparkled as he waved back at her.

"Marissa!!"

Chapter 2

A BOLT OF HAPPINESS SHOT THROUGH Marissa's heart as she saw Arthur at the entrance to Komodo. He was an unkempt mess; his suit was filthy and frayed at the hems, and his hair was damp from both sweat and the swampy humidity. He was a far cry from the well-dressed, distinguished royal who had escorted her to a fancy party the night before. But Marissa saw her joyous relief reflected in his forest-green eyes, and to her, he had never looked so magnificent.

But just as Marissa sprinted towards him, ready to embrace him in a tight hug, a giant figure slithered in front of her. Ezrinth pulled a dagger from his waistband and thrust it toward Arthur's neck, stopping just inches from his Adam's apple. Marissa froze in horror as Arthur's throat clenched, his body shaking as he desperately tried not to stumble backwards. He was locked in place, his face grimacing and his eyes squeezed shut.

<How *dare* this filthy human barge into our territory.> Ezrinth growled, raising himself up so he leered over Arthur's terrified frame. His serpentine eyes darted toward Marissa. <Do you know this intruder?>

<Yes, please, I'm begging you.> Marissa's voice shook as she stood helplessly off to the side, struggling to hold back tears. Seeing Arthur with a knife to his neck awoke a desperate, protective urge, one that flooded her entire body with adrenalin and fear.

<Boss, sir.> One of the Varan tapped Ezrinth's scaled shoulder. <You may want to see this.>

Marissa held in a panicked shriek as Varan handed Ezrinth the armor.

Ezrinth was initially confused, staring at the glittering object like it was an alien artifact, but as soon as he plucked it from the Varan's claws and ran his fingers over the Naga hide, his slitted eyes ignited with fury. Marissa lunged towards him, desperate to explain, but Ezrinth's snake-like reflexes had Arthur coiled in less than a second.

<Slitting your throat would be too kind, human.> The deep anger radiating from Ezrinth's thoughts made Marissa shudder. <And my venom won't kill you fast enough. It looks like we'll be doing this the old-fashioned way.>

Arthur gagged and sputtered for breath as Ezrinth's serpentine body tightened its grip, his face flushing bright red.

<Stop!!> Marissa pleaded. <Please!! Let me explain!!>

She grabbed Ezrinth, attempting to loosen the deadly coils wrapped around her closest friend, but the infuriated Naga shoved her away with his scaled claws.

<What could you possibly have to explain!?> Ezrinth's thoughts roared. <What sort of horrid mutilation is this!? Do you not understand that these are your kin, being mercilessly slain for vanity!? This is why we must exterminate every human in Squamata.> Ezrinth turned toward Arthur, who was half-buried in his grasp. <Starting with this one.>

Marissa's breaths came in shallow gulps as she struggled to assess the situation. Arthur was quickly disappearing in Ezrinth's coils – she could no longer hear his strained breaths and feared he was unconscious. There was no time to reason with Ezrinth. *I need to make him let go, now.*

She was half his size; she couldn't overpower him, and her venom would have no effect. She ran her tongue over her fangs and took a deep breath. *I'm already a criminal in the humans' eyes - what's one more bite?*

Ezrinth's scales were a lot tougher than human flesh, but Marissa could still taste the sour tang of blood as she sank her fangs into the Naga's arm. A sharp hiss echoed from his throat, his eyes widening in shock and betrayal. Marissa almost felt guilty for biting her own father, but that feeling was quickly replaced with relief as Ezrinth loosened his grip and a pale, limp Arthur collapsed into the sandy dirt.

"Arthur!!" Marissa cried out, bolting toward him. He was weak but conscious, gasping for breath as he lay on the ground with his chest heaving. Marissa hovered over him, placing her hands on his shoulders. She was grateful that he was alive, but the harrowing thought that she'd almost lost him sent deep pulses of distress through her mind.

But she could feel the Naga's looming presence behind her. She turned around, her thin frame still protectively hunched over Arthur, and stared at Ezrinth as he gripped his bloody forearm. The wound was superficial; deep enough to draw blood but small enough to heal in a day or two. Marissa tensed, expecting him to lash out in anger. But the shock of having his own daughter attack him to save a human seemed to quash his fury, which was instead replaced by a mixture of frustration and remorse.

<Fine.> Ezrinth huffed. <Explain.>

<It's true, the humans have been poaching reptilians to turn their scales into armor.> Marissa sighed. <But this human didn't do this, nor did he come here to hurt you. His name is Arthur. He's a herpetologist.>

Ezrinth frowned. <A *what*?>

<A reptile expert. He's devoted his life to studying reptilians, and he admires and respects them. Both of us have been trying to find you, to keep you safe from the humans as you went searching through the outer villages. But most importantly, Arthur is my friend. He's come here to help us. Please, I swear, not all humans think the reptilians are monsters.> Marissa took a deep breath, her eyes locked on Ezrinth. <I know my mother didn't.>

Ezrinth's gaze fell as Marissa's final sentence sent a pang of realization through his heart.

<I beg you, let him in to Komodo.> Marissa continued. <We need his help.>

Ezrinth didn't reply. His uncertain eyes flicked from Marissa to Arthur, and after a moment of silence, he hissed, scooped up the armor, and slithered off, muttering about finding Rathi.

Marissa and Arthur turned toward the Varan guards. They seemed to accept Ezrinth's lack of a response as a reluctant approval, and they shrugged and stepped aside.

Marissa stepped forward, her eyes looking over her shoulder at Arthur. "Are you alright?"

Arthur nodded, wiping strands of sweaty hair from his forehead. "Yeah, I'm fine. Certainly got the wind knocked out of me though."

Marissa turned back toward the guards, "I guess they're letting us through."

"It would seem that way." Arthur nodded as he stepped forward.

"Are you sure you want to do this?" Marissa asked. She didn't want to hinder him, but she still feared for his safety. Ezrinth may have relented, but there was still an entire village of reptilians beyond them. She didn't know how tolerant they would be of a human's presence.

But Arthur nodded, a shaky but bright smile on his face. Marissa returned the smile. She knew he loved the reptilians. He'd taken this risk before, and would happily do it again, especially in these dire circumstances. But at least this time, she would be there to protect him.

"I am," Arthur gestured Marissa forward. "Let's go."

ARTHUR'S EYES WIDENED IN WONDER AS THE sprawling huts came into view, but Marissa's jaw was locked in a tense frown, her shoulder pressed against his as they ventured into Komodo. Her fierce blue eyes shot daggers into the dozens of gawking Varan as they passed, warning them not to harass the strange human wandering through their village. Arthur sensed her stress and shook his head, snapping out of his dreamy fascination and keeping his gaze locked on the ground.

Marissa peered over at Arthur and sighed. *He's so happy to be here, yet he's so ostracized by the beings he's devoted his life to studying.*

"I knew the armor would make them upset," Arthur's voice was barely a whisper, even though the reptilians couldn't understand him. "But I had to bring it here. They deserved to know the truth."

"I know." Marissa's fingers brushed against his wrist. She wanted to grip his hand tight to reassure him, but she was too nervous.

All that time in Brennan and the outer villages, he kept me safe. Now he's the outcast. It's my turn to protect him.

Marissa felt her chest loosen as they ventured to the edge of the village, near a wild unkempt garden bordering the swampland. Rathi and Aina's home was just a few hundred feet away, and Marissa kept a sharp eye out for any signs of Ezrinth.

"Here." Marissa took a seat on a worn bench and patted the space next to her. "I have a lot I need to explain to you."

As they sat together on the bench, their hips just barely touching and the sun slipping further down the sky, Marissa described her eventful day. She watched Arthur's concerned expression deepen as she explained that she collapsed once she made it to Copperton, the reptilians brought her back to their territory, and, most importantly, that Ezrinth was her father and was plotting to destroy Brennan.

"Your *father*!?" Arthur exclaimed, in a manner similar to Marissa's when she received the news. "And he's gathering pieces of a mythical artifact to summon a *god*?"

"Goddess, actually." Marissa corrected. "I know it sounds insane, but hear me out. If the humans are this adamant on war, they know the reptilians are plotting something. It sounds like a fairy tale, but we all know that there are bits and pieces of magic in this world. It's what allows us to cure wounds with oranges and hang eucalyptus in our homes during the summer to keep us cool. Maybe summoning a goddess isn't that far-fetched."

Arthur shook his head. "I bet you're right. In fact, there's something I need to tell you. When I fled the Castellas' home last night, my brother Ramsey tried to stop me. I'm never going to support destroying the reptilians, but there was one thing he said that haunted me."

"What was it?"

"He said, *'the reptilians aren't who you think they are'*. But he was so... cryptic, like he was barred from telling the truth. I'm certain the king has him under his thumb. But I understand what it means now. My family knows, Marissa. And as long as the reptilians wield that sort of power, there will never be peace in this valley."

Marissa swallowed and clutched the edge of the bench in her palms, disheartened. War was simpler when the sides were black and white; good and evil. But Marissa sympathized with both humans and reptilians, and she and Arthur were stuck in the middle - crushed by the anger of two species desperate to destroy each other.

I know I'm naïve. I know this seems impossible. But there must be a solution. I must find a way to end this war before it consumes the whole valley.

"We steal the idol pieces and destroy them."

Arthur sat up straight and raised his eyebrow, amazed at the boldness of Marissa's declaration.

"Well, we *could*, but I'm assuming it won't be that easy. What sort of measures has your father taken to guard those bits of rock?"

"They're hidden deep within the chieftain and chieftress's home, in a room flanked by two guards. We could always come up with a distraction. What if-"

<Marissa?>

Arthur stopped mid-sentence as Marissa shot out of her seat. A familiar, friendly-faced Varan stepped towards them, her pace indicating hesitance to interrupt them.

<Hello, Aina.> Marissa greeted.

<Hello my dear. I've been looking for you everywhere, hoping you didn't wander too far... anyway, your father has planned a festival to celebrate your return, and we were hoping to fetch you both before dinner begins.>

Just as Aina finished speaking, the deep, gurgling growls of Marissa's stomach echoed through the gardens. Marissa gripped her torso, embarrassed. *I still haven't eaten today.*

Aina chuckled. <I believe your stomach agrees with me. I'll see you both there.> The petite Varan turned around, her long tail nearly swatting Marissa's feet.

Marissa peered back at Arthur, and he nodded, gesturing her forward.

"Come on, let's go enjoy the festival. We can discuss our plans later."

As they made their way back to the village square, the smell of fresh meat and sound of unfamiliar yet comforting music flowed through Marissa's senses. Dozens of Varan were gathered around a bonfire, eating, chatting and dancing. Several of them were gathered in a semicircle around the perimeter, tapping their scaled hands on drums and plucking at odd string instruments with their claws.

Marissa noticed that the previously unclothed lizardfolk were now adorned in colorful garments. The females wore long, flowing dresses like Marissa's, handwoven and dyed in bright strips of color, while the males wore waistcloths tied tightly around their torsos. Both sexes were adorned in strands of beads made from seashells, which gave off faint earthy chimes as they danced around the bonfires. They were surprisingly nimble for such large creatures, their clawed feet leaping effortlessly through the air. Even with their long tails that dragged on the ground, they never stumbled into each other. Their spotted scales seemed to glow in the fiery orange light of the sunset.

Despite being half-human, Marissa felt a deep, comforting warmth wash over her, as if she were finally home after a long journey. As soon as the dancers caught sight of Marissa, they swept around her like a whirlwind; a multitude of excited thoughts babbling in Marissa's mind. Several of them lifted strands of shell beads from their own necks and placed them around Marissa's. She was so overjoyed that all she could do was smile as their thoughts flooded her head, even as the weight of nearly a dozen necklaces sank into her scaled shoulders.

But one Varan carried something else towards her. And when she saw him, coiled around the lizardfolk's arm with his happy tongue flicking like a dog, she nearly leapt with joy.

<NIM!> She exclaimed, joyfully unraveling her pet snake from the Varan's forearm and looping him around her neck. She noticed that the little python's body felt tense, and at he lifted his head, Marissa noticed his eyes were coated in a milky blue film.

<He's in shed,> she sighed, and the Varan nodded.

<He'll probably be out of commission for a few days.> The lizardfolk noted. <Just keep him safe in the meantime. Snakes can't see with their eye caps clouded over.>

Marissa nodded, offering Nim a reassuring head pat. Despite his blindness, he raised his head to meet her palm, contentedly flicking his tongue against her fingers.

She suddenly realized how bare her neck had felt with his absence. He was a part of her, an extension of her own being. And she was overjoyed to have him back.

The Varan tried to pull Marissa toward the musicians, but with hunger broiling in her empty stomach, she promised she would dance with them after she'd eaten. She took a seat next to Arthur, who sat cross-legged in the sandy dirt several feet away from the rest of the Varan.

"I must say, even if I'm an outcast here, this is an absolute dream." He smiled, the fiery glow of the bonfire reflected in his green eyes. "I've never been this immersed in reptilian culture. If only I had my notebook..."

Arthur's ponderings were interrupted as one of the Varan stepped towards them. The reptilian handed a large wooden platter to Marissa, who set it on the ground between her and Arthur. Arthur eyed it curiously, his fingers outstretched but reluctant to touch the platter's contents. "Ah, I forgot that the reptilians prefer their food raw."

Marissa's nostrils flared as she leaned toward the platter. The meats were arranged in thin strips of various thicknesses and colors; she wasn't sure which pieces belonged to which animal. Back at the orphanage, with Beatrice's finances dwindling, fine cuts of meat were never on the dining table. Once Marissa moved out to the storehouse, her meals mainly consisted of grains and dairy, with the occasional piece of fruit. For most of her childhood, rodents were her only source of meat.

Even raw, the filets were mouthwatering to Marissa. As she plucked a dark liver-colored piece from the edge of the platter, she felt like a royal about to bite into a steak. She peered over at her human companion, who eyed her with a smile and a raised eyebrow. She shook her head. *Arthur's reluctance to even touch the platter makes me realize how much my reptilian instincts are emerging.*

With a swift gulp, Marissa tossed the piece of raw meat in her mouth, trying to imitate the Varan by chewing as little as possible. She heard giggles coming from Arthur's direction, and she turned her head away, embarrassed.

"Sorry," Arthur chuckled. "I didn't mean to poke fun at you. It's just amazing, really, how much you blend in with the reptilians now that you've met them."

Marissa quickly swallowed her food, biting her lower lip. The meat had a soft, almost rubbery texture with little flavor, but as soon as its deep, rich fattiness hit her forked tongue, she craved more of it. She longed to grab another piece and silence her ravenous stomach, but she was self-conscious about Arthur observing her.

"Relax, Marissa." Arthur picked up on her anxieties and handed her another piece of meat. "You're starving – you need to eat. And I told you a while ago that I'm not going to judge. I've devoted my entire life to studying reptilians. You can never be anything but fascinating to me."

You can never be anything but fascinating to me. Arthur's kind words and warm smile reminded her she had nothing to worry about. *With any other human, I'd be embarrassed by my reptilian nature. But not Arthur. I can always be myself around him.*

For a moment, as she gazed into Arthur's forest-green eyes, the anxieties of the impending war faded away. A soft autumn breeze swept against her body and tickled her reptilian nose. She realized how foreign the wind on her scales felt - her arms and legs were no longer covered by long clothing, and her face was no longer masked by a scarf. She was free, surrounded by delicious food, rejoicing reptilians, and the most incredible human she'd ever met.

Arthur grinned, sending a warm bolt of electricity through Marissa's heart. *I swear, no matter how dark the future may be, I will never forget this moment.*

Her hazy reverie was interrupted by a soft *thud* against her thigh. Normally she would've jolted at the foreign feeling, but in her relaxed state she simply peered down and noticed a small leather ball against her leg. Faint shouts echoed behind her, and both she and Arthur spun around.

A group of juvenile Varan ran across the village square, scrabbling to be the first to grab the ball that had bounced so far away from their court. Arthur chuckled and rose to his feet, scooping the ball up in a single clenched hand. With little effort, he dropped the ball from chest-height and kicked it with his foot, sending it straight into one of the juvenile's outstretched claws.

Marissa's eyes widened. Arthur noticed her amazement and grinned, his hands shoved in his pockets and his face tinged slightly red with embarrassment.

"Hey, I wasn't always a bookish geek," Arthur laughed. "When I was a child, my parents enrolled me in sports to curb my reckless energy. My throws are alright, but kicks have always been my real strength. And from my observations." He peered back over at the Varan children, who had stopped a few feet in front of them. "You're not allowed to use your hands in this game."

Marissa eyed the juveniles curiously as they stood still in front of Arthur. Unable to speak to them, he gestured a small 'you're welcome', grinning nervously as they stared at him in awe. As he went to settle back into his seat, he nearly cried out in surprise as one of the older juveniles grabbed him with a scaly claw and pulled him upright.

Arthur stumbled to his feet and turned toward Marissa. "What are they saying?"

"Nothing." Marissa grinned, her fangs gleaming in the setting sun. "But I can tell that they're impressed and want you to join their game."

"Oh, uh..." Arthur's eyes flicked back over to the eager children. He was taller than all of them, but they were still bulky lizards with sharp claws and long tails. "I appreciate it, but-"

It was too late. Arthur's words slipped away as the Varan children yanked him toward the court, squabbling amongst themselves over whose team he would play on. Marissa scooped up the remainder of the meat platter and settled cross-legged on the edge of the court, eager to observe their game.

Dinner and a show. Marissa grinned as she tossed another bite of meat into her mouth.

She had never watched sports, but she was able to conclude after a few minutes of play that the objective was to get the leather ball through the opponent's stone hoop without using your hands. The Varan children, with their giant scaled feet, were able to kick the ball great distances. But they also bounced it with their tails and bopped it off their heads, careful not to let their dorsal spines pop the ball.

As the opposing team scored their first goal, Marissa made another observation – this game was incredibly physical. Whoever was in control of the ball was subject to kicks, tail slaps, and sometimes full-body tackles. While Arthur had impressive footwork, he couldn't keep up with the speedy lizards, and he was too afraid of being injured to do much defense of the ball. At one point, he was just a few dozen feet away from the opponent's hoop, and Marissa rose out of her seat, cheering him on with glee. But with a sudden kick, a Varan from the opposing team was able to slip the ball away from Arthur's feet and hurdle it straight across the field. Miraculously, it dove through the other hoop, giving the opposing team a second goal.

Arthur huffed, his shoulders slumping. His teammates grinned and patted him on the back, too amused by their human teammate's fumbles to be upset.

They lined up in the center of the court, both teams staring each other down, and this time Arthur's gaze was different. His eyes were aflame with a fierce determination that made Marissa smile with pride. *You've got this.*

A soft horn blow echoed through the court, and chaos erupted. The ball spiraled up in the air in a straight line, causing several Varan to fumble in a cluster near its landing point. Arthur hung back, his body tensed and ready to run. Marissa wondered what he was doing, until she noticed the way his eyes studied the Varans' scaly tails.

As the ball plummeted to the ground, Arthur charged. Before the other Varan could react, he skidded across the grass, kicking the falling ball through the space between two Varans' tails with his outstretched foot. The ball soared several dozen feet onto the opponent's side of the court, giving Arthur's teammates the opportunity to take the lead and charge after the ball. Arthur bolted after them, his legs pumping and chest heaving. Once he and two of his teammates were approaching the goal, one of the teammates kicked the ball towards Arthur.

<We believe in you, human!> Marissa heard one of the children's words echo through her head. <Score us this goal!>

Arthur froze for a moment, surprised. They were still about thirty feet from the hoop, and their opponents were rapidly catching up to them. Marissa knew that Arthur had a decision to make. If the Varan caught up to him, he'd be easily overpowered. He had one chance, now.

Marissa saw the stress burned across his face as he reared back, then shot his leg forward and sent the ball soaring across the court. His teammates froze, keeping their eyes locked on the flying bit of leather as it sailed through the sunset-soaked sky. To everyone's amazement, it swept straight through the hoop at the edge of the court.

Goal!

Arthur's teammates cheers screeched so loudly in Marissa's mind that she winced. But as she pressed her palms to her head, her pained expression erupted into joyous laughter. She watched as Arthur jumped up and down and threw his fists up toward the sky, in pleasant disbelief over his victory. As Arthur's teammates charged towards him, their shouting thoughts became coherent in Marissa's mind.

That was the tenth and final goal. She realized. *Before Arthur joined the game, his team was at nine points. Once he joined, the opposing team scored two goals, also putting them at nine points.*

Arthur just won them the game.

And he was elated. Marissa had never seen his face so flushed with happiness as his teammates swarmed him. But his joy quickly turned to confusion as the gleeful Varan children tackled him to the ground in a victory pummel. Marissa rose to her feet, alarmed, but her fear dissipated as she heard Arthur's laughter under the dogpile of lizardfolk.

"Guys, guys..." Arthur's grunting voice echoed through the air. "You're kind of... crushing... me..."

Marissa shook her head. *I'm sure he'll be fine. After all, this means they've accepted him. I bet this is one of the happiest moments of his life.*

<I understand now.>

The sudden words interrupting her own thoughts made her jolt. She sensed a towering presence behind her, and she turned around to see Ezrinth a few feet away, his lower body coiled in a circle around his torso. His coppery gaze was sharp; his slitted irises widening at the impending darkness. *The ridge of scales above his eyes always makes him look so stern.*

But she could tell his anger had dissipated. It had been several hours since she'd last seen him, and the armor set was gone – likely stowed away somewhere in Rathi's home. His eyes darted over to Arthur, who was being led back to the bonfire by his new Varan friends. Marissa could tell by Ezrinth's deep, unwavering stare and the stony look of contemplation on his face that he wasn't sure how to feel about the human.

<I understand why you don't want the humans destroyed.>

Marissa felt her shoulders lighten, wondering if Ezrinth had reconsidered his plan.

<What do you mean?>

<That human boy... you're in love with him, aren't you?>

<*What!?*>

Marissa recoiled, not realizing that in her shock, she'd projected her thoughts aloud to Ezrinth. The Naga gave a snide hiss, doubting her surprise at his accusation.

<Why else would you demand he be let into Komodo, biting your own father to defend him!? And I saw you both sitting around the fire, staring at each other with those sappy eyes. It's pathetic.>

<I am *not* in love with him. He's just my friend.> Marissa retorted, her reptilian nostrils flaring. <And do you forget I'm half-human? Even if I was in love with

29

him, how would that make me any different than you? My mother, who you said you loved, was a human too!>

Another hiss, this one louder and sharper, echoed from Ezrinth's throat. But Marissa could tell his disgust was deflated by her accusation of hypocrisy. He lowered his head, dropping his gaze to the ground, and the pair stood in silence for several minutes.

Which was enough time for Marissa's head to swirl with dismay. *First feelings, now love!?* Ezrinth's claim was even more nerve-wracking than Thomas's. Her face flushed with distress, worried that she'd made her attraction too obvious. She could no longer deny that she had feelings for him, but *love* was such a foreign concept that it seemed impossible.

Her naive mind pondered what it meant to love, and to be loved by someone. She had never experienced such a feeling; only read about it in books. In *Nim's Forest*, Nim's wolf friend Casper fell in love with a female wolf named Delilah. He even took a bullet from a hunter to save her. *Maybe that's what love is,* she thought. *Caring so much about another being that you're willing to put yourself in harm's way to make sure they're safe.*

Her conclusion caused a bitter memory to surface – Thomas hunting a Varan to save his wife's life. *No.* She quickly shoved the thought out of her mind. *Love or not, Thomas is a murderer.*

But with all her uncertainty, she did know that love took time, and she'd only known Arthur for two weeks. Her scales burned as she imagined what life would be like if she did fall in love with him. *Days spent running the Menagerie together, tending to reptiles, feeling the snakes' joy as they slither around my wrist...*

No. Her heart fell. *It's impossible.* Not only was she a homeless half-Naga, banned from the kingdom, but she had a war to survive. She knew that her chances of finding peace were slim, and she worried that any alternative ending would result in her death.

She turned back to the silent Naga beside her. She remembered her promise to hug her parents if she ever met them. It had been nearly twenty-four hours, and the only physical contact she'd had with Ezrinth was her fangs in his flesh. She couldn't see him as her father – only as a monster. A deeply tormented, mistreated one, but a monster nonetheless. She knew parents loved their children, but Ezrinth's love didn't feel real - it was corrupted by his horrid ideals. *He's willing to destroy so much, claiming it's all for me and my mother, offering us everything we could ever want...*

And I want none of it.

<I'm headed to Gharian territory with Rathi in the morning.> Ezrinth's sudden words broke the heavy silence in the air. <Several of the Varan guards will be joining me. Aina and the others have been instructed to keep an eye on you. I want you to remain here, safe. Do you understand?>

Just as Marissa's response began to form in her mind, she turned her thoughts off like a door slamming shut. She needed to stay quiet. She and Arthur still need to come up with a plan to take the idol, and they couldn't let Ezrinth get suspicious.

<And I want that human gone by morning.> Ezrinth huffed. Marissa remained quiet, but she noticed that the Naga's attention was piqued by an approaching guard.

<Ezrinth, sir. We have another group of visitors.>

Ezrinth groaned. <Why so many visitors? Hmph. Fine, who is it and what do they want?>

<It's a group of Naga, sir.>

A spark of anger flared in Ezrinth's eyes. <Tell them to leave. I have no interest in speaking with those worms.>

<They're led by a female, sir, and she was adamant that I tell you her name.>

<Well, what is it?>

<Um, her name is Nathara, sir.>

The anger in Ezrinth's eyes was now ablaze. However, instead of shooing the guard away, he bolted toward the village entrance, leaving a snaking trail of dirt behind him.

Marissa turned toward the guard, who shrugged in unknowing confusion. She frowned and slowly paced after her father, following the serpentine path left behind by his tail. Her human eyes struggled with the heavy darkness of the night, and her mind was burning with questions.

I don't understand. Who is Nathara? And why is her presence making Ezrinth so upset?

Chapter 3

$\mathcal{A}$S THE ENTRANCE TO KOMODO CREPT INTO view, Marissa crouched in a patch of tall grass. She hoped that even with the Nagas' powerful night vision, the shadowy darkness of the swampland would be enough to conceal her.

Her eyes struggled to comprehend the scene a few dozen feet away. The soft orange glow of the Varan guards' torches was the only source of light in the inky sky, and the cluster of figures arguing with the guards were nothing more than murky shadows. As they moved, Marissa could make out serpentine heads, arms, and tails – there appeared to be four Naga, led by a slender female. She was shorter than the other Naga, but still much taller than any human. The flickering torches made her coppery eyes glow like bonfires.

Ezrinth had swept up to the scene in a whirlwind of slithering coils, and his whole body froze as he caught sight of the female Naga. He raised a torch to her face, and from a distance Marissa could make out her features. Her black-and-brown scales glowed like gemstones, and she had a slimmer face than Ezrinth, with more rounded eyes. Despite her serpentine features, her soft expression made her eerily beautiful.

Marissa noticed the female Naga's eyes lit up with a glimmer of hope.

<Ezrinth.> Her thoughts were soft and gentle. <We->

<What do you want?> Ezrinth hissed, his harsh tone causing the female Naga's face to drop. <Are you here to try and stop me?>

Marissa craned her neck, trying to get a better view amidst the tall reeds that broke up her vision. Ezrinth and the female Naga – who Marissa assumed was Nathara – clearly knew each other. And despite her gentleness and his fury, they both had a pained look in their reptilian eyes. Like they once shared a bond that was now broken.

<No.> Nathara replied softly. <In fact, we are here to help you. We want to join your cause.>

The other three Naga nodded in solidarity. Ezrinth reeled backwards, clearly surprised by their request. His eyes flicked toward the ground as he pondered their thoughts, seeming both eager and hesitant.

<I don't understand.> He scowled.

<Let us come into the village.> Nathara slithered toward Ezrinth, but he backed away. <I promise, we will explain everything.>

Ezrinth turned away, his scaled hand clenching into a fist.

<Please, Ezrinth.>

<Fine.> Ezrinth grumbled, still refusing to look Nathara in the eye. He slithered back toward the village, stopping once he reached Marissa. The sickening burn of fear crept through her veins, and her muscles tensed as she tried not to budge.

<I know you're there, daughter.> He huffed. <It's alright, you don't have to hide.>

Marissa bit her lip, rising slowly from the spindly reeds until her eyes locked with Ezrinth's. He smirked, but Marissa could still see a tinge of sadness in his eyes. In the distance, the four Naga were slowly catching up to them.

<Come with me.> He extended his hand. His crescent-shaped claws glinted in the torchlight. <You're a Naga - you should be a part of this.>

Marissa stood up, brushing dirt off her scaled knees. She stared at Ezrinth's extended hand for a moment before brushing past him. He huffed, upset at his daughter's indignance, but they walked back toward the village side by side.

<I don't understand.> Marissa noted softly as they approached Komodo. <Who are they?>

<The other three Naga?> Ezrinth replied. <I don't know, most likely villagers from Nerodia. I haven't been allowed back there since you were born. As for the female- >

<You know her.> Marissa accused. <The way you two looked at each other... who is she?>

<Her name is Nathara.> Ezrinth sighed, confirming Marissa's suspicions. <She's my sister.>

MARISSA'S HEAD SWIRLED AS SHE FOLLOWED Ezrinth and the others into Komodo. She was so lost in thought that the village commotion was a just a blur of noise in her ears. *Nathara is Ezrinth's sister... that means she's my aunt.* Her longing mind had only ever focused on her parents. It had never occurred to her that she had an entire extended family, both human and reptilian. *Aunts, uncles, cousins, grandparents...* She even wondered if she had siblings, but the idea seemed far-fetched. *Ezrinth clearly doesn't have any other children, and my mother... did she ever find anyone else? Did she become an outcast like her forbidden mate, or did she blend back into human society, putting this all behind her?*

Marissa's old storybooks described motherhood as one of the strongest feelings of love any being could ever know. All day long, she'd seen female Varan nurturing their bumbling hatchlings, rocking them in their bulky arms and snuggling them against their chest as they walked. It made her stomach sick with longing as she thought back to her days at the orphanage. There, they were all abandoned children, discarded remnants of what was supposed to be an unbreakable bond. And among them, she was the child that shouldn't even exist.

A sudden shout pulled Marissa out of her wistful haze. She spotted a familiar human face among the group of Varan clustered around the bonfire.

"Marissa! What's going on?"

Arthur jogged up to her, even as she kept pace with the others. As he approached, dressed in baggy Varan ceremonial clothes with shell-bead bracelets wrapped around his bicep, Marissa saw Ezrinth turn his head. A soft hiss of disgust echoed from the Naga's throat.

"Not now," Marissa whispered in a stern but gentle tone. "I doubt Ezrinth is going to let you into Rathi's home, and you won't be able to understand anyone. Stay here with the other Varan. I promise I'll explain everything later."

Arthur sighed but nodded, turning back toward the bonfire. Marissa couldn't help but smile as he plopped down next to his newfound friends. The Varan juveniles were clustered in a circle, teaching Arthur some sort of board game involving shells and wooden pegs. They waved their hands and pointed in silent gestures, but Arthur seemed to understand the rules. As Marissa continued walking and lost sight of them, she heard a victorious shout of joy echo from the crowd.

They really have accepted him, even though they can't speak to each other. I guess it proves that friendship knows no bounds.

Once they reached Rathi's sprawling abode, the group gathered in a large, central room comprised of wooden benches in a loose circle around a small firepit. Aina knelt in the center of the room, tending to the flames as smoke rose above her narrow face and plumed out of a large hole in the ceiling. Her head shot up as the group entered, startled to see the four Naga. Nathara gave a small smile and a friendly wave, which Aina returned with uncertainty.

Marissa watched the tension unfold through the gap between Rathi and Ezrinth. She was the last one in the room, and it gave her a chance to fully observe her surroundings. *Me, Ezrinth, Rathi, Aina, and four Naga, including my long-lost aunt. We certainly are a strange bunch.* Her gaze flicked toward the two guards flanking the entrance as she took a seat.

Once everyone was seated, all eyes were on Nathara. Marissa could see the tension in the Naga's face.

<I'm sure you're wondering what caused us to come all this way.> She began. <Please, allow me to explain.>

Marissa noticed that Nathara's speech seemed to be directed toward Ezrinth, who sat with his cheek propped on the back of his scaly hand and his body curled tightly around the bench. His slitted eyes glowered at his estranged sister, but within his coppery gaze, Marissa could see a tinge of sadness.

<My dear brother, our father knows about the idol. You didn't exactly cover your tracks when you stole it.>

Ezrinth huffed, although he seemed unsurprised. <And?>

<He's decided to evacuate the Naga from Squamata.>

Ezrinth's sour face dropped for a moment, before returning to its usual hardened grimace. <I don't know why I'm surprised. Our father is a coward, always has been.>

Nathara's sigh demonstrated that she didn't disagree.

<The problem is that his decision has divided our people. Some of the Naga want to leave with Orami, others want to stay and fight. But those who want to stay are terrified. Since their numbers will be smaller, they fear that the humans will overpower them.>

<We want protection.> One of the other Naga, a young male, piped up. <In return for joining your cause. Squamata is our home – we won't simply abandon it like our pathetic chieftain. Let us fight together, all of us.>

With his final sentence, the Naga raised a fist in the air. The others returned the gesture, with shouts and cheers erupting from the small group. As the joyful banter filled Ezrinth's head, Marissa saw a small, satisfied smile creep onto his face.

And it made her nauseous. But as the crowd continued rejoicing, Marissa realized she wasn't alone. While her Naga companions were thrilled, Nathara's face was expressionless. She looked lost in thought, and not in a wistful manner. *She doesn't agree with this. But then why did she come all the way to Komodo?*

The enthusiastic chatter continued for a few minutes as the group filed out into the dark, star-speckled air. While Aina led the four Naga to their accommodations for the night, Ezrinth and Rathi stayed behind – Marissa assumed that they were discussing their plans to leave in the morning.

Crap. I still need to talk to Arthur about our plan to steal the idol pieces.

As she scoured through Komodo in search of her friend, her stomach twisted over itself in nervous knots. Thoughts of the festival floated through her mind. *The food, the merriment, the first feeling of relaxation in a long time...* it was all a charade, gone in a puff of smoke. There was still war on the horizon, and even if Marissa managed to successfully steal the idol pieces, the fate of the entire valley would be in her hands. *It's enough to make anyone sick with anxiety.*

"Marissa?"

She'd been so lost in thought that she hadn't realized where she was. Her head spun around as she tried to pinpoint the shout – all she could see around her were clusters of lush foliage. *I must be in Rathi and Aina's back garden.* It was so dark that the plants were nothing more than black silhouettes against the indigo night, but in the distance, she could make out a shadowy human figure perched on a bench.

She smiled.

"Arthur!"

She took a seat next to her friend. It was dark, but up close she could make out his facial features. He was still adorned in his oversized ceremonial clothing, with his shell-bead bracelets chiming in the still night air. His choice to wear a vibrantly colored tunic instead of being bare-chested like the Varan sent a deep feeling of disappointment through Marissa, who scolded herself for having such thoughts.

"There you are." Arthur grinned. "I know it's dark outside, but did you notice there's a horse here?"

He pointed to a clearing beyond the gardens. A few hundred feet from where they sat on their bench was a small paddock, fenced in with bamboo poles. And within the paddock was a large, four-legged creature, its long wispy tail flicking in the darkness.

"A horse?" Marissa remarked, confused. "Wait a minute... that's Arrow! He's safe! Thomas let me borrow his horse to get here. Good gods, I completely forgot about him... and Thomas..."

Arthur seemed confused. Marissa realized that not only was she showing pity for someone she previously hated, but Arthur also likely hadn't heard the news.

"I should probably explain. I ran into him when I fled the Castellas' home."

"You did? What was he doing in Brennan?"

"He and Marian evacuated, along with the rest of Copperton. The Varan burned down their village to get revenge."

"They *burned it down*?! All of it?"

"Yes. The reptilians have every right to be angry over the poaching, but all those people, their cries, the burn wounds... it was a horrible thing to see."

Arthur was silent, but Marissa noticed he was hunched over, hands on his knees, fingers clasped around the loose fabric of his waistcloth. *He knows how much this will escalate the war. He's scared.* Marissa felt the urge to take his white-knuckled hand in hers, tell him that everything would be alright... but she shook the feeling away.

"It's hard to believe, especially after seeing them so kind and carefree at the festival. But between the Varan mourning those killed by poaching, and Thomas taking such drastic measures to save his wife... things are getting very ugly. And complicated."

"That's why we need to steal the idol and destroy it." Marissa sighed. "Things will only get worse if we don't. Speaking of which, what are we-"

<Um... niece?>

Marissa's craned her neck around. Behind her was nothing but darkness, but between her hesitancy in calling Marissa *niece*, and the softness of her thoughts in Marissa's mind, Marissa knew exactly who was approaching them.

<Nathara?>

Marissa could see rows of dark scales illuminated by the soft white moonlight as the Naga slithered into view. Her clawed hands were folded in front of her torso, and Marissa noticed that her previously slit irises had expanded to near-circles in the gloomy night air. It gave her serpentine face a gentler, more human-like expression.

Upon hearing her name, Nathara froze a few feet from the bench.

<Ah, I imagine Ezrinth told you about me. Well, am indeed his sister, and by extension your aunt. I know you don't know me, and my appearance is rather sudden, but... could I have a moment with you alone?>

Marissa would've normally been nervous to be left alone with a large, imposing reptilian in near-black darkness. But ever since Marissa first spotted the kindly Naga at the entrance to Komodo, her intuition had told her that Nathara could be trusted.

"Arthur?" she turned toward her friend, whose gaze was tilted up at the towering Naga. "Do you mind giving us some time to chat?"

"Are you sure?" Arthur raised an eyebrow, clearly sharing Marissa's initial hesitancies.

"Yes. I never told you about her, did I? This is Nathara, she's Ezrinth's sister and my aunt. I really think I can trust her. She's family."

Marissa felt her intuition scoff at her last sentence – she knew from her mother's disappearance and Ezrinth's foul plans that family wasn't always well-intentioned. *But I saw how Nathara reacted to the cheers at Rathi's home. I need to learn what her real intentions are.*

"Ah, I see." Arthur stood up from the bench, brushing off his knees and craning his neck upwards at the towering Naga. "Well, I'll leave you two to it. I'll be back at the village square if you need me."

Arthur wandered down the sandy path out of the gardens, disappearing into the darkness. Marissa wondered if he really was going back to the village square, or if he planned on creeping into the dark brush to keep an eye on her. But as she turned toward her towering relative, she felt a strange stillness in the night air that made her assume they were completely alone.

<I'm amazed to see you.> Nathara's sudden thoughts broke the silence. She slithered around Marissa, her long, trailing tail creating circles in the soft dirt. <To be honest… I didn't realize you were still alive. I always wondered what a half-Naga would look like. The body of a human and the scales of a snake… I must say, you are truly incredible.>

Marissa smiled, her heart burning with warmth at her aunt's compliment. Nathara was the only being besides Arthur to ever comment positively on her appearance.

<My dear niece.> Nathara continued. <I don't think I've gotten your name?>

<I'm Marissa. It's wonderful to meet you, Nathara. Thank you for being so kind to me.>

<Of course. Marissa... that's a lovely name. A human one, I noticed. I take it you were raised by them?>

<Yes, I was.> Marissa nodded sadly. She hoped her aunt wouldn't ask too many questions about her past. She hated reliving her childhood memories, so she attempted to change the subject.

<Nathara, aunt... if you don't mind, may I ask you a question?>

<Of course, my dear. I'm sure you have a lot of them.>

Too many to comprehend, Marissa sighed. The past twenty-four hours had sent her mind reeling with new discoveries.

<Come.> Nathara ushered her toward the bench. <Let us sit and discuss.>

Marissa settled down on the far edge of the seat, as Nathara's long coiled body took up nearly the entire bench. *She's huge.* Marissa observed. She realized that Nathara was slightly taller than Ezrinth. She assumed that maybe female Naga were larger than males, but then she remembered how massive Nathara's three male companions were back at Rathi's home.

She sighed. <It's about Ezrinth... why is he here, in Varan territory? Should he be with the other Naga?>

Nathara exhaled, her reptilian nostrils flaring. Pain emblazoned her face – it seemed that she'd dreaded Marissa asking this question.

<It's a very long, complicated story. But in short, Ezrinth was exiled from Nerodia by our father, Orami, many years ago. He's been an outcast for a long time.>

Marissa frowned. As much as she was disgusted by the scheming Naga, she felt her heart sink. *An outcast for a long time... just like me.*

Then, the realization hit her.

<It was because of me, wasn't it?>

<Well... yes.> The pain in Nathara's face deepened. <But please, do not put blame on yourself. Like I said earlier, my father is a coward. Ever since my mother died, he's been a broken, bitter old snake. I'll admit the truth – Ezrinth's plans are monstrous. But Orami was just as monstrous for abandoning his own son.>

<Once Ezrinth left... did you ever see him again? Did you ever try to find him?>

Marissa's black lips burned as the words escaped her mouth. *You fool. Stop being so trusting – she's a stranger. She's not going to like such personal questions.*

Nathara chuckled sadly, a deep remorse in her eyes.

<It's quite alright.> She seemed to notice Marissa's anxiety. <I don't mind explaining things - you've been left in the dark for a long time, my dear. The truth is, not really. I've caught glimpses of him over the years, but tonight was the first time I've spoken to him since you were born.>

Marissa was quiet, her palms resting upright in her lap. She remembered her shock upon learning Ezrinth was her father, her fury at his horrid plans, and her disgust at the way his eyes glowered with hatred. But she also remembered seeing bits of despair behind his fiery copper gaze. Eighteen years in exile had corrupted Ezrinth, steeping him in wrath and anger. She needed something – or someone – to mend the damage done to his soul.

Once again, she thought about her mother. Marissa sighed. *As soon as I've destroyed those damn bits of rock, I swear I'm going to find her.*

<Nathara?> Marissa took a deep breath. *I must ask her. I must take this risk.*

<Yes, my dear?>

<I couldn't help but notice that you seem... hesitant about everything. You weren't cheering like everyone else back at Rathi's home.>

Nathara huffed. <I noticed you weren't either. I could see it in your eyes from the moment I met you. You're a half-breed, torn between two worlds. And in this war, you don't want to take sides, do you?>

<No.> Relief washed over Marissa's scales. It was as if Nathara's thoughts were poured directly into her soul. <And as impossible as it sounds, I just want to stop this war before it begins. Before more humans and reptilians die. I want peace.>

<Well it's a good thing we found each other.> Nathara smiled. <Because that's exactly what I want as well. The truth is, I grew up brainwashed into thinking all humans were evil. They were murderous demons, everyone said, and all they did was take – destroying the swampland to build their overblown kingdom. But once

I found out about Ezrinth's secret life – and the child that came from it – I had to confront my own prejudice. My own brother loved a human, so clearly, they weren't as terrible as I'd been told.>

<Nathara.> Marissa spoke up, emboldened by Nathara's words. <I could use your help.>

<Of course, my dear. What is it?>

<I need to steal the idol pieces and destroy them. To put an end to Ezrinth's horrible plans.>

Marissa expected Nathara to be shocked, or sickened, or outright refuse her request. But she was surprised when the Naga's expression contained only sadness.

<I'm afraid we can't, my dear. The idol pieces are indestructible.>

<What!? I don't understand... then how did they break in the first place?>

<We don't know. It all happened eight hundred years ago. The idol was made by the great serpent goddess Vaipera, crafted in the heavenly realm of Reptilia, far away from this world. When our ancestors couldn't agree on whether to summon her, some of them attempted to destroy the idol. They fought and fought, to no avail... until a bolt of lightning emerged from the sky, shattering the idol into four pieces.>

Marissa's eyes widened. <That means...>

<Yes, my dear. It means that the only person capable of destroying the idol is Vaipera herself. As to why it shattered that day, none of us know. The gods are fickle beings – their true motives are a mystery to us mortals.>

Marissa's heart sank. She'd been reassuring herself all day, every time the impending war broiled her stomach, that all she had to do was destroy the idol. And now she couldn't. No one could.

Except...

<Vaipera can destroy the idol.> Marissa declared.

Nathara's face fell.

<Marissa, I know what you're thinking.> She warned in a low tone. <Vaipera is the goddess of chaos, and her personality reflects as such. One teenage half-Naga is not going to change her mind after eight hundred years of turmoil.>

<But what if- >

<I know, Marissa.> Nathara lowered her head. <But I have a better idea. Listen, my dear, the truth is that I didn't come here to side with my brother. I came here to find *you*. How much do you know about what happened eight hundred years ago?>

<Very little.> Marissa frowned.

<Well, the truth is a well-kept secret, known only by the descendants of the four reptilian leaders who first attempted to summon Vaipera. They made the long, dangerous trek up to the top of Mount Krait, where the barrier between Squamata and Reptilia is said to be at its thinnest. It's where reptilians go to have their prayers answered. They were ready to summon the great serpent goddess and destroy the humans once and for all... until one reptilian stopped them. It was the chieftress of the Testudo, a young female named Mata. And rumors have been swirling around for years that she is still alive.>

<*Still*? How long do Testudo live?>

<They have the longest lifespans of any reptilian, up to three hundred years. Mata still being alive sounds absurd, but maybe not impossible. The Testudo are a highly secretive race, living deep in underground burrows and avoiding outside contact. Anyone who visits them is turned away. But after learning that my brother had stolen a piece of the idol, I became desperate for answers. So I tried my luck and traveled there.>

<Did they let you in?>

<Well, no, but when I asked about Mata, they didn't deny her existence. Instead...> A smile broke out on Nathara's face. <They told me to come back later... and to bring them the half-reptilian girl.>

<*Me?*> Marissa was bewildered. <But why? What does that mean?>

<I don't know. But clearly Mata sees you as important. Who knows, maybe you are the key to ending all of this. So I ask you, please, come with me to Testudo territory. We need to speak with her.>

Marissa's gaze shifted past Nathara, back toward Komodo. The faint rumble of activity had slowed, with music and laughter being replaced by the buzzing of nocturnal insects. Tired Varan shuffled into their huts, extinguishing their torches as the once bustling village succumbed to the stillness of night.

And there was no sign of Arthur. Marissa assumed he too had settled into one of the huts. *He needs rest. He must be exhausted.* And although Marissa enjoyed the time alone, getting to know her long-lost aunt, she wished Arthur was still with them. *Even if he can't understand Nathara, he needs to be a part of this.*

But he wasn't. Marissa needed to make the decision for them both.

<Alright.> She agreed after a long pause. <But Arthur comes with us.>

<Excellent.> Nathara broke into a relieved grin. Marissa was amazed at the softness of her smile, despite the sharp fangs lurking behind her lips. <And are you referring to your little human friend?>

<Yes. He's a herpetologist, and he's devoted his whole life to helping the reptilians. I want him with us.>

<I see no problem with that. I certainly wouldn't want to separate you two.>

Nathara's previously sweet smile became devious with accusation, and Marissa huffed.

<Stop it. He's just my friend.>

<Whatever you say, my dear.> Her tone indicated that she doubted Marissa's words but wouldn't push the subject. <Anyway, I agree that we should still swipe the idol pieces. I certainly don't want them remaining in my brother's vicinity, and the Testudo are aware of what he's plotting. They will fight beak and claw to defend their piece of the idol, and will do the same for the other two once we hand them over.>

Marissa knew it should've been reassuring that three of the four idol pieces would be deep underground, protected in a secluded maze of a village by some of the toughest reptilians in the valley. But instead, it made her nauseous. Not only did she envision her father's wrath at discovering that his own daughter stole the idol pieces, but she feared the drastic measures he would take to reclaim them. *He wouldn't possibly harm the Testudo, his fellow reptilians... or would he?*

But Nathara was right. Despite the risks, Testudo territory was the safest place for the idol pieces to remain hidden.

<It's a plan.> Marissa declared. <But we still need to figure out *how* to steal the idol pieces. Ezrinth has that room protected by two guards.>

<I have some ideas.> Nathara grinned, her body rising from the bench and slithering onto the garden path. She gestured for Marissa to join her. <Come along, let's go find your little human friend and discuss our plans. Plus, you need rest – we'll have a long day ahead of us tomorrow.>

MARISSA DIDN'T KNOW WHAT TIME IT WAS, BUT she imagined it was well past midnight. She, Arthur, and Nathara were alone, each sprawled out on a simple wooden bed. Nathara was fast asleep – Marissa could see her shadowy figure rise and fall as her lengthy serpentine body spilled onto the floor. Varan beds were large by human standards, but still too small for the massive – and very long – snakefolk.

There was a heavy stillness in the air, not just from the eerie darkness but from the daunting weight of their mission. Marissa couldn't sleep – she'd laid wide-eyed in her cot staring at the palm-thatched ceiling for the past several hours. Her mind was too busy scouring every step of their plan to succumb to sleep.

Even if we're not caught stealing the idol pieces, we still have to transport them across the valley. If we travel through human territory, Nathara is in danger. And if we travel through reptilian territory, Arthur is. As for me, who knows...

I might be in danger no matter which choice we make.

The soft sound of shifting palm fronds interrupted her anxious thoughts. She knew Arthur was also still awake – he'd been tossing and turning in his bed all night. Yet they hadn't spoken a word to each other since they finalized their plan with Nathara many hours ago.

<*I'll create a distraction for the guards, and you two sneak in and steal the idol.*> Nathara had declared while Marissa translated her thoughts to Arthur. <*I'll rope the juveniles into it. I won't tell them what it's for, of course, but they do love playing pranks on their elders. No one will suspect a thing.*>

Marissa wanted to believe her aunt. But she was terrified that they would be caught. Despite Ezrinth's horrid behavior, Marissa knew Ezrinth cared about her and would never cause her harm.

What truly scared her was what Ezrinth would do to Arthur.

"Are you alright, Marissa?"

Arthur's sudden voice nearly made her jolt.

"Uh, yes, I'm fine," Marissa stuttered, sitting upright in her bed. "What makes you ask?"

"You're grinding your fangs together – I can hear it. You've been doing it all night."

Marissa raised a hand to her mouth, pressing her fingers against the sharp, needle-like protrusions that sat on either side of her two front teeth. *I really do act just as nervous as I feel.*

"Well, to tell you the truth." Marissa sighed. "I'm not fine. I finally found my father only to discover he's a horrible villain, he's on a mission to destroy Brennan at the expense of thousands of lives, and the only way for me to stop all this is to carry two pieces of rock dozens of miles away and hope the Testudo can seal them away forever. It's a lot to process."

"I know. It's okay to be stressed. It was foolish for me to pretend that you aren't." He sat upright so that they were face to face, sitting on the edges of their beds just a few feet away from each other.

"The worst part." Marissa's throat tightened. "Is that one thought keeps gnawing away at me. What if this is all my fault?"

"What do you mean?"

"When I spoke with Nathara earlier, she mentioned that Ezrinth has been an outcast for the past eighteen years. And it's all because of me. If I was never born, Ezrinth would still be with his family. Maybe he wouldn't be so vengeful, and..."

"No, Marissa." Arthur's tone was sharp. "Don't go there. This is not your fault. Outcast or not, Ezrinth is responsible for his own actions. He caused this, not you."

Marissa nodded and sighed. She was being absurd; she knew it wasn't her fault. She felt as if the weight of the valley were on her shoulders, and it was clouding her judgment. Not only was she anxious about their daunting mission the next morning, but she had a massive number of new revelations to process. The fact that Ezrinth, the troublesome Naga they'd scoured the valley for, was her long-lost father still seemed unreal.

Eighteen long years... maybe if I'd found him sooner, this wouldn't all be happening...

Her blue-eyed gaze fell to the floor. She remembered one night at the orphanage when she was very young, and she'd received a particularly bad scolding from Beatrice for stealing an extra dinner biscuit. She'd spent the whole night huddled under a scratchy old comforter in the cramped storage closet that served as her bedroom, fantasizing about running away. She traced her petite fingers across the raindrops that streaked the filthy old window. *My parents must be out there somewhere.* She doubted they'd ever come back for her, but maybe if she found them instead...

"You seem lost in thought."

Marissa jolted. She had been so engulfed in her memories that she forgot she was still seated on her bed, face-to-face with Arthur. She peered up at his dark figure, barely able to make out a smile on his lips. A faint, gauzy bit of moonlight streamed into the hut and reflected in his forest-green eyes, making them glitter like jewels against his shadowy face.

"Oh, sorry." Marissa lifted her scaled feet so that she sat cross-legged in her bed. "I was just... thinking about our plans tomorrow. That's all."

"I assumed such. It's alright to be nervous. I am too. But..." His eyes drifted toward the slumbering Naga coiled around her ill-fitting bed. "I think we have to trust Nathara. I know her plan seems shaky, but I really do believe in the juveniles. I know it sounds ridiculous, especially when I can't even speak to them, but last night I truly felt like I had close friends... for the first time in a while."

Arthur gave a sad smile, his head lowering. Marissa reached out and placed a hand on his shoulder. To her, it was another reminder that she wasn't the only one who felt like an outcast among others.

Marissa saw Arthur's sadness fade away as her fingers pressed against his skin. His smile began to glow with a warmth unfamiliar to Marissa, as Arthur raised a hand to his shoulder and placed it over Marissa's. He slowly, gently, trailed his fingers up her wrist, until he reached the place where her human skin faded away and her reptilian scales emerged.

"Your scales are so soft," Arthur's voice was barely a whisper, one laced with a trace of desire.

The feeling sent hot quivers down Marissa's spine. Arthur had touched her many times before, but something about the way his breath slowed as he traced the outline of her scales further up her arm was different. Everything, from her chest down to her stomach to the tips of her toes, was on fire with a longing she'd never felt before.

Just as quickly as it began, it stopped. Arthur, as if he suddenly realized what he was doing, jerked his arm away in a sudden, swift motion. Marissa flinched, surprised by his sharp recoil. They locked eyes, and despite the gloomy darkness, Marissa could tell that his face was flushing red from embarrassment.

"We... we should go to sleep." Arthur quickly laid down and tossed a blanket over his legs. "Thank you for everything today, Marissa. I'll... see you in the morning."

Marissa still wasn't ready to sleep. She wanted to talk, but after a few moments of stewing quietly in her bed, she decided against it and rolled onto her side. She knew that she would never forget the way she felt for those few moments, and she couldn't decide if she was desperate for more or never wanted such emotions to surface ever again.

Either way, it was all she could think about until her overwhelmed yet exhausted mind finally succumbed to sleep.

Chapter 4

WHEN RAMSEY HAD AWOKEN EARLIER THAT same day, all he could feel was nausea.

He rolled sluggishly out of bed, rubbing his crusty eyes and running his clammy hands through his dark brown hair. The blanketed lump next to him continued snoozing – Ramsey decided it was best to let his wife Charlotte sleep in. She hadn't been feeling well lately, and he wanted to make sure she recovered quickly from whatever illness had struck her.

He didn't feel well either, but for entirely different reasons.

He stumbled into the bathroom, a glowstone lamp flickering to life as he entered. The soft white light was usually gentle on his eyes, but today it felt blinding, and he could see searing flashes of red under his eyelids as he shielded his face. Once his eyes recovered, he slid his palms down his cheeks and peered at himself in the mirror.

In his reflection, he saw a sallow, bleary-eyed man, his face puffy and pale and his sweat-stained hair sticking to his forehead. He'd had another nightmare in his sleep, and at this point, he feared they'd never end.

Some future king I am. He huffed as his reflection, fighting back the urge to ram a fist into the mirror. He imagined King Gabriel in his throne room, the pinnacle of confidence and poise, always alert and impeccably groomed. But then his thoughts turned back to the night before, where the king's haggard appearance nearly matched Ramsey's current state.

Maybe this is what King Gabriel meant what he said that if I wanted to be king, it wouldn't be easy. He splashed cold water on his face and glimpsed back up at the mirror, watching water droplets trail down his still-sallow cheeks. *Is this really the cost of being a monarch?*

He'd have to wait to find out. King Gabriel had given Ramsey a mission – track down his troublesome younger brother Arthur and persuade him to hand over his mysterious half-reptilian companion. He had no moral issues with hauling the strange girl back to the palace, especially after her bite nearly killed one of the Castellas' sons. She was clearly dangerous, and Ramsey feared what sort of manipulative trickery she'd used to wrap Arthur around her finger.

What he did dread was the inevitable confrontation with his brother. Like many siblings, they'd had their fair share of conflict over the years. But beneath their tangled web of quarrels and disagreements, there was no doubting their bond. Arthur always knew how to make Ramsey laugh when he became a bit too uptight, and Ramsey always knew how to shield Arthur from the more severe consequences of his antics.

Until now. Ramsey could still feel his heart fall out of his chest every time he thought of Arthur jumping through the Castella's window. His brother had dug himself a grave so deep that Ramsey questioned if he'd ever be able to help him out of it. But he would try. Someday he would be king, and with that power, he would fight with every fiber of his being to keep his younger brother in his life.

Because he loved him, and no war would ever change that.

Ramsey would've eagerly set off at dawn, but King Gabriel had requested that he not depart until the next day. Some sort of 'extra preparations'. Ramsey huffed, patting his sour face with a fluffy white towel. Despite his reservations about finding Arthur and the half-reptilian girl, having to delay his journey filled him with even more dread. *Am I supposed to just loaf around the castle for the next twenty-four hours?*

A sudden knock at the front door interrupted his thoughts. Ramsey scrubbed his face with the towel, hoping to bring some color back to his pallid cheeks. As the future king of Brennan, he certainly didn't want to answer the door looking like a ragamuffin.

He strode brisky through the apartment – a sprawling three-bedroom abode with high ceilings adorned with elaborate crown molding. The apartment was tastefully decorated with fine artwork and hand-crafted furniture that screamed opulence. And despite being an apartment, one of the dozens throughout the palace, it was larger than many of the houses in Silverkeep.

A meek yet cheery-faced servant greeted Ramsey as he swung open the heavy front door. She bowed curtly before spouting off a message directly from King Gabriel – Ramsey was supposed to spend the morning and afternoon attending a meeting of the king's court. Ramsey was familiar with the affair – all his dour-faced old relatives sitting around drinking tea and bantering about politics. It sounded dreadful, but Ramsey hoped their conversations would be enough to distract his fraught mind.

They weren't. An hour later, once he'd had time to freshen up and wipe the last traces of anxiety off his face, Ramsey sat in a plush velvet chair around a ridiculously large table with a dozen other royals, all much older than him. Above the table, Ramsey was the peak of politeness and elegance, listening diligently to his companions' conversations with a calm expression. But out of view, Ramsey gripped the edges of his chair cushion until his knuckles turned white. He feared it was the only thing keeping him from bursting out of his seat and telling the old royal clique what absolute fools they were.

We're on the brink of war, Ramsey growled in his head. *Preparing for the worst conflict this valley has ever seen. The reptilians are trying to summon a god, for heaven's sake. Yet they're sitting here, sipping tea and bickering over royal gardening budgets like nothing is wrong.*

But there was nothing he could do. As heir to the throne, this was part of his future duties. Not to mention that voicing his true opinions would get him in trouble with the current monarch.

So he waited, feeling the minutes pass like hours, painfully aware of every second-hand tick of the giant antique clock that hung on the wall in front of him. But eventually that clock struck noon, and Ramsey's elders announced an hour-long break for lunch.

Ramsey nearly leapt out of his seat.

He doubted that King Gabriel wanted him leaving the castle, but Ramsey was desperate for fresh air. He strode toward the glittering palace foyer at a brisk pace, snatching a cloak from one of the storage closets in the hallway. They were meant for the servants to wear when running outside errands in the valley's brief winter, which meant it would be a perfect disguise for a sneaking royal.

He pulled the cloak's hood over his head as he jogged down the palace steps, making sure his face was mostly concealed. Not that anyone wandering around Augustree would think much of him – until a few days ago, he'd been a distant royal, insignificant to passersby. But he knew that as the newly declared heir to the throne, it wouldn't long until Brennan's citizens started recognizing his face.

But for now, he was anonymous, just another cloaked figure wandering through the merchant's district. And it allowed him some time to breathe.

Once he could no longer see the palace looming in the distance, he took a seat on a rather chilly wrought-iron bench. Behind him was a row of buildings with large front windows, revealing the glittering trinkets for sale within. But in front of him was a small park – a tiny patch of greenery in the limestone jungle. A few children scrabbled in circles around a playground, nearly getting kicked in the face by a toddler on a swing set. An older man pushing a vendor cart came to a rolling stop in front of the park, and a series of delighted shrieks erupted. Ramsey realized that the vendor was selling ice cream, and the children quickly formed a line, each clutching a single copper coin in their hands.

It was a beautiful yet mundane scene, an ordinary part of everyday life in the kingdom. As a royal, Ramsey had spent much of his youth in the palace, sheltered from such events. It usually caused him to relish these moments alone, wandering undetected amongst the common folk, taking a break from being his usual prim-and-proper self.

But right now, it only brought nausea bubbling back up his throat. Because it was all a reminder of what was at stake. Ramsey knew that the royal guard was patrolling in full force, with droves of them marching through the southern gates and into the wilderness every morning. For right now, they would keep the reptilians at bay. *But if they do summon their god...* Ramsey shook his head. He didn't dare imagine what sort of monstrous deity would come tearing down the kingdom walls.

He peered down at his watch, groaning as he realized he had fifteen minutes to walk back to the palace, jog up two flights of stairs, and return to the stifling courtroom. He stood up and strode briskly away from the park, just as the cart vendor finished serving the line of eager children.

He walked quickly, nearly breaking into a jog all the way back to the palace. By the time he strode up two giant winding staircases, he struggled to keep from panting. The worst part was, once he was settled back in his seat, he realized he had five minutes to spare.

I could've at least bought some ice cream, Ramsey huffed. *Done something with my free time other than stew about my current predicament.*

But now lunchtime was over, and Ramsey was mentally preparing himself for another several hours of political banter fraying his few remaining nerves. The heavy wooden doors swung open, and at first, he hardly paid the new arrival any attention. He figured it was another gruff elder returning from lunch.

"Ramsey?"

He looked up. It wasn't a court member – it was a servant. One that clearly had a message for him.

"His Highness has requested your presence in the gardens. Please, come with me."

RAMSEY'S RELIEF AT FREEDOM FROM THE SUFFOcating courtroom was overshadowed by fraught anticipation of what the king had in store for him. *Why the gardens? What are these 'extra preparations' he mentioned? And when will I be permitted to set out in search of my brother?*

He was so lost in thought that he hadn't realized they'd reached the rear entrance to the castle, which resulted in him nearly tripping on the staircase that led into the gardens. Ramsey could tell that the servant, who strode several paces ahead of him, was aware of his distractedness. But per royal protocol, the servant did not say a word.

King Gabriel stood in the center of a circular path, admiring a tall stone fountain as it bubbled and plumed. He turned around as they approached, and Ramsey noticed that while he was dressed in fine clothes, he lacked his cape and other regalia that he typically wore around the palace. Even the petite female guard that normally followed the king around was gone. In the finer districts of Brennan, he would've blended in perfectly.

And it made Ramsey wonder where they were going.

"Good afternoon," The king greeted in a smooth, deep voice. The servant bowed deeply before excusing himself and returning to the palace. Ramsey snapped to attention, attempting to shake off his anxiety and carry himself with the proper poise of a future heir.

"Good afternoon, Your Majesty. It's a pleasure to see you."

A soft chuckle rumbled through his throat, "It's alright, Ramsey. Relax. I know you have a lot on your mind. And since I know you are wondering, I have plans for you to set off with several other members of the royal guard tomorrow morning. I want you well-rested and prepared for your journey, so I hope the courtroom was a bit of a mental reprieve."

Ramsey fought back the urge to scowl at that statement.

"In addition, I had some matters to attend to this morning," King Gabriel continued. "Which is why I've summoned you here – I have something to show you. Let us go for a little stroll."

As they walked, the king elaborated on the events of the past few days. He told Ramsey that in addition to border patrols, there had been several strategic ambushes by the royal guard, resulting in multiple destroyed Varan and Naga villages.

"An excellent start to seizing the remaining land in the valley." A satisfied grin stretched across the king's face. "But we must push even harder. We don't want to give the beasts the opportunity to flee through the mountains and summon their god in distant territory. They must be fully eradicated for our kingdom to survive."

A wretched knot formed in Ramsey's stomach, tightening with every word King Gabriel spoke. This wasn't just a war; this was genocide. *Even if the reptilians surrender and agree to leave the valley forever, that won't be enough for the king. He wants them dead.*

Stop it. Ramsey forced the thoughts out of his mind. *Why are you empathizing with those beasts? We must destroy them. Don't you realize that they have the capacity to destroy us if we don't?*

As Ramsey stopped fretting and turned his attention back to the king, disappointment flooded through his veins as King Gabriel mentioned that they were yet to find any of the idol pieces. Not only would obtaining them keep the kingdom safe, but deep down Ramsey hoped that it would prevent the reptilians from being fully massacred. *If they can't summon their god, maybe King Gabriel will let them surrender and flee.*

Ramsey realized that they were headed in the direction of Everwind, the industrial district. The sounds of clanking metal and hissing steam rose above the buildings, which were shrouded in a faint cloud of smog. As they got closer, a sour mixture of chemicals scorched the inside of Ramsey's nostrils. He fought to hold back a sneeze.

It was early afternoon, meaning that the various blacksmiths, carpenters, and other trade workers were in full production mode. King Ramsey led the way, sweeping past stony-faced laborers that carried stacks of cut timber over their shoulders. Ramsey noticed that the workers hardly paid the king any attention. *Maybe they don't know who he is. Or maybe... he comes here often.*

They were approaching a large blacksmith's shop, one that sprawled across several storefronts and was many stories high. Ramsey noticed that it was one of the largest businesses in the area, more of a factory than a mere shop. Coming and going through its doors was a sea of workers, mostly metalworkers but also, strangely, leatherworkers and a few seamstresses.

A deep chill trickled down Ramsey's spine. He knew exactly where he was. He'd visited this place several times back when he was a teenager. But it had never been this busy.

"Welcome to Castella Metalworks." The king stood in front of the entrance, peering over his shoulder at

Ramsey. "If I remember, it's been a long time since you've visited this place."

Ramsey nodded, the tense lump in his throat preventing him from replying. Without a word, he followed King Gabriel through the entrance, where they were met by a man with deep olive skin and a head of thick yet greying black hair. Like the king, he was dressed in subtle yet formal clothing, his impeccable grooming setting him apart from the scruffy laborers. Despite his appearance being so out of place at a busy blacksmith's, the workers paid him no attention. In fact, they seemed to skitter past him with their heads down.

"Lorenzo Castella," King Gabriel greeted in a hearty tone. The two men shook hands, and Ramsey tried his best to appear dignified as the king ushered him forward.

"Ramsey," Lorenzo held out a hand, and Ramsey reluctantly took it, feeling a jolt up his forearm as the Castella patriarch squeezed with a bit too much force. "I can't believe how much you've grown. You're what, twenty-five now?"

Ramsey nodded.

"And what a fine young man you've turned out to be. King Gabriel chose the perfect successor. Well, my friends, shall I give you a full tour?"

Ramsey lagged a few paces behind as Lorenzo and the king walked around the factory. They strode shoulder-to-shoulder, joyfully conversing like old friends. Ramsey picked up on faint bits of their conversation, but he was mostly peering around at the factory as they went from room to room.

Waves of heat prickled Ramsey's skin as they passed by the blazing forges, their coals burning white-hot in a sea of roaring flames. Beyond the forges were rows of anvils, which rattled Ramsey's eardrums like gongs as the crafters pounded bits of hot glowing metal into various shapes. His eyes flicked across the room, and he took inventory of what the workers were making. He saw plenty of half-finished swords and various parts for guns, but also buckles, chains, and other embellishments - ones that would normally go on armor.

Metal armor. Of which there was none in sight.

Then it hit him. Ramsey knew what was coming – why the king had brought him here. But his stomach still twisted as they walked into the next room.

"We've had to bring in plenty of leatherworkers," Lorenzo remarked as they entered. "Beneath those scales is still skin, after all. It's proven tricky to work with, but even without our initial prototype, each set made so far has held up to rigorous testing. It's half the weight of metal armor, and much thinner and more flexible. I'm sure your men will be satisfied with the results, Gabriel."

Even without our initial prototype. Lorenzo's words rattled through Ramsey's mind, dredging up painful memories of his brother jumping through the window with said prototype. Ramsey wondered where Arthur took it. He feared the worst – that it was in the reptilians' furious, vengeful hands. Ramsey understood the king's strategy, and he did believe that the reptilian-scale armor would be more effective than metal suits. But enraging the reptilians would only make them fight back harder. *Meaning bloodier battles, and more dead soldiers.*

Ramsey shuddered as the trio strolled through the back door, bathing Ramsey's skin in sunlight. He frowned, craning his neck to peer past Lorenzo and the king. They were now in a dirt-filled, barren backyard. It stretched on for at least a hundred yards, ending in a shoddy, abandoned building. *Wait a minute.* He remembered this place. *It used to be a lumberyard... there's even still bits of timber amongst the dirt.*

He shuffled his feet as they walked, kicking at the splintery stands of wood flaked across the ground. *They look fresh*, he noted. He could even smell a faint whiff of sawdust in the air.

Then he looked up and saw it – a long, thin building made entirely of timber, with a low roof and no windows. Ramsey wondered how he could've been so blind to it before. He shook his head, scolding himself for being so distracted by his racing thoughts.

As they approached, Ramsey noticed more workers skittering in and out of the odd building. Ramsey was confused as to why it was made of timber – most of the buildings in Brennan were limestone, and wood was susceptible to fire and storm damage. *But one big advantage of using wood,* Ramsey noted as they entered. *Is that it makes the building process much quicker.*

The sour smell of freshly cut wood overpowered Ramsey's nostrils as they entered. But despite its considerable size, the building was nearly empty.

Except for... Ramsey froze as his blood chilled in his veins.

It was impossible to miss, towering in the back corner in its horrid magnificence. While the king was quick to fawn over the armor set, running his fingers over the scales and fiddling with the shining metal buckles, Ramsey held back. Even from a distance, he couldn't deny its beauty – the scales were polished to a fine gleam, not a single tear in the hide or a stitch out of place. Despite his initial disgust, he soon found himself raising a finger to touch the mottled black-and-brown scales.

This is Naga hide.

"Isn't it a beauty?" Lorenzo grinned, revealing a gold glint in the corner of his mouth. "It was built by the finest crafters in the whole factory. Only the best for the future king."

Ramsey froze just as his fingers touched the scales. A jolt ran through his nerves, as if the armor had shocked him. But he fought the urge to pull away. He narrowed his eyes, hardening his emotions, and pressed his whole hand against the armor.

This is mine. My armor.

Naturally, King Gabriel was insistent that Ramsey try it on. He felt a deep chill prickle his skin as Lorenzo slid the cuirass over his head and settled it over his torso. He winced as the chestpiece was tightened and buckled into place. As much as he tried to force his sympathies for the reptilians out of his mind, he couldn't deny the morbidity of wearing another sentient beings' skin.

The pauldrons were slid over his shoulders, and the greaves fitted over his legs. The armor fit like a leather glove, perfectly tailored to fit the future king, but to

Ramsey it felt suffocating. Finally, the helmet was slid over his head, and it reeked of freshly cured leather.

Ramsey clenched his throat, fearing he would vomit.

But as he turned around, he realized that King Gabriel was beaming. He wore the largest, proudest smile Ramsey had ever seen. It reminded Ramsey of the way his own father looked at him, when he performed a perfect piano recital or gave an immaculate toast at dinner.

Or when he eventually told him that his oldest son was going to be king.

Lorenzo ushered Ramsey in front of a wall-length mirror, and a wave of surprise and shock washed over him as he caught a glimpse of his reflection. Morbid or not, the armor set looked fantastic. It was light-weight, flexible, and incredibly durable. A faint sliver of light peeked in through the ceiling beams, and Ramsey couldn't help but grin as a thin line of Naga scales glittered in the light.

I am a future king. He repeated it to himself like a mantra, forcing himself to believe it. *I must hold myself with the composure of one. And that means doing whatever it takes to defend my kingdom from those monsters.*

King Gabriel appeared behind Ramsey, placing a hand on his shoulder.

"I couldn't have my own heir venture into the swampland without the finest armor available to him." the king grinned. "I hope you like it, son."

Ramsey beamed, taking a deep breath to keep from shaking.

A few minutes later, Lorenzo and the king helped to remove the armor set and placed it back on its stand. Ramsey gave it a final, forlorn look of admiration as they left the building.

The rest of Lorenzo's 'tour' passed in a blur. Ramsey continued pacing behind the chattering duo, a small smile sneaking its way onto his face. By the time the tour ended, Ramsey's anxiety was gone, and he'd come to detest his previous emotions. *Fear, disgust, even sympathy for those damn beasts.* It made him feel sick, as if those thoughts were betrayal. *No more of this*, he huffed. His loyalties would rest with the king, his family, and most importantly, the kingdom he would someday rule.

If any more whispers of doubt creep into my mind, he growled to himself as he and King Gabriel departed the factory and made their way back to the palace. *I will quash them in an instant.*

It was nine o'clock, nearly time for bed, and yet Ramsey found himself once again staring bleary-eyed into the bathroom mirror.

Charlotte was already tucked into bed, wearing her finest silk nightgown with her long blonde hair unraveled from its usual braid. When they first arrived home, she'd announced that she had a surprise for him. Normally, Ramsey would've been eager to hear it. But he found himself deeply distraught when he looked into his wife's joyful eyes and felt nothing. No excitement, no happiness, just fear and worry for the coming days ahead.

That was when he decided to excuse himself to use the restroom.

He splashed cold water on his cheeks and buried his face in a fluffy white hand towel, resisting the urge to scream into it. He'd been fine for a few hours – trying on the macabre yet beautiful armor had infused him with pride and confidence. But as the tour of the metalworks factory concluded and evening activities ensued, his joy was quickly replaced with impending dread. Because with every hour that passed, he was that much closer to leaving the safety of the palace, venturing into reptilian territory, and confronting his brother.

There was a debriefing shortly after the metalworks tour, and Ramsey swore he didn't take a full breath for the entire hour. He met his comrades from the royal guard that would be joining him, having to force about a dozen cheerful greetings and handshakes. They were a decent-sized group – small enough to not draw too much attention, but large enough to fend off any angry reptilians that blocked their path.

Then came the king's speech. King Gabriel was an elegant public speaker, his deep voice adding an impressive bravado to his words. Ramsey knew the king was attempting to rally confidence, but all it did was make Ramsey's stomach churn with anxiety. And as he peered around at his stone-faced companions, he wondered if they felt the same.

Thankfully, dinner was quieter. The entire royal family was invited to a feast nearly large enough to be considered a banquet. And of course, King Gabriel chose that time to announce who his new successor was.

After that, all attention was on Ramsey. Charlotte, being the beautiful sweetheart she was, doted on him the whole night, beaming with pride as the others told her she was a lucky woman. *A fine future queen,* they said. And the whole night, there was a certain glisten in her blue eyes, as if her husband being king wasn't the only revelation she was excited about.

She waited until they were alone, having just locked the door to their apartment, before announcing that she had a surprise.

And now I'm hiding in the bathroom like a damn fool. Ramsey scrubbed his face until his cheeks turned red, tossing the towel on the marble countertop. He couldn't focus on being king. He couldn't even focus on his wife.

All he could think about was Arthur.

No one had mentioned his name all night. As Ramsey's family sat around and feasted on far too much food, it was as if his younger brother didn't even exist. Ramsey wondered where he was. *Human territory? Reptilian? Is he safe? Injured?*

Is he still with that half-reptilian girl?

His blood sizzled at the thought of her. This was all her fault – the monstrous witch had manipulated Arthur and torn him away from his own family. *I don't understand why he's so insistent on defending her.* Ramsey growled. *She's an evil half-breed who nearly killed a human. She does not belong in this world.*

Despite his fears about confronting his younger brother, Ramsey knew one thing was certain - he'd take great satisfaction in dragging that horrid creature back to the palace for her execution.

"Ramsey? Are you all right in there?"

Charlotte's sudden knock caused Ramsey to jolt. After a few seconds, he relaxed, took a deep breath, and tried to regain his composure. He sighed. He'd been neglecting his poor wife the whole day, barely speaking to her about his newfound future as monarch. *Our future,* he reminded himself. *She'll be queen.*

"Yes, my dear," Ramsey forced a cheery demeanor. "I'm alright."

After taking a deep breath, he opened the bathroom door. Charlotte stood barefoot in her nightgown, her long, curly blonde hair beautifully disheveled after taking it out of her intricate updo. She was bare-faced, her cheeks still pink from wiping off her makeup, and her blue eyes glittered with a deep, emotional happiness.

"Are you ready?" she reached for Ramsey's hand. He loosened his tense posture, allowing his wife to pull him back onto the king-sized bed. She sat cross-legged on the comforter, wrapping a crocheted blanket around herself like a cape.

"Yes, I am. What did you want to tell me?"

The grin on her face widened, as if she'd burst with excitement at any moment. Anticipation filled Ramsey's stomach.

"Ramsey, my sweet husband, I'm so proud of you. With you now as heir to the throne, our whole lives are going to change."

Ramsey nodded robotically, his mind swirling with questions.

"But my dear, that's not the only thing that's going to change," Charlotte sat up straight and pressed a hand against her stomach. "Sometime in early spring, the apothecary says. That's why I haven't been feeling well."

The frantic spinning gears in Ramsey's head began to click together as it all made sense. His stomach dropped as if he were in freefall, but the overwhelming tidal wave of shock quickly simmered into a mixture of disbelief and joy.

"You mean..." he could barely sputter the words.

"Yes," Charlotte beamed. "It finally happened. We are expecting a child."

Ramsey assumed she was amused by the dumbfounded look of shock on his face, because she immediately swept Ramsey up in her arms, laughing and cheering with tears brimming in the corners of her eyes. Her beautiful laugh was infectious, and before long Ramsey was rejoicing with her, picking his wife up and twirling her around like when they were newlyweds.

He'd wanted this for years. His marriage to Charlotte was an arranged one, just like everyone else in the royal family. But they'd known each other since they were children, with Charlotte being the daughter of one of King Gabriel's most esteemed guard captains, and Ramsey was secretly thrilled when their betrothal was arranged when they were eighteen.

He'd always had a crush on her – with her petite, pale figure, blonde curls, and stunningly blue eyes, she was an incredible catch for any man, even a royal one. Their attraction to one another certainly made the arrangement more appealing, but they had quickly learned that marriage was never that simple.

But in the six years since their wedding, Ramsey was proud of how far they'd come, both as individuals and as a married couple. He could truly say that Charlotte was his best friend and greatest supporter, and while their marriage had its difficulties, she was truly the love of his life.

But the largest of those difficulties had been their inability to conceive. For the first two years, Charlotte would come home in tears after every apothecary visit ended in disappointment. *She's not infertile,* they said. *Sometimes these things just take time.*

As the years passed and the couple became increasingly swept up in their royal duties, Charlotte's apothecary visits became less frequent, and discussions of children became nearly nonexistent. Ramsey had worried about it for a while. *Maybe she's given up. Or maybe she's decided she doesn't want children after all.* But for the past few months, between joining the royal guard, dealing with his brother's traitorous behavior, and most importantly, becoming the future heir to the throne, he'd been too distracted to broach the subject.

But now it had happened, and with impeccable timing. Not only was Ramsey heir to the throne, but he now had his own heir to surpass him.

But now that the initial excitement had settled, the reality of his current situation made his mind whirl in circles like a spinning top. *The reptilians, my mission, Arthur...* in an instant, everything had changed.

Ramsey's life was no longer about him. He peered up at Charlotte, imagining his beautiful wife holding their newborn child, their heir... and anger began to boil in his veins. The more he feared his child being born into a chaotic world, full of violence and bloodshed at the hands of reptilians wielding the power of gods, the more he understood King Gabriel's actions. Every scrap of sympathy he had for those creatures earlier in the day quickly dissipated. *They must be destroyed. All of them. I will not let them hurt my child, my family, or my kingdom.*

"I know."

Charlotte's soft voice loosened his fraying nerves. Her empathetic smile showed that she understood Ramsey's fears, and she wrapped her husband in a tight embrace.

"I know you're scared. I know that we're on the brink of war, and as future king you now have enormous responsibilities. But just remember, I'll always be here for you."

She reached out and grabbed Ramsey's hand, placing it on her stomach. "*We'll* always be here for you."

Now Ramsey could feel his own tears hanging on his lower eyelids, threatening to descend at any moment.

"Thank you, my dear. I love you."

Ramsey needed sleep, but between the upcoming war and his upcoming parenthood, he was far too anxious to relax. So he spent the next few hours lying in bed, resting his head on Charlotte's chest as they discussed everything from baby names to what their child's teenage years would be like.

But neither of them brought up the war. Or Arthur.

As midnight approached and Charlotte succumbed to sleep, Ramsey realized just how fragile his promise to save his brother truly was. He swore that he would salvage his relationship with Arthur, keep him in his life... but that was before he discovered he was about to be a father. He couldn't endanger his child's future by protecting a traitor to the kingdom. The horrid truth was that no matter what Ramsey did, no matter how hard he fought for his brother, Arthur's loyalty was to the reptilians. It always had been.

And as Ramsey lay in the darkness, the soft downy comforter doing little to warm his frigid nerves, all he could do was pray. Pray that somehow, with enough persuasion, his brother would let go of his delusions and return home where he belonged.

Because, Ramsey shuddered. *I'm terrified of what I'll have to do if he doesn't.*

Chapter 5

WHEN MARISSA AWOKE THE NEXT MORNING, Arthur was gone.

She sat upright in bed, still woozy and disoriented from her anxiety-filled slumber. She pressed her fingertips against the scales that lined her aching forehead and peered around. Arthur's bed was empty; the blankets neatly folded and the freshly fluffed pillow perched against the headrest. It was like he was never there at all.

In the other corner of the hut, Nathara was still asleep. She was nothing more than a massive lump half-covered by a blanket, with her tail descending onto the floor and coiling around one of the bedposts. The blanket was pulled up above her head, completely concealing her serpentine face. Marissa realized why – not only were Naga semi-nocturnal, but they had no eyelids.

Nathara was using the blanket to shield her unblinking eyes from the morning sunlight.

No wonder I'm not a morning person. Marissa chuckled and slid out of bed, planting her feet on the cool dirt. She remembered the many days spent traveling with Arthur, where he'd be wide awake with the sunrise, sipping his morning coffee and reading the newspaper. A lump formed in her throat. Maybe he wasn't avoiding her – after all, he woke up early every morning. *Even with our stressful night of sleep, today is likely no different.*

A warm tingle ran down Marissa's scaled back as she stepped out into the dewy morning air. It was well past sunrise, which meant the valley was engulfed in a soothing warmth that soaked into Marissa's dark scales. A hint of an autumn breeze trickled through the village, making her long black hair curl around her arms and neck.

She paced around the village, weaving through clusters of busy Varan. She caught glimpses of their activity – they were arranging a communal breakfast of assorted insects and small brown eggs that appeared to be from some sort of lizard. She watched as the lizard-folk grabbed handfuls of bugs in their claws and tossed them into their mouths like popcorn. The eggs were swallowed whole, with the Varans' throat muscles bobbing as they gulped them down.

Marissa bit her dark lips, her mouth watering. She was hungry, and while she was unsure about trying insects, the eggs looked appetizing. *Although I'd prefer to cook mine...*

A sudden, faint shout snapped her attention away from the Varan. Marissa spun around, then smiled and shook her head. Several juveniles were on the outskirts of the village, chasing a small, strange lizard that was desperate to skitter away from them. As it came closer, Marissa noticed that it had a similar body shape to a bearded dragon, but with a vibrantly red head.

"Got it!"

Marissa jolted. *That voice wasn't a reptilian.* Her heart froze as Arthur emerged from the scrabbling crowd, pouncing on the lizard and grabbing hold of the back of its neck.

As Arthur finished rejoicing and the cheers subsided, Marissa saw him catch a glimpse of her. He smiled briefly and turned away, distracted by his friends, but she jogged towards him anyway.

"Good morning," Marissa greeted in a friendly, inno-cent tone. "You were up early."

"Varan are early risers," Arthur shrugged. "Unlike snakes. I'm glad you slept in though. You were up late last night."

Marissa chewed on her bottom lip, her face burning. She didn't want to bring it up, but clearly Arthur wasn't going to either. His nonchalant tone made her mind swirl with worry. *Is he embarrassed? Regretful? Does he want to pretend that last night never happened?*

"Check it out," Arthur held up the wriggling lizard, his words breaking the awkward tension in the air. "It's a red-headed agama. Must be a male, look at those colors! Bright blue body and a blood-red head. Can't believe I outran the others," he grinned at the juveniles behind him. "Anyway, is Nathara awake yet?"

Marissa shook her head.

"Ah. Well once she is, she said she'd do the reptile-mind-communication-thing with these guys. Then our plan should be all set."

Marissa gulped. While their plan was important, Arthur's oblivious words were like knives in her ears. Her heart was melting to a puddle at her feet, and it sent scalding embarrassment through her body. *Stop brooding. It was nothing. It means nothing. I'm a snake, and he's a human. That will never change.*

"Marissa?"

Her mind snapped back to reality. She peered up at Arthur, who was pointing behind her.

"It looks like your father and his entourage are leaving."

Marissa spun around and saw Ezrinth, Rathi, and a small group of Varan cutting through the village. They each wore leather sacks stuffed with supplies, and Ezrinth had both a bow and quiver on his back and a dagger strapped to a belt around his waist. While the Varan had determination in their eyes, chatting quietly amongst themselves as they walked, Ezrinth's attention was elsewhere. His slitted eyes scanned the village, flicking in all directions.

He's looking for me.

"You'd better go say goodbye," Arthur continued. "Be curt but polite. We don't want to arouse any suspicion. Then we'll be ready to put our plan into action."

Marissa stepped away, keeping an eye on Ezrinth but keeping his eyes off of her. She wanted to give Arthur enough time to retreat, so she could pretend he'd already left the village. In reality, she knew he was sneaking off toward Rathi's home, ready to await the next phase of their plan.

But she could only keep Ezrinth away for so long. Eventually, the Naga caught sight of Marissa as she stepped toward one of the firepits. He immediately broke away from the group of Varan and slithered towards her.

She froze, forcing herself to maintain a relaxed demeanor. In the corner of her eye, she could see Arthur scrambling towards Rathi's home, constantly peering over his shoulder for onlookers.

<Good morning, my dear.> Ezrinth's thoughts were soft, but to Marissa they were full of venom. <I'm surprised you're awake. You know, us Naga are meant to rise late and stay up with the moonlight. I suppose you've had to acclimate to human schedules, haven't you?>

<I'm fully rested.> Marissa fought back to urge to hiss her thoughts.

<Excellent. Well, I hope you've found Komodo to be as enjoyable as I have. Please make yourself at home while you're here. Aina will be keeping an eye on you – let her know if you need anything.>

Ezrinth extended a scaled hand and cupped Marissa's chin, making her stomach clench. She knew the Naga meant for it to be a tender gesture, but she fought not to flinch as his claws slid across the scales that lined her lower jaw.

<It won't be long, my dear.> A smile crept across his serpentine face. <I just need two more idol pieces and to

retrieve your mother from that filthy human kingdom. I've wanted my family back for so long... I can't believe it's finally happening.>

The emotion behind his words nearly made Marissa's tense posture soften. As genuine as Ezrinth's love was, it was mixed with too many other hideous emotions for Marissa to appreciate it. *He has a heart all right, but it's a heart full of venom.*

Despite her disgust toward Ezrinth, she felt an unsettling longing in her chest as he slithered away into the swampland. He and his companions' figures were slowly engulfed by the sea of tall grass that swayed in the autumn breeze. Then they were gone.

Marissa shook her head, snapping her mind back into focus. *I need to hurry.* She scampered off toward Rathi and Aina's home, careful to avoid catching the attention of any wandering Varan. The sprawling abode was situated in the back of the village, bordering the waterfront and surrounded by palmetto bushes. It gave Marissa plenty of privacy, and as she crept around the front entryway, she saw no signs of Aina. In fact, Marissa hadn't seen her all morning.

Odd. I thought she was supposed to be watching me.

Marissa shrugged it off and stepped into the hut. The woven pine rugs draped across the floor bristled under her bare feet. She grimaced as a stray pine needle pricked the underside of her toe. *I wish I had my boots.* She'd been barefoot since she arrived in Varan territory. Reptilians didn't wear shoes, and she still had the scabby remains of blisters from the beautiful yet painful stilettos she'd worn to the party. Her dependable yet haggard boots were a world away, likely still slumped in a dark corner of Arthur's now-abandoned apartment.

This place is a maze. Marissa frowned as she crept through the home. *I need to be careful that I don't accidentally run into the guar- wait.*

Marissa froze. In front of her, in a hallway bordering two rooms, were two massive woven storage baskets, each several feet tall. This was part of Nathara's plan; she had noticed them while assisting Aina with cleanup from the festival the night before. *<They're in the perfect location.>* Nathara had insisted. *<It's just two rooms away from the idol pieces, and guards will be forced to run through this hallway to reach my distraction.>*

Marissa chuckled as she approached one of the baskets and lifted the lid. *How did Nathara figure all of this out? She must have a mind like a steel trap. I'm completely lost - I have no idea what part of the house I'm in.*

"Psst."

The sound was barely a whisper; it could've easily just been a rustling leaf or a creaky hinge on the basket lid. But as Marissa crept inside the giant woven structure and shut the lid behind her, she knew that the sound was coming from the other basket.

Arthur.

The baskets, like much of the rest of the home's furniture, were made from woven palm fronds. And through the gaps in the intertwined plant fibers, she could see broken bits of a human silhouette, so shrouded by the basket that no fleeting passerby would ever notice. Even Marissa would've been unsure if Arthur was in the other basket, if not for a sliver of his forest-green eyes peering back at her.

All they could do was wait. Even if the Varan couldn't understand human speech, the lizardfolk still had excellent hearing and would detect their mumblings. They had to be still and silent, not making a sound or saying a word.

Which gave Marissa's mind plenty of time to stir up memories. It all seemed surreal – only a few weeks earlier she'd been a reclusive orphan, tucked away in a storeroom behind a decaying mansion with little human contact. She reflected on the sights she'd seen, the people she'd met, and the new experiences and emotions that had set her heart on fire with longing. *The Valley of Scales is a wild, strange, broken world, but every bit of it is worth saving.*

Maybe Nathara was right. Maybe Marissa's dreams of peace weren't so far-fetched. Maybe after this was all over, she wouldn't be an outcast anymore. She could have a life of her own. *A home, friends, family...*

Arthur's eyes were no longer on Marissa, but she couldn't help but gaze at the basket that concealed him. *I've only known him two weeks, but it's felt like a lifetime. I just wish he didn't feel so distant right now...*

Wait...

Thoughts were forming in her head. Panicked yelps and shouts, combined with worried chatter and distress. They were faint yet painfully loud at the same time. Marissa pressed her head against the side of the basket, desperate to decipher the jumbled reptilian thoughts.

What's going on?

Just as anticipated, the two guards from the idol pieces' storeroom came jogging around the corner, passing the inconspicuous baskets without a second thought.

Is this Nathara's distraction? But why does it sound so... panicked?

The shouts continued, but now the sound of a whimpering juvenile chimed in. Marissa peered over at Arthur. He was calm, his green eyes devoid of the wild panic that flashed through her blue ones. *He can't hear any of this.*

She took a deep breath. She kept trying to tell herself that this was just Nathara's distraction, and all was going to plan. But her aching intuition told her otherwise.

"Marissa, no!" Arthur whispered harshly as Marissa lifted the lid on her basket to peer out a nearby window. Blood pounded in her temples. She knew this was dangerous; the guards were gone, but someone could still come charging through the home and spot her at any moment.

The scene was closer to the village square, the large cluster of Varan just tiny figures in Marissa's vision. She squinted, and within the chaos she could make out a familiar Varan cradling a young juvenile.

Aina? Where was she this whole time?

Standing next to Aina were several other juveniles, younger than the ones Arthur had hung out with the night before. Pain emblazoned their reptilian faces. They hunched over with their arms crossed in a petrified stance, trying to maintain composure. There was no sign of Nathara.

<Keira!> A male Varan darted out of the crowd, hurriedly scooping the injured juvenile out of Aina's arms. <What happened? Is she alright? Where is her mother?>

Aina's gaze lifted from the ground. In her eyes was the agonizing hollowness of a being that had just witnessed an indescribable horror.

<Tavi, I'm so, so sorry.> Aina could barely utter her thoughts. Her frail posture made it appear as if she could topple over at any moment. <Your mate and I were out gathering pine needles with a few of the juveniles when we came across human guards. They... they attacked us.>

<I... I don't understand.> The male Varan's reptilian face paled as he cradled his daughter. <The border is miles from here. What were those humans doing so close to our territory!?>

<I don't know. But Tavi, your mate... she's gone. They killed her.>

It was as if all blood flow stopped in Marissa's body. Her nerves felt like ice as she watched the devastated father crumpled to the ground, his somber cries chilling her heart. His daughter was too young to fully comprehend what was happening, but Marissa could see the distress in the child's eyes as she listened to her father's sobs.

It was then that Marissa noticed the bloody gash on the juvenile's arm. To her, that wound was what made it all so terrifyingly real. It was a reminder of what the humans were capable of. *Whatever Nathara's distraction was... this wasn't it.*

It even made Marissa wish that Ezrinth and Rathi hadn't left yet. *Maybe they could've prevented this...*

"Marissa? What's going on out there?"

The lid on the basket next to Marissa's rose a few inches, exposing a concerned pair of green eyes. Marissa was too horrified to acknowledge Arthur – it was as if her body had turned to stone. Arthur noticed the panic in Marissa's eyes and rose slowly, placing a hand on her bicep as the two stood wide-eyed just inches from the window. Marissa's eyes flicked to her right, and saw Arthur's face fall in horror as he observed the distraught Varan still crumpled in the center of the village. The crowd had dispersed, leaving only a few of Tavi's relatives to console him. Marissa watched as an older female Varan, her own face lined with anguish, placed a sympathetic hand on Tavi's shoulder.

"Good gods, Marissa... what happened?"

His words were soft with disbelief. But Marissa didn't have time to answer – the familiar sound of belly scales sliding across the pine-needle mats quickly snapped their attention away from the window. Nathara was scrambling down the hallway. Her frantic pace causing her long body to tumble behind her in coils, her tail bumping into furniture as she scrambled towards them.

Nathara froze as she caught sight of Marissa and Arthur standing in the baskets. Their dismayed faces and the Varan's cries echoing from the window behind them told the Naga all she needed to know. She sighed, her reptilian nostrils flaring.

<I take it you saw what happened?> Nathara's eyes flicked over to Marissa.

Marissa gulped and nodded. She couldn't speak; her throat felt like dried leather.

<I wish we could do more to help them, but we need to get out of here. Do you have the idol pieces?>

Marissa's eyes widened in panic. She'd been too immersed in shock and sorrow to follow through with their plan. But the guards were still gone, at least for a little while longer. Marissa forced herself to move, stepping one shaky leg after another out of the basket and onto the ground. With her nerves on fire, she bolted down the hallway.

She nearly sneered with disgust when she saw them – two pieces of carved rock sitting atop a pedestal in an empty room. *Ezrinth and Rathi took off with the Varan's best guards. They abandoned the village and left everyone vulnerable, all for their vain little quest to cause more violence.* Anger at Ezrinth's actions caused her blood to boil as she firmly scooped the idol pieces into her palm. She wished she could've smashed them right there and then.

Nathara and Arthur weren't far behind her. The pair appeared in the doorway, gesturing for Marissa to hurry. But as the trio dove back down the hallway, ready to make their escape, Marissa's eyes locked back onto the window.

Tavi... he's still sitting there in the middle of the village... mourning his mate...

<Marissa.> Nathara realized her niece had fallen behind and sighed. <I know. But there's nothing we can do. We can't bring his mate back. And if we don't bring these idol pieces to the Testudo, it's only going to get worse. Much worse.>

Marissa winced and peeled her gaze away from the window, realizing Nathara was right. The best way to avenge the Varan's death was to prevent even more bloodshed.

A new sense of determination burned through Marissa's heart as the trio made it through the maze of rooms in Rathi's home and approached the exit. No matter what it took, she would get these idol pieces to the Testudo. She gripped the two pieces of rock, one in each palm, when a sudden realization stuck her.

"Arthur?" <Nathara?>

The two of them spun around, just a few feet from the front door.

As she still struggled to communicate in both human and reptilian, one after the other, Marissa moved both idol pieces into one palm, and made an inserting motion with her other hand.

Arthur and Nathara immediately peered down at their bodies. None of them had any satchels or bags in which to carry supplies. *Or more importantly, the idol pieces.*

"I'll search the room." Arthur declared as he began combing through the entryway, opening baskets and scouring through shelves. Nathara quickly followed, tossing decorative pillows over her shoulder as she searched.

<Found one!> Nathara exclaimed a few moments later. She triumphantly held up a satchel in her left fist. It was about the size of a hardcover novel, made of rough leather with a long strap for wearing across ones' shoulders.

Marissa grinned, her fangs gleaming. It was a small bag, but it would at least keep the idol pieces safe. *I'm certainly not going to carry these in my hands through dozens of miles of swampland.*

Their plan was nearly a success. Relief washed over Marissa's body like a cool stream of water. All they had to do now was walk through the front door and take off into the swampland. Rathi's home was on the edge of the village, meaning that no one would spot them while they escaped.

<Marissa?>

The thought was too shaky and panicked to be Nathara's. A hot flood of anxiety burned through Marissa's veins as she turned around. Standing in the front doorway, with a mixture of grief and exhaustion on her face, was Aina.

All three of them froze in panic. Marissa's mind scrambled to think of an excuse, any way to get them out of this situation... but it was too late. Marissa still held the idol pieces in her hands, and they were the first thing that Aina's eyes fell upon.

<Aina.> Nathara took a deep breath. <We can expla-.>

<Do you really think you can do this?>

Marissa was silent, her palms sweating as they clasped the idol pieces. The sentence sounded accusatory, but her tone did not. Her voice had the weary softness of a heartbroken, exasperated soul, steeped in too much pain for anger.

<Do you really think you can stop this war?>

Marissa was frozen in shock. <I... I don't know. I hope so.>

<Then that's good enough for me. Marissa, my dear, there's something I need to tell you. Your father coming here, the idol pieces... it's all because of my daughter. My girl Mikara was killed by a poacher just a few weeks ago. It nearly broke me; I couldn't bear to go on without her. Neither could Rathi, but unlike me, his grief morphed into hatred and vengeance. I never wanted to ally with Ezrinth – it was all my mate's doing. The truth is, all I want to do is move on in peace. I don't want this, and my daughter wouldn't have either.>

Marissa was in disbelief. The truth was piecing together like a puzzle in her mind, and she was horrified by the results. *Rathi and Aina's daughter was killed by a poacher... that's what caused the Varan to ally with Ezrinth.*

Thomas...

Good gods...

He started all of this.

But Marissa didn't have time to dwell on her realization. Aina was giving them an opportunity to escape, and they needed to take it quickly – before the guards came back.

<Go, hurry.> Aina ushered them out the front door. <I'll make sure no one else comes this way.>

Aina went to turn away and run back towards the village square, when she suddenly pulled Marissa into a tight hug. Marissa was stunned by the Varan's sudden action, but she felt a deep sense of comfort with Aina's scaly arms wrapped around her.

<Good luck, Marissa. I believe in you.>

Aina pulled away, and within a few moments she was gone. Nathara smiled at their kind moment, but urged Marissa to keep moving. As she ran, she placed the idol pieces in her new satchel and slid it across her shoulders so that the bag rested on her hip. She placed a protective hand over the satchel as they disappeared into the forest, the sounds of village activity becoming fainter until all they could hear was the chatter of the murky jungle.

I cannot fail. I cannot let the goddess be summoned. For Arthur, Nathara, Tavi, Aina, Mikara... even my own parents. For all of us.

MARISSA WAS TOO LOST IN THOUGHT TO COM-prehend where they were going.

All that surrounded her and her companions was dense foliage, woven together in a mess of tangled vines and ratty underbrush that crunched under her bare feet as she walked. Up ahead, Nathara seemed to have no trouble navigating the dizzying jungle, her body and tail gliding effortlessly across the ground. Arthur wasn't as fast as the massive Naga, but as an experienced researcher who had many expeditions under his belt, he was able to easily keep up.

Marissa was the one that lagged behind. She paced aimlessly behind them, her attention lingering deep in the recesses of her mind. To her, the scenery all blurred together like an ocean of green. *I have no idea how Nathara can navigate through all this.*

Marissa assumed it been about an hour since they left Komodo, but the forest seemed to distort both her sense of direction and time. It was an uncomfortable slog of a journey, but she was too distracted to worry about the vines snagging her heels or the sandspurs pricking her toes.

All she could think about was death.

Ever since their journey first began, she felt like she'd been surrounded by it. Various haunting memories screeched through her mind. Thomas's anguished cries as his body was ravaged by Naga venom at the apothecary. The painful moans of the burn victims at the church in Alistar. But the most horrid sound, the one she could never forget, were Tavi's mournful howls. The sound that was still painfully fresh in her mind.

Yet as much as death permeated the valley, Marissa had never truly experienced it. She couldn't begin to imagine what it looked like up close; seeing a reptilian corpse stripped of their scales or a human cadaver scorched from the inside by Naga venom. Seeing Tavi's outburst of anguish at learning of his mate's death was heart-wrenching, and Marissa knew his grief was far from over. It was a never-ending wound - no healing, no resolution, only the endless passage of time with the realization that the one you once loved was truly *gone*.

Marissa ran her palm over her wrist, slowly tracing her fingers up her arm. Her human flesh faded away near her wrists, slowly being consumed by the scales that spread up her arm. Skin and scales had different textures, yet they were both smooth and soft in different ways. While scales were tougher, they were far from impenetrable, and her musings on death reminded her just how vulnerable she really was. *Human or reptilian, we are all mortal. Nothing in this life is guaranteed, even life itself.*

<Marissa!> A sharp hiss cut through her thoughts. <Get down!>

She shook her head, her mind snapping back to reality. She realized that Nathara, about twenty feet ahead of her, was crouched between two trees. Her forearms touched the ground as her long, serpentine body lay flat against the foliage, her winding tail disappearing into the thick brush. Arthur couldn't understand reptilian thoughts, but unlike Marissa he'd been paying attention to their surroundings. He too was hunched behind a bush, his knees scuffed with dirt.

Marissa peered around, confused, when she felt a sharp tug on her arm. Arthur yanked her out of the open forest and pulled her behind him, gesturing for her to sit down. Marissa flinched, not fond of someone – especially Arthur – being so rough with her. But as soon as she realized what Arthur and Nathara had their eyes locked on, she was grateful for his sudden action.

Guards. Her scales prickled as a deep chill settled over her. The silhouettes of the pair of humans were barely visible against the emerald hue of the forest. Marissa's stomach dropped as she realized the crucial detail as to why the trio hadn't spotted the guards earlier. Normally, the soldiers would've been easy to spot, marching around in their bright purple-and-gold regalia. But now they wore muted, earthy colors, making their figures easily blend with the scenery. It was if they didn't want to be seen.

Marissa noticed Arthur's breaths came in deep pants, his shoulders rising and falling with every exasperated breath. He was trying so hard to be silent, but Marissa knew his panicked thoughts were the same as hers. *This isn't about guarding the borders. They're wearing camouflage so they can sneak around reptilian territory and commit murder.*

Marissa's shaky breaths lingered in her chest as she tried to stay quiet. The guards were moving, but slowly, whistling and chatting amongst themselves as they walked. Their hands were bare, but Marissa could see two weapons either side of their belts; a gun and a sword.

She bit her lip. All she could think about was Aina and the others' deadly encounter in the forest that morning. *Did Tavi's mate try to fight them? Chase them off? Or did the guards just kill her unprovoked?* She thought of the female Varan's tiny child, watching helplessly as her mother was murdered. She would live the rest of her life without her, and she was so young that she'd have few solid memories left of them together. But she knew by the anguish in the child's eyes back in Komodo that her mothers' death was something she would never be able to forget.

No child should ever have to feel that sort of pain.

"They're gone," Arthur whispered. The guards had slipped out of sight, the sound of their footsteps now just a faint pattering in the distance. Arthur turned toward Marissa and pressed a finger to his lips. She nodded, and the pair ambled carefully through the brush, keeping their backs hunched in a near-crawl as they traveled in the opposite direction of the guards.

Marissa and Arthur's pace was slow, but Nathara was as swift as a fish in water. She kept her body nearly parallel with the ground like a true snake, her long figure trailing across the ground with barely a rustle. Marissa and Arthur struggled to keep up as they followed her winding tail through the brush.

<Alright, I think we're safe.> Nathara stopped, raising the upper half of her body like a cobra until she was back in her regular Naga form. Marissa and Arthur came to a fumbling halt behind her. Arthur wiped the sweat from his forehead and panted like he hadn't taken a breath the entire time.

"Good gods, what are the guards doing way out here?" Arthur exclaimed. "This is bad. We're still miles from the border. Clearly the king has sent his men on a hunt."

Arthur turned toward Marissa, his face falling into a deep melancholy, "That's what you saw earlier, wasn't it? Did those Varan encounter the guards?"

Marissa nodded. Arthur chewed on his lower lip. He didn't need to ask for further details – the sight of the male Varan crumpled to the ground in grief was enough for him to understand.

<Arthur says the border is still miles from here.> Marissa relayed the information to Nathara. <What are we supposed to do? Those guards could be lurking anywhere. Maybe we should travel deeper in reptilian territory. We'll be safer there.>

<We're in trouble either way.> Nathara huffed. <If we travel through human territory, we risk those village

oafs catching sight of a giant Naga, which won't end well for me. But to get to the Testudo, we'd have to travel south and then cut west through Naga territory. Not only is it a longer journey, with your human friend being in danger the entire time, but there's risks for me as well.>

<What do you mean?>

<The truth is... I wasn't supposed to leave my village. My father Orami knows I've run off and is likely on the hunt for me. If he captures us, not only will I be in trouble, but it won't bode well for you or your friend either. My father detests humans, even if they're half-Naga and his own grandchild.>

Marissa took a deep breath and rubbed her temples. She turned toward Arthur, who was eagerly awaiting her to translate the information for him.

She did, and Arthur's face turned pale.

"We really are in a heap of trouble, aren't we?" Arthur sighed. "Nowhere is safe for us. And since both options have risks, I say we leave it up to you. Human or Naga territory, you decide."

Marissa's mind spun with indecision and worry. She hated being tasked with deciding their fate. And if they were caught on either route, Marissa knew she would endlessly blame herself. She peered up at her serpent-faced aunt, then down at Arthur's chestnut brown hair and thin glasses. She couldn't bear the thought of risking either one of them.

<Arthur says it's up to me to decide.> Marissa turned toward Nathara. <Both options are dangerous, but human territory is faster. So that's my choice.>

<Works for me. I'm in danger either way. At least your friend will be safer.>

Marissa grimaced, knowing Arthur wouldn't be. Like Nathara, both options were dangerous for him. Not only was he unwelcome in Naga territory, but to Brennan he was now a wanted criminal, a scourge who dared to bring a half-reptilian into human society. Marissa shook her head, deciding it wasn't best to relay her entire history with Arthur to her aunt. *Especially the part about him being a royal.*

"Human territory it is," Marissa relayed to Arthur. "But we still need to get past the guards."

"Well, as much as I spent my college years traipsing through swamps, I'd ask your aunt for ideas," Arthur replied. "She's probably better acquainted with the wilds of the valley than I am."

Marissa agreed. She turned toward Nathara. <I know you're not as familiar with Varan territory, but you're the expert on sneaking through the jungle. Do you have any ideas on getting past the guards? They're probably patrolling all over the place.>

<Well...> Nathara mused, running a claw over her scaly chin. <I do know of one place in Varan territory that the humans won't touch. It's called the Monitor River.>

<Monitor River? What's that?>

<Exactly what is sounds like, except it's more of mucky, nearly stagnant stream than a true river. But it is full of monitors - some of the largest lizards in Squamata. They don't like humans, which means it would be difficult for guards to patrol that area. I passed

a Varan village next to the river on the way up here. We can swipe one of their canoes.>

They don't like humans. Marissa grimaced. Nathara's plan did seem like a valid strategy to sneak past the guards, but she feared Arthur would balk at the idea. She peered down at her nervous hands and traced a finger over the skin on her knuckles. *Human skin. I don't know how the monitors will react to me either.*

But the rest of Varan territory was too dangerous, and Marissa decided the monitors were a more favorable enemy than the guards. They had to take the risk.

She turned toward Arthur, who once again awaited her translation, and sighed as she gently relayed Nathara's plan.

"The Monitor River!?" Arthur's reaction was exactly what Marissa had dreaded. "*That's* your aunt's idea? Is she trying to get you and I killed?"

"Well, it's the lizards or the guards," Marissa frowned. "And honestly, it's our only option. You and I are both wanted by the royal guard. If we're caught, you'll be imprisoned, and me and my aunt will likely meet a far worse fate."

Arthur clenched a palm to his forehead, distraught by the danger of their plan and frustrated that Marissa was right. "Fine. But it's still a major risk. Those canoes better be sturdy. And bite-proof."

Marissa turned to Nathara and nodded. Nathara noticed the grim look on Arthur's face, but she still clapped her scaly hands together with feigned enthusiasm.

<Excellent. The river isn't far from here. I'll lead the way.>

As Nathara slithered ahead, keeping a sharp eye out for guards, Arthur stayed back with Marissa. The pair walked side-by-side, dead leaves and moss crunching under their feet.

"Better to let her take the lead," Marissa acknowledged. "You know, I never actually explained what the Monitor River was. And yet you knew. I take it you've been there before?"

"Yes, unfortunately," Arthur grimaced. "During my university studies, me and a few other biology majors went on an expedition on the outskirts of human territory. Nothing major, we just wanted to document some of the flora that grew in that area for a project. Everything was fine... until we ventured too far downstream and ended up in Varan territory."

"Is that where the monitors started appearing?"

"Yes. They're smart enough not to venture into human territory – they'd be easy targets for hunters. And don't get me wrong, I love monitor lizards. They're some of the most beautiful and intelligent creatures in the valley. But they don't like humans, and they fiercely guard the river from intruders. They nearly capsized my group's boat."

Marissa gulped, remaining silent as they ventured through the jungle. Marissa could feel moisture under her bare feet – the ground was getting damper. Most of the valley was barely above sea level, meaning that much of the region was a flood zone. And with all the rain they'd had recently, the low-lying soil often held water long after the weather dried up.

<Marissa! Up here!>

Nathara made a sharp left turn and disappeared into the brush. Marissa followed her, brushing away branches and maneuvering her feet through thorny vines. She winced as one of the sharp protrusions pricked her toe, splattering tiny red droplets that sank into the damp earth.

"Are you alright?" Arthur nearly bumped into Marissa as she stopped and gripped her foot.

Marissa groaned. "Yes, I'm fine. I really need shoes though."

"Too bad you don't have scales on your feet," Arthur chuckled, but Marissa was too frustrated by the pain for humor. She huffed and kept walking.

Nathara frowned as Marissa and Arthur emerged behind her in a clearing, with Arthur tearing a tangled clump of vines off his shoe.

<I need to teach you how to move like a true Naga.> Nathara's slitted eyes shot over to Marissa. <You're too slow.>

<In case you haven't noticed.> Marissa crouched in the dirt. <I'm half-human. I have legs. And feet. Feet that really need shoes right now.>

Nathara sighed as she watched Marissa pick up her left foot and wipe more blood off her toe. <Maybe we can find something in the Varan village.> She suggested. <Which, speaking of, is right over there.>

Marissa peered around her aunt. About a hundred feet away, tucked deep into the jungle, the tops of thatched-roof huts peaked over the trees.

<It's a small village.> Nathara remarked as they ventured closer. <Probably just a few dozen Varan living here. Here, let's sneak through the forest. The river's on the other side, along with the boats.>

<Sneak? Wait a minute, we're not stealing a boat, are we?>

<What else are we supposed to do?> Nathara hissed. <March up there and ask to borrow one? In case you haven't noticed, not only do the reptilians not like humans, but we don't tend to have much interaction with each other. A Naga venturing into a remote Varan village unannounced is going to cause problems. Not to mentio- >

"Um, Marissa? Nathara?"

The quiver in Arthur's voice immediately made Marissa snap her attention on him, even as her aunt obliviously chattered on. He had been walking several feet behind Marissa and Nathara, but he was now stopped and staring wide-eyed at the ground.

As Marissa got closer, she realized why.

Blood.

It was a dry, dark rust color, at least a day old, but easily distinguishable as it splattered the dead leaves. A thin trail of it snaked its way up to the entrance to the Varan village.

"Good gods," Marissa whispered. "What happened here?"

The three of them peered over at the village. It was still late morning, and Varan were diurnal creatures. The village should've been full of activity – cooking, cleaning, crafting. Instead, it was eerily silent. Marissa realized that normally, they would've never been able to get this close without being spotted.

Something's wrong.

<We need to go investigate.> Marissa declared to her aunt. <Maybe we can help them.>

Nathara sighed, her tone eerily serious. <Judging by how quiet it is, I don't know if there's anyone left to help.>

<Maybe they evacuated?>

<Let's hope most of them did.> Nathara peered down at the trail of blood. <But I fear some weren't so lucky.>

"We're going to go investigate," Marissa turned towards Arthur. His face was grim, his steely eyes locked on the silent village. He shook his head, breaking himself out of his anguished daze.

"I'll stay here and keep an eye out for guards."

"Are you sure?"

"Yes. Even if there are survivors, I don't think they'd take kindly to seeing a human right now. At least you're half-reptilian."

Marissa nodded sadly, realizing that he was right – it would be wise to have someone keep watch for guards. If Arthur spotted them, he could slip away into the village and let them know. But Marissa feared what would happen if the guards spotted him first – Arthur had no weapon, and he was still dressed in colorful Varan clothing that was beginning to fray at the hems from trekking through the forest.

"I'll be alright," Arthur said softly, as it he could detect Marissa's thoughts. She knew he'd spotted the worried look on her face. She sighed and stepped away, ready to join her aunt.

<Stay safe.> Nathara peered over her scaled shoulder at Arthur as they crept into the desolate village. He remained silent, his back to them as he peered out at the vast jungle.

<You know he can't understand you, right?>

<Of course I do.> Nathara huffed. <It's moreso for my sake. I'll admit he's a decent human, and I don't want to see any harm come to him.>

The sound of Marissa's footsteps and Nathara's slithering body were the only noises in the hushed air. The grass and dead leaves under her feet were nothing but soft crunches, but the noise pounded in her ears like gongs. The village had the same choking aura of death as the Black Market, as if all oxygen had been sucked out of the air.

And as the first few huts crept into view, Marissa realized another reason that Arthur wanted to stay behind. And it nearly made her run back to join him.

Lifeless, stagnant bodies slumped against the thatched walls at odd angles, contorted in ways that they never should've been. Between that and the crusty blood that drenched every corpse, it was difficult to tell who was human and who was reptilian. But Marissa knew it was a mix of both. A jolt of horror shot through her body as she nearly stepped on a torn bit of flesh - one with speckled Varan scales still hanging off the edge of it.

Marissa squeezed her eyes shut, trying to keep her stomach contents from erupting out of her throat. She clenched her sweaty palms to her forehead, uncertain if she could take another step.

<This was recent.> Nathara remarked. <Either late last night or earlier this morning.>

Marissa peered up as her aunt's thoughts interrupted her nauseated panic. She noticed that while Nathara's face was somber, she was much more composed at the gruesome sight than her unaccustomed niece. It sent a pang of sadness through Marissa's heart – clearly this wasn't her aunt's first experience with death.

She closed her eyes again, another wave of nausea broiling in her stomach. In her childhood, she'd read plenty of fantasy novels full of violence - fiery spells, swordfighting, and heroes slaying villains. But she'd never realized how gruesome death truly was. All her earlier musings on the subject came rushing back, but as a tidal wave instead of a trickle. She wished she could rip the horrid images out of her own brain, but she knew it was now burned into her memory forever.

No one ever forgets something like this.

<I know it's hard.> Nathara placed a palm on Marissa's shoulder. <But I need you to compose yourself and keep walking. You're not going to be able to help me find survivors if you faint or lose your breakfast.>

Marissa opened her eyes and nodded sadly. She knew that Nathara was sympathetic, but the Naga's reptilian practicalities outweighed the instinctual horror that Marissa's human half felt. *Nathara is right. Stop standing here and trying to pretend this isn't happening. If you're going to stop a war, you need to be stronger than this.*

She stepped cautiously around the thatched homes, her nerves jolting every time she came across another corpse. In the center of the village was a large firepit, the charred remains cool and stagnant in the damp air. Small flakes of chalky white ash scattered in the breeze and speckled the bloody ground. Marissa wanted to scream, not only because of the horrid scene, but also in futile hope that someone – human or reptilian – was still alive and could hear her. But all she could hear was the rattle of anoles in the trees overhead, a single, pitiful sign of life in a decrepit village full of death.

<Marissa!>

She craned her neck over her shoulder and saw Nathara a few dozen yards away, her slithering body settled in a coil by the shoreline. Marissa noticed two more bodies at her feet, one human and one Varan. But a trail of bloody, clawed footprints extended past the scene of death, stopping at the edge of a crude wooden dock. The dock was lined with cleats, but no canoes. The woven ropes that once held them dangled in the murky water.

<There's only one boat left.> Nathara pointed to a canoe slumped on the shoreline, half-hidden by trees. <Clearly some of the Varan managed to escape. And if any of those bastard guards tried to follow, let's hope they were swarmed by monitors.>

Nathara chuckled, but her face fell as she peered down at Marissa, who had her solemn eyes locked on the corpses at her feet.

<Alright, maybe I'm a bit too harsh. Poor souls.>
Nathara bent down and inspected the human and Varan bodies. Marissa was frozen, her scales shivering as her eyes fiercely studied the deceased human. Her face was damaged beyond recognition, but Marissa could tell it was a woman, which was unusual for a member of the royal guard. She was very petite, pale-skinned, and likely middle-aged. With trembling hands, Marissa gingerly brushed a lock of long raven-black hair away from what remained of her features. Marissa's throat tightened as she noticed a single glassy, widened eye, in a vibrant shade of pure blue.

Marissa jolted as she heard a rustle from the deceased Varan. Her gaze shot over to Nathara, who was removing the corpse's holstered dagger and tying it around her waist.

<Nathara!! What are you doing!?>

<What do you mean?> Nathara's tone was calm as she finished securing the dagger around her scaled body. She sighed. <This Varan is dead. Gone. He doesn't need this anymore.>

<It's still horrible! You can't just steal from a body!!>

Nathara gave a small, sad sigh. <Marissa, reptilians don't think that way. We're not sentimental creatures. Once our souls have left Squamata, the materials we leave behind are meant for the living. This Varan is already on his way to Reptilia, where he will be guided by the great god Sauria and reborn into a new life. But you and me, we're still here, and we're on a mission to prevent this from getting worse.> She lifted the dagger, which was made from carved bone, out of its sheath.

<And even if this weapon couldn't save his life, maybe at some point on this journey it will save ours.>

Marissa's eyes flicked from the dagger back down to the deceased Varan, her face lined with uncertainty.

<Where do humans go when they die, anyway?> Nathara asked.

<I... don't know. There's a lot of theories. Different people believe different things. Honestly, I've been seeing and experiencing death a lot more lately, and it scares me to not know where I'll end up if it happens to me.>

<Well, regardless of who we are or what we believe, I trust that our souls do not cease to exist when we pass. All of nature is a cycle – an end is always a new beginning.>

Marissa nodded, appreciative of her aunt's words. She noticed the slight glint in the deceased guardsman's boots and peered down at her own feet. They were caked in dirt, with grubby toenails and callused soles. A small scab had formed on the bottom of her toe from where she'd pricked it earlier.

She couldn't bring herself to take them, but Nathara noticed Marissa staring and began removing the guard's boots herself.

<Wait.>

Nathara froze, her scaled hands clasping the heel of the left boot.

<Us humans, when bad things happen, we pray. If I'm really going to take her shoes, I want to thank her properly.>

<Ah. Excellent idea.> Nathara raised her body into a standing position and slithered next to Marissa, so they were shoulder-to-shoulder. <I do have some training from Nerodia's shamans. You pray for the human, and I'll pray for the reptilian.>

Marissa bowed her head and clasped her hands low at her hips. Nathara's rhythmic chants echoed in Marissa's head. She couldn't understand them, but they were both powerful and soothing, like the smooth flow of a river. She then retreated deep into her own mind, struggling to find the proper words to say. She'd never been a religious person, and while growing up Beatrice had few books on the subject.

Royal guardsman, I'm so sorry I don't know your name. I don't know your story, or what brought you to this place. But whoever you are, and no matter what you believe in, I hope you've found peace beyond this valley. I really do hope that Nathara is right, and that an end is always a new beginning. Please go find yours.

<I must say, I do feel better now.> Nathara remarked once she'd finished her own prayer. <I'm so sorry, Marissa. I realize now that I was callous. It's just... as future chieftress of the Naga, I'm often at the forefront of these conflicts. I've seen death more times than I can count, and it's numbed me emotionally. I guess it must, otherwise the grief would drive my soul mad.>

Marissa felt a deep, sympathetic pain for her aunt as the Naga finished removing the boots from the deceased guard. She already knew that Nathara had lost her mother, and her brother had been exiled. But Marissa's intuition told her that more pain hid behind her aunt's slitted eyes, pain that she wasn't yet willing to discuss.

<Here you go.> Nathara handed the boots to Marissa, who slid them over her dirty feet. The shoes were slightly damp and a bit too large, but Marissa felt relief once she was able to take a few steps forward without pine needles prickling her bare toes.

<Let's go fetch your little human friend.> Nathara declared, slithering back toward the village entrance. <We need to get going. Hopefully that last canoe is still watertight.>

ARTHUR WAS STILL STANDING WITH HIS BACK TO the village when they returned, having barely moved since they left. A lump formed in Marissa's throat at the sight of him, his body nearly frozen in place. She could tell by the stiffness of his posture that he was desperately trying to hide his emotions, as if any sign of weakness could ruin their mission.

The colorful, woven clothes that draped over his lean frame rustled as a small breeze crept up behind them. Marissa thought back to the day before, when she first saw him adorned in his gift from the Varan juveniles. How happy he was among the reptilians that he so deeply admired. And now a slaughter lay behind him.

"Arthur?"

He turned his head slightly to the right, so Marissa could barely see his profile. A single forest-green eye took notice of Marissa's boots and the pile of clothes folded in her outstretched palms. He sighed, his shoulders falling.

Nathara wasn't far behind. The Naga slithered up to the pair with a rucksack full of scavenged goods. Nathara was insistent that they needed to search the desolate village for supplies, and despite her hesitancies, Marissa agreed. After all, they'd left Komodo in a hurry with nothing but a tiny satchel containing two pieces of rock.

Marissa insisted all she needed were shoes, and as they searched the village, she became even more grateful for the boots she'd taken from the slain female guard. The Varan didn't wear shoes, and the rest of the guards were men with boots far too large for a petite eighteen-year-old woman. It would've been a long, painful journey to Testudo territory in bare feet.

Despite scavenging the entire village, and watching Nathara accumulate numerous supplies, Marissa was only willing to swipe one item - a change of clothes for Arthur out of one of the guard's satchels. It was a simple outfit – a long sleeve cotton shirt and a pair of sand-colored trousers, but at least it was clean and comfortable. And Nathara had immediately snatched up the satchel to carry the rest of their acquired goods.

As Marissa stood in front of Arthur, the clothes nearly folded in her hands, he gave a sad nod. "I see. I suppose it's best for me to not wear Varan clothing while traveling through human territory. Although me traveling with two reptilians might make that obvious."

Marissa tried to smile at his subtle joke, but her stomach was too clenched in knots for any positive emotions. Amid so much anguish, Marissa worried that she wouldn't be able to express joy again for a long time.

Arthur crept behind a tree, and quickly changed into his new outfit. Marissa felt her face flush as she stood awkwardly in the clearing, pretending that Arthur wasn't completely undressing just a few dozen feet away. She huffed as she noticed a smirk creep across Nathara's scaled face.

<You can't hide it, can you?> She teased.

Despite only being half-Naga, Marissa gave her best effort at a serpentine hiss, which only made Nathara's snicker.

Once Arthur emerged, his colorful Varan clothing folded in a pile and placed in Nathara's satchel, the trio crept back through the village toward the docks. But as they approached the first set of homes, where the blood trails led to their gruesome ends, Arthur stopped.

"Arthur?" Marissa turned around as she noticed her friend's footsteps cease behind her.

"I'm not looking forward to this."

Marissa noticed the sorrow in his eyes and the way his mouth hung open, unable to squeeze out another word. She knew that deep within his mind, he was holding back a massive tidal wave of emotion. *I know exactly how he feels. The fear, the horror, the sense of desperately wishing you were anywhere but here.*

"I've never truly seen death before," His hoarse voice was soft. "I don't know if I'm ready to see it today. But I guess war doesn't give you a choice, does it?"

"It doesn't," Marissa replied, remembering the severity of her own nausea when she first walked through the village.

"How are you feeling about all this? Are you alright?"

Marissa paused for a moment, pondering how to answer. Whether to admit how much this had affected her mental state.

"No," she sighed. "But like you said, war doesn't give us a choice. I'm scared to walk back through that village too. But at least-" She took Arthur's hand and squeezed it tight. "We can do this together."

"Of course," Arthur nodded, forcing a sad but genuine smile. "Always."

Marissa sighed as she stepped forward, and Arthur gave her hand a reassuring squeeze. They paced through the village, side-by-side, the same horrid scenes of battered bodies and blood trails creeping into view. But this time, Marissa didn't feel the same sense of stomach-twisting shock. She felt a deep sense of pain and anger mixed with determination. *I swear, to all of you, I will get these idol pieces to the Testudo. I will end this.*

She noticed that Arthur was silent and stone-faced as they walked. His eyes were wide and alert, taking in the same scenes she was, yet his emotions were hidden behind a mask. But Marissa knew they were still there. Just like Nathara, shock and pain lingered deep inside his soul, even though it wasn't expressed on his face.

"It's worse than I expected," Arthur eventually remarked, once they were almost to the docks. Nathara had already slithered past them and was hauling the single remaining canoe into the water.

"A lot worse," Marissa admitted. "A lot of bodies, a lot of blood. It's horrifying. And I don't blame you for not wanting to see this. The truth is, I wish I hadn't. But I can't unsee it now."

They finally made it to the docks, and Arthur loosened his grip on Marissa's hand. She shivered as they watched Nathara slide the canoe into the water and fetch two wooden paddles from the edge of the dock. Her distress seemed to amplify the bitterness of the breeze that swirled around her.

"You know," Marissa continued. "When I was a child, still living at the orphanage, the headmistress Beatrice was a widow. She used to say that once you've seen death, it changes you permanently. You never view the world the same way again."

Arthur opened his mouth, but Nathara quickly slithered up to them before he could respond.

<Are you two ready?> She asked.

<Yes.> Marissa replied. She turned to Arthur and gave him a knowing glance. He nodded, his face still strained and pale.

Nathara slid her satchel off her shoulder and plopped it in the boat, her serpentine body following. The wooden canoe lurched under her weight, swaying back and forth in the murky water.

<Give this to Arthur.> Nathara handed a large blanket to Marissa as she stepped into the canoe. Marissa stared at the heavy, dark cloth in confusion, but quickly realized that it was meant to conceal him from the monitors. She wondered where Nathara had obtained it from, until she caught sight of a clothesline further up the shoreline. It

was mostly full of rags and tunics, with a suspiciously large gap in the center framed by two empty clothespins.

<What about me?> Marissa asked as Arthur stepped into the canoe, lying down in the middle and disappearing under the hefty blanket. <Won't they notice that I'm not fully reptilian?>

<You smell more Naga than human.> Nathara replied, her nostrils flaring. <Most of your body is covered in scales. Let's hope it's enough for the lizards to let us through. Besides.> She plucked an oar from the inner wall of the canoe and handed it to Marissa. <We need two people to row.>

Marissa had never been in a boat before, but she mimicked Nathara's swift scooping motions with her own oar. The wooden paddle cut through the calm water like a knife, propelling the canoe downstream. A tiny wake formed behind the boat as they rowed, with Marissa padding on the left and Nathara on the right.

Being on the water made the jungle seemed even more primordial. The tree canopy curled around the stream in a u-shape, nearly blocking out all sunlight. The water was almost pitch-black and very stagnant, with only the slightest current aiding them in their journey. Marissa took a deep breath, her reptilian nostrils expanding as she inhaled. The air had an earthy yet sweet scent, a mixture of decaying leaves and damp soil after a rain shower. It reminded Marissa of her swim in the stream after their troublesome encounter with Thomas, and it caused the same feeling of nostalgia to pour over her. For someone who hadn't grown up around water, it certainly made her feel at home.

But within a few minutes, Marissa's pleasurable sense of calm was swamped by a mixture of awe and fear. Even with their camouflage, their massive, hulking bodies were impossible to miss. They were all at least several feet long, basking on the shoreline and lounging in low-handing tree branches. Their narrow, dragon-like faces and eerily human eyes made them seem mystical, as if they contained the power of the gods themselves. Even without seeing them, Marissa could feel them – their curiosity pulsed through her mind and felt just like her own.

<They're beautiful.> Marissa breathed in awe as they paddled. She noticed that Nathara didn't look at them with the same glint of wonder in her eyes.

<They certainly are, but let's not get too comfortable.> She warned. <We need to get through here as quickly and discreetly as possible.>

Marissa nodded, but her mind was flooded with questions. She decided not to ask them until they were further downstream, where the sandy shoreline disappeared and was overtaken by clusters of deep-rooted trees. She noticed that far less monitors lurked in these parts of the river.

<I guess they let us through.> Marissa remarked. <Do they normally only let Varan through?>

<Well yes, but they generally leave other reptilians alone. It's humans they're concerned about. The Varan, like all reptilians, live in a symbiotic relationship with their kind. In this case, it's the monitor lizards, their closest relatives. But not all monitor species that you see along the river are native to Squamata. Some of them are dumped pets from other regions that ended up establishing their

species in the valley. But all reptilians, whether native or introduced, are connected. No matter where we come from, Reptilia is what binds us – we all come from the same plane of existence, and it's where we all go after we pass.>

<All of us come from Reptilia? But what about- >

<Wait, Marissa.> Nathara gripped the side of the canoe. <Did you feel that?>

Marissa froze, her question still hanging on her dark lips. But she did feel it – a bump on the back of the boat. Marissa's heart pounded as she prayed that it was just a floating branch or a rough patch of water. But then a second bump slid under the boat, far too deliberate to be an inanimate object.

Then they saw it – a boiling swirl in the water, followed by dark scales sliding across the surface. Faint hisses echoed through the air – Marissa and Nathara peered around and noticed that the previously quiet section of the river was now full of monitors. Some gathered at the water's edge, their hefty bodies swaying as they stomped forward. Others emerged from the murky water, their sharp, slender faces pointed directly at the canoe. They were all different species – a swarm of colors and sizes. She recognized some of the species from Arthur's teachings at The Menagerie.

I see several water monitors... a massive blackthroat monitor... even some tiny Ackie monitors by the shoreline...

"What's going on out there?" Arthur whispered, his face peeking partway out of the blanket.

<Foolish human!> Nathara snapped, smacking the top of Arthur's head with her tail. <We're surrounded! Now is not the time for you to poke your head out!>

Arthur flinched and immediately retreated under the blanket. As much as Marissa feared for their safety, she wished Arthur could see the monitors. The scene was both incredible and terrifying.

But there was still the question of what bumped their boat. Marissa could see bits of its dark, scaled form slipping in and out of the water. It was clearly much larger than the other monitors, and the emotions that it emanated were different. While the other monitors leered, their eyes flashing with intimidation, the giant one was calm. It gave off an ancient, wise aura, which to Marissa made the creature feel like an old friend.

It finally stopped in front of the boat, a few bubbles appearing at the tip of the bow. The water gurgled as its massive head emerged - wide and bulbous like an alligator's and covered in crisscrossed scars. Its dark, gentle eyes, locked firmly on Marissa, seemed to reflect a single question, <Who are you?>

Marissa froze, her chest quivering. She had no idea how to respond.

<It's a Komodo Dragon.> Nathara breathed in disbelief. <The oldest, largest, and wisest of the monitors. The Varan believe that they are messengers for the great lizard goddess Acantha. And it seems to be very interested in you.>

<I swear it's asking me, 'Who are you?' But I don't know what it means by that.>

<It's concerned because you smell both human and reptilian.> Nathara replied. <The other monitors see you as a threat, but this one knows better than to assume hostility. It simply wants an explanation.>

\<But how am I supposed to respond? Will it even understand me?\>

\<Remember, reptiles are different than reptilians.\> Nathara instructed. \<Their communication is simpler, but relies heavily on how they *feel*. You need to channel your answer into a single emotion, something that can be felt regardless of intelligence.\>

\<I thought you just said Komodo Dragons were the smartest of the monitors?\>

\<I said *wisest*. Intelligence and wisdom are two separate things.\> Nathara corrected. \<Now, focus. We need them to let us through.\>

Marissa closed her eyes, retreating deep into her mind. *I must explain that I am both human and reptilian, and that we mean no harm and just wish to pass through. What emotion would convey that?*

Think... think...

Her head pounded and her temples throbbed as she struggled to decipher the question. *It can't be a forceful emotion, it has to be calm, peaceful...*

Her eyes flicked down towards her hands in her lap. She was still wearing the woven Varan dress, which covered most of the scales on her arms. Only her fleshed wrists and hands peeked out from her sleeves.

If I can't tell it, I'll show it.

Marissa crept up to the front of the boat, struggling to keep her balance as the canoe bobbed in the water. She locked eyes with the massive monitor, whose head hadn't budged an inch since it first emerged. She held up her forearm and rolled her sleeve back, exposing her mottled black-and-brown scales.

But the monitor's question only deepened in her mind. Her reveal only made it want more answers. Marissa exhaled, trying to hide her frustration. *I don't understand. How am I supposed to explain myself with a single emoti-*

Then the realization hit her, pouring over her mind like the smooth waves lapping the shoreline. She hadn't imagined the 'Who are you?'. It's message to her wasn't just her mind guessing its intentions. Its thoughts weren't as clear as those of true reptilians, but they weren't vague emotions either. This creature sat somewhere in-between on the spectrum of intelligence. Not a reptilian, but not a true reptile either.

<I am a half-Naga.> She declared, attempting to imitate the Dragon's own unique communication method. It blinked knowingly, as if to say 'Go on.'

<I know I'm part human, and that you generally don't let humans through. But someone who I care deeply about said I'm special. That I exist for a reason. And right now, that reason is to stop this war. Please, great Komodo Dragon, let us through.>

A warm pulse crept through her mind, seeping through her soul like a drop of ink spreading in water. The Komodo Dragon almost seemed to smile. A mysterious sparkle flickered in its rust-colored eyes as it sank back under the water, leaving only a swirl of bubbles behind as it disappeared. Slowly, the other leering monitors retreated, the unnaturally fierce postures relaxing into sluggish indifference.

"That was incredible," Arthur whispered. Nathara whipped around, ready to scold Arthur for once again poking his head out of the blanket. But upon watching the monitors disappear, she groaned and decided otherwise.

<I think the human is fine to come out now,> Nathara declared. <We've received a Komodo Dragon's blessing, so clearly the monitors won't bother us on the rest of our journey.>

Nathara turned back around and continued padding, and Marissa did the same. Once he was convinced that Nathara was no longer paying attention to him, Arthur emerged fully from the stifling blanket and stretched his arms over his head.

"But seriously, Marissa, we were surrounded by lizards, you had a staring contest with a giant Komodo Dragon, and they all left. What did you do?"

Marissa smiled. Her arms were growing weary from the weight of the water under her paddle, and her scales were slick with moisture from the humid swamp. She didn't know if Komodo Dragons truly were divine messengers, but something about her encounter with the great beast seemed to awaken her mind. It was as if the Komodo Dragon already knew who she was, and wanted her to come to terms with her own identity and importance.

"To be honest, I don't know," Marissa explained as Arthur sat in the middle of the canoe, his fascinated eyes fixated on her. "I'm still trying to figure that out. But I will say, you're right – it truly was incredible."

Chapter 6

S EVERAL HOURS LATER, THE TRIO REACHED TO the end of the Monitor River. The shallow, dark, slow-moving water pooled into a small lake that bordered a clearing – the first bit of open terrain they'd seen in miles. Marissa's eyes lit up as she noticed a dilapidated farmhouse next to a sandy dirt path.

We made it.

This was the first clear sign that they had crossed between the two realms, although they'd likely already been in human territory for a while. About an hour earlier, Marissa had noticed that the amount of monitors basking in the trees and on the shoreline had plummeted. But Nathara had explained that the mile or so stretching between human and reptilian territory was barren of occupants, a disputed zone where frequent border squabbles had caused the area to become abandoned.

<Even the wildlife doesn't want to be here,> Nathara had noted as they paddled downstream. Marissa had noticed that the jungle had become eerily silent without the barking calls of the geckos that scampered through the trees.

But now it was definite – the river had ended, and bits of human civilization were visible in the distance. Marissa peered back over at sandy trail that snaked its way around the farmhouse. She knew that every carriage path in the outer villages eventually made its way back to the main road.

The path that we can't take. Marissa sighed as Nathara rammed the canoe against the shoreline, slithering out once she concluded its bow was firmly wedged on land. Arthur quickly followed, but Marissa held back, eyeing her companions with a disheartened glance.

She translated her concerns to both Arthur and Nathara – they would need to stay in the forest and out of sight, which was a problem because it would prevent them from following the main road. Marissa knew Nathara had a sharp sense of direction, but she was unfamiliar with human territory. And Arthur admitted that he wasn't quite sure which direction they needed to travel in.

"I know that Testudo territory is west of Varan territory, but that river was disorienting," Arthur frowned as they trudged across the clearing, leaving their canoe hidden behind a cluster of trees.

"Well, when you went on your research expeditions, how did you find your way around?" Marissa asked.

"A compass and a map," Arthur replied. "Neither of which we have right now. Our best option," Arthur peered up at the sky, shielding his eyes as he squinted. "Is to navigate the old-fashioned way. It's well into the afternoon, and the sun sets in the west. So, I say we let the giant glowing ball in the sky lead us onward."

The next hour or so of trekking through the dense jungle was quiet, which Marissa hated. Distractions were what kept her sane; the silence allowed too many harrowing memories to surface. The gruesome scene at the Varan village still burned through her mind, making her temples throb and her stomach lurch with every step forward. She swore she could still see blood-stains sprayed across the ground in front of her, and she flinched at every stray branch, fearing them to be more dismembered limbs.

She peered up at Arthur, who walked a few paces in front of her. She couldn't see his face, but could tell by the angle of his head that his gaze was focused on the sun. She was grateful that she was with him on this journey. When they passed through the slaughtered Varan village, the feeling of his hand clasped in hers was an anchor to sanity. Whether they remained just friends or became something more, one thing was certain - he was her rock. A faint beacon of security and peace in a world that was falling apart.

"You alright, Marissa?"

He'd turned around, his soft green eyes flickering with concern. Nathara was a few dozen feet ahead of them, but she too had stopped and was peering over her shoulder at them.

"Y-yes, I'm fine," Marissa fumbled her words, determined to reassure him that he didn't need to worry about her. But she knew her posture said otherwise. She walked with her body hunched in on itself; shoulders pressed inward and her arms crossed protectively over her chest, as if she were trying to comfort herself. Her pace was slower than her two companions, and she knew her sallow complexion revealed her nausea.

Arthur had managed to keep his composure, and Nathara had seen it too many times. But for Marissa, her first glimpse of death was a sickening nightmare that she couldn't push out of her mind.

Arthur gave a sympathetic nod, understanding her pain but knowing that Marissa didn't want it acknowledged.

"We'll only go a few more miles. The sun is starting to set, so we'll need to find a place to rest for the night."

They continued on, with Marissa's sickness still boiling in her stomach. But Arthur now walked alongside her, which gave her mind some ease. She appreciated how skilled he was in offering a subtle sense of comfort. He was there if she needed him, but it was also okay if she didn't.

<Marissa!>

She froze, her blood chilling at the uneasy panic in Nathara's thoughts. Up ahead, Nathara had hunkered down with her slithering body pressed against the earth. Her wary eyes were locked on something off to the far right.

<What is it?> Marissa asked, creeping deeper into the brush as she approached her aunt. Arthur followed behind her – he couldn't hear Nathara's thoughts, but he could tell that something was wrong.

<It's a human village,> Nathara replied. Marissa watched as the Naga slithered a few feet closer, her body still low to the ground. <But I don't see any humans, and... wait a minute.>

<What?>

<This village, all the buildings... they're *burned*.>

Realization pulsed through Marissa's veins like ice, and she spun around to face Arthur.

"Nathara sees a burned-down village up ahead," she explained. "It must be Copperton, right? I remember it being close to Varan territory."

Arthur's eyes widened. "You're right. At least that means we're headed in the correct direction."

Marissa explained the situation to Nathara, whose tense posture softened as she realized the village was abandoned.

<So *this* is the village that my brother and the Varan burned down?> Nathara sighed. <Good gods, I hope the scene here isn't quite as gruesome.>

<It shouldn't be.> Marissa reassured her. <Everyone made it out alive, there were no casualties.>

<Then we should go investigate.> Nathara declared, slithering off toward Copperton. <Hopefully we can find more supplies.>

Marissa reluctantly followed, Arthur's footsteps echoing behind her. Like before, she disliked the idea of rummaging through an abandoned village, but at least this one wouldn't be littered with corpses. And as much as it made her uncomfortable, she understood Nathara's foraging mentality. Reptilians were resourceful beings, more concerned with survival than sentiment. Marissa just needed to shift her mindset away from her human half.

Copperton looked much the same as it had a few days ago. It was still a barren graveyard of charred and splintered homes, but the embers no longer burned and most of the smoke had dissipated. White ash swept across ground like ghostly dust, and the remains of a flag, its design too charred to be recognizable, waved desperately in the faint breeze. The air had a stagnant, eerie aura just like the Varan village, but this one reeked of anger and pain, not death.

<I can't believe everyone survived, considering the damage,> Nathara remarked as she slithered between the charred homes, picking through piles of blackened belongings. <Fire is truly a horrific weapon when it burns in the wrong hands.>

<There were many injured, though,> Marissa sighed and knelt next to a charred object splayed across the dusty ground. Her throat soured as she realized it was the doll she'd noticed while riding Arrow through Copperton a few days earlier. She felt a sudden urge to turn it over, and with gentle fingers she rolled the doll onto its back. She immediately wished she hadn't – its face was nothing more than an ashy crater encrusted with burned bits of stuffing.

It reminded her of the deceased guard's massacred face. *That long black hair... framing her one remaining blue eye...* Marissa staggered away, her vision blurred from nausea. She took a deep inhale, hunched over with clammy hands clasping her scaled knees. But between ragged breaths, she noticed a second object next to the doll, one almost completely concealed by the sandy dirt.

She clasped the small, round object in her hand, scraping the dirt off with her fingernails. It was a toy whistle, one made of clay and shaped like an unusually plump turtle. Unlike the doll, this trinket had been untouched by the fire, its fine details and carved shell patterns still in mint condition. She curled her fingers around it, the cool clay sending soothing pulses down her palm. Amidst so much destruction, the intricate little whistle was like a tiny beacon of hope.

Slipping the toy into her satchel, Marissa was able to regain composure and walk away. She was determined not to let Copperton break her the same way the Varan village did.

She also didn't want to worry Arthur or Nathara, who were both warily poking around the decrepit remains in search of supplies. Nathara had her back turned and was rifling through a charred crate, but Arthur waved Marissa over as soon as he noticed her.

"Check this out," Arthur grinned, plucking a small round object from his pocket. "I found a compass!"

Marissa smiled as she took the small round object from Arthur and examined it in her palm. A thin spiderweb of cracks wove through the glass, but its needle still bobbed reassuringly to the west, pointing toward the setting sun.

They had been heading in the correct direction. She grinned triumphantly, her fangs gleaming in the hazy orange sunset.

<Hey Marissa, come here!>

A sudden shouting thought pulled her attention away from Arthur. Nathara appeared from behind a pile of burned timber, clutching a long, shiny object in her clawed hands.

<Look what I found!> she waved her prize in the air, peering down its metallic barrel with a single slit eye.

"A gun!?" Arthur exclaimed, his voice shrill with panic. "Good gods, Nathara, that's not a toy!! Put it down!!"

But Nathara couldn't understand him, and before Marissa could relay Arthur's warnings to her aunt, Arthur leapt toward the Naga and snatched the gun from her claws.

She hissed sharply in protest, but Arthur ignored her and stormed away, settling down on a wooden crate next to a collapsed roof. He ran his dirt-lined fingers across the weapon, inspecting it like a soldier.

"It's a blunderbuss," he announced as Marissa walked up to him. Nathara soon followed, her long body slithering behind her. "A pretty basic one, definitely not the royal guards'. Probably owned by one of the higher-ups in the mining camp. It's hefty, and quite a large caliber. When loaded this could do some serious damage."

Arthur stood up, holding the gun at his waist. He glowered at Nathara, "Explain to your aunt that the number one rule for handling guns is to always assume it's loaded. Which means *not pointing the muzzle at one's face.*"

Nathara huffed as Marissa relayed Arthur's warning. <Well, was it loaded?>

<I don't think so.> Marissa replied. She then asked Arthur, who shook his head.

"So, what should we do?" she asked. "Nathara and I don't know how to fire a gun. Do you?"

"Somewhat," Arthur sighed. He stood up and began digging through the crate he'd been sitting on. "I've always preferred bladed weapons, so I'm probably not the best teacher. But I don't want to just leave it here. Also-" he pulled his arm out of the box, revealing a half-full powder horn, several round musket balls, and various other instruments Marissa didn't recognize. "It looks like this village still has the equipment to fire it."

He stared at the gun for a long, silent moment, rubbing the shoulder strap with his fingers. He then slung it over his torso, securing it snugly in place, with the powder horn looped over one shoulder. Marissa knew Arthur was right – as three fugitives sneaking through human territory, they needed to take any opportunity to arm themselves. But seeing her closest friend, a man who sought peace as strongly as she did, with such a nefarious weapon sent uncomfortable quivers down her spine.

"Oh, and Marissa," Arthur reached back into his pocket. "I found something for you when I grabbed that compass."

The cloth seemed to endlessly pour out of Arthur's pocket, and Marissa immediately realized what it was. She appreciated the gesture, but clutching the dusty maroon scarf in her hands gave her dreadful memories of being homeless on the streets of Brennan. For the past few days, she'd been free to wander unmasked, and it gave her a renewed sense of energy. The thought of covering the lower half of her face made her entire disposition sink.

Not to mention that once she did press the scarf to her reptilian nose, she began gagging. The musty cloth still reeked of smoke and ash.

"No," she declared, letting the snaking scarf fall to the ground. "I'm not going to cover my face anymore. Not only do I hate it, but there's no point. I'm already traveling with a wanted man and a full-blooded Naga – it's not like the scarf is going to make me blend in."

Arthur nudged the dusty scarf, now crumpled in a pile on the ground, with the toe of his shoe, "You're right. Besides," he peered up at Marissa. "You look much happier now."

His words twisted her stomach into confused knots. *Happier? How?* She felt horrible - she'd seen nothing but death and destruction since they left Komodo. She'd seen things that would be burned into her mind for the rest of her life. Things that no being should ever see.

But then she remembered the moments in between. The joyful celebration with the Varan the night before. The beauty of the jungle as they floated down the Monitor River. The awe that settled in her heart as she came face-to-face with a Komodo Dragon. She realized that her mind was swirling in both misery and happiness. She was finally free, but at what cost?

Life was difficult back at the Thorburn Estate. But it was also easier. She may have been a lonely outcast, forced to cover up her body and face, but at least she was safe. She remembered the lazy afternoons spent basking in the sun - reading books, chasing lizards, and weaving pine needles into little dolls. But those days were gone. Hopefully there would be better ones ahead of her, ones where her existence was no longer a secret... but first she had to overcome the greatest challenge of her life... *stopping this war.*

She sighed and shook her head, ridding her mind of her stray thoughts. Arthur and Nathara had wandered off, and in the distance, she could see them setting up shelter in the skeletal remains of a burned-down house. Marissa wondered if it could've been Thomas's, but all the homes were too badly damaged to tell.

She huffed as she walked toward her companions. The sun was setting, and they needed her help. Her frantic worries could consume her mind later.

Tonight, the destruction would be their shelter.

I just hope we stay safe.

THE SKY WAS BEAUTIFUL THAT NIGHT – AN END-less dome of deep indigo speckled with stars that glittered like diamonds. As Marissa lay on her back with her arms sprawled above her head, she tried to focus on them – her mind struggling to remember the constellations that she'd read about in her childhood books. She chuckled softly to herself as she strung together the stars in her mind, realizing that any combination could always be interpreted as a snake.

It brought her a brief bit of happiness. And more importantly, it helped her focus on something other than the events of the past two days.

Her body was exhausted – she lay sprawled out on a dirty bedroll she'd found in a cabinet that somehow survived the fire. Her limbs felt like lead, and her eyes struggled to stay open. It was her rampaging mind that refused to let her sleep.

She rolled her head to the side and peered over at Arthur. He was fast asleep, his chest rising and falling in deep snoozing breaths. She imagined he was just as stressed as she was. *Although, the horror hasn't affected him as much. Or at least, he doesn't show it.*

Being a semi-nocturnal Naga, Nathara was still awake, keeping watch and occasionally tossing more twigs in their crackling fire. Marissa was tucked away in a corner near a collapsed roof, not wanting her aunt to know that she was still awake. *I need to sleep,* she huffed, attempting to coerce her rampant brain to settle down. *I need to get some rest so I can keep watch later. Nathara can't stay up all night alone.*

Although, Marissa contemplated. *Maybe talking with my aunt will help calm my nerves.*

<I can tell you're still awake.>

Despite her exhaustion, Marissa nearly bolted upright upon hearing Nathara's voice in her head. Instead, she sat up slowly and locked eyes with her aunt, who was poking the smoldering campfire with a long stick.

<Us reptilians can sense each other's emotions, just like we can with reptiles.> Nathara explained as Marissa stood up and wandered toward the fire. <You are way too anxious to be asleep.>

Marissa sat cross-legged in front of the fire and scratched her head, confused. <I guess I have been able to pick up on the Varans' joy. And Ezrinth's twisted emotions. But you're the one I've spent the most time around, and I've never been able to feel anything from you.>

Nathara hissed, although it sounded more like a sigh. <It's like I said at the Varan village, I've seen too much. I push my emotions too deep down to be detected. And I know that someday my father will step down as chieftain, and I will lead the Naga. But I have no one to rely on, and it makes me feel that I must bear this enormous burden alone. My mother and my mate are dead, my brother is a vengeful outcast, and my father is a useless coward. Trying to stop this war is the only thing that gives me hope. I feel like if I can bring peace to the valley, then being a leader all on my own won't be so terrifying. Maybe I'll finally be happy.>

<Nathara...> Marissa's heart ached for her aunt. She'd never realized that the massive, powerful Naga that had led them on their journey carried so much pain.

Nathara shook her emotions away. <It's alright. And I'm sorry if I've been hard on you. The truth is, you amaze me. You're incredibly brave, but you also have a gentle heart full of empathy – something I'm struggling to reclaim. But I'll give one word of advice...> Her eyes drifted toward Arthur's snoozing figure in the distance.

<What's that?>

\<Never let fear keep you from those you care about.>

Marissa's face burned, but she cocked her head, feigning obliviousness.

\<You know exactly who I'm referring to.> Nathara huffed. \<I know you haven't known him very long, but you two share a bond that I haven't seen in a long time. When the time is right, don't be afraid to tell him how you feel. My biggest regret in life was not telling Kadina that I loved her more often.>

\<Kadina? Was that your mother?>

Nathara chuckled, \<No. Chumana was my mother – and therefore your grandmother. Kadina was my mate.>

\<Kadina was your mate?>

\<Yes.> Nathara shook her head, a wry smile across her face. \<I've never been one for males. But she passed a long time ago, and I haven't brought myself to love since. The truth is, all those corpses at the Varan village... it reminded me of the day she was killed by humans.>

A knot formed in Marissa's throat. Nathara's coppery eyes were wistful, like she was dreaming of her younger years. Her tone wasn't one of sorrow or anguish – perhaps time had patched her pain. But Marissa still didn't dare to press for more details.

\<A big reason why I can't sleep is because of that village.> Marissa hugged her knees to her chest as she sat with her aunt in front of the fire. \<All I can see are those bodies. They're burned into my mind. I'm afraid even if I do get some sleep, it will be wrought with nightmares. And there's this...>

A tidal wave of emotion choked up her words.

\<What is it, my dear?>

<I just can't stop thinking about it. There was this soldier, the only human woman there, that was among the dead. She had long black hair, and while most of her face was missing, she had this single blue eye, and...>

<I saw her too. That wasn't your mother, Marissa, if that's what you're worried about.>

Marissa froze, her mind locked in disbelief. She was relieved by Nathara's words, but also startled that her aunt was so skilled at deciphering her fears. And although she'd been too afraid to admit it, the lingering thought that the deceased soldier looked a bit too similar to her had frayed her mind all day.

<Your mother didn't look much like you,> Nathara continued. <She did have blue eyes, but she was very short, shorter even than you, and had long wavy brown hair. She also had a birthmark on her neck, which the dead soldier didn't have.>

<Wait a minute, how do you know this?>

Nathara grinned. <Well, the truth is... I saw your mother once. Together, with Ezrinth.>

<*You did!?* When? And where was this?>

<It was a long time ago, well before you were born,> Nathara continued. <They were just teenagers, out swimming in the wetlands between human and reptilian territory. I wanted to confront them, tell my brother what a foolish snake he was... but I couldn't bring myself to do it. I never ended up telling anyone about them.>

<Were they happy?>

Marissa's question seemed to surprise Nathara. She sat silent for a moment, her eyes glittering as they gazed into the cracking fire.

<Why yes, they were. And to be honest, that's why I didn't say anything to our parents. My brother was the happiest I'd ever seen him, and, well... that was something I rarely saw. And someday... I hope I will see it again.>

Three decades earlier

 VER SINCE CASSANDRA WAS A CHILD, SHE
wanted to be a hero.

As the youngest of five children, her home was full of warmth, love, laughter, and chaos. Her family owned the only inn in their small town of Live Oak, just a few miles from Naga territory, and all seven of them squeezed themselves into a three-bedroom apartment on the third floor. The inn was always bustling with activity, and with her parents busy tending to its many patrons, Cassandra was often left upstairs in the company of her two sisters that she shared a bedroom with.

But while Alice and Penelope were busy styling each other's hair and stealing their mothers' jewelry,

Cassandra poured her attention into books. They were hand-me-downs, their pages yellowed and their spines peeling from dozens of hours of reading. Her sisters sometimes joined her, and all three of them would gather around and read each line aloud.

Her sisters always wanted to be just like the princesses in the books, and would spend hours pretending that their cramped bedroom was a royal palace, complete with plastic tiaras and old, chipped tea sets that were swiped from downstairs. Cassandra always enjoyed her sister's antics, and felt beautiful every time they adorned themselves in their pretend finery.

But deep down, she didn't want to be the princess that the knight rescued.

She wanted to *be* the knight.

She brought this up with her sisters once. She was eight years old, while Alice was ten and Penelope was thirteen. Penelope was exhausted – their parents had decided she was old enough to start helping out with the inn, and Cassandra and Alice were trying to cheer her up with one of their favorite books.

"I want someone to rescue me too," Penelope noted, pointing at the pink-adorned princess being pulled from a tower. She brushed away her sweaty bangs as she lay slumped on the floor with her head against a pillow. She wore a plain tan dress with a recently mended hole in the shoulder, and her stained apron was a far cry from any royal adornments.

Cassandra nodded, "But what if we didn't need someone to save us?"

Alice and Penelope immediately lifted their heads, gawking curiously at their younger sister.

"What do you mean?" Alice asked.

"Well, what if *we* were the ones dressed in armor and wielding a sword? What if *we* were the ones that slayed the evil Naga? We'd be the heroes!"

Penelope pointed to the armor-clad figure on the next page, who had the princess swept up in his arms, "But aren't knights *guys*?"

Cassandra's face flushed, "I mean... they don't have to be."

Penelope rolled her eyes, crossing her arms above her head and using them as a pillow, "You're missing the point, Cassie. Princesses get to live a life of luxury. They never have to scrub gross dinner dishes or serve stew to old sweaty guys covered in dirt. Being a knight is hard work. Something I'm not a fan of."

"What did you say you're not a fan of?" Cassandra asked.

"*Hard work*."

"Ah, okay."

Penelope turned her head toward her youngest sister, her frustration replaced with concern, "You've been doing that a lot lately."

"Doing what?"

"Not hearing everything I say. You ask me to repeat myself all the time. Is something up with you?" Penelope pointed at her own ear.

"No," Cassandra muttered, her face flushing with embarrassment again. "I'm fine."

But Cassandra knew that Penelope had a point. Lately, her ears had ached more than usual, and sometimes a few stray words in a sentence would get fuzzy. At first, she'd dismissed it, passing it off as nothing. But the more it occurred, the more it scared her, and the more difficult it became to hide.

"I dunno," Alice piped in. "I think we may need to talk to Mother and Father about this. Something's wrong with your ears, Cassie."

"SHE'S LOSING HER HEARING."

Cassandra, being only eight years old, didn't quite understand the gravity of the apothecary's diagnosis. But her parents, Cadence and William, were silent, their bodies stiff as boards, and that sent alarm bells through her mind.

Cadence held her close, smoothing her hair while William conversed with the doctor. Insisting there must be something they could do. Some sort of treatment, or maybe even a cure. His worried, elevated tone of voice sent shivers down Cassandra's spine, and she squeezed her mother tighter.

"I'm afraid there isn't," the apothecary replied solemnly. He was a specialist, one that they'd traveled all the way to Brennan to see. "There's still a lot us healers have left to learn about hearing loss. It will progress through her teen years, and she'll likely have little residual hearing by the time she's twenty."

Cassandra peered up at her father. His eyes were wide with disbelief, and it made her stomach lurch. Her father was usually a calm, jovial man, always behind the bar at the inn, smiling and chatting with the customers. She'd never seen him like this before. *I don't understand. Is he mad? Did I do something wrong?*

"While we don't have a treatment or cure, we do have options," the apothecary continued. "As her condition progresses, she'll need to learn new ways to communicate. Lip-reading is common among those with hearing loss. It's a tricky skill that can take many years to acquire, but it will allow her to maintain conversations with those around her."

"Alright," William's tense posture loosened as he sat upright. "And what else?"

"Well, there is a school for deaf and hard-of-hearing children. There are two locations – one here in Brennan and one in the town of Sanford, not far from your inn. There, she'll be able to interact with other children with hearing loss, and receive special instruction catered to her condition. In addition, they teach an entirely new method of communication – one that uses hand motions and facial expressions. It's called 'sign language'."

William raised an eyebrow, "And how much does this school cost?"

Cassandra frowned. She knew that while her parents gave them a comfortable life in their cozy inn, money was often tight. And this special school sounded expensive.

"The location in Sanford caters to many families in the outer villages, and they offer need-based scholarships to those who cannot afford the cost. I highly recommend applying."

Cassandra focused on the rows of potions on the far side of the room while her father continued his conversation with the apothecary. She drowned their voices out – steadying her shaking chest while studying the colors of the bubbling mixtures within the vials.

She felt like she couldn't breathe. Or was about to be sick. This was too much to process all at once. *I don't understand. Why is this happening to me?*

But she had perked up when the apothecary mentioned the school. She loved school – it had lots of books and other kids to play with. Getting to know other children who were also losing their hearing sounded reassuring. Like she wouldn't have to deal with this alone.

After what seemed like an eternity to Cassandra's young, restless mind, she and her parents left the apothecary and found themselves wandering the streets of Augustree.

"Hold my hand," William instructed firmly. Cassandra took his large, callused palm in hers, not only because he asked her to, but because it was *packed*. The apothecary's shop was located in the busiest part of the merchant's district, and not only were the whimsical trinket stores bustling with people, but a line of them congregated parallel to the cobblestone streets.

"What's going on?" Cassandra asked, her hand slipping out of her father's grasp as she attempted to peek through the crowd of people.

"Cassie, stay with me," William curled his hand around her arm and pulled her along. "I don't want to lose you. And I think there's a parade going on today."

Parade? Cassandra's eyes lit up.

"I wanna watch!"

"Cassie, sweetheart," Cadence interjected. "We have to get back to the inn before the dinner rush."

"Just a few minutes!" Cassandra pleaded. "Please?"

William and Cadence stopped and stared at each other for a moment, exchanging knowing glances. William sighed.

"Alright, Cassie, five minutes. Here, it looks like the royal guard is about to start their march."

"Hooray!" Cassandra jumped up and down, her heart exploding with delight. She'd heard stories of the royal guard in school, and seen illustrations of their purple-and-gold regalia in her history books. She knew that they were soldiers who guarded both the city and the royal family's palace. But to her, perched atop marching white horses in their celebration finery, *they* were the royals.

"Come here sweetheart," William scooped Cassandra up and hoisted her onto his shoulders. He grimaced. "You're getting a bit big for this."

But Cassandra didn't care. She's gone from a diminutive child to a giant overlooking everyone's heads, with the greatest view of the parade she could've asked for. She held both hands up in the air, waving them in big, sweeping circles at every guard they passed.

And one guard, a woman with jet-black hair swept back in a tight bun, smiled and waved back at her. And it set off fireworks in her stomach.

"Daddy! Daddy! She's waving at me!"

"I see that," William chuckled, shifting his daughter's weight on his shoulders.

There *were* female guards. Cassandra focused on that moment for the entire parade. Even as the newly crowned king and queen passed, dressed in sparkling finery with their gleaming crowns, she barely paid them any attention.

She really could do this. She would become a member of the royal guard. She would march down the kingdom streets on the finest horses in the valley, protecting Brennan from the dangerous reptilians that lurked beyond their borders.

She would be a hero.

That had always been her dream. And she would never let something like hearing loss get in the way of it.

AS THE YEARS PASSED AND CASSANDRA'S CONDI- tion progressed, there was no denying it – her hearing had deteriorated to the point where she needed help.

She could still understand conversations in a quiet room, when she was close to the person, and they spoke in a strong, clear voice. But bustling around the tavern was like being submerged underwater – her ears swimming in a sea of blurry noises that were impossible to decipher.

With their two older sons reaching adulthood and moving out of the inn, Cadence and William needed their daughters' help more than ever. Once Cassandra turned twelve, she spent every evening after school scrubbing dishes and shuttling sloshing mugs of mead between tables. It was dirty, grueling, exhausting work, and she had considerably less time to play with her sisters or read her favorite novels.

But at the end of each night, despite the fatigue weighing on her weary bones, she would sneak outside to the makeshift sparring dummy she'd built and practice.

At first, all she had were sticks, until her oldest brother Robert dug through his old toys and found her a wooden play sword. It was small and flimsy, meant more for childhood make-believe than to be used as a practice weapon. Cassandra swiped some books on melee combat from her school's tiny library, and within a few months she was able to perform a many of the basic moves with ease.

But no matter how skilled she became with a sword, she'd always be disadvantaged by the fact that she couldn't hear clearly. She had difficulty with high-pitched tones, and sometimes couldn't tell which direction a sound was coming from. Not to mention being unable to understand shouted orders by her superiors.

Her father had bought some books on lip-reading and practiced with Cassandra, but to her it felt futile. Lip-reading was *hard*. It involved having a full view of the person's face, and having them speak clearly and intently. Which didn't often happen in a schoolroom full of squabbling twelve-year-olds. She struggled to understand her teacher even when seated at the front of the class, and her classmates avoided her at best and were bullies at their worst. She lost count of the number of times some crude boy would sneak up behind her and shout as loud as they could.

Finally, after coming home from a parent-teacher conference one night, William made an announcement – they were going to apply for Cassandra to attend the school for children with hearing loss. She spent the next few days high on excitement, floating through her routine as if she were on a cloud. Even scrubbing dirty dishes in the inn's kitchen couldn't bring her down. She was finally going to get the help she needed.

But unfortunately, applying for a new school, not to mention a scholarship program, took time. As the days blended into weeks, Cassandra's excitement dissipated. After a month, she rushed out to check the mailbox less frequently. Her impatience was causing her to stew in frustration, and her parents were taking notice.

"Give it time, Cassie," William reminded one morning, her as he sat at one of the inn tables sipping coffee. Cassandra had just come back in from her daily mailbox check, and as usual, she slumped over one of the chairs in frustration.

To alleviate her anxiety, she shifted her focus back to her combat practice. She was starting to get the hang of some of the more advanced maneuvers in her combat books, and she was able to easily defeat her peers in practice swordfights behind the schoolhouse.

"You're dead," she leered at a boy as she pointed her weapon directly at his neck. "I win."

Granted, they were just playing with sticks they'd found in the forest, but having half the schoolhouse watch Cassandra conquer one of her worst bullies gave her a smug, sinister sense of satisfaction. She was convinced that he'd never mess with her again.

And it was on that day, as she skipped home with pride still bubbling in her heart, that it arrived.

"Cassie!" her mother exclaimed the minute Cassandra walked through the front door. She didn't even have time to hang up her schoolbags before her mother swept her up in an all-encompassing hug.

"Uh, mom," Cassandra grunted. "You're squishing me."

"Sorry, sorry," Cadence chuckled and set her down. "But look what arrived!"

Cadence waved a thick parchment envelope in her hand, and Cassandra immediately knew what it was.

It was a letter.

The letter.

"You've been accepted, sweetheart!" Cadence exclaimed. "I apologize, I know I should've waited until you got home to open it, but I'm just so happy for you!"

Cassandra's jaw fell open in an astonished grin. She was so overjoyed that she launched herself forward for a second hug, nearly tackling her mother in the process. But Cadence didn't scold her. She laughed as her daughter broke their embrace and danced across the room, skipping and shouting and jumping with a level of enthusiasm she hadn't had for years.

Cassandra hadn't heard most of what her mother said. At this point in her life, she'd grown accustomed to only understanding parts of conversations, and her mind was usually able to piece the rest together.

But she had definitely heard the word "accepted", and at that point, that was all she needed to hear.

Next fall, when she turned thirteen, her new life would begin.

The first few weeks at the Valley Academy for the Deaf swept by in a blur, mainly because Cassandra was so engrossed by her new surroundings. The school was two towns over in Sanford, meaning that she couldn't just walk there like she did to the Live Oak schoolhouse. Thankfully, her father discovered that one of his longtime customers also had a daughter with hearing loss, and he arranged for Cassandra to catch a ride with them.

And the man's daughter, Lucy, quickly became Cassandra's best friend.

It was a thirty-minute ride to the school by horse-drawn cart, which gave Cassandra and Lucy plenty of time to get to know each other. Lucy had been completely deaf in one ear since she was a toddler, and had been attending the Valley Academy most of her life.

"So you speak the hand language?" Cassandra asked on their first day of school. The girls rode in the back of the cart while Lucy's father Jonas drove up front.

"You mean sign language?" Lucy responded. Cassandra noticed that Lucy had a unique voice, one that sounded different from those with no hearing loss.

"Uh-huh."

Lucy made two quick, deliberate gestures with her hands as a wide grin stretched across her face.

"Wow! What did you say?"

"I said 'of course'!" Lucy laughed. She was clearly happy to show off her skills. "Here, let me teach you some basic signs."

From that day on, every morning while Jonas drove them to school, Lucy would teach Cassandra new signs. After just a few weeks, Cassandra was giving simple, single-word responses. Lucy beamed with pride, always applauding her when her signs were correct.

Cassandra caught on quickly. Not only was she learning new signs from Lucy, but she had a dedicated sign language class every day, and many of her teachers, who also had hearing loss, taught only in sign. The building was divided into several classrooms, with much smaller class sizes than the one-room schoolhouse back in Live Oak. The classes were specifically designed for deaf and hard-of-hearing children. The lights were brighter, there were minimal noise distractions, and the instruction was much more visually-oriented. In addition, instead of being in rows, the desks were arranged in a semicircle, so everyone had a perfect view of the teachers.

Cassandra no longer struggled to understand what was being taught. And since she could fully understand the lessons, she devoured them with an enthusiasm that she hadn't had in a long time. Over the past few years, between incomprehensible lessons and obnoxious bullies, Cassandra had grown to hate school. Now, she loved it again.

She was especially excited one early winter morning, when her parents announced that they were taking an overnight trip to Brennan to run supplies up to a vendor.

Cassandra found it strange, as her parents rarely left Live Oak, much less venturing all the way to the kingdom. But her confusion was quickly masked by excitement when she learned that she would be spending the night at Lucy's house.

Lucy lived in Vale, which was the next town over from Live Oak. Cassandra's mind spun with questions as she sat in the back of Jonas's cart, an overnight rucksack in her lap and Lucy sitting next to her. She asked Lucy lots of questions about her home and family, but she noticed that Lucy always seemed vague and evasive with her answers.

Which is why it confused Cassandra when the cart stopped in front of a beautiful, well-kept vintage estate, two stories high with rows of large windows bordering an arch-shaped doorway. The estate was bordered by lush flowerbeds that swooped their way across the front lawn, their dark, earthy mulch bordered by waves of perfectly aligned stones.

"It's beautiful," Cassandra signed to Lucy, and she grinned and nodded.

Cassandra's second surprise was when Jonas opened the front door and a swarm of squabbling children, most of them younger than thirteen-year-old Lucy, clamored for Jonas's attention. Cassandra was bewildered, but Jonas simply laughed and scooped a plump toddler into his arms.

"Beatrice, we're home!"

A tall, thin woman appeared in the foyer. Her almond hair was pulled back in a tight bun, and she wore gleaming gold earrings that contrasted her simple dress and flour-covered apron.

"Oh, excellent, dinner is almost ready," Beatrice noted, sounding exasperated. The small horde of children flocked in her direction upon hearing the word 'dinner'. "Well, come on in girls, make yourselves at home. Cassandra, was it?"

Cassandra nodded.

"That's the thing," Lucy signed once they went upstairs. "This is an orphanage. Jonas and Beatrice aren't my birth parents."

"But they took you in?" Cassandra signed back, wondering if her grammar was correct. While she had memorized hundreds of individual signs over the past few months, she was still learning how to string together complete phrases.

"Yes. My parents died when I was a baby. They were killed by..." Lucy made a sign that Cassandra couldn't remember the meaning of. Lucy held her fingers in an s-shape, followed by two clawed fingers pointing down.

Almost like fangs.

"Naga," Lucy spoke aloud, which surprised Cassandra. Lucy preferred sign and rarely spoke unless it was necessary. She even signed to Jonas while on their rides to school. "They were killed by Naga."

A horrid shiver made Cassandra's shoulders hunch. The monstrous snake creatures lived on the edge of the human world, not far from Live Oak. As her hometown was so close to the border, she'd heard many stories of conflicts with their beastly neighbors. They were the

monsters that the knights vanquished in her childhood stories.

She'd never seen one in person. But if she wanted
to join the royal guard, they were the enemy that she
would have to protect the humans from.

"Lucy?" Cassandra signed.

"Yes?"

"Can I tell you a secret?"

"Of course."

"Someday," Cassandra paused, searching for the right
signs. "I want to join the royal guard. I want to be a hero
and fight the Naga."

"That sounds wonderful," Lucy signed back enthusiastically. "I'm glad you're my friend, Cassandra. The ride
to school is so much better now that you're with me."

Lucy's signs warmed Cassandra's heart. While she
had friends back at the schoolhouse in Live Oak, her
relationships with them suffered as she lost her hearing.
It had been difficult to keep up with their conversations,
and she constantly felt left out.

But attending Valley Academy, meeting Lucy,
learning to sign... it all made her feel so included and
wanted. Lucy was the closest friend she'd ever had, and
it pained her to know that she'd kept such a large secret
about herself.

It made her desire to join the royal guard
even stronger.

Therefore, the next day, the last day of the semester
before winter break, Cassandra decided that she wanted
to spend recess swordfighting.

Sadly weapons of any kind, even toy ones, were prohibited on school grounds, so once again she and her classmates had to make do with sticks. Cassandra easily defeated her first few opponents, pressing her stick against their chest or throat within seconds. Some of the boys put up a tougher fight, but it wasn't anything Cassandra couldn't handle. They were brutish fighters, preferring to plow headfirst into a fight and come at Cassandra with everything they had. And while she was a very thin, petite child, she was also far nimbler and more dexterous, simply dodging their vigorous attacks until they tired themselves out.

"I declare myself the victor," Cassandra boasted triumphantly, waiting for her weary opponent to raise his head so she was certain he'd see her sign. He replied with a hand motion that Cassandra was fairly certain was a swear word before stomping away.

As the crowd dissipated, a boy named Clayton continued watching her. He was a shy child, one of the few that hadn't challenged Cassandra, and he rarely said a word in class – in speech or sign.

Cassandra peered up at him, and as soon as he realized he had her attention, he raised his hands and began to sign.

"Why?"

Cassandra's eyes narrowed.

"What do you mean?" she signed back.

"Why do you do this?"

Cassandra let out a faint chuckle. She did know that it was unusual for a preteen girl to insist on sword-fighting everyone in her grade.

"Because," she grinned. "I want to join the royal guard."

Clayton's flat expression didn't change. "But you're a girl."

Cassandra huffed and signed furiously, cutting him off, "Who cares if I'm a-"

"You also can't hear."

And with that, he walked away, joining the other children at the playground.

Cassandra stood dumbfounded in the now empty field, not sure if she wanted to scream or cry. Scream because Clayton was a rude little scutch, and cry because as much as she hated it, he was right. Very few woman joined the royal guard, and she had no idea if a hard-of-hearing person had *ever* joined.

Maybe I'll just have to be the first one.

She sighed and lowered her swordfighting stick, tossing it in the bushes as she walked across the field to join her classmates. *Who cares what Clayton says? I can still do this. I know I can.*

Besides, Cassandra grinned. *Hearing or not, I just kicked everyone's butts.*

Chapter 8

*T*HE FOLLOWING DAY WAS A LONG, WEARY, and tedious one, spent trudging through the forest in human territory. By late afternoon, the sound of rustling branches and crunching leaves made Marissa's temples throb, and her hands and ankles were itchy and raw from snagging on vines. It was a monotonous journey, but at least it was an uneventful one - they hadn't come across any guards.

"Most of them are probably clustered at the borders," Arthur explained as he walked a few paces in front of her. "I bet that's their primary concern – keeping the reptilians from crossing into human territory."

She could tell that he too was fatigued – his pace was slowing, and his shoulders drooped with exhaustion. Nathara, on the other hand, was full of energy. Her lithe, serpentine body slipped through the brush with far more finesse than her two-legged companions. She also made a lot less noise – Marissa could tell that her aunt was becoming frustrated by their slow pace and stomping footsteps.

Before they set out that day, Nathara had asked to carry their looted gun. Her reasoning was that with her superior sight and smell, she would slither ahead as their scout and needed a way to defend them if she spotted humans. But when Marissa relayed this to Arthur, he vehemently opposed – mainly pointing out her inexperience with the weapon. Guns were fickle tools, slow to load and fire. Mistakes could easily be fatal, with Arthur heavily emphasizing that *she pointed the muzzle directly at her eye yesterday*.

With Arthur being so unwavering in his answer and Marissa growing frustrated from translating their argument, Nathara had backed down with a begrudging hiss. Arthur had kept the gun firmly strapped to his torso the entire journey, but he did admit that the Marissa and Nathara needed to learn how to fire weapons.

"I know you're not very experienced with them," Marissa replied as they walked. She noticed that the once bright blue sky was beginning to dim – their daylight was waning, and they would need to find shelter soon. "But you may be the only teacher we have."

"I haven't fired a gun since I was a teenager."

"Well, how much do you remember? It's not like we can go find a human for shooting lessons with a giant Naga in tow."

With her last sentence, Marissa peered up at her aunt, and her blood immediately chilled in her veins. Nathara was stopped in her tracks, her reptilian eyes wild with horror and her body recoiling at something on the right side of the forest. Marissa bolted past Arthur, and she too froze at the unnerving sight.

There was a Naga lying in the brush, its coppery eyes glazed over with the stagnant mask of death. Its body was stiff, but its scales were still fresh and glossy in the dim evening light.

<This was recent.> Nathara extended a scaled, shaking hand to touch the corpse, but drew back at the last second. <I don't understand. This is a young male, and he has no injuries. What killed him?>

<I... I don't know. Maybe- wait, Nathara, do you hear that?>

Nathara wove her head around, attempting to catch a glimpse of activity between the dense trees. <I don't. Us full-blooded Nagas don't have very good hearing. No external ear openings, see?> She pointed at the side of her scaled head and flicked her tongue. <But I do smell a faint bit of human.>

<And more Naga.> Marissa added. <And I hear shouting, both human and reptilian. There's some sort of conflict going on up ahead.>

Nathara rose her long body upwards, preparing to dash forward. <Stay here. I'll go investigate.>

<I'm coming with you. I swear I'll make my footsteps quieter.>

<Marissa, this isn't like the Varan village. This is an active confli- >

<I don't care. You're not doing this alone.> Marissa huffed, her face masked with determination. She took a step forward. <Now let's go.>

Nathara gave a soft hiss of frustration before slithering off through the forest. Arthur had caught up to them, and his face immediately fell. He too saw the deceased Naga and heard the violent commotion in the distance.

Marissa quickly grabbed his hand and pulled him forward as she ran after her aunt.

"What's going on here?" Arthur asked, his question intermixed with huffing breaths as they sprinted through the forest.

"We don't know. That's what we're going to find out." Marissa gulped. "But be prepared for the worst."

"Wait, Marissa."

Arthur stopped, forcing a sharp tug on Marissa's arm to stop her from running forward. Marissa initially resisted, desperate to keep sight of her aunt slithering in front of them, until she realized what Arthur had pulled out of his pocket.

A scarf. Just like the one from Copperton, except this one was a deep shade of royal purple.

"I know you didn't want to wear one," Arthur held up the thin scarf, bits of hazy orange sunlight glittering through the woven fabric. "But I found this shortly before we left this morning. It doesn't reek of smoke, and I just wanted you to be safe…"

The glint of worry in his eyes gave Marissa a sudden urge to hug him. Despite her newfound bravery, she realized how foolish she'd been to not have a backup plan. A human and a Naga running into a conflict was one thing…

but Marissa revealing her existence would be a bombshell greater than any battle.

"No, it's okay." She threw the scarf over her neck, wrapping it around the lower half of her face. "Thank you, Arthur."

There was no time for further gratitude; a sudden spattering of gunshots had permeated the shouting. Marissa and Arthur both jolted, instantly ducking and wrapping their arms protectively over their heads. A few dozen feet ahead, Nathara recoiled and crouched low to the ground, her serpentine body as stiff as a log.

"Stay low," Arthur whispered, his voice strained from concealing his fear. "And use as much cover from the forest as you can. I think I can see a human village up head."

Marissa squinted. With her human eyes, she couldn't see well in the rapidly darkening maze of trees. The sun was a blazing beam of orange sitting low in the sky, barely giving off any light. Only the fiery muzzle flashes, permeating the dim air like fireworks, gave Marissa a sense of where the conflict was.

Her heart hammered in her chest as she followed Arthur's dark silhouette through the forest. She was terrified to keep moving forward, but she was also terrified to stay in one place. The gut-lurching fear that a stray bullet would strike her body at any moment sent waves of terror through her shaky limbs.

Her breaths were shallow and rapid. Panic flooded her brain, and she wanted to do was close her eyes and make it all go away – the gunfire, the smoke, but most importantly, the screams. They sent spasms through her chest and melted her ears like lava. It took a tremendous amount of restraint for her to not let out her own cry of horror.

Then it happened. A dark figure behind them, a brief flash of mottled scales – and Arthur was instantly coiled.

It happened so quickly that he couldn't even scream – all Marissa heard was a faint gagging sound. She spun around, nearly tripping in the process. This Naga clearly wasn't Nathara – it had much lighter eyes, almost yellow instead of brown, and a more triangular head. In its scaly, clawed hand was an unsheathed dagger.

Marissa's mouth fell open in helpless horror.

<NATHARA!!!!> Her mind shrieked in desperation.

The sun was nearly gone, just a buttery orange sliver above the horizon. The smoky, crackling air was almost pitch-black, with the Naga and Arthur being little more than inky silhouettes against a greyscale forest. Marissa had no idea where her aunt was, or where *she* was. To her, the darkness was a disorienting nightmare.

A faint glint in the Naga's yellow eyes glittered in the darkness. Arthur was silent, having vanished in its scaly coils. But the Naga wasn't hostile towards Marissa – in fact, it was confused.

Realization chilled Marissa's scales. *It heard me shout for my aunt. In reptilian.*

Its voice was soft yet gravely in Marissa's mind, clearly belonging to a female. <How can I understa- >

A long, shadowy figure lunged for the Naga before she could finish her sentence. Marissa fell and scrabbled across the forest floor, crawling on all fours and dragging a gasping Arthur away from the conflict. The Nagas' hisses sounded more like shrieks as they fought, clawed arms and slithering bodies lunging at each other, until Nathara swiped the dagger from the strange Naga's hand and pointed the tip of the blade at her neck.

<Please, wait!!> the Naga howled in panic and fear. Her eyes darted back toward Marissa. <This human... I could understand it! How!? Who are you!?>

<You first.> Nathara hissed, pressing the dagger into the Naga's scales. Nathara looked down, and with her other arm she lifted a pendant from the Naga's chest. <You're from Agkistra. That's miles from here. What are you and the rest of your village doing in human territory?>

The Naga's fiery yellow eyes flickered with anger. <We had to do something! My cousin lies dead not far from here, poisoned by those filthy humans!>

<Poisoned!?> Marissa and Nathara exclaimed simultaneously. Marissa's eyes widened as it all clicked in her mind. *The dead Naga... who didn't have a mark on him...*

<But that's enough chatter from me.> The Naga's voice hardened, and her slitted eyes leered at Marissa. <I want to know what's going on with that human. I clearly heard it speak as if it were a reptilian. And why is its face covered?>

<You're imagining things,> Nathara hissed. <She's just a-

<I am a half-Naga.>

The two Naga immediately spun towards Marissa, Nathara's face flashing with anger while the other Naga's eyes widened in disbelief.

<W-what?> she stammered. <That's impossible. But... wait a minute, your face...>

The Naga extended a scaled hand towards Marissa, whose limbs froze in fear. But just as the giant snake's claws skimmed across the scarf cloaking the bottom half of her face, Nathara pressed the dagger further into the Naga's neck.

<Do. Not. Touch. Her.> Nathara growled. The Naga whimpered as the tip of the blade indented the skin around her throat, threatening to draw blood if Nathara pressed it any deeper.

Marissa's nerves loosened, and she raised her hand and cupped it over her lower face. As the long skeins of cloth pressed deeper against her nose and mouth, the slightest scent of smoke burned through her reptilian nostrils. She swore could still feel the strange Naga's claw scraping her chin. It was already risky to *tell* her the truth – but to *show* her could cause even more chaos. Marissa's blue eyes flicked around. *Plus, we're in the midst of a battlefield. I don't want any other humans or Naga to see me unmasked.*

Seeing Marissa's reaction, the wild-eyed fear began to fade from the Naga's face, and she huffed.

<Who are you anyway?> she leered at Nathara. <What sort of depraved Naga attacks their own kind to defend a *filthy human?*>

Just as the Naga's last word trickled into Marissa's mind, a blisteringly loud gunshot crackled through the air, causing all four of them to flinch and duck their heads. Marissa bit her lips to keep her fangs from chattering.

<Look,> Nathara grumbled at the Naga as the group slowly rose. <Since my niece has inexplicably chosen to

reveal herself, I promise I will explain everything. But *later*. We're currently in the middle of an active battle-field, and my current priority is to figure out what's going on so I can end this.>

The Naga scowled in disbelief. <You really think you can get us Naga to back down after what they did to us? They sent *poisoned* rats to our village. Baiting us like we're animals... they deserve to suffer like we did.>

Nathara looked confused, but a sudden memory made Marissa's eyes light up. *Wait a minute. When I was a young child, and Beatrice was out gardening, she mentioned having a rat problem...*

<Miss,> Marissa stepped toward the Naga, which made her recoil in surprise. <May I ask your name?>

The Naga hesitated at first, but then let out a reluctant huff. <I'm Ahira. Who're you?>

<My name is Marissa. And this is my friend, Arthur, and my aunt, Nathara. Please, I think I can help both your village and the humans. I believe this may be a misunderstanding.>

<Wait a minute,> Ahira turned toward Nathara, golden eyes wide in disbelief. <You're *the* Nathara? Future chieftress of the Naga? And this half-human is your *niece*!?>

Nathara nodded, <Indeed, I am. And yes, she is. And if you want this conflict to end, I recommend you listen to her.>

Ahira peered back over at Marissa, a low, guttural hiss echoing from her throat. <Alright, fine. Follow me. But be warned, I guarantee no one's safety. Those humans are relentless with their murderous fire weapons.>

MARISSA QUICKLY UNDERSTOOD JUST HOW DIRE Ahira's warning was.

The group snaked through the trees, crouching low to avoid the raging Naga as they charged through the forest toward the humans. Marissa had previously declared that she would never be afraid of her own kind, but seeing their sinister silhouettes, raising daggers in the air and brandishing their fangs in the moonlight, she had to force herself not to shudder.

As they crept closer to the battle scene, the extent of the damage became clearer. Slivers of the human village could be seen through the trees – the candlelit windows of the village inn provided bits of shadowy orange light that illuminated the humans' faces. They stood in a multi-layer firing line surrounding the inn, picking off the Naga as they charged out of the forest. Marissa's throat quivered as she watched a small, round bullet tear through a Naga's chest, causing him to stumble backwards. She could see his body pulsing with pain, but he pressed onward with a staggered slither. He managed to make it to the humans before they could reload, slashing his attacker across the chest in a spray of blood before collapsing.

Panic erupted as the humans' firing line was breached. A tidal wave of Naga charged the inn, the humans abandoning their synchronized gunfire and defending themselves with close-range weapons. Bayonets clashed against daggers, with the humans using their long muskets to stay out of the Nagas' strike range. But some Naga still went straight for biting, attempting to inject the humans with venom to make them flee. But Marissa cringed as one of the Naga received a bayonet blade to the throat for their attempt.

As the battlefield descended into chaos, Marissa's reptilian ears picked up on faint shouts and cries from beyond the demolished firing line. She squinted, and through the inn windows she could see glowing silhouettes scrambling inside the building. The voices sounded mostly like children. Her throat locked up in horror.

They were defending the rest of the villagers, those who were too young or old to fight.

<We must do something.> Marissa insisted. <Ahira, please, do you have any ideas on how to stop this?>

Marissa saw Ahira's jaw tighten as her yellow eyes fixated on the frenzied crowd.

<It must be you, little half-human.> Ahira declared after a long moment of silence. You're the only one that can get both the humans' and the Nagas' attentions.>

Marissa forced down a swallow, her throat quivering as she watched the grisly scene. There were no longer gunshots piercing the air, but the sight of metal blades ripping through scales and flesh was far more gruesome. Bullets pierced their attackers – a direct shot to the head or chest led to a quick death. But blades did far more damage – they tore and sliced and stabbed, leaving bits of their victims' bodies exposed in ways they never should've been.

With every strike of their blades, Marissa felt her chest throb as if she'd been the one stabbed. She would have to walk into an active battlefield, somehow get everyone's attention, and pray that they didn't kill her in the process. It seemed impossible, but she knew that she had to do it. Yet her fearful body wouldn't allow her to take a step forward.

"Marissa?"

Arthur was just a few feet away from her, but his face was barely visible. Without the pulsing, smoky light from the gunshots, the night air had darkened significantly. Marissa didn't respond, but Arthur noticed the fear glistening in her eyes, because he took her hand and gripped it tight.

"I have to do this." The fear in her throat nearly made her choke on her own words. "Ahira said I'm the only one that can stop this. And she's right."

Arthur sighed and nodded, chewing on his bottom lip. Marissa had explained everything to him between gasping breaths as they'd ran across the forest – who Ahira was, what killed the Naga they'd found earlier, and – more importantly – what she thought was causing the entire conflict.

Marissa gripped his hand tighter, squeezing away all her anxieties until her knuckles nearly turned white. She knew how difficult it was for Arthur. Since he was unable to communicate with the reptilians, Marissa had to constantly explain things to him. She could barely imagine the fear he'd been hiding behind his steely eyes – having to dive right into dangerous situations with no idea what was happening. It made her realize how much he trusted her.

She remembered Arthur's words the night they were at Sienna's cottage, after they confronted Thomas. *You're braver than I am, Marissa.*

She turned toward him, forcing a smile despite her fears. *I'm not so sure of that, Arthur.*

"You know," he spoke, his voice low. "When I was a teenager and fired a gun for the first time, I was very scared. And you know what my father told me? He said that when you're afraid to do something, but you must do it, you just empty your mind. Don't worry, don't stress, just do it. Without even thinking. And it worked. I pulled that trigger and hit the clay bird right in the chest before I even had time to question it."

"Then that's what I'll do." His words made a lot of sense to Marissa. Her anxiety would only hold her back. "I swear, I'm going to end this."

Her eyes locked back on the village. The bodies, both human and reptilian, were piling up, but the Naga still hadn't managed to breach the inn.

Don't think. Just do it.

She was already halfway across the open field leading up to the inn before her worried thoughts caught up to her. She pushed them out of her mind and kept running. A few Naga caught her attention, and they released deep, angry hisses before being distracted by the combative humans flanking them.

Marissa slowed her pace, then stopped. It was quieter without the constant booming gunshots, but she'd still have difficulty being heard over the raucous sounds of battle. She lifted her hand and opened her clasped fist – in her sweat-stained palm was the turtle whistle she'd found back at Copperton. She took a deep breath and slipped the instrument under her scarf.

She placed the clay tip and her mouth and exhaled as if her life depended on it.

The loud, high-pitched shriek soared through the village and echoed off the surrounding forest. Several humans who weren't in active combat cringed and covered their ears. The Naga barely flinched, but several coppery slit-eyed gazes still flicked in Marissa's direction.

Yet for most of the crowd, blades still slashed against metal and flesh. A lone human with a whistle wasn't enough to stop the battle.

Marissa clasped a hand to the side of her head. She'd never spoken in both human and reptilian, but believed it could be possible. Her breaths slowed as she attempted to concentrate. *Just one word, say and think it at the same time.*

<"STOP!!!">

It felt like her mind was erupting like a volcano. Her temples throbbed as she clutched her head, feeling her racing heartbeat pounding in her skull. Yet, it worked. It was enough to catch the humans' attention, but more importantly, the Naga were in disbelief.

Marissa heard one of their voices creep into her aching head.

<Did that human... just *talk* to us?>

Marissa released her grip on her head as the pain began to recede. She heard faint shouts in both human and reptilian behind her – she spun around and saw Arthur, Nathara, and Ahira slowly emerge from the forest. She then turned back toward the stunned crowd, immediately pocketing the whistle and raising her shaking hands in a gesture of peace. She noticed one very large Naga sheathe its dagger and slither forward.

<Who are you?> she asked. Yet as she noticed the approaching figures behind her, her reptilian eyes widened.

<Ahira? Good gods, where have you been?>

<Mother,> Ahira greeted in a flat tone as she slithered up next to Marissa. <I know this sounds insane, but listen to me. This is Marissa. You can understand her because, well, she *is* a Naga. Or rather, a half-Naga. Please, listen to her. She wants to help us.>

Marissa gulped as the large female Naga, easily a foot taller than Ahira, slithered in circles around her. She was an older Naga, with leathery scales and criss-crossing scars over her stomach and chest. Her golden eyes flicked over Marissa, surveying her like prey. But thankfully, she made no attempt to roll up Marissa's sleeves or pull her scarf off her face.

<You do smell a bit reptilian,> she noted, pausing in front of her. Her thoughts were deep and gravely in Marissa's mind. <Alright, half-human. What do you have to say?>

<Thank you, ma'am. Um, I- >

<By the way, my name is Agama. I am chieftress of the Agkistra.>

Marissa noticed the Naga's eyes soften as she introduced herself, and the tension in Marissa's shoulders began to loosen.

<Okay, Agama. Well, to begin,> Marissa stammered, tripping over her words. <I understand that poisoned rats have made their way into your village. Am I correct?>

<Yes,> Agama huffed, a sharp hiss echoing up her throat. <The poison took the lives of several of our own, including my young nephew. We traced the rodents' scent back to this village. We've never bothered this village, and yet they attempt to kill us!>

Marissa could feel the venom in Agama's final sentence. The Naga's nostrils flared, her slitted eyes flicking back towards the humans. Panic flooded Marissa's veins as she feared another outburst of violence. But as she watched the wary humans take a few steps backwards, she noticed several marked crates stacked next to the inn visible between their stumbling legs.

"Everyone," Marissa gathered the humans' attention. "My name is Marissa. I mean no harm – I am here to seek peace and end this conflict. Now, the Naga have explained that consuming rats that came from this village resulted in several deaths. And, if I'm not mistaken, are those crates behind you full of rat poison?"

Several people in the crowd peered back over their shoulders at the crates. One man nudged them with his foot.

"And why should we tell ya anythin'?" a rowdy voice echoed from the crowd. "Are ya seriously tellin' us that ya can speak to those snakes?"

"Indeed, I can," Marissa took a deep breath. "Because I am one. I am a half-Naga."

With Marissa's reveal came an explosion of muttering disbelief amongst the crowd.

"She's a *what*?"

"Is that even possible?"

"But she looks human!"

"I say she's lyin'! Why should we believe 'er?"

"Rodger is right. We still need to get these damn beasts off our land, and she's just gettin' in the way!"

The chatter increased in volume and fervor, anger and frustration mounting amidst the rabbling crowd until the Naga became visibly agitated. Shouts, jeers and hisses mixed in Marissa's head, making her temples pulse and muddling her own thoughts. She placed a hand against her nose, the thin, smoky cloth suddenly feeling scratchy against her face. She peered behind her – Nathara, Ahira, and Arthur all looked confused. Marissa was the only one who could speak to both parties – the only one that knew the full story.

She closed her eyes, remembering Arthur's words. *Don't think. Just do it.*

Marissa nearly tore the brittle scarf as she pulled it off her face, the long skeins of cloth falling in a coil at her feet. It took a few moments for the crowd to realize what had happened, but once they did, silence fell over them like a dampening blanket. Dozens of wide-eyed glances, mouths hanging open in disbelief... Marissa had never felt so exposed. Her heartbeat pounded in her throat, and nervous sweat stained both her forehead and her clammy palms.

"Look." A sudden burst of adrenalin allowed her quivering throat to speak. "I know what you're thinking. *She's a monster, isn't she?* Well, I don't care. I don't care if you think I'm a freak, I don't care if you're disgusted

175

by me. I can help you fix this without more violence. Unless you'd prefer to continue killing each other on this damn battlefield."

Shock melted into worry. Soft mutterings broke the stunned silence as the villagers wrung their hands. Marissa could hears bits of their whispers – they were clearly struggling to decide on what to do.

"We had to!!" A sudden, pained voice cried out. Marissa realized it was the same man who had accused her of lying. He stepped forward – a scraggly-haired man of about fifty dressed in dirty, torn breeches. "Those damn rats are eating all our crops! Our families 'er on the verge of famine, we had to do somethin'! Please, tell the Naga that we didn't mean to harm 'em! We didn't realize this would happen!"

Marissa's heart sank into her stomach as the man confessed, his weary voice nearly cracking as tears pooled in his eyes. She noticed the rest of the villagers' heads lower as a wave of remorse washed over them.

<Agama.> Marissa turned back toward the Naga chieftress, whose eyes were locked on the guilt-ridden faces of the villagers. <They poisoned the rats because they were consuming all their crops. They didn't mean to harm the Naga.>

The chieftress was lost for words. Her thoughts seemed to be miles away as her slitted eyes flicked over the bloodied battlefield.

<That means this battle, all this death... this never should've happened. Good gods... what have we done?>

<It's not your fault.> Marissa reassured Agama, even though she herself was on the verge of tears. <You had no way to communicate with them.>

<No wonder they see us Naga as monsters.>

The deep, regretful pain in Agama's thoughts crackled through Marissa's chest like a lightning bolt. She knew that much of the strife between the humans and reptilians came down to an inability to communicate, but this conflict showed her how dire of a need it really was.

Arthur had insisted she was special since they first met, but Marissa was beginning to realize just how important her abilities truly were.

"Um, miss, half-Naga? Marissa, right?"

She looked up. A young woman with thick blonde hair dry as straw stepped forward.

"What are we supposed to do? We still need a way to keep the rats away from our crops. Otherwise, we won't have enough food for the upcoming winter."

Marissa paused, focusing her attention deep in the back of her mind. *Crap, she's right. How else can they keep the rats out of their village?*

Think, think...

Then, a sudden thought hit her mind, like a drop of water breaking the surface tension on a smooth lake.

I have an idea.

<"I know how to fix this."> Marissa temples throbbed from communicating in both human and reptilian, but she felt it was essential to tell both groups at once. She kept a hand pressed against her aching head, determined to force out her words and thoughts.

<"The humans should let the Naga come through the fields a few times a week and hunt down the rats. Then they won't need to use poison. It's a win-win – the Naga get an easy meal, and the humans don't lose their crops to pests.">

"It's that simple?" The straw-haired woman peered up at Agama, who gazed back with a sliver of a smile on her face.

Marissa couldn't believe it – the humans and the Naga stood in front of the inn, face-to-face, for once seeing the other side as something other than monsters. Marissa noticed that the warm glow in their eyes and soft expressions on their faces were remarkably alike. It was as if beyond the scales and flesh, they weren't that dissimilar.

Marissa was even more shocked when Agama extended a scaled hand toward the woman.

<Marissa, can you please tell this human that we'd like to accept this deal and propose a truce?>

The woman turned toward Marissa, uncertainty lining her eyes. Marissa broke into a grin, her reptilian fangs gleaming in the dim moonlight, and a sad smile crept across the woman's face.

"I wish things were different," she sighed. "But as the wife of the village head, I swear that I will never allow this violence to happen again."

Her slender human hand gripped Agama's giant one, scales against flesh as they shook hands on their agreement. Both the humans and Naga were relieved, but a deep, remorseful sadness still penetrated the chilly night air.

Marissa turned back toward her companions. Nathara and Ahira were overjoyed, and while Arthur hung back, he had a prideful smile on his face.

<I can't believe it!> Ahira exclaimed. <You actually stopped the battle! Marissa, the Agkistra are forever in your debt. Every human and Naga standing here tonight is alive because of you. You are truly our hero.>

But as she now faced her cheering companions, Marissa could also see the shadowy battlefield behind them. She may have brought peace, but she couldn't forget the dark silhouettes lying crumpled in piles, the surrounding grass slick with still-fresh blood. She couldn't forget that despite ending the conflict, she couldn't erase the aftermath of the battle.

The dead were still dead.

A lump formed in Marissa's throat. She didn't feel like a hero.

She felt sick to her stomach.

Chapter 9

*H*OURS LATER, MARISSA SAT ALONE OUTSIDE the village inn, still staring into the inky abyss of the battlefield. The bodies were gone – the humans and Naga had spent most of the night clearing them away. The humans hauled the deceased off the battle-field while the Naga, being much larger and stronger, dug the graves. It was a gruesome, bloody reminder that they'd been enemies just a few hours earlier. They may have made a deal to benefit them both, but there were still a lot of fresh wounds, both physical and emotional.

Yet they still worked together to clear away the after-math. The humans treated the deceased Nagas' bodies with as much respect as their own kin, burying them deeper in the forest so that they wouldn't be put to rest in foreign territory. And as the night hours deepened and the last of the corpses were buried, the two groups simply parted ways. The Naga slithered back into the forest to return to Agkistra, and most of the humans settled into their homes.

But a few of them, driven to insomnia by the traumatic events, decided to spend the night drinking at the inn. It turned out that the straw-haired woman, Emma, was the wife of the inn owner, a slender olive-skinned man named Lukas. He'd been inside the inn during the battle, keeping the doors barred in case the Naga tried to burst through. He'd happily invited Marissa and her companions inside, offering them a hot meal and complimentary overnight stay for their heroics. But while Arthur and Nathara took advantage of Luka's generosity and scarfed down large plates of fresh venison, Marissa had excused herself and stepped outside.

Her empty stomach screamed for food, but she was too anxious to eat.

She'd been sitting cross-legged on the front porch for nearly twenty minutes. All her weary mind could do was stare out at the empty field. She could still pinpoint where all the bodies had been, yet now all that remained were dried bloodstains that splattered the grass. On the other side of the inn, rows of oval-shaped patches of dirt sprawled out behind a run-down church. The once pristine place of worship was now crumbling in on itself, bits of white paint flecking off the exterior and exposing the shoddy construction work. It was so decrepit that Marissa wondered if anyone had been inside the building for years.

The faint yet joyous racket of the inn activity broke the silence in the heavy night air. It reminded Marissa of her first night on her own, huddled under an awning in the pouring rain listening to the inn patrons in that tiny village. She remembered how alone and ostracized she felt. Now, not only did she have Arthur and Nathara, but she had a whole village that viewed her as a hero.

So why do I still feel so alone?

<Marissa?>

Her biceps quaked at the unexpected voice in her head. A single lit torch cut a burning sphere of light through the darkness, illuminating a familiar scaled face.

<Ahira? You came back?>

<Um, yes...> The Naga looked visibly nervous, her slitted pupils flickering around. <On my mother's orders. She wanted me to speak to you to um, discuss the details of our arrangement with the humans.>

<Oh, of course.>

It made sense to Marissa, which made her confused as to why Ahira's whole body was as tense as a skittish anole. The expression on her scaled face was like that of a human whose cheeks were turning red.

<Well, thank you. But I must ask,> Ahira seemed to shake off her anxiety as confusion set in. <What are you doing out here? Aren't you the hero of the town?>

Marissa huffed, her uneasy fingers tracing circles on the porch steps as she sat cross-legged. <I don't feel like a hero.>

Ahira frowned, giving a sad, sympathetic nod. She slithered up next to Marissa, her body coiling around her as she settled on one of the steps. <I get it. As the

youngest daughter of Agkistra's chieftress, I've seen a fair number of battles myself. When I was a child, I'd watch my mother and older sisters charge off to fight border disputes with the humans, and they would always boast about their victories. But it didn't make sense to me. I'd think, 'Why are they celebrating killing?'. Eventually, I became old enough to fight alongside them, and came to terms with it. I realized it was an ugly reality of living amongst strange, hostile creatures that we couldn't communicate with. But I was never proud, and I certainly never felt like a hero.>

<It's certainly a lot more gruesome than my childhood fantasy books make it out to be,> Marissa remarked. <I hate it.>

<But Marissa, your situation is different. You *should* feel like a hero. You didn't end the conflict by killing the enemy. Instead, you risked your own life to charge onto an active battlefield and use your communication skills to stop the fighting. In my fifty years of life, that's the bravest thing I've ever seen.>

<But people still died. If I had made it here earli- >

<Marissa,> Ahira cut her off with a sharp hiss. <Stop. Look, I get it. As a half-Naga, I bet you feel a tremendous amount of pressure to help everyone. But you can't put the weight of the whole valley on your shoulders. You saved lives today. Yes, we lost some souls. But you need to focus on the fact that without you, we would've lost a lot more.>

Marissa's throat quivered as her head sank into her palms.

<I do want to feel like a hero,> her thoughts shook as she clenched her chest to hold back her emotions. <All I want to do is go back inside the inn, be with Arthur and Nathara, and enjoy not feeling like an outcast for once. But I can't. It feels so wrong, as if it's not fair to those who died...>

<It's called survivor's guilt.> Ahira placed a scaled hand on Marissa's hunched back. <I get that too.>

They sat in silence for a moment, the weight of Ahira's large scaly palm on Marissa's back soothing the bundle of nerves in her stomach. It was nearly midnight, and she was exhausted. She felt the fatigue of the long, tumultuous day deep in her aching bones.

She was so relaxed that she nearly fell asleep, her weary body melting into the porch steps. But as soon as the front door to the inn opened, a bolt of adrenalin shot through her veins.

It was Nathara. The tall, slender snake greeted her niece with a sad yet warm smile of sympathy.

<Marissa, my dear, I know how you feel.> Her serpentine body cascaded down the porch steps until she was on the same level as Marissa. She went to take a seat, but stopped when she realized her niece wasn't alone.

<Ahira?> Nathara looked puzzled. <What are you doing here?>

Marissa noticed that the anxiety had returned to Ahira's scaly face. Her fingers fidgeted in her lap, and the gaze in her coppery eyes was a mixture of unease and... *awe?*

<Oh, uh, Nathara, it's a pleasure to see you again.> Ahira raised her body up off the porch step. She was

a large, imposing Naga, with a bulky triangular head and a wide body, but was still a few inches shorter than Nathara. <I was just wondering if I, uh, could come inside…. I needed Marissa's help to speak with the inn owner about our deal with the humans.>

<Ah, I see.> Nathara smiled, which only seemed to make Ahira more nervous. <Of course, I imagine the villagers would like the fields cleared of rats as soon as possible. Both of you, please, come inside.>

Marissa nodded sadly. She knew that Ahira was right – she needed to focus on her victories and not fret about the things she couldn't change. As much as she yearned for peace, she knew that in a region torn apart by war, not everyone could be saved.

Also, her eyes flicked toward the two Naga slithering up the stairs in front of her, engaged in conversation. *I want to know why Ahira is acting so strange.*

The previously faint clamor of the inn activity roared across Marissa's ears as the heavy wooden doors swung open. Bright orange light from the flickering wall sconces stung her night-drenched eyes, but through her squinting she could see clusters of boisterous men and women clinking heavy beer mugs in the air and gobbling down plates of calorie-rich food. The tone was a joyous one of celebration – an explosion of cheers echoed through the room as the villagers caught sight of Marissa. But to her, the exuberance barely masked the heavy cloud of grief that hung in the air. She could see it reflected in the villager's eyes, especially the ones who'd had too much alcohol.

Even Arthur had a tinge of sorrow on his face as he caught sight of them. Yet his eyes still sparkled at the sight of Marissa, and he quickly waved her and the two Naga over to the table.

"I see that Ahira is back," Arthur noted as they took a seat. The circular wooden table was surrounded by six seats. Nathara and Ahira were so large that they each used an extra chair to support their long, serpentine bodies. Marissa peered around and noticed that despite there being two Naga in an inn full of humans, *she* was the one they were all staring at.

"At least a dozen patrons have offered to buy you a drink," Arthur told Marissa, shaking his head. He pointed at his own mug, which contained only water. "It's a kind gesture, but I don't think alcohol is the best idea after a night like this."

"It didn't stop the townsfolk," Marissa sighed, her eyes drifting over to the gambling tables. It was mostly men, and several of them still had bandaging from fresh wounds. They stood still, beer mugs in hand, their eyes locked on the dice as they clattered across the table. Marissa noticed that they only smiled when they won their bets. Otherwise, their eyes seemed distant, as if their minds were still on the battlefield.

"Where are we anyway?" Marissa asked.

"Apparently the village is called Canterbury," Arthur replied, taking in deep gulps of his water. His plate was empty – nothing more than venison drippings and cornbread crumbs. "Lukas said that in the daytime, way off in the distance, you can see the very top of Mount

Krait. That means we're almost to Testudo territory. Hopefully we can finish our trip tomorrow."

Marissa peered across the table at Ahira, wanting to ask if she still needed help. Yet Marissa couldn't get the Naga's attention; she was deep in conversation with Nathara, a misty gaze in her reptilian eyes.

"What brought Ahira back anyway?" Arthur asked.

"She wanted to speak with the innkeeper about the Naga coming through to clear out the rats, and she needed me to translate."

"Odd that she'd come back so late at night. Well, I suppose Naga are semi-nocturnal," Arthur reached across the table and rapped his knuckles on the wood. Ahira immediately stopped chattering away and looked up at Arthur. Marissa noticed the slight disdain on her face.

<Does your human friend need something?> Ahira asked.

<I was wondering.> Marissa scooted forward in her seat. <If you still needed my help translating with Lukas.>

<Oh, yes, of course.> Ahira slithered off the chair, nodding a quick goodbye to Nathara. <Come along, little half-human.>

The pair walked and slithered up to the bar, where Lukas frantically kept up with beer orders. He caught sight of Marissa and Ahira and gestured that he'd be with them in a moment.

While they waited, Marissa noticed that Ahira was eyeing her like a zoo exhibit.

<I still can't get over you being a half-Naga,> she remarked. <Where exactly did you come from? And where are your parents?>

These were questions she'd heard many times over the past few weeks. But while she'd previously been able to block the thought of her parents out of her mind, now her veins seeped with venom every time she thought of Ezrinth. She hated being reminded of her father's actions. The idol pieces, hidden away in the satchel slung over her shoulder, seemed to burn as they pressed against her upper thigh.

<Wait a minute,> Ahira continued before Marissa was able to stop her. <You're Nathara's niece. That means... is her troublesome younger brother your father?>

Marissa didn't respond, her face burning. Ahira noticed her bright red cheeks and recoiled.

<I'm right, aren't I?>

<How much do you know about him?> Marissa grumbled.

<Enough to not like him. Like every other village in Naga territory, Agkistra has been split in two. Some of our own snuck off in the night to join Orami and his cowardly band of deserters. But the rest of us want to stand our ground and defend our home. I will admit, at first, I was enticed by Ezrinth's plans. But tonight showed me that peace isn't impossible. My mother feels the same – we won't abandon Squamata, but we won't support your father either.>

<I hate him,> Marissa growled, yet she was surprised by the malice in her own thoughts. She knew that, like her, he'd been an outcast with a heart full of pain. But unlike Marissa, he'd let his anger overtake him. He wanted revenge, a concept that Marissa was never able to fathom.

<Can't say I blame you.> Ahira slithered forward, resting her scaly elbows on the bar counter. <But I've been wondering... what are you three doing out here? A half-breed, a human, and a Naga, traveling through reptilian territory on some sort of mission?>

A deep chill ran through Marissa's limbs, and the weight of idol pieces suddenly felt heavy on her shoulder. *No.* She told herself. *Who knows who Ahira will do if I tell her? Even if she's on our side, another Naga that isn't might find out. No reptilian can know about this. It's too risky.*

<We're just looking for safety,> Marissa responded. <We're all sort of outcasts right now, just looking to find peace wherever it may be.>

<Well, why don't you stay in here in the human village?> Ahira suggested. <Or better yet, you can stay in Agkistra. Both communities view you three as heroes – we promise to keep you safe.>

<We can't,> Marissa sighed. She peered around the room at the cheerful inn patrons. Night was quickly melting into morning, and the group was thinning – many of them had already stumbled out the door to try and get some rest. Yet those who remained waved at her with glowing smiles on their faces.

Deep down, she didn't want to leave.

<Sorry, Ahira, but we can't.> Marissa's head lowered as the noticed the disappointed look on the Naga's face. <At least, not right now. We have some business to attend to elsewhere. For now, can we just focus on talking to the innkeeper?>

With impeccable timing, Lukas sauntered over to the far edge of the bar, away from the rambunctious crowd, and plopped his hairy elbows on the counter.

<I see that one of our Naga friends has returned,> he remarked. <May I interest her in any alcohol?>

Marissa relayed this to Ahira, who huffed, <Naga don't drink, at least not that human swill. I'm fine, unless this gentleman happens to have any pints of rat blood behind the bar.>

Marissa's face paled, and she decided that it was best not to translate Ahira's question.

Thankfully, the conversation quickly turned to the earlier events, how the Naga were faring back at Agkistra, and most importantly, how to enact Marissa's mutually beneficial plan.

Between the conversations with Nathara and the innkeeper, Marissa was realizing that Ahira was a very animated, talkative snake. She struggled to condense Ahira's swift yet lengthy sentences into human speech. After ten minutes, Marissa's head was beginning to ache, but at least Lukas and Ahira had come to an agreement – the Naga would visit twice a week, gulping down all the rats they could find and preventing the vermin from consuming the humans' crops. The crates of rat poison would be shipped back to an alchemist in Brennan, never to be used again. The two communities, at least for now, would be at peace.

"I appreciate your help, Lukas." Marissa smiled at the innkeeper. "And thank you for the food. And the inn room. You and your wife are very kind."

"Of course!" he replied in a warm tone as he lifted the empty beer mug he was cleaning into the air. "Oh, and one last thing. Tell the Naga that they're always welcome back at the inn after the rat clearing. I'll have to find out what Naga like to drink... Marissa, do you kno-"

"Thank you, Lukas!" Marissa strolled away curtly, pushing Ahira ahead of her. Back at the table, several drunken men were palling around with Arthur, shaking his shoulders with their grubby palms and trying to push sloshing beer mugs into his hands. Arthur played along with their driveling jokes, but politely refused their offering of alcohol. As soon as Marissa approached the table, his eyes subtly pleaded for help.

"Ah, the fine lady of the evenin' has returned!" one of the men exclaimed. He held up his half-full mug, some of the pale wheat-colored contents splashing onto the stained wooden floor. The man turned back toward Arthur. "Ya know boys, I think someone's a bit starry-eyed for the lil' lass."

Arthur hunkered in his seat, his face turning an alarming shade of red.

"Aw, look at 'em! That's quite tha blush. I guess ya prefer scales over flesh, my friend?"

Arthur faked a chuckle, yet the unease on his face only deepened. Marissa stood next to the table, stiff as a board and her scales scorching with embarrassment. She could barely look Arthur in the eye. Even Ahira and Nathara hid snickers behind their scaled hands.

"She's got 'em everywhere, all the way down 'er arms and legs." One of the men eyed Marissa, his bulbous nose cherry-red as the alcohol burned through his system. "Ya know, I bet she even has 'em dow-"

"That's enough." Arthur's tone was as sharp as a freshly forged sword, yet he barely raised his voice. He took a deep breath, regaining his familiar noble-bred sense of composure, and turned toward the men. "I appreciate your company, gentleman, but if you don't mind, I'm quite weary from our long day and wish to retire for the evening."

There was a low drone of disappointed mumblings, but the cluster of drunken fools slowly disbanded as they returned to the gambling tables.

"We really do need to get some sleep." Arthur turned back toward Marissa as the drunkards' racket faded away. "It's almost one a.m. I believe the bar closes soon, and I'm exhausted."

"Me too. Should we ask about our room?"

"Excuse me, Emma?" Arthur grabbed the attention of the innkeeper's wife as she swept through the crowd, stacking beer mugs into an impressively tall tower that she carried in one palm. "Should we speak with you or Lukas about checking in to our room?"

Emma bit her lip, pushing wisps of blonde hair away from her face with a free hand, "Well, that's the thing. After offering y'all the room, I went through the books, and, well... we only have one room available for the night, and it's only got one bed."

Marissa noticed Emma's eyes drift toward Ahira and Nathara, who were once again engaged in conversation. Even while seated, the giant snakes still dwarfed the nearby humans. Marissa knew they had to each weigh several hundred pounds – even a queen-sized bed would only fit one of them.

I suppose I could always sleep on the floor...

"Ah, I understand," Arthur replied. "Well, let me discuss with my companions, but we'll likely be checking in shortly. It's been a long day."

Emma nodded and strolled away, the lofty stack of glasses wobbling slightly as she walked. Arthur heaved his elbow onto the table and groaned, propping the side of his face on his open palm.

"Well, that's a less-than-ideal sleeping situation. What do you think the chances are that we can persuade Nathara to sleep on the floor?" He chuckled faintly at his own joke, until he realized that Marissa was barely paying attention.

"Uh, Marissa? You alright?"

Arthur's words wafted past her oblivious ears as her eyes locked on the front door. A disheveled man had just stumbled into the inn, his thick auburn hair stringy from sweat and his heavy boots leaving behind a trail of dirt. He looked familiar.

Too familiar.

It can't be... what would he be doing all the way out here?

Marissa wasn't sure how to react. As much as she wanted to turn back around and pay attention to Arthur, she couldn't keep her eyes off the irritated man as he hauled his weary body into a barstool and gestured to Lukas with little more than a grunt.

Once he had a mug of beer in his filthy hands, he swiveled around on his barstool to observe the rest of the inn. He consumed his drink in deep gulps, as if he were trying to soothe both a parched throat and a heavy heart.

Yet as soon as he saw her, sitting with her scales exposed in the middle of the inn with two massive Naga, his heavy glass mug nearly fell to the floor.

"Marissa!?"

As Thomas approached their table, gawking at the two Naga with a mixture of disbelief and awe in his eyes, Marissa knew she had a lot of explaining to do.

Ahira and Nathara were too lost in conversation to acknowledge him. After all, the humans and Naga were now at peace, and the two chattering snakes had little reason to be concerned about his presence. Marissa had no idea where Thomas had come from, but he'd clearly missed out on the tumultuous events of the evening.

"I..." his voice trailed off as he fought to string together his myriad of questions. "Yer mask is off... those Naga... good gods, what did I miss?"

"Ya missed an awful lot, Thomas!" one of the men from the gambling tables walked past them, chiming in on their conversation as he chugged down the last of his drink. "These four are Canterbury's finest heroes! They saved us!"

The man then erupted in a coughing fit – Marissa assumed some of his beer must've gone down the wrong pipe. He walked away clutching his chest as he wheezed, but he still had a joyous twinkle in his eye.

Thomas turned back toward Marissa, the growing look of incredulity in his eyes demanding an explanation.

"Look, I promise I will explain everything," Marissa reassured him. "But you first. What brought you to a little village on the border of Naga territory at one-fifteen in the morning?"

"I live here," Thomas grumbled. "At least, my folks do. We had nowhere else ta go after the fire."

"Your parents live here in Canterbury?" Arthur was also surprised by the coincidence.

"Yep. And ya wanna know what's happened ta me these past few days?" he took a long swig of beer, as if he were mustering up the courage to have this conversation. Marissa noticed that the glimmer of awe in his eyes was gone, and the sorrowful grief had returned. "I went off and got tha cure, just like I said I would. The whole way home, I'd never been happier. Marian would finally be feelin' better, and we could rebuild our lives 'ere in Canterbury. Once I handed her the vial, I expected 'er to be overjoyed. But she wasn't. Instead, she demanded to know how I'd gotten ahold of so much money."

"Did you tell her the truth?" Arthur asked.

"I could'a lied," Thomas's voice crackled with emotion. "I could'a said I stuck it big gamblin' or somethin'. But I swore on our weddin' day that I'd always tell 'er the truth. And ya know what she did? She called me a monster and ran off."

"She left? Where'd she go?"

"I assume off to 'er parents again. Or maybe to 'er sister's... anyway, she left earlier today. Took my folks' only other horse and cart, so I was left chasin' 'er down on foot like a fool. Lost track of 'er after a few miles. The road split a few times and the cart tracks 'ere disappearin'. Then it started gettin' dark, and I was horribly lost for hours - I ain't familiar with this area. I thought I was gonna get ambushed by reptilians and die out there..." His eyes flicked over to Ahira and Nathara. "But apparently they ain't fightin' us anymore?"

"At least not here in Canterbury," Marissa corrected.

"Yeah, that's the part I don't get," Thomas set his beer mug on the counter. It was already almost empty. "Can ya explain to me what happened?"

Just as Marissa went to speak, a rattling chime echoed through the inn.

"Bar's closing!" Lukas shouted, a small yet surprisingly loud cowbell clutched in his hand. "Last call for drinks!"

Marissa peered around. Only a handful of patrons were left in the bar, most of which were clustered around the gambling tables. Disappointed mutterings rumbled through the small crowd. Despite their foolish, drunken behavior, Marissa felt their pain. Without the jolly alcohol-soaked atmosphere, they'd be forced to go to bed for the night – the perfect opportunity for their minds to torture them with recollections of the earlier battle.

"I get it," Thomas sighed, tipping his head back and pouring the last few drops of beer down his throat. "Y'all are tired. I see that Arthur's startin' ta fade."

Marissa turned toward her companion and realized why he'd been so quiet - his elbows were folded in front of him, making a pillow for his weary head as it pressed against the slick wooden table. She doubted he was already asleep, but she knew he wouldn't be able to stay up much longer.

He was human, after all. He didn't have half-Naga blood to keep him awake late into the night.

"Y'all got a place ta stay tonight?" Thomas asked.

Marissa peered over at Arthur, who looked just as uncertain as she was.

"They offered us a room tonight," Marissa continued. "But it's-"

"Lemme guess." Thomas's bloodshot eyes flicked over to the two chattering Naga. "Yer giant snake friends ain't gonna fit."

"Well, I think Ahira will be heading back to Agkistra tonight, but yes, the room only has one bed."

"I'll tell ya what," Thomas sighed, standing up with a groan and rubbing his back. "The snake stays here tonight, and you two c'mon back to my place. We've got a spare bedroom, and my folks are outta town, so it'll just be us three."

Marissa hesitated. Admittedly, she wasn't nearly as averse to Thomas as when they first met. Perhaps, with great hesitancy, she could even call him a friend. But one long glance at Nathara made her sigh. Naga needed a lot of support for their long, hefty bodies, and Marissa wanted Nathara to get a good night's sleep in a proper bed. After all, she'd saved Arthur's life.

But the thought of spending the night lying on a hard, cold, dirty floor made her nauseous. She'd had enough of it while she was homeless on the streets of Brennan, and she was growing used to sleeping in a comfy bed.

"Alright," Marissa replied. Thomas grinned, a faint glint of silver reflecting off one of his back molars. Arthur exhaled deeply – he seemed relieved that he too wouldn't be sleeping on the floor.

"Lemme pay my tab and we'll be off," Thomas walked over to the bar. "Tell the two Naga that we're leavin'."

Marissa turned around and froze before she could begin to relay her thoughts to Nathara. She and Ahira had been chatting all night, but Marissa hadn't paid much attention to their discussion until now. She realized that the pair were deep in conversation about their childhoods, comparing growing up as daughter of chieftresses. They spoke about their relationships with their parents, siblings, other members of their villages... deep thoughts that were typically only spoken between close friends. Nathara rested her chin on her fist, smiling warmly at Ahira as she talked. And Ahira... she was in absolute awe. Her eyes sparkled as if Nathara was the most beautiful creature she'd ever seen. There may as well have been no one else in the bar – they were lost in their own realm.

Marissa had never seen two beings so happy to be in each other's presence. She felt her heart tinge with happiness... and longing.

Then she noticed that Arthur was watching them too.

"I can't understand them," he remarked. "But I will say... now I think we all know the real reason why Ahira came back."

Marissa turned to face him. He too was touched by the scene, a pure, sweet smile stretched across his face, his forest-green eyes twinkling. Then realization struck her heart like a lightning bolt, sending burning emotions down her throat.

The way they're looking at each other... I've seen that look before...

I get it from Arthur...

All the time...

"Alright, tab paid," Thomas marched back up to the table. "Y'all ready?"

"Yes," Marissa stood up. As much as she enjoyed the heartwarming feelings that the two Naga gave her, she was exhausted. It hit her the second she stood up – a flood of dizziness causing her scales to shake.

Once Marissa regained composure and forced herself to remain energetic, she explained to Nathara that she and Arthur would be staying with Thomas for the night. This way, she'd have the inn room all to herself, and no one would end up sleeping on the floor.

Nathara was fine with the arrangement, as she, being a Naga, intended to stay up longer anyway. Marissa didn't even bother asking what time Ahira planned on heading back to Agkistra. She had a creeping suspicion that Ahira didn't plan on leaving at all... and that Nathara wouldn't be sleeping in the inn room alone that night. But Marissa knew that it was none of her business, and simply gave her aunt a happy smile before heading out the front door with Arthur and Thomas.

Chapter 10

HE HALF-MILE WALK TO THOMAS'S PARENTS' cottage was a dark and gloomy one. For the first few minutes, the trio walked in silence, too overwhelmed by fatigue for conversation. Marissa noticed that air felt so still and so alive at the same time – the three humans walking through the fields may have been quiet, but the rest of the forest wasn't. The buzzing of insects mixed with various reptilian squawks and chirps that echoed through the pitch-black forest and up into the milky, star-spotted night sky. The loudest ones were the Tokay geckos, bellowing out their distinctive 'to-kay' barks. Marissa watched as one of the vibrantly colored creatures scampered down a nearby tree trunk, its blue-and-orange scales popping against the dull tan color of the bark.

"I got bit by one of those once," Thomas remarked, his eyes flicking over towards the gecko in disgust. "Wasn't pretty. They got nasty jaws and some of the worst temperaments of any lizard I've seen."

He then stopped, his chin arched over his neck as he waited for Marissa and Arthur to catch up. He sighed, and Marissa noticed dark, puffy circles under his drowsy eyes.

"I know it's late and y'all are exhausted, but can ya at least gimme a summary of what happened tonight?"

Marissa's thoughts were beginning to fall apart, so she was relieved when Arthur spoke up and recapped the events of that evening. What caused the Naga to attack, how they came across the battle and met Ahira, and, of course, how Marissa managed to stop the whole thing.

"Good gods, no wonder yer a hero," Thomas turned toward Marissa, amazed. She merely shrugged, her eyes locked on the ground as they walked. "The craziest part of it all is that, when ya really think about it, y'all didn't have t'do this. Ya coulda just snuck around the battle and kept goin' instead'a riskin' yer lives."

Thomas's words sent a small jolt through Marissa's heart. *He's right. We could've just kept traveling. But that would go against everything we're trying to accomplish. Peace is worth the risk.*

"Speakin'a which," Thomas continued. "Where are y'all headed? Last I saw Marissa, she said she was headin' to lizard territory. That'sa long ways from 'ere."

"Well, uh..." Arthur fumbled his words. "We're headed, um, to..."

Marissa's nerves tensed. She hated having to lie to everyone about where they were headed.

"Testudo territory," she interjected, which made Arthur's eyebrows rise in alarm. "We have some business to attend to there."

Not technically a lie. Just not the entire truth.

Thomas gave Marissa a quizzical look, and the knot in her stomach tightened.

"Testudo territory, eh?" he pondered. "Well... whatever yer doin' out there, I won't pry. But ya do know that their burrows are a secret, right? Nobody knows where the entrances are."

As Thomas spoke, Nim stirred around Marissa's neck, periscoping his triangular head above her shoulders. The dull bluish tinge of his shed had faded earlier that day, and his onyx-black eyes glimmered in the darkness. His eyes were locked on the forest, and a sharp, stabbing pulse of panic echoed through Marissa's mind.

Nim... is something wrong?

"What's yer little striped beastie doin'?" Thomas asked, eyeing the brightly colored snake.

"Nothing," Marissa patted Nim's neck, gesturing for him to settle down. He reluctantly lowered his head and repositioned himself back around Marissa's neck. But even as Nim calmed down, Marissa could still feel the tension in his muscles as his body gripped her collarbones.

"Well anyways," Thomas raised his arm and gestured off in the distance. Marissa noticed that it was in the same direction that Nim's head had been pointing. "There's the place. Cozy, ain't it? We'll be there shortly."

SEVERAL HUNDRED FEET AWAY, SHROUDED BY THE black silhouettes of the forest, Ramsey was just as exhausted as the trio he was spying on.

He shook his head and rubbed his eyes, twitching his shoulders to readjust the fit of his scale-mail armor. He was grateful to not be wearing a heavy metal suit, but the stiff leather still wasn't very breathable. And after days of wearing it nonstop, it was straining his torso like an ill-fitting corset.

In the two days that they'd been traveling, he was too afraid to take it off. The first few miles of their journey, as they passed through the southern gates and into the villages closest to Brennan, all was calm. The chaos of the war was yet to spread so close to the main kingdom, and it nearly lulled Ramsey into a false sense of security.

It wasn't until they were nearly to the reptilian border that they first saw the bodies.

The closer they got to the beasts' territory, the worse it became. Entire villages reduced to bloody graveyards, with the few ghastly-faced survivors barely able to sputter out what had happened. And the few bits of information the traumatized villagers were able to provide were futile – they were never sure who started the battle. Some survivors even swore it was the royal guard attacking the villagers unprovoked.

Lies. Ramsey had hissed to himself, refusing to believe it. But deep in the recesses of his mind, he knew it might be true. After all, the royal guard had been enacting wartime laws to seize weapons and other supplies from the villagers, and Ramsey knew how belligerent some of the guard members could be when they didn't get their way. Out on the edges of human society, so close to the reptilian border, it was every person for themselves. And that meant more than a few villagers would've been unwilling to give up their guns.

But amidst the chaos, Ramsey was determined to keep his wits and do as much investigating as possible. But he faced a conundrum – he couldn't simply go around asking if anyone had seen a half-Naga girl. Because human-reptilian hybrids weren't supposed to exist, and Ramsey didn't want to reveal the truth to the whole valley. They'd either be horrified by the possibility, or they'd dismiss Ramsey as a fool for believing such things.

So he stayed silent, mainly relying on the other guard members to handle the aftermath of the battles. His mind was always focused on watching, scanning, trying to detect any piece of evidence that his brother or the half-Naga could've been through each village.

But his mind also wandered elsewhere. In the long stretches of time between villages, plodding down the main road on their horses, all he could think about was Charlotte. They'd spent the seven years of their marriage in sweet, contented bliss, fluttering around the castle and attending to their royal duties. Yet each night, they always returned to their cozy apartment, full of peace and luxury, and fell asleep in each other's arms.

And in the short span of time since he'd been declared the future king of Brennan, all of that seemed to fall apart.

He'd never felt so distant from her – they'd barely spoken since he came back from the temple in Naga territory. Something had broken inside of him. He was too stressed to enjoy the finer pleasures of the castle like he used to. He was so anxious and under so much pressure; everything around him seemed darker and twisted. The hallways were menacing, the throne room a prison, and even his own beautiful apartment seemed cold and gaudy.

His mind kept circling back to the last night before he left, lying in bed with Charlotte after she'd announced her pregnancy, and how their conversation brought a bit of happiness back to his battered heart. He'd barely known about his impending fatherhood for two days, and yet he was already determined to give the world to his future child.

Yet, he told himself. *None of that will matter if the reptilians destroy Brennan.*

And that paralyzing fear, the thought that his future heirs would inherit a kingdom in ruin if he didn't succeed on this mission, was what made him persevere. Even in moments like this, when he and his companions were hiding in a dense forest at two a.m. and all he could think about was sleep.

They'd finally found them. Off in the distance, walking down a thin dirt path toward a large cottage nestled between the trees, was Arthur and the half-reptilian girl. Ramsey and his companions – a dozen other high-ranking guard members – were crouched within the shadows of the surrounding forest, watching Arthur and his wretched companion like tigers stalking their prey.

Ramsey's cohorts were ready to pounce, and they were eager for him to give the signal. But Ramsey hesitated. Not only were they traveling with a large auburn-haired man who could possibly be armed, but a single phrase uttered by the half-reptilian girl turned Ramsey's blood to ice.

"Testudo territory."

It was a reply from the auburn-haired man asking where they were going. And it made Ramsey's mind swirl with questions. Testudo territory was a mystery to humans, a barren mixture of muddy marsh and pine scrub with no reptilians in sight. But Ramsey knew the tortoisefolk were there – hiding deep within their elusive burrows that no human had ever managed to find.

Until now. An idea sparked in his head.

"Um, Ramsey, sir," one of the other guardsmen muttered in a whisper. "Shouldn't we stop them before they enter that cottage?"

Ramsey hesitated for a moment, spinning together the plan in his head. He knew this was the right decision.

"No," Ramsey replied, standing up from his crouched position as Arthur and his companions vanished inside the cottage. "They mentioned that they're headed to Testudo territory. Which means I have a better idea."

"What is it, sir?"

Ramsey paused, rubbing his chin as he formulated a plan. "There is a guard training camp not far from here, correct?"

"Yes," one of the guardsmen piped up. "Just a few miles from the Testudo territory border. Three, maybe four hundred recruits are currently stationed there."

But would that be enough? Uncertainty prickled Ramsey's throat. They would have no idea what they were up against until they found the burrows, but it was a risk they would have to take.

Besides. He reasoned. *We have guns to even the odds.*

"You two," Ramsey pointed a finger at the guardsmen who spoke up, as well as the guardsmen seated next to him. "Go to the camp and tell them to send every able-bodied soldier they have. King's orders."

"As for the rest of you," Ramsey addressed the weary crew. "We're going to follow my brother and his wretched companions there in the morning, and then we'll finally find out where those tortoises have been hiding all these years."

The warm, sweet satisfaction of an easy victory snaked its way through Ramsey's chest. It would be a win-win – they could flush the elusive Testudo from their burrows and reclaim the land for Brennan, and easily capture Arthur and the repulsive half-reptilian girl in the process.

After all, there would only be so many entrances to the Testudo burrows. It would be easy to trap them underground.

King Gabriel will be thrilled.

As Ramsey stood, he noticed his companions' eyebrows raise and their faces light up as they realized the ingenuity of his plan. Ramsey grinned, a wicked, toothy smile flashing across his face.

"Then it's decided," Ramsey brushed the dirt off his scale-mail armor before retreating deeper into the forest. "Come along, let's set up camp. Get plenty of rest – we'll need to be up earlier than they are. Then, we follow them straight to the Testudo."

Chapter 11

$\mathcal{T}$HE SPACIOUS YET HUMBLE BUNGALOW WAS tucked between dense clusters of trees, giving it plenty of privacy from the neighboring homes. Marissa noticed that while many of the homes in the outer villages were made of wood, this one was made of limestone, its craftsmanship rivaling some of the buildings in Brennan. The home was strictly middle-class by Brennan standards, but it was still clear that Thomas's parents had more money than the other townsfolk in Canterbury.

"What did you say your parents do again?" Arthur asked as they approached the front door.

Thomas chuckled as he reached into his pocket and fiddled with an old copper key, the door squeaking open on creaky hinges. Two large, tawny-colored dogs barreled toward the entrance, jostling each other and leaping up on two legs as they whined for affection. They were shaggy-coated mutts - a mix of scent hound and some sort of herding breed.

"Argus, Willow, down!" Thomas barked at the wily dogs, commanding them to sit. "Sorry 'bout that. Anyway, why don'tcha see for yerself?" Thomas stepped to the side, holding onto the dogs' collars and gesturing for Arthur and Marissa to enter.

The small foyer, which led into a cozy living room with earth-toned furniture and hand-crocheted blankets strewn across the couches, wasn't what caught their eye. It was what was up above: wrought-iron gun mounts in various shapes and sizes were stacked across the walls in neat columns. A few of them held elaborate blunderbusses – weapons made of dark wood with finely etched gold-and-silver filigrees, their craftsmanship fitting of the royal guard. Yet most of the mounts were empty, hanging ominously in the dim light like dark metal skeletons.

"Ah, I remember now," Arthur remarked as he paced through the room. "Your parents are gunsmiths, aren't they?"

"Indeed," Thomas stepped behind him, admiring several of the guns. "Their workshop is down the hall to the right, and they even have a target range out back. Growin' up, I learned to shoot at a young age. Even won some contests – I consider myself an expert marksman."

Marissa hung back, studying the guns from afar. As beautiful as they were, the presence of so many weapons in such a homey, innocuous living room sent a chill up her scaled back.

A sudden question popped into her head. "So Thomas, if you're so experienced with guns... why didn't you have any back at your home in Copperton?"

Thomas turned around, a grim, sad shadow over his face. "Well, let's just say that when yer depressed and drinkin' every night, it ain't a good idea to have such deadly weapons around."

Marissa's stomach fell, and she immediately regretted asking such a question. It made her realize how lucky she was that Thomas merely pulled an arrow off his shelf when Marissa attacked him... and not a gun. She shuddered, reminding herself to be less impulsive with her emotions.

"So why are so many of the mounts empty?" Arthur asked, his eyes locked on a particularly elaborate musket. Despite the dim light, its dark wood finish gleamed like polished stone.

"The guns 'ere seized by the royal guard," Thomas grumbled, thumping his boot against a table leg in frustration. "They've been knockin' on the doors'a every gunsmith in the valley, takin' all their weapons and payin' 'em a pittance. The only ones left on 'ese walls have got somethin' wrong with em." Thomas removed the musket that Arthur had been admiring, flipping it around to reveal a sizable dent in the tip of the barrel. "But my folks stashed a few under the floorboards out in the storage shed, just in case."

Marissa's face twitched as she remembered the blistering crack of the muskets earlier that day as the villagers fought against the Naga. *They must've known about the gun stash.* As much as she had hated seeing the snakefolk's bullet-riddled carcasses, deep down she was grateful that the humans were able to defend themselves. *Without those guns, they would've been no match a horde of angry Naga.*

A sudden rustle of footsteps came from the dark hallway beyond the living room. Arthur and Marissa dove behind the couch, with Marissa hastily pulling her scarf out of her pocket and throwing it over her face. Thomas gestured for the two of them to stay hidden, and slowly crept toward the approaching footsteps.

Then they stopped. A small female silhouette was visible in the shadowy hallway.

"Thomas?"

Her voice quivered on the brink of tears. Thomas didn't even need to see her face to know who it was – he dove toward his wife in an instant, his arms curling around her back in a deep embrace.

"You came back," Thomas's voice was soft with disbelief as his wife burst into tears.

The pair stepped out of the shadows, and in the soft orange glow of the living room, Marissa was able to get a better glimpse at Marian. As Marissa's bright blue eyes peeked around the arm of the couch, she noticed that Marian's face was soft and peachy – full of life even as her cheeks became blotchy with tears. It was a far cry from her gaunt, sallow complexion just a few days earlier. The bruises on her arms were gone, and while she was still thin, it was no longer to a deathly degree. Even her long brown hair seemed thicker and shinier in the gentle light.

But Marian's remarkable recovery wasn't the only thing that soothed Marissa's weary heart. As Thomas broke their embrace, his hairy hands cradling her elbows as he gazed deep into his wife's eyes, Marissa studied the way the couple looked at each other. It was different than the starry haze of infatuation that she'd seen on Nathara and Ahira's faces. Instead, through their glistening eyes, Marissa saw years' worth of affection, pain, and perseverance, all melded together. To Marissa, it was a foreign blend of emotions, but the essence they radiated was remarkably clear.

Is this... what love looks like?

"My dear," Marian placed a hand on her husband's scruffy cheek. "I'm so sorry. It was wrong of me to run off like that. I'm grateful for what you've done," Marian gestured toward the empty potion bottle on the table. "I really am. But..."

"It's alright," Thomas sighed, releasing his grasp on her arms. "What I did was wrong. There's no gettin' 'round that. And it's gonna haunt me for the rest of my life. But I just can't believe it," Thomas's voice choked with tears as he admired his rosy-cheeked wife, a red-lipped smile blooming on her face. "You're cured! Good gods, I missed seein' ya this way. It's like yer a lil' lass again, like when I first met ya'."

They embraced again, with Thomas spinning his joyful wife around in his arms as she laughed. Yet as she spun and locked eyes with Marissa, her glee quickly turned to confusion.

"Um, Thomas, dear," Marian broke their embrace and stepped forward. "Who is this behind the couch?"

Marissa turned around and sat hugging her knees, biting her lip as she tried not to make a sound. Next to her, Arthur did the same, having to crouch much lower due to his height.

"Arthur, Marissa."

Their muscles clenched as Thomas said their names.

"It's alright. Y'all can come out now."

Arthur stood up, but Marissa crawled forward, still hesitant to fully reveal herself.

"My goodness, y'all were the folks at the apothecary last week," Marian looked confused. "May I ask what you're doing all the way out here?"

"They stopped the battle between the humans and the Naga," Thomas explained, a proud smile on his face. "I agreed to give 'em some lodgin' for the evenin'."

"*That's* what was going on?!" Marian exclaimed. "Once my weary heart had me turn around, I figured you'd be back at the inn drinking. But I stepped one foot through the door and immediately slammed it shut, running back to the house with my nerves in a frenzy. There were two giant Naga sitting at a table, and nobody seemed to care! What has this valley come to!?"

Marissa, Arthur, and Thomas all gave each other knowing, exasperated glances.

"I know we have a lot of explainin' to do," Thomas sighed. "But it's well into the early mornin' hours, and we're all exhausted. Let's allow my friends to wash up and head for bed, and I promise I'll explain everythin' while we're doin' the same."

Relief washed over Marissa's body. Despite her Naga half's nocturnal tendencies, the toll of the long, strenuous day was starting to weigh her body down like lead. All she wanted to do was let her tired limbs sink into a soft, puffy bed and wrap the blankets all around her.

"Oh, one last thing," Thomas noted as he led Marissa and Arthur to the guest bedroom. Marissa noticed a mischievous twinkle in his eye, and it made her uneasy.

"Yes?" Arthur asked.

Thomas pressed on the door, the guest bedroom slowly creeping into view. Marissa's throat immediately felt parched.

Thomas noticed Marissa's pale expression and grinned, "'Ere's only one bed. Anyway, have a good night, you two. I'll see ya in the mornin'."

TEN MINUTES LATER, MARISSA WAS STILL standing in the doorframe, dumbfounded by the large yet very singular bed. It did look inviting, with its rustic wooden headboard, soft downy comforter, and pile of decorative pillows. It seemed to beckon for her weary body to lie down, yet she was hesitant to step anywhere near it.

"I'm sure it'll be fine," Arthur's voice from the other side of the bathroom door made Marissa jolt. He'd decided to wash up for bed first, and the sound of running water and scrubbing brushes echoed from the little room while Marissa fretted over their sleeping situation.

"It's just for one night," he continued. "Besides, we're both so exhausted that we'll be passed out before we know it."

Marissa bit her dark lower lip, questioning Arthur's statement. She was definitely drained – her limbs felt heavy and her mind was beginning to cloud over. Yet she feared that the events of the past few days would keep her tossing and turning for hours. The gruesome scenes still struck through her mind like a dagger stabbing its way through her skull.

But sleeping together? It brought implications that made Marissa's stomach swirl. She'd even seriously considered curling up on the dog-hair-covered couch. But when she'd peeked in the living room a few minutes earlier, Argus and Willow were already nestled at either end, their gentle yet firm eyes signaling that they were not willing to move. And Marissa didn't dare to creep into Arthur's parents' room – the only other open bed in the house.

Yet as much as she wanted to avoid her swirling emotions for Arthur, she secretly longed for his touch. She feared it was the only thing that would allow her to escape her tormenting thoughts. Arthur was her dearest friend, but as much as she enjoyed his company, their blooming closeness made her more afraid. When she was a child at the orphanage, relationships only brought her pain. Her half-reptilian blood had always kept humans at bay – even the woman that raised her treated her with disdain. It was all she'd ever known... but now that was starting to change.

The squeak of metal door hinges shook her out of her musings. She looked up and saw Arthur emerge from the bathroom, the sweet, clean humidity of steam and soap sinking into her scales. Yet as soon as he turned around and she caught a glimpse of the triangular patch of chest hair peeking out of his nightshirt, her skin nearly turned white.

Her eyes flicked down toward the ground. She hoped that the scales spreading up her cheekbones would help conceal the fact that her face was turning bright red. Arthur wore a loose white nightshirt with a deep V-neck and a pair of linen shorts that barely covered his knees. His calves were muscular yet lean and covered in light brown hair. He raised a hand to his forehead, running his fingers through his scalp, before removing his wiry glasses and setting them on the nightstand.

"Well, do you need to wash up?" Arthur asked. His seemed oblivious to the fact that Marissa's whole body was quivering. "Or are you ready for bed?"

"No, um, I'm alright," Marissa stepped toward the bed, her legs feeling unsteady under her. Just before she reached the edge, she stopped. "But... I must ask. I'm concerned... isn't sleeping together only for married couples?"

"One night isn't going to do any harm," Arthur grabbed the edge of the comforter and tossed it aside, preparing to slide under the covers. "I promise I'll stay way over on my side."

"But... isn't that how children are made?"

Arthur froze, his foot hanging in mid-air as he prepared to step onto the bed. His body became surprisingly rigid, until he finally took a step back and awkwardly scratched his head.

"Um, what are you talking about?"

"Well, when I was at the orphanage, the other teenagers talked about married couples 'sleeping together'. They said that's how babies were made. The couple would sleep in the same bed, and the woman would end up expecting a child."

Arthur exhaled deeply, burying his face in his palms in a mix of embarrassment and frustration. "Marissa... no. That's not how it works. It's um... sort of accurate... but there's more that goes into it than just sleeping in the same bed together."

Marissa's innocent glance remained, and Arthur grimaced.

"And no, I'm not explaining it tonight. I promise you will not end up with a baby after this. I don't know if that's even possi- um, never mind. Let's just go to bed."

With her concerns at least somewhat dissipated, Marissa crawled into bed and pulled the thick comforter up over her scaled legs. She felt her whole body sink into the plush mattress, so exhausted that she feared she'd never be able to stand back up.

"Um, Arthur?" Marissa's voice was barely a squeak as Arthur turned off the oil lamp next to the bed.

"Yes?"

"Am I too naïve?"

As they were now alone in the darkness, several feet of space between them with each of their bodies hugging the edges of the bed, Marissa couldn't see Arthur's face. But she could sense from the tension in the air that her question was a heavy one.

"No, Marissa, you're not," he replied after a few moments of silence. "And naivete isn't a bad thing. You're not stupid. You just haven't had as many experiences as other humans."

"It does make me feel like a fool sometimes." Marissa pulled the covers up to her neck. "My whole life, I basically never left the orphanage. I didn't have friends, or go to school... I barely even know how to read."

"You're incredibly smart though," Arthur noted. "Intelligence isn't just how much you know. It's also how you interact with other people. You're very kind, idealistic, and in tune with others' feelings. In fact, I'd say you have more emotional intelligence than most other people I've met."

"Really?" Marissa's heart bloomed with a warmth that nearly brought tears to her eyes. No one had ever given her such a compliment.

"Yes. And I swear, Marissa, once this is all over, we will find a place for you in this world. Somewhere that you can feel accepted and wanted, not clinging to the edges of society."

"I thought I was going to help you at The Menagerie?"

That question brought a thick, dampening tension over them. It was as if the already pitch-black room suddenly got even darker.

"Marissa," Arthur's voice quivered with harrowing emotion. "I don't know if there will be a menagerie to return to. I'm an outcast now too – gods know what my family has done with my shop and my apartment."

Arthur's words sent a cold chill through Marissa's heart. She remembered when Arthur made the offer on their first night traveling together, lying on the dirty bare floor of an abandoned inn. Now they were in a plush bed, surrounded by comfort, while outside the whole valley was falling apart. Working at The Menagerie was always wishful thinking – a faint promise shattered by the war.

She thought of her single day spent working there, cleaning the snake tanks and feeding the chunky bearded dragons with Arthur. Surrounded by reptiles, their one day of domestic bliss, where for a few hours the world didn't seem like such a tumultuous place.

It was right before they went to the Castella's party, where their whole lives were thrown into turmoil.

Marissa felt her sorrow burning on her face, and before she knew it, tears were slipping from the corners of her eyes and spilling onto the sheets. She lay in pitch-black silence, afraid to make a sound and give away her distressed state. But after a few minutes, an incriminating sniffle gave her away. Her scales quivered as she felt Arthur shift closer to her.

"I know," Arthur's voice was tense and fraught with emotion. "It's hard. I'm feeling it too. Once I left the palace, The Menagerie was my sanctuary. I was finally able to do what I loved away from the prying eyes of my family, surrounded by my animals... and now it's all gone. And Aurora..."

His words trailed off as his own sniffle permeated the heavy air. Sympathy choked Marissa's throat. She knew how much Arthur loved Aurora, and having Thomas's two rambunctious dogs greet them at the front door likely sparked somber memories of her. Arthur was probably right – The Menagerie would've been seized by the royal family once Arthur fled the kingdom and was declared a wanted man. She had no idea where Aurora – or any of the other animals – would've ended up.

She remembered when she was kicked out of the abandoned building when she was homeless and lost her possessions. It wasn't much, but she knew the gut-wrenching feeling of having all someone had in the world torn away from them.

Marissa's thin veil of composure broke, cracking like a shattered eggshell as her soft sobs permeated the room. She squeezed her eyes shut, embarrassed. *Gods. I can't believe I'm crying.*

Marissa felt Arthur inch his way across the bed, as slowly and silently as possible, before finding her hand in the darkness and lacing his fingers through hers. Marissa felt his breath slow, knowing he likely feared her pulling away or lashing out. But as soon as his fingertips touched hers, Marissa chest loosened as a wave of relief washed over her body. Deep down, this was what she'd wanted the entire night. What she needed.

Sensing her reaction, Arthur pulled Marissa into his arms, curling his large yet thin-fingered hands around her scaled back. All her anxiety about sleeping in the same bed melted away. Forget keeping a safe distance – they both needed comfort after the day they'd had.

Marissa was too stunned to move. Arthur clasped her slender torso as if it were the only comfort in the world. She could feel the worried tension in his arms begin to unravel, as warm pulses of comfort radiated through both of their bodies. Marissa shivered as he raised his chin, cradling her head underneath it.

She didn't dare say a word, as if speaking would break their embrace. She was scared yet calm, flooded with both unease and tranquility, her body slowly becoming aware of every inch of her bare scales pressed against his skin. She released her breath, loosening the knot in her chest, as she allowed herself to relax fully, melting into his arms.

Yet along with the relaxation, a burning warmth radiated through her heart and down her stomach, past her navel and into unfamiliar territory. It both intrigued and terrified her, but despite her blooming affections for Arthur, she forced the urges back up into her fluttering stomach. Her mind began to wonder if those feelings were related to 'sleeping together', but her young mind couldn't comprehend how it all worked.

She sighed. *No. No more of these thoughts. Tonight, I sleep in Arthur's arms, and that is all. Nothing more.*

She closed her eyes. Arthur was already dozing off – his breaths were laced with faint traces of snoring. Marissa realized she was too, which amazed her considering the harrowing events of the past few days. It was as if Arthur's embrace was a shield, protecting her from the horrifying memories that always flashed through her mind at night. In his arms, she was safe, even from her own thoughts.

As she settled into slumber, a small yet warm smile spread across her dark lips.

Good night, Arthur. And thank you. For everything.

Chapter 12

AS THE YEARS PASSED AND CASSANDRA grew into a teenager, her grades, confidence, and friendships blossomed. Within a year she was fluent in sign language, able to easily keep up with her peers. She loved the language – it allowed her to express herself quickly and efficiently while being able to understand her classmates' conversations. No more struggling to lip read – all she needed were her eyes to understand. And according to the apothecary, her vision was nearly perfect.

She noticed that while her hearing continued to degrade, her perception of the world had been altered. She was much more visually perceptive than when she was a child – able to catch a glimpse of a single coin dropping all the way across the inn. She was hyperaware of her surroundings, always on the lookout, as she couldn't rely on auditory cues to tell her what was happening in the world.

By the time Cassandra was fifteen, she had lost the ability to understand direct conversations, and relied solely on lip-reading to communicate with her family and the inn patrons. And she hated it. She'd tried for years to teach her parents sign language, and while they knew a few basic signs, they were always too busy for more in-depth lessons. Cassandra understood – after all, they needed to run the inn to pay the bills – but she always felt a bubble of resentment when her father grew frustrated at his inability to get her attention while she was waitressing.

She didn't interact much with the customers other than bringing them their orders – it was too difficult to lip-read in a dimly lit, busy tavern with people constantly swiveling their heads around. But there were two patrons, Isaac and Curt, who took an interest in her, eager enough to converse that they would speak clearly and directly for her to lip-read. She even taught them a few basic signs, and her sisters always let her handle their table when they arrived.

Cassandra was fascinated by them; not only were they a pair of cheery, enthusiastic older men, but they were retired members of the royal guard. Once Cassandra got to know them, she broached the topic, and they were eager to share their stories.

But what she loved most about them was that they never questioned her dream of enlisting herself. It didn't matter that she was a girl, or that she had little hearing left.

"You wanna know the truth about the royal guard?" Isaac spoke slowly so Cassandra could lip-read, gesturing her forward while she served them their bill for the night. He paused, struggling to remember, before making three distinct signs.

Skill, dedication, bravery.

"Those are the skills that matter to the royal guard?" Cassandra asked. Her hearing loss had progressed to the point where she could barely hear herself speak, and she knew that her voice was changing, sounding more and more like Lucy's.

"Indeed. Anyway, here's our tab," Curt interrupted, placing a small pile of copper on the table. "And of course, a tip for our favorite server."

Cassandra beamed, having clearly read the word "tip" on Curt's lips. Usually, any monetary tips that Cassandra received went straight to her parents. She understood – they needed the money. But Isaac and Curt, having noticed this, started tipping her with gifts instead. Small trinkets, like candy from street vendors or woven bracelets from the merchant's district. They made frequent trips into the kingdom, and Cassandra was always enthralled with what they brought back for her.

But this time, it wasn't candy. Isaac placed a small orange vial on the table, and Cassandra picked it up, holding it up to the light and studying the strange substance.

"It's orange paste," Isaac explained. "Vital for all members of the royal guard. It allows for rapid wound healing. Sorry it isn't something more novel, we were in a bit of a rush on our recent trip."

Cassandra didn't make out everything Isaac said, but she did understand that the vial contained a healing balm. She'd heard of orange paste before – her parents bought it from an apothecary once when Alice fell from a tree and cut her leg open. It was a miraculous substance – her sister's injury had healed in less than a day.

"And on top of that," Isaac continued. "We'll have an even better tip for you tomorrow."

"What is it?" Cassandra asked.

"That's the thing – it's a surprise. But we know it will be something you really like."

Cassandra spent the rest of that evening and her time in bed at night pondering what the surprise could be. What object could they bring back from Brennan that she would truly enjoy?

She sat with her arms folded behind her head as a makeshift pillow, staring up at the dark, vapid ceiling. It was just her and Alice now, as Penelope had left when she turned eighteen. Her brothers were both married, the oldest one with a baby on the way. And with only the youngest two children left in the Warden household, they each had their own bedroom.

She enjoyed the privacy, but she also missed Alice. And Penelope. The room that was once crammed with three beds and a mountain of ragged old toys now contained only a single bed and dresser. It felt so sterile and lifeless.

Is this what growing up is supposed to feel like? Hard work and sadness?

She closed her eyes and shook the creeping thoughts out of her head. After all, growing up wasn't all bad. She still had the Valley Academy, her best friend Lucy, and her friends at the inn.

And whatever mysterious object they are bringing me tomorrow.

From the time she awoke the next morning, she pondered it all day. Lucy commented that she was quiet on the ride to school. Since they were both now teenagers, Jonas trusted them to drive the cart themselves, and it was just the two of them watching the swampland pass by. Cassandra even found herself not paying attention during her sign language class, which was her favorite hour of the day. She couldn't even focus during a surprise pop quiz, although thankfully she only got one answer incorrect.

Her parents were confused by her eagerness to start her shift that evening, but they didn't question it. She made sure that Isaac and Curt's usual table was polished to a glossy sheen, and kept glancing at the front door between customers, waiting for their arrival.

Eight o'clock. Nine. Ten. The sun was long gone, and the pair's usual table was now crammed with guests. *Where are they?*

This wasn't like them. Isaac and Curt were staunch regulars at the inn, coming in every night except Sundays. Even William took notice and made a comment about it while Cassandra was passing by with an armful of dirty dishes.

Finally, the clock struck eleven, and the inn began to wind down for the night. Cassandra found herself longingly staring at window, hopelessly anxious and confused, as her father came up behind her and flipped the OPEN sign around to read CLOSED.

"I'm sorry, sweetheart," William patted her on the shoulder. "Maybe something forced them to stay in Brennan overnight. I'm sure they'll be back sometime this week."

That makes sense, Cassandra reasoned as she hopped away from the window. *There's lots of things that could delay their journey home.*

But as she laid in bed that night, she knew that it wasn't true. Something was wrong.

Once it was well past midnight, and Cassandra was certain that her parents were asleep, she slipped out of her bedroom window and slid down the sloped roof, plopping on the ground in a frog-like crouch. Once her aching joints recovered from jumping ten feet, she snuck around to the storage shed behind the inn, snatched an oil lamp and some matches, and took off across town.

She knew that Isaac and Curt lived on the edge of Live Oak, near the swampland that signaled the end of human territory. She felt the ground dampening under her boots as she crept through the trees. The palmetto fronds swayed and crunched under her feet, and although she couldn't hear them, she knew she was being far from stealthy.

But there's nothing to fear, she reasoned. *They're fine. I'm sure once I arrive at their cottage they'll greet me at the door, mad at me for taking the-*

The toe of her boot thumped against something hard, something that definitely wasn't part of the forest.

She peered down, waving her lamp at the ground, and nearly fell back screaming.

A body. Not just any body – she knew those vacant, lifeless blue eyes and steely grey hair. It was Isaac.

Once Cassandra managed to stop trembling, she took a deep breath, as if she were about to plunge underwater, and shined the lantern in his direction again. Beyond his empty-eyed stare, a row of giant claw marks was raked across his chest, leaving his shirt tattered and soaked with blood.

Cassandra whimpered, stepping away from the corpse. She had noticed a second shadowy figure lying next to Isaac, but she couldn't bring herself to step toward it. She already knew it was Curt.

Pain and fear overtook her frail body, and she crouched down, her howling cries erupting from deep within her lungs. She was too in shock to leave, despite the danger. She knew she should've never left the house and wandered through the woods in the dark. Not only was she a child, but the inky darkness of the night sky was difficult to see through, even with a lamp. That, combined with her hearing loss, made her incredibly vulnerable.

Vulnerable to whatever killed her friends.

This was no human... she gulped. The image of Isaac's torn-open torso was burned into her mind like a branding iron. *Those claw marks... this was a monster.*

Fear snapped Cassandra out of her grief as she realized how much danger she was truly in. *It could be watching me in the shadows right now... stalking me...*

And I'd never be able to hear it coming.

She stood up, waving her lantern wildly in all directions. The forest was dark and sinister, composed of the blackened silhouettes of trees. But that's all that surrounded her – trees. She didn't catch a glimpse of anything living.

But what she did notice was a blood trail. At first she assumed it was Isaac or Curt's blood, but as she followed the trail a few paces, she realized it belonged to someone else. Someone that was once here and had stumbled away, clearly badly injured.

Every square inch of her gut screamed at her to run. Flee to the safety of the inn, crawl back into bed, and forget any of this ever happened. Isaac and Curt were dead – there was nothing she could do for them. And she had to make sure she didn't meet the same fate.

But stronger than anything, even her fear, was Cassandra's desire to be a hero. If she wanted to join the royal guard one day, she would have to face situations like this. Heroes didn't run away and hide in bed. Whoever made the blood trail needed help. This was her chance to save someone's life.

So she stepped forward, once again shining her light on Isaac's body. She gingerly removed the freshly sharpened sword from the scabbard at his waist, its blade gleaming in the soft orange light of the lamp. It was much larger and heavier than the sticks and toy swords she'd practiced with, but she braced her arm and pointed the blade in front of her, refusing to let her hand shake from the weight.

She paced forward, step by step, following the blood trail as it grew from a row of splattered droplets into a small, flowing stream. The sight of it made her nauseous, and she focused on looking straight ahead, steadying both her breathing and the shaky sword in her hand.

"Hello?" Cassandra called out into the night. "Can anyone hear me?"

She couldn't even hear herself, and she wouldn't know if someone responded back. But she had to at least reassure them that help was on the way.

She continued forward, just a few more paces, until the blood trail abruptly ended at a dark figure slumped on the ground.

"Hello?" Cassandra repeated. The lump stirred, its head rising.

"It's alright, I'm here to hel-"

She lunged backwards. Because as soon as the faint glow of the oil lamp cast its light on the figure, all she saw were scales. The creature was massive - long and slender, the lower half of its coiled in a circle with its torso looming above. It was like every childhood novel she'd ever read, where the hero snuck into the dark forest only to be greeted by a pair of slitted, glowering eyes. This was a real, true monster, leering just feet away from her.

She knew exactly what it was, even though she'd never seen one in person, only as illustrations in her childhood novels.

A Naga.

She wanted to run. She could feel her blood lurching in her veins and her stomach plummeting through her abdomen. She wanted to scream. Hide. Or possibly just vomit from fear. But as she stood frozen in shock, her mind racing as she contemplated her situation, she noticed that the Naga didn't lunge towards her. She'd fully expected it to attack and deliver a venom-filled bite to her neck. Instead, it barely even moved.

She slowly realized that the haunting glare in its eyes wasn't a threat. This creature was in pain.

With unsteady fingers, she waved the lamp in front of its coiled body. A massive, gaping wound tore through the flesh from its lower abdomen and trailed several feet down the length of its tail. Cassandra didn't know for certain if this was the creature that attacked Isaac and Curt, but if it did, the two men had certainly put up a fight.

And, based on the amount of blood staining the dark foliage and the Naga's inability to move, it would likely meet the same fate as her friends. Slowly, painfully, and alone.

But there was always the chance that there were others nearby, ones who could come and rescue the injured Naga. There were palm fronds rustling in the distance, but they could've easily just been the wind, or a few Tokay geckos scrambling about.

This is my chance to be a hero, she thought, peering down at the sword in her other hand. *To slay the Naga that killed my friends.*

She gulped, keeping her eyes locked in the injured Naga. As she stared into its copper-colored eyes, hatred boiled in her stomach. She gripped her sword tighter, raising it to chest level and stomping toward the injured snake.

She expected it to be hard. She expected the creature to put up a fight, or painstakingly attempt to flee. It would've made killing it more difficult, but somehow also easier, as if her naïve teenage mind could better rationalize slaying a hostile creature. What she didn't expect was for the Naga to wince, lower its head, and turn away, bracing itself for what it knew was coming.

It's just going to... surrender?

It still had its fangs and claws – it could easily kill Cassandra with one hit from either. Yet it chose not to fight. Cassandra froze, realizing it made sense. Even if the Naga killed her, it wouldn't change its own fate. It would still be stuck in the dark forest, mortally wounded and unable to slither away, waiting in unbearable pain for its inevitable death from blood loss.

Pain. That was all she could see in the Naga's eyes. She'd never seen such a grotesque wound – not even the claw marks on Isaac's body compared to this.

Why does being a hero have to involve killing?

Cassandra slowly lowered her sword. Maybe it didn't have to. Maybe being a hero wasn't just about killing monsters and saving princesses. Maybe bravery involved more than just conquering one's enemies.

She remembered her father's words a few years ago, when she complained about how she was being bullied by one of the smartest kids in the class. She had told William how she wished she could be more like him, especially since she was still struggling in the local schoolhouse.

"No," William had firmly objected. "Who cares how smart he is? Let me teach you something, Cassie. Out of

all the character traits in the world, the most important one isn't intelligence. It's kindness. You can be the smartest, strongest, most successful person in the world... but if you don't have empathy for others, then none of it matters."

And empathy was exactly what she felt for the despondent, hopeless, gravely injured creature in front of her. The world may have viewed Naga as monsters, but at that moment, killing the creature would've made *her* feel like a monster.

But what else can I do? I can't exactly drag it over to the apothecary.

Apothecary...

Wait...

She placed her sword on the ground, which caused the Naga to raise a confused eyebrow, and dug around her pocket until she pulled out the vial of orange paste. She'd brought it just in case she got a cut or scape while trudging through the forest to Isaac and Curt's home. She knew it wasn't nearly enough to mend such a gaping wound, but maybe it would heal the area enough so that the Naga could slither home.

The Naga flinched as she approached, a deep, guttural hiss echoing from its throat. Cassandra looked up, locking eyes with the monstrous creature. Its eyes were a glistening shade of copper, full of swirls and flecks, with its void-black pupils spread wide in the evening darkness. The eyes were so alien, so inhuman... yet she knew the exact emotion quivering through them. Not anger, not rage... but fear.

"I'm. Not. Going. To. Hurt. You," Cassandra signed, being slow and deliberate with every movement of her hand. Her facial expressions were just as gentle.

She knew it had no idea what she was saying. According to her parents, reptilians had no grasp on language at all. *They are simple beasts*, they'd said, *barely more than animals.* But even if the Naga had no idea what she was signing, her intentions were clear – she meant no harm. And that was enough to make the panic in the snake's eyes dim.

Now satisfied that the Naga wouldn't take a swipe at her head with its massive claws once she looked away, she knelt and pulled the vial of orange paste out of her pocket. Her stomach lurched as she applied the salve to her finger and pressed it against the Naga's wound. It was horrifically slimy and oozing, the snake's beautiful scales falling away to reveal a crater of exposed tendons and muscle.

It hissed again, the sharp noise echoing through the dark forest. But this time, it was from pain.

More and more blood leaked onto Cassandra's hands. It dripped onto her pajamas, staining them with dark crimson splotches, and it left a red tinge on the vial of orange paste. The vial that was quickly emptying.

It wasn't nearly enough. Cassandra wasn't even able to cover half of the wound. She bowed her head, debating whether she should spend her allowance at the local apothecary and come back with more paste the next morning... when she felt a firm, scaly hand on her shoulder.

She looked up. The Naga pressed its fingers gently against her collarbone, its coppery eyes glowing with the warmth of a smoldering campfire. Cassandra swore it was smiling.

It was happy for her help.

Let me at least get it somewhere safe for tonight, Cassandra reasoned, standing up and wiping the dirt off her clothes. She knew that there was an old, abandoned shack nearby, right where the forest met the swampland. She and her sisters had turned it into their personal clubhouse when they were young. Back then, it was littered with paper airplanes and origami figures, the shabby walls covered in their doodles and handprints. Cassandra swore they must've each signed their names on those walls a dozen times over.

That was years ago, before border disputes with the reptilians forced them to stay away from this part of the valley. But maybe the shack was still standing.

Cassandra grasped hold of the Naga's palm, amazed that it wasn't cold like she'd expected it to be. She wrapped its arm across her shoulder, prepared to help drag the hefty creature out of the forest. But after a few steps, the Naga seemed to understand their massive size difference, and gestured with its hands that it would be able to slither unassisted.

But it was still a long, painful journey. Cassandra tried the best she could, but the Naga was right – it was far too large for her to be of much assistance. Because the wound trailed down its tail, every winding, s-shaped slither across the ground took a great deal of effort. Cassandra wished she could reassure it, that they didn't have much further to go, but of course the Naga wasn't intelligent enough for such things.

Or is it? Her interactions with the injured creature had her suspecting that wasn't entirely true. Sure, it couldn't speak, but its gestures and facial expressions displayed that it was far more understanding of the situation than Cassandra would've believed. When she'd first encountered the Naga in the woods, she was certain she wouldn't walk away alive. *After all, they are monsters, right? They're the villains in every story I've ever read...*

Finally, she saw it – just a splintered silhouette in the distance, where the trees gave way to dark, glassy, perfectly still water that glistened under the half-moon. It was especially ominous under the thick midnight sky – as a child, she'd been taught to fear the swamplands that surrounded the human realm. Because it was where the monsters lurked.

Monsters. Like the one currently slithering next to her. The one that she'd saved from certain death.

She climbed up the steps, struggling to figure out which ones were safe and which ones would give way like brittle, waterlogged crackers under her feet. She jolted in surprise when the Naga grabbed ahold of her hips and hoisted her all the way above the old, precarious stairs. She signed a quick 'thank you' to it, and it nodded in return. This time, it knew exactly what she had said.

They both ventured inside, the floorboards creaking ominously below feet and scales. It was pitch-black inside, the moon barely visible through the cracks of a boarded-up window, and Cassandra's dimming oil lamp only allowed her to see the room one corner at a time.

There was no doubt the shack was falling apart – there were far more loose shingles and moldy floorboards than there were all those years ago. Yet Cassandra was amazed that it was still standing at all. The valley had experienced several years of bad thunderstorms, and even a nasty hurricane that tore apart half of Live Oak when she was ten. But she could still trace her fingers along the drawings she and her sisters had etched across the walls as children. She paused when she came to a series of notches in one corner. They were marked with the sisters' names and the date – July 25th, seven years ago. Cassandra pressed her body against the notches – hers was the one all the way at the bottom. At only five feet tall, the mark came up to the top of her ribcage. She was destined to always be small and wiry like her mother.

Which was a stark contrast to the Naga currently resting in the far corner. Even with its coils wrapped around itself and its torso slouched against the wall, it was still far taller than any human. Especially one as petite as Cassandra.

She approached the Naga, watching as its scaly mouth twisted into something resembling a smile. Its face was distinctly reptilian, with armor-like scales and slitted, unblinking eyes - a far cry from a human's gentler features. Yet its expressions were eerily similar to her own.

Cassandra shined the oil lamp on its long, coiled tail. It was difficult to tell, but she swore the wound was beginning to heal.

Crap, she sighed. *I have to somehow get it to understand that it needs to stay here.*

She pursed her lips in thought, pointing first at the Naga and then down at the floorboards. She signed the word 'stay', hoping that the gesture, which involved making it look like her hand was frozen in place, would be understood by the creature.

To her surprise, it nodded eagerly. It had no eyelids to close, but Marissa could tell by its dull, glassy gaze that it was exhausted.

"Me. Back. Morning," she signed, cursing herself in the process. *This is hopeless. It doesn't have that level of intelligence. It...*

The Naga nodded. It raised a hand, making the same gesture she had made earlier, when it had helped Cassandra up the stairs.

The sign for 'thank you'.

Disbelief washed over Cassandra. The Naga knew nothing about human society and had no grasp on any form of human language, spoken or signed.

Yet it understood. It knew that the gesture was a sign of thanks.

She signed a quick 'thank you' back, stumbling out of the shack in an astonished daze. Not only did she come out of the whole ordeal alive and unharmed, but she was beginning to suspect that the Naga were not the mindless monsters that the valley made them out to be.

She didn't care if it took every last coin of her allowance. She had to bring the Naga more orange paste tomorrow.

"MY GOODNESS, SOMEONE IS HUNGRY TODAY," William chuckled as Cassandra shoved bite after bite of pancake in her mouth, barely giving herself enough time to swallow.

True, after the night she'd had, she awoke the next morning starved for food. And while she usually loved her family's Saturday morning pancake breakfasts, she didn't have time to savor the fluffy, syrup-covered treats.

Because it was the weekend, which meant that other than helping prepare and clean up breakfast, Cassandra was chore-free for the day.

And she needed to slip away to the apothecary and return to the Naga as soon as possible.

Not only was she hungry, but she was also exhausted. She'd tossed and turned for half the night, her mind reeling from both her revelations about the Naga and her fears for the one currently hiding in a shack in human territory. Despite having so little orange paste, she prayed that it closed the wound enough that the Naga was able to rest. That it didn't succumb to its injuries overnight. The thought of it dying, after all she'd done to save it, made her feel surprisingly awful.

She lay awake for hours after returning home, not succumbing to sleep until the early-morning sun was already peeking its way over the horizon. And she swore her dreams lasted five seconds before Alice banged on her door.

"Mind if I just clean my own dishes today?" Cassandra asked timidly, placing her sticky, syrup-coated silverware next to her empty plate. "I... have somewhere to be after breakfast."

She cringed as William cast a suspicious eye in her direction, complete with a raised eyebrow. Her breath slowed, praying he'd heed her request and not pry further.

After a few seconds of silence, he chuckled, "Alright, go ahead. You've done enough at the inn this week. You deserve a break."

Cassandra leapt out of her seat before her father even finished his sentence, scouring her plate with a soap-covered brush in mere seconds. She quickly stacked it away in the cupboard, creating a racket of shifting ceramic, and bolted out the door before her father could object to her hasty cleaning job.

Thankfully the apothecary was open on Saturdays, and her intuition was correct – it took nearly all her allowance to buy a single vial of orange paste. One that, disappointingly, was about the size of the one she'd obtained from Isaac and Curt.

It would have to be enough.

The apothecary, a cheery, elderly gentleman with long braided hair and wire-rimmed glasses, wished her the best of luck as she scurried out the door with her purchase. It made her chuckle slightly as she jogged down the road, headed back through the forest and towards the swampland. She knew the man would say otherwise if he knew who – or rather, what - the orange paste was for.

Her heart was caught in her throat during the entire trek through the forest. Would the Naga still be there? Would it still be alive? Or worse... would it decide to attack her now that it was no longer dying?

The shack was still there, a dilapidated, rotting building half-swallowed by the surrounding trees. The stilts that held it above the water were partway disintegrated, and Cassandra wondered how structurally stable it was. One hard hit to those stilts would probably send the whole building crumbling into the water.

But that was the least of her worries. Besides, it had held up overnight with a several-hundred-pound Naga resting inside. Certainly her petite frame wouldn't tip the scales.

It was still dim inside the shack, but the bits of daylight peeking in through the exposed doorframe and slits in the boarded-up windows allowed Cassandra to see the whole room. And as soon as she stepped inside, her heart plummeted.

The Naga was gone.

She stepped cautiously through the one-room shack. She couldn't hear the floorboards creaking under her feet, but she could feel how unstable they were. Every time they wiggled under her feet, it sent jolts of fear down her arms and into the tips of her fingers.

It's gone. It's not safe for me to be here. I should...

She screamed before she even realized what had happened. All she knew was that she was falling... and a splitting pain rocked her thigh and pelvis. A rotting floorboard had collapsed under her left foot, and she was now stuck with her entire leg dangling ten feet above the water below.

She braced her palms against the surrounding floor and attempted to hoist herself up, but the splintered wood surrounding the hole dug into her thigh like needles. She went to scream but immediately snapped her mouth shut, reminding herself that she needed to be quiet. She was right on the cusp of Naga territory, and she knew not all of the snakefolk would be as friendly as the one she'd helped the night before.

She squeezed her eyes shut, on the verge of tears as she dug deep into her mind and tried to formulate a plan. She had to get out of this, somehow, even if it meant having the splinters cut into her thigh like a thousand tiny knives.

She took a deep breath, preparing to hoist herself up again, when she felt a familiar scaled palm grabbed ahold of her bicep.

She opened her eyes. Clawed fingers were scraping at the wood surrounding her stuck leg, tearing away the splinters with little effort. She noticed that the Naga's thick, scaly palms seemed to protect it from injuring itself.

After a few seconds, the Naga wrapped its large arms around Cassandra, hoisting her out of the hole. She started panting from exhaustion and relief as soon as the Naga set her down on a less dilapidated section of the floor.

She never thought she'd be so happy to see a Naga. It was definitely the same one from the night before, and its coppery eyes glistened with concern.

"I'm alright," Cassandra signed, along with a thumbs-up. The Naga mimicked her hand motions, fascinated by the language.

Where was it? How did it get here so fast?

The Naga knelt down, its tail coiling around its body. Its claws traced the cuts around the edge of Cassandra's thigh, from where the splintered wood had dug into her flesh.

"I'm okay," Cassandra signed, nodding her head enthusiastically.

But the Naga still seemed concerned. Its eyes flicked over to the vial of orange paste, which had fallen out of Cassandra's pocket and rolled across the floor.

"No, no..." Cassandra spoke, protesting as the Naga fetched the vial and scooped out a bit of the salve with its claw. "That was meant for you."

She craned her neck, peering over at the Naga's tail while it applied the paste to her thigh. It was still injured, but the wound was half the size it was the night before, and covered in a thick layer of scabs.

I don't understand... I'll be fine... it needs it more than I do...

But the Naga was adamant. Cassandra's cuts weren't too deep, and they closed completely within ten minutes of the orange paste being applied. During that time, Cassandra sat on the floor while the Naga slithered around the room, studying the scribbles along the walls. It seemed particularly fascinated by one section in the far corner, where Cassandra and their sisters had signed their names next to their own handprints. Cassandra watched as the Naga placed its clawed palm over her tiny, child-sized hand. The Naga's massive hand was more than twice its size.

Once Cassandra healed, the Naga helped her up and led her outside, to a small deck on the opposite side of the shack, bordering the water. The Naga turned toward her, the side of its mouth twisting into a sly grin, before its long body leapt off the dock and trailed into the water with a faint splash.

It surfaced a few seconds later, flicking its tongue and staring curiously at Cassandra. It cocked its head and extended a claw, and Cassandra shuddered.

She appreciated its help, but there was no way she was jumping into a reptilian-infested swamp with the Naga. She barely even knew how to swim.

But she was glad it was feeling better, and was healed enough to return to the rest of its clan. She signed a 'thank you' to the Naga, and it signed it back.

She chuckled. She would have to teach it the sign for 'you're welcome'.

If she ever saw it again.

And as the Naga swam away, disappearing under the watery horizon, Cassandra realized that she *did* want to see it again. Now she knew that the Naga weren't hostile, mindless monsters – or at least, that this one wasn't. She'd saved its life the night before – and this morning, it had possibly saved hers.

And she left the shack, venturing through the forest back toward her home, she had a feeling that this wouldn't be the last time she saw the Naga.

She really hoped it wouldn't be.

Cassandra couldn't stay away.

She knew that the chances of the Naga returning to the shack were slim. She also knew that it was a rotting, unstable mess of a building and that she was risking her life just venturing in there. But she longed to return once she finally got a chance to slip away from her hectic routine of school and chores.

By this point, news of Isaac and Curt's death had spread, and Cassandra's stomach was in knots the entire time she and her family stood outside the town church for the funeral. The pastor's gentle words offered her some comfort, but that feeling was quickly soured once his speech turned into a tirade against the evil Naga lurked at their borders. Cassandra remembered how angry and sickened she felt upon seeing those claw marks on Isaac's chest... until she saw the gaping wound torn across the Naga's own flesh. She had no idea what had caused her slain friends to attack the Naga, or what even started the conflict. Her interactions with the creature had her questioning everything.

She mourned her friends, and held back tears as their coffins were lowered into the ground. But the potential of seeing the Naga again gave her an idea. Clearly it was an intelligent being, capable of learning sign language. If she taught it enough signs, maybe it would be able to tell her what really happened that night.

After all, wasn't the main reason why there was so much fighting because they humans and Naga couldn't communicate?

Despite her lifelong desire to join the royal guard, she realized that maybe swords weren't the true answer to conflict. Communication was what held all the power.

That became even more apparent when she ventured into the shack a few days later. Not only was the Naga there, but it was busy pounding a nail into a plank of wood with a hammer made out of animal bone. Its scaly brows were furrowed, clearly deeply focused on its task.

But as soon as the Naga looked up and saw her, its entire expression changed. A huge grin spread across its face, its eyes glittering with disbelief. Clearly it hadn't expected her to return, and it was thrilled to see her.

Cassandra chuckled and offered a friendly wave, and the Naga immediately slithered towards her, clasping a scaly palm around her wrist and pulling her forward. It enthusiastically pointed at the hole where she'd fallen a few days before, which was now patched with planks of scrap wood.

Where did it find these?

The Naga seemed to read the confusion on her face, because it once again grabbed ahold of her wrist, this time leading her out of the shack and deeper into the forest. Cassandra was confused, but didn't pull away. She could feel the incredible strength in the Naga's grip – but at the same time, it was remarkably gentle.

Her eyes widened as the Naga slithered to a halt. She'd never wandered this far past the shack, and was amazed to see an entire *village* being swallowed up by the forest.

"Wow," she whispered, wandering between the collapsed homes and inspecting the ancient, filthy belongings scattered across the ground. A shattered hand mirror, a rotting teddy bear with stuffing pouring out of its neck, even a set of royal guard figurines dumped in a box next to an open doorway. She picked up and inspected the pieces, the few remaining flecks of metallic purple-and-gold paint glinting in the sunlight.

The Naga slithered over, curious about what she'd found. It plucked out of the soldiers from her cupped hands, scowled in disgust, and tossed the little figurine on the ground.

Cassandra's stomach flipped, but she couldn't blame the Naga. She then took notice of another figure still lying in the box. It was a giant Naga, with mottled black-and-brown scales just like the one currently with her. Except this figure's eyes were bright red, and its mouth gaped wide open, revealing rows of needle-like teeth.

She decided she wasn't a fan of the figurines either, and dumped the rest of them back in the box and walked away.

She went to check on the Naga, who was inspecting its own reflection in the shattered hand mirror. It traced a claw along its scales, as if unfamiliar with its own features. It looked up at Cassandra as she approached, flicking its tongue in a long, slow gesture. It froze for a moment, as if deep in thought, before pointing at the mirror.

Cassandra cocked her head, confused.

The Naga pointed again, this time making a gesture with its other hand.

Oh, Cassandra realized what it was asking for.

"*Mirror*," she signed slowly, repeating the gesture a few times until the Naga caught on. It mimicked the sign before clasping the metallic rim with both palms. As it did so, a few loose pieces of the shattered mirror tumbled to the ground.

It continued picking up more and more objects, each time asking for the respective sign. *Ball, hairbrush, cooking pot*. With each new sign, the Naga caught on faster and faster. Once they came across a second set of cooking equipment ten minutes later, it pointed and enthusiastically signed, 'pot'.

Technically, it was pointing at a cast-iron skillet, but Cassandra decided she'd correct the Naga later.

Once the Naga ran out of steam and had pointed at nearly every object in the ruined village, it then raised a claw and pointed at itself.

Something about the gesture shook Cassandra to the core. Learning the signs for basic household objects was one thing. But this... the Naga wanted to know what it was. What *she* viewed it as.

"*Snake,*" Cassandra gestured, which involved holding up two fingers to make a modified S-shape.

The Naga repeated the gesture, but still didn't seem satisfied. Cassandra, still holding up her hands, then added two "fangs" with her other fingers.

"*Naga.*"

The creature seemed even more confused, wondering how its entire existence was represented by a single hand sign. Cassandra realized that no matter how enthusiastic or fast of a learner the Naga was, having a full-on conversation with it was going to take a *long* time.

But it wasn't that long ago that she was in the same position, struggling among her hearing classmates as the world continued to grow muffled around her. She too felt ostracized and misunderstood. She too had to learn a whole new method of communication.

If she could do it, so could the Naga.

This time, it was her that wrapped a hand around her companion's wrist. She smiled – a true, genuine, beaming smile, and felt her heart flutter as it was reflected in the Naga's serpentine face.

She began leading him back to the shack on the water's edge. It was still early in the day, and she wasn't due back home for a few more hours.

Which meant they had plenty of time for sign language lessons.

Chapter 13

$\mathcal{T}$HE FOLLOWING MORNING, MARISSA ONCE again woke up alone.

She opened her groggy eyelids and sat up, peering around as she rubbed her tired face. She was surrounded by sprawling sheets, far too rumpled to have been slept in by just one person. She peered down at her hands, her fingers spread out and her palms upright. She could still feel his hand clasped in hers, his chest pressed up against her scales, and his chin perched atop her head. Arthur was gone, yet she knew it wasn't all just a brooding dream.

Sadness was replaced with a hint of anger, which felt bitter in her throat. She thought back to the night in Komodo, where Arthur sat close to her, running his hands up her scales, only to disappear the next morning and leave Marissa questioning her own sanity.

Why does he always do this?

She huffed and tossed the comforter off her legs, revealing the bare scales lining her calves underneath her dress. She knew why. She knew exactly why, and it made her stomach churn and nausea rise up the back of her throat like acid. She was a half-Naga, an oddity at best and a monstrosity at worst. Maybe Arthur did have feelings for her. Maybe he thought she was a kind and empathetic soul, full of intelligence and bravery, but he just couldn't get past her appearance. But even if he *was* attracted to her snake-like features, Marissa knew the harrowing implications of a royal, even a minor one, becoming involved with a reptilian.

It probably crept through Arthur's mind the entire night. And even if Arthur was now an outcast, Marissa knew that he could never truly forsake his family. Maybe he was hoping that someday he'd obtain forgiveness, and announcing to his parents that he was courting a half-Naga would severely hinder that process. Marissa knew what it was like to be alone, with no family, and she didn't want Arthur to endure the same hardship.

Her lips quivered. *Even if that means I can't be with you.*

A faint knock on the door made her bolt upright, scrambling to cover her scaled legs with the hem of her dress.

"Marissa? It's me, Marian. May I come in?"

Thomas's wife. She doesn't know about...

Marissa leapt out of bed, ransacking the room in search of her scarf. Her blood curdled in horror when she realized she'd left it out in the living room. That meant that standing between her and the bit of fabric that covered her half-snake face was the woman who had no idea she was a reptilian.

She clasped her palms to her forehead, running her fingers through her thick bangs. But as Marian knocked again, the bubble of panic in Marissa's stomach began to settle. She released her grip on her dark hair, letting her hands fall to her sides as she realized that maybe she didn't need to worry. The past few days had taught her that humans discovering her secret was no longer a death sentence. *Arthur knows. Thomas knows. The entire town of Canterbury knows... and they didn't kill me. What's one more person?*

"Come in," Marissa's strained voice was halfway between a whimper and a croak.

The door cracked open, with a friendly, rosy-cheeked face peeking in. Marian's appearance revealed that she hadn't been awake long – her wild chestnut hair was frizzy, and there was a faint puffiness around her eyes. But she still looked leagues better than she had just a few days earlier.

"It's alright." The softness in her voice was reassuring. The door creaked the rest of the way open, and Marian stepped into the room. "Thomas explained everything to me last night when we were getting ready for bed. You have no idea how grateful I am for you. Saving my husband's life with your venom, stopping the conflict last night... you are a truly a wonder."

She stepped toward Marissa, her eyes alight with fascination. "Your scales are lovely. They look like polished stones along your skin, and their color really compliments your dark hair."

A warm, gleeful disbelief bloomed in Marissa's stomach and crept up her throat, preventing her from being able to even sputter a 'thank you'. But the glistening happiness in her eyes made Marian chuckle.

Marian's smile was laced with a hint of sadness, and her face suddenly turned grim, "But I will say, what truly makes you a miracle is how you treat my husband. He committed a horrible crime against your people, and yet you've forgiven him. In fact, I-"

"No," Marissa growled. Marian's words offered more pain than comfort. No matter what Thomas said or did, Marissa could never forget that he killed a reptilian.

She took a deep breath, her expression softening. "I haven't forgiven him. But I don't believe you have to forgive someone to show empathy. I appreciate everything he's done for us, but the fact that he committed murder will never change."

But as she spoke, her mind swirled with contemplation. When she'd first confronted Thomas about his crime in Copperton, he'd asked if Marissa would do the same for her own family. At the time, Marissa thought she had no family. But now, even if her father was a rage-filled villain and her mother was nowhere to be found, maybe the definition of family wasn't as rigid at Marissa once believed. She thought about her companions – Nathara was blood, her own aunt, and the closest thing she'd ever had to a mother. Despite her reservations about Thomas, he and his wife were kind and accepting souls who'd let them spend the night. And Arthur...

As usual, her stomach swirled at the thought of him. Despite his recent flighty behavior, he was the one who her heart beat the strongest for. She adored him, wanted him... and she began to wonder if this was what love felt like. She knew that it was a powerful emotion. It was what bound souls together, made families of those not related by blood. She'd only known Arthur a few weeks, but she knew deep in her soul what she'd be willing to do if his life was in danger. Thomas and Marian had been together for years – Marissa couldn't even begin to fathom how strong of a bond they had.

For the first time in her life, Marissa was forming relationships, and as much as she hated it, she was beginning to understand Thomas's motivations for killing the Varan girl.

Her reptilian nostrils flared. *But understanding isn't the same as forgiving. It never will be.*

A slight rustling sound caused Marissa to look up. Nim had awoken from his cozy spot in the curtain rod, and he was now slithering down the gauzy curtains in a spiral pattern, showing remarkable strength as he descended toward Marissa. His glossy black eyes were locked on her as she extended an upturned palm. Like an eager puppy, he wound his way across her arm and settled in a coil around her neck.

Marian tilted her head and smiled, eyeing the slender-bodied snake as he flicked his tongue in her direction. Up above, dangling from the curtain rod like an ethereal ghost, was his freshly shed skin.

I'll have to get a stool and grab that later.

"I must say, once you get past your initial fear, they're such beautiful creatures." She gently stepped forward, raising a hand toward Nim and giving Marissa a quizzical look. Marissa nodded eagerly, signaling that Nim meant no harm, and Marian gingerly pressed her fingertips against the vibrant black-and-yellow scales on the snake's neck.

"He's so soft. It's funny, as a child, I thought reptiles were slimy." Marian chuckled. "Anyway, I imagine you're hungry. Care for breakfast?"

Marian's question immediately caught Marissa's attention. She tilted her head around Marian, attempting to see down the hall. "Are Arthur and Nath-"

"Your friends? Yes, they are. Arthur's having his morning coffee and reading the paper at the table. He's been awfully quiet... anyway, the Naga lady came in early this morning. Gave me quite a spook, but Thomas and Arthur explained that she's your aunt. She's lovely – she's been helping my husband cook in the kitchen. It's a shame we can't understand her. But... you can, can't you?"

"Yes." Marissa nodded. "May we go out and join them? I'm quite hungry, and I'd like to see how Nathara is doing."

"Of course," Marian stepped to the side, gesturing for Marissa to step out into the hall. "Follow me."

As Marissa entered the cramped yet cozy kitchen, the first thing she noticed was that her massive Naga aunt's head nearly touched the ceiling.

Nathara was slithering around the kitchen, pulling various cooking utensils off hooks and eyeing them quizzically before handing them off to Thomas. The auburn-haired man was still dressed in his nightclothes, but his bright eyes indicated that he'd been awake for some time. He was hunched over the stove, the warm popping and crackling sounds of grease filling the air the air. It smelled rich, meaty, and salty, and Marissa curiously craned her neck over Thomas's shoulder to see what he was cooking.

In one cast-iron skillet was a familiar sight – pancakes. They'd been a staple at the Thorburn Estate, and they were one of the foods Marissa missed the most when she was cast out into the storehouse. The sweet smell of butter and raw dough filled her reptilian nostrils, but what caught her attention the most was the savory scent emanating from the other skillet.

She recognized the thin strips of meat, oily and sizzling as they curled up into crispy ribbons. They'd never had such delicacies at the orphanage, but she'd seen – and smelled – the same food being cooked at some of the vendor stalls in Brennan.

"G'mornin', Marissa," Thomas greeted in a hearty voice. He flicked his eyes toward her head, which was just inches from his shoulder. "I see that yer a fan of bacon. But ya might wanna step back before ya start droolin' on my stove."

Marissa stumbled backwards, shaking off her embarrassment and wiping her mouth just in case. Behind her, Nathara was still fumbling around the kitchen. From what Marissa had seen, reptilians ate their food raw, so the sight of meat cooking on a stove was likely an unfamiliar experience for her aunt. And apparently so were human kitchens, because her attempts to help Thomas were barely more than futile. She couldn't understand human speech, but Thomas made an effort to communicate by pointing at the various pots, pans, and utensils that hung on a row of racks above the kitchen drawers. It was a guessing game – Nathara would point her claws at them one by one, confused by the whole charade, until Thomas finally gave a thumbs-up when she'd selected the tool he needed. Marissa could tell that Thomas was growing frustrated, but he played along due to Nathara's happiness at being able to assist him.

Marissa then noticed another source of Thomas's frustration – Nathara was distracted. She seemed to periodically get lost in thought, her mind clearly reminiscing on a place far from Thomas and Marians' humble kitchen. A small smile crept onto Marissa's lips as she noticed the infatuated glow on her aunt's face.

She knew exactly where Nathara's mind was wandering off to. But there was no sign of Ahira, so she'd clearly already departed for her home village.

Marissa wondered if Nathara missed her already.

But with Thomas busy cooking and her aunt bustling around the kitchen trying to help, Marissa decided it was best to stay out of the way, and she took a seat at the kitchen table. But her stomach immediately twisted itself in a knot when she noticed the large, unraveled newspaper hovering in the air at the opposite end of the table.

The newspaper slowly lowered, revealing a familiar pair of green eyes and a head topped with sandy brown hair. Arthur was silent as he gave Marissa a welcoming smile. His eyes twinkled with their usual warmth, but his upturned lips were pressed in a stiff line. It was a 'we'll talk later' smile, one that barely masked the reluctant, conflicting emotions that crept across his face. And it made Marissa's stomach boil with frustration. She was tired of this. She wanted to talk *now*.

She pressed her back against her chair, taking a deep breath and let her burning face cool off. As much as she hated it, Arthur was right. They needed to wait for the right time to discuss things. Which wasn't in Thomas and Marians' house. If anyone overheard them, not only would it cause a scene, but everyone would know that they – Marissa quivered – *slept together*.

And as much as Marissa craved his affection, admitting her feelings was an entirely different beast. One she wasn't sure she was ready to confront yet either.

So she kept her mouth shut, forcing herself to pry her eyes away from Arthur. He pulled his outstretched newspaper back up, completely concealing his face.

"When did Nathara show up?" Marissa asked, twisting around in her seat so she was facing Thomas.

"Quite early this mornin'," Thomas remarked as he flipped a pancake with a doughy *splat*. "It surprised me, as I thought the snakefolk were nocturnal. I think she was worried about ya. Although she gave my wife quite a scare chargin' up to the door with that gun slung over 'er shoulder."

A shock of remembrance jolted Marissa's brain. *The gun. Nathara's not wearing it.* She sat up straighter in her chair, craning her neck in an attempt to locate the weapon. She froze as her eyes locked on one of the gun racks. The plain, worn-out musket was a stark contrast to the shining, elegantly designed weapons made by Arthur's parents.

"Don't worry," Thomas chuckled. "I wasn't concerned. She wasn't wearin' it right, and she had no powder horn or buckshot on 'er. She doesn't even know how to fire it, does she?"

"Um, no," Marissa replied, cringing as the image of Nathara pointing the gun barrel at her eye a few days earlier flashed through her mind. "We passed through Copperton on the way here. Nathara found it among the wreckage."

"I see," Thomas sighed, his eyes turning steely at the thought of his burned-down village. He turned around, glancing over at the weapon hanging on the wall. "In that case, it must've belonged to one of the supervisors. Which means it's an older gun, got a snaphance instead of a flintlock."

Marissa cocked her head, "What does that mean?"

"It uses an older firing mechanism," Thomas continued. "Flintlocks are the newer guns - simpler and more reliable. Means that it ain't worth teachin' ya to shoot with that old thing."

"Teach?" A slight chill ran across Marissa's scales.

"I was thinkin' 'bout that," Thomas slapped the last pancake atop a pile of them. He and Marian then began loading the table with food – from the fluffy pancakes and the fatty, crispy bacon to plump strawberries and freshly-squeezed orange juice.

"I'm just concerned," Thomas remarked as he plopped down at the table, plucking several pieces of bacon off the communal plate and onto his own. "Testudo territory is still another half days' walk. And I dunno if y'all have noticed, but there are guards lurkin' everywhere. We're lucky they weren't around to interfere last night. And I still don't know what y'all are after in the tortoises' land. From what I've heard, they ain't very hospitable to outsiders."

Marissa lifted her head, watching Arthur out of the corner of her eye as he lowered his newspaper and chewed on his bottom lip. She placed her hands in her lap, fiddling with the straps of the satchel that held the idol pieces. She hadn't let them out of her sight since they left Komodo – she even slept with the satchel tucked next to her. To the rest of the world, it was a simple bag, likely carrying a few important yet ultimately trivial possessions. Only her, Arthur, and Nathara knew the truth.

And Aina. The Varan chieftress slipped into Marissa's mind. She shuddered as she remembered the pain in the Varan's eyes as she allowed them to escape.

Her eyes flicked over to Arthur. Forget her brooding about their night together – he was her partner, and she needed his help.

Arthur's green eyes glittered with worry. Marissa knew he understood what her gaze meant. He hesitated, a tense expression on his face, before giving Marissa a weary yet definitive nod.

Tell him.

Marissa gulped. *Sure, he did stab me with an arrow... but otherwise Thomas has done nothing but help us.*

She peered back up at the burly man, with his thick auburn hair and plump mustache. His arms were scarred, and his face was lined with far too many wrinkles and spots for being only thirty-one.

Marissa never thought she'd trust a murderer. But her few weeks outside the orphanage had taught her that life was far more complicated than she'd ever imagined.

"Thomas." Marissa squeaked, forcing her words out of her tense jaw. "Let me show you something."

In one swift motion, she placed the bag on the table, undid the button holding it shut, and pulled it away to reveal the idol pieces hidden inside. It was a moment that sent cold chills down her scaled back, but Thomas and Marian only looked confused.

"Two... bits of rock?" Thomas asked quizzically.

Marissa lifted the idol pieces and stacked them, revealing that the two bits of rock were shaped like the bottom half of a serpent. "It's way more than that. According to the Varan and the Naga, this is two of the four pieces of an idol capable of summoning a goddess."

Marian recoiled; her face contorted with bewilderment. Thomas nearly choked on his orange juice.

"Excuse me," he let out a few gasping coughs and clutched his chest, setting his half-empty glass on the table. "I'm not sayin' I don't believe ya, but I'm not gonna lie... that sounds insane."

"I know it does," Marissa sighed. This was the exact reaction she'd expected. "But think about it. The Naga that ransacked Copperton and bit you has at least one, possibly both of the other pieces. He wants to summon the goddess to destroy Brennan. And the royal guard knows - why else would they be this adamant on war? The only ones I can trust to keep these idol pieces safe are the Testudo, and if I don't make it there, the humans and reptilians are going to destroy each other. It will be the most disastrous war the Valley of Scales has ever seen."

Marissa's stomach clenched with anxiety as she outlined the seriousness of their situation. She hated thinking about the dire consequences of failing. She hated thinking about the royal guard, the impending war... but most of all, she hated thinking about Ezrinth.

While explaining everything to Thomas, she deliberately left out that the destructive Naga was her father. She wanted as few people to know that fact as possible.

"Well..." Thomas was lost for words. He took a few moments, sitting up straight in his chair and couching into his fist. "All I can say to that is... all the more reason for shootin' lessons. Y'all are gonna need to borrow some of the muskets for yer travels."

Marissa realized that Arthur must've noticed her quivering, because he immediately turned toward her. "I know that look. You don't like the idea of bringing guns into reptilian territory. I know it will make the Testudo wary of us, but Nathara will have one too, and she's a reptilian. It's just in case we run into the royal guard. Besides, the tortoisefolk clearly view you as important. Guns or no guns, I bet they'll want to bring you straight to Mata."

Arthur's words reminded Marissa that her mind was still swirling over the mysteries surrounding the Testudo. *Is Mata truly alive? How does she know that I exist? And what does she want with me?*

"Alright." Her faint voice was laced with uncertainty.

"Excellent," Thomas clapped his hands together before scooping up his knife and fork. "Well in that case, everyone eat up. Y'all have a long day ahead of ya."

"I'll clean up after breakfast," Marian offered. "There's a small gun range out back for y'all to practice."

It was decided. As Marissa gulped down fluffy mouthfuls of pancakes, she couldn't help but observe the scene around her. Arthur continued to read his newspaper as he ate, gulping down his second cup of coffee. Thomas and Marian were lost in conversation, their eyes sparkling as if their relationship was the best it had been in years. And Nathara, being a carnivore, had lined her plate with only bacon. She was hesitant at first, plucking a piece in her claws and eyeing it suspiciously, but her scaled face lit up with surprised joy after her first bite.

Marissa smiled. She realized that it had been a very long time since she'd enjoyed breakfast at a dining table. And this time, she was unmasked, surrounded by those who fully accepted her.

Three humans, a half-breed, and a Naga all enjoying a meal together.

264

A few weeks earlier, Marissa never could've imagined it possible.

A NAGGING UNEASINESS CREPT INTO MARISSA'S stomach as she stepped out into the backyard. It settled slightly as she noticed that in addition to being gunsmiths, Thomas's parents were avid gardeners – an array of overflowing flowerbeds bordered a straight gravel pathway. Marissa noticed that they were all native plants – lush, tropical beauties that despite not being in bloom, remained a vibrant green even in October. At the back of the garden was a row of tall sabal palmettos whose fronds ruffled in the gentle breeze.

Marissa flinched as they walked, realizing that beyond the row of palmettos, the path led directly to the shooting range. It was a small open field, a few dozen feet wide, and she could catch glimpses of rusting metal targets between the tree trunks.

As they got closer, she was able to decipher the silhouettes. To her relief, the targets weren't shaped like humans or reptilians. Instead, an array of alligators, monitor lizards, and tightly coiled snakes lined the back of the shooting range, their dark metal figures riddled with jagged holes. The thought of firing at reptiles didn't bring her much solace, but she was just grateful she wouldn't be shooting at something humanoid. Since reptiles made up most of the fauna in the valley, they often ended up as food for humans. Despite her deep connection with the creatures, Marissa had understood and accepted this from a young age. Those living in the outer villages often had little money, and hunting wild reptiles was what kept families fed.

But the thought of putting a hole through the metal figures' bodies still made her stomach lurch.

She stood awkwardly next to Arthur and Nathara as Thomas went to fetch several guns from the storage shed where his parents had hidden them. Thankfully, they'd all been returned after the battle the previous night. *But that means now I must learn how to fire one,* Marissa gulped.

She felt like a tense child dreading a trip to the apothecary, thinking of any excuse to extract herself from this situation. But like going to the apothecary, Marissa knew this was something she needed to do, whether she liked it or not. A dagger in her hand and Nim around her neck only provided so much defense. If she encountered Ezrinth, she'd never be able to overpower him, and even if she could, her venom would have no effect. But what scared her even more was the thought of coming across the royal guard. All Ezrinth would do was kidnap her and drag her back to Komodo. The kingdom, on the other hand, wanted her dead.

Or worse. Marissa shivered, squeezing her eyes shut. If they kept her alive and hauled her away to Brennan, she might meet an even more horrid fate. *Being tortured for information, or being experimented on, or...*

"Got 'em," Thomas's gruff yet cheery voice pulled Marissa away from her mounting dread. He was carrying a large, rectangular case with a leathery exterior.

As he walked up to the shooting range, he placed the case on top of a chest-height table, where unlatched the locks and opened it gently.

Inside were three guns. Marissa didn't know much about weaponry, but she did notice that they were smaller than the ones she'd seen the villagers using the night before. Much smaller.

"They're so little." She couldn't help but comment out loud.

Thomas chuckled at Marissa's unknowing remark. He lifted one of them out of the case, allowing the metal gun barrel to gleam in the dewy morning light. Marissa noticed that these were simple weapons, without the fancy wood or elaborate filigrees of the guns hanging inside the house. She also noticed how Thomas handled them with great caution and care, as if they were both valuable and deadly treasures.

"These ain't muskets. They're pistols," Thomas explained. "And yes, they're small, but they're a whole lot more versatile. Y'all ain't gonna be in a firin' line defendin' a buildin' like the villagers were. Yer gonna be marchin' through reptilian territory – ya need somethin' more mobile if the guard comes after ya."

Marissa peered over at her companions. Arthur seemed to completely understand. Nathara, on the other hand, looked bewildered, staring at the guns as if they were alien technology. Marissa assumed that this was partially because of her inability to understand Thomas, and partially because of her inexperience with the weapons. Thomas had forced her to leave the old, ineffective gun she'd found back at Copperton inside the house, much to her dismay. She knew her aunt's reptilian senses were questioning the effectiveness of such small pistols.

"Besides," Thomas noted as he stepped off to the side, one of the pistols still clutched in his hand with the muzzle pointed at the ground. "Those muskets can weigh up to twenty pounds. Y'all ain't gonna wanna carry all that weight through tortoise land."

Marissa's wary eyes followed Thomas as he collected more supplies. Horn-shaped containers full of gritty black powder, wet gobs of cotton stacked in a sticky pile, and several long metal rods were laid out on the table in a meticulous fashion. Marissa realized that guns were a lot more complicated than she'd expected.

"Alright," Thomas laid the final metal rod on the table. "Who's up first?"

Nathara, being unable to understand Thomas, didn't respond. Marissa turned toward Arthur with pleading eyes, but his gaze was firm. It may have been a long time, but he already knew how to fire a gun. And unlike Marissa, he wasn't the one that had a fear to conquer.

She gulped, taking the slightest step forward.

"Excellent!" Thomas's enthusiasm seemed to boom through the entire shooting range as he clasped his hands together. He gestured for Marissa to follow him, leading her to the edge of the wooden platform, directly in front of the targets.

"Alright, first rule of gun safety," Thomas gestured toward the pistol in his right hand, which was still pointed at the ground. "Always keep the gun pointed in a safe direction. Only point it at something you intend to shoot."

A few feet behind them, Marissa noticed Arthur shoot a dagger-filled glare at Nathara. But the towering Naga was oblivious, watching Thomas curiously with her clawed hands folded behind her back.

"Alright, now to load the gun." Marissa watched as Thomas took one of the horn-shaped containers and poured the gritty black powder into a small metal tube. "This is called a powder horn, and it holds the gunpowder. You pour the gunpowder into this measuring flask, which is just the right size for this model pistol. And that brings me to my second rule of gun safety," Thomas remarked as he dumped the contents of the flask down the barrel of the pistol. "Never pour gunpowder directly down the gun barrel. Always use the flask."

Thomas continued his instructions, his voice firm and methodical as he spelled out every detail of the process. *He'd make an excellent teacher,* Marissa thought. But his clear directions didn't prevent her head from spinning. As he continued loading the gun, placing a bit of soaked cloth down the gun barrel before loading the round lead bullet, Marissa began to question her ability to follow his instructions. *What if I mess something up? Will the gun explode? What if my terrible mistake gets myself or my friends killed?*

"Alright," Thomas grunted as he shoved one of the metal rods down the gun barrel. "In there nice and snug. Now we're ready to fire."

Marissa gulped. Her legs felt like stiff wooden boards underneath her shaky body. Not only was loading the gun complicated, but even if Marissa managed to perform all the steps correctly, she'd still have to actually *shoot* it. And pray she didn't miss.

Her hands shook as Thomas wrapped them around the gun handle. Marissa knew he sensed her nervousness, because he looked her right in the eyes with a reaffirming glance.

"You can do this," he kept his hands clasped around hers to stop them shaking. "Deep breaths."

Marissa closed her eyes. She refused to think about the fact that she was holding a gun, the fiery weapon that had killed so many beings, both human and reptilian. Instead, she focused on steadying her hands, gently loosening her nerves until they stopped shaking.

"Excellent," Thomas pulled out another flask of powder and poured a tiny amount into a metal socket on the top of the gun. He gave her a final reaffirming nod before stepping back.

"Focus on keeping the gun as level as possible. Be prepared for the kick after it fires, and whatever you do, don't let go of the gun while it's firing."

Marissa forced a swallow, doubting her ability to heed that final warning. Her hands may have been shaking before, but now they were trembling. The muzzle bobbed and twitched in the air as Marissa's nerves prevented her from keeping her aim on her target – the large coiled snake. Her fingers suddenly felt like they were made of rigid iron. She could barely move them an inch, much less pull the trigger.

Slowly, shakily, her hands lowered. The powder on top of the gun spilled off and sprayed across the grass.

Tears welled in her eyes as Thomas stepped forward.

"I can't do this." Her fraught voice was barely a whisper.

She was too afraid to look behind her – she dreaded seeing the look of disappointment on her companions faces. But she swore she could hear Thomas sigh.

"Yes, you can."

His voice was firm, but it wasn't laced with anger or frustration like Marissa had expected. She turned around, and in the gruff-faced man's eyes was a mixture of sadness and determination. He knew exactly why she was afraid. And his gaze told Marissa that it was exactly the reason why it was so important for her to do this.

She peered down at the weapon, still clasped in her left hand. She knew that she and her companions were in constant danger, from both humans and reptilians, and they may run into a situation where firing a gun would mean the difference between life and death. But she still couldn't shake the previous evening out her head. The booming sounds of gunfire, the bright flashes and smoke, the bullet-riddled corpses that smelled sickeningly of fresh blood. When she'd been looking down the barrel of the pistol at that snake-shaped metal target, all she could imagine were living, breathing figures. Both human and reptilian. Both halves of her.

"Look, Marissa," Thomas continued. "I know yer scared."

"It's not just that." She frowned. "Ever since I've left the orphanage, I've been terrified of guns. I've seen what monstrosities people are capable of when given one – the poachers, the royal guard, and yes, the dreadful battle that occurred last night. They're what give humans an advantage over reptilians. And, most importantly, they're what would end up pointed at my face if the wrong human found out what I really am. To me, guns are humankind's most horrific creation, made for one purpose - to kill."

"Marissa," Thomas sighed. "I understand ya, believe me. But ya have this all wrong. My whole life I grew up around guns, and my father taught me a very important lesson. Yes, they may be weapons, capable of killin', but they're also tools. For those of us in the outer villages, life can be tough. Guns are what allow us to hunt and gather food. They allow us to defend our homes from bandits. Yes, they are an enormous responsibility, and they can cause havoc when given to the wrong person. Trust me, I know what that feels like."

A deep, choking pain washed over Thomas's eyes, and he took a step backward. Marissa's scales quivered at the memory of his crime against the reptilians. Thomas used a bow, not a gun, but Marissa wondered what was going through his mind, and how he felt, right before he released that arrow.

But she began to understand the importance of his words. *Guns are tools*, she repeated in her mind, attempting to force the paradigm shift through her skull. She peered back down at the pistol, studying its sleek wooden grip and shiny metal barrel. *And I refuse to be afraid of a mere tool.*

Her breaths grew in strength as she forced herself to remain calm. There would be no more 'I can't do this'. She was a half-Naga, born from scales and flesh, her human and reptilian mind capable of connecting two worlds that couldn't communicate. The night before, she'd run into an active battlefield and stopped two villages from attacking each other. By comparison, firing a gun at a simple metal target should be easy.

With her newfound confidence, Marissa positioned herself in front of the snake-shaped target, raising both her arms and clasping her hands around the gun. Thomas refilled the powder on the metal top and stepped away, her companions watching with their breaths held.

She hesitated for a moment, repositioning her grip. Her hands were no longer shaking, which allowed her to focus on her aim. She slowed her breathing to a near standstill, and attempted to empty her mind of any intrusive thoughts. All she allowed to float through her brain was Arthur's advice from the previous night's battle.

Don't think.

Just do it.

A slight click, a hiss, and brief flash of fire culminated in a sickeningly loud crack that shot through Marissa's reptilian ears and bounced around her skull. A small plume of smoke wafted past her, souring her reptilian nostrils. But as the echo of the gunshot faded, Marissa was left in stunned astonishment. *I did it. I actually fired a gun.*

Her hands were shaking, but not with fear. Something about the booming sound of the gunshot combined with the recoil seeping through her palms had flooded her body with adrenaline. But it wasn't the tense, fearful kind. It was an overwhelming, exhausting feeling of satisfaction.

A small chorus of claps echoed behind her. Marissa turned around. Thomas was cheering, his eyes crinkled in the corners like a proud parent, and Arthur was beaming. Even Nathara had a satisfied smile on her reptilian face.

Marissa laughed. She didn't know how else to express her relief and joy in overcoming her fear. She lowered the gun, remembering to keep it pointed at the ground, before shielding her face with her hand as she squinted off in the distance.

"Um, Thomas?"

"Yes?"

"Where did the bullet go?"

His cheers turned to raucous cackling, and Marissa's face began to burn. Once his laughter subsided, Thomas noticed Marissa's sour face and shook his head.

"Pro'ly off in the woods somewhere," he replied, a cheeky grin still on his face. "It's alright, we just gotta work on yer aim. In fact." Thomas stepped back toward the gun case, where he removed two more pistols before turning toward Arthur and Nathara. "So does everyone else. C'mon now, step forward you two. We ain't got a lotta time though. Y'all should plan on leavin' for Testudo territory by noon."

AN HOUR LATER, MARISSA FINALLY MANAGED TO strike the target.

She pumped her fist with joy as soon as she saw it hit – a high shot that punctured the very top of the snake's head. But her victory was overshadowed with the grim reality that it had taken her eight shots to hit a metal target. One that wasn't alive, or even moving.

She gulped. In a real-life situation, she would've long since been dead.

Eight shots in an hour. Marissa huffed and lowered the gun. Prepping and loading the pistol was a slow, meticulous process, made even slower by Thomas having to double-check everything before she fired. She was getting the hang of the process, but she still didn't fully trust herself, and she certainly didn't want to discover the consequences of an improper load.

At least somewhat satisfied with her progress, Marissa took a moment to breathe and observe her surroundings. Arthur and Nathara were each spaced about a dozen feet away from her, firing their own pistols. Arthur hadn't taken long to reacquaint himself with firearms, and he'd easily shot several holes in a large metal alligator target. Nathara, on the other hand, was struggling. Her scaly reptilian hands were too large for the gun, and like Marissa she was having difficulty with her aim. Marissa had to translate when Thomas was first teaching Nathara how to load the gun, and Thomas's current attempts to communicate without words was like a jumbled game of charades.

Marissa scanned Nathara's face as she once again aimed her gun, attempting to decipher her aunt's emotions. Nothing. Her coppery eyes were cold as iron. Whatever she was feeling, it was hidden deep within her serpentine mind.

A loud, popping crack echoed out of her pistol. The resulting plume of smoke wafted around Nathara's coiled body, giving her an almost ghostly appearance. And as Marissa watched the smoke dissipate, she saw a small, triumphant smirk spread across her aunt's scaled face.

It was a low shot, piercing the base of the lizard target's tail. But it was still a hit.

Despite her and Nathara's long-awaited victories, Marissa noticed the hint of apprehension on Thomas's face. Arthur had no trouble with a gun, but Marissa and Nathara had struggled for an hour to hit a single target. It probably made Thomas question the trio's ability to make it through their mission alive. She knew that despite meeting under troubling circumstances, there was no denying that some semblance of a bond had formed between the four of them. *He's worried about us.*

And it made Marissa's stomach sink like a rock.

"Hello!" A cheery voice wafted through the gardens, quashing some of Marissa's anxiety. Marian's pink-cheeked face peeked out from behind one of the sabal palms. As she stepped cautiously into the shooting range, Marissa noticed a large basket cradled in her arms.

"I've packed a few supplies for your journey," Marian turned toward Marissa and handed her the basket. It was quite heavy, and through the cracked lid Marissa could see leftover strawberries and oranges, along with fresh bread and several cheeses and jams.

"Anyway," Marian continued. "It's nearly noon. Shouldn't you and your friends be on your way?"

Marissa turned around. Arthur had set his pistol down and was walking over to join her, but Nathara was busy reloading her gun, a look of worried determination on her face. Marissa noticed the tense, jerking motions of her aunt's scaled arms as she hurriedly prepared her pistol for another shot. *She's desperate to hit the target again. To prove it wasn't just a fluke.*

To prove that her and I aren't completely worthless at shooting.

Marissa's last thought made her throat tense up.

"Yes, we should get going," Arthur chimed in as he reached the others. He gave Marissa a firm but sad nod, signaling that it was time for them to leave, whether they were ready for it or not. It had already been three days since they left Komodo – today needed to be the day they finally reached Testudo territory.

Three whole days. Marissa then wondered if Ezrinth had already made it to Gharian territory. To secure the third piece of the idol. *He may already be on his way back to Komodo, where he'll discover we fled with the idol pieces...*

Suddenly the feeling of urgency in her stomach became much stronger.

"Let me help you get ready," Thomas packed away Marissa and Arthur's pistols, and eventually managed to persuade a frazzled Nathara that shooting lessons were over. The Naga reluctantly plopped the pistol in Thomas's outstretched hand and slithered away with a faint huff of frustration.

The next half hour was a blur. Marissa ran through the motions of packing up their belongings, but her mind was elsewhere – frantically anticipating what they'd encounter once they made it to Testudo territory. *If we even make it there.*

Once they'd brought their meager belongings out of the cottage, Thomas appeared with two heavy cases in his arms. Six pistols in total – the three they'd been practicing with plus an additional case of three - were loaded onto a wooden cart stored in the old barn.

"Just in case," Thomas remarked about the extra guns as he loaded them onto the cart. "If the Testudo are the only ones y'all can trust to keep those bits'a rock safe, ya might wanna have some extra protection. I bet Arthur can teach those tortoises to shoot."

"Um, Thomas?" Marissa's voice shook as Thomas fumbled with a pair of leather straps. Next to them, a small grey mare stood lazily with her neck hung low, waiting to be hitched to the cart. Arthur was outside the barn speaking to Marian, and Nathara stood next to him – leaving Marissa alone with Thomas.

"Yes?"

Marissa cleared her throat, struggling to spit out the words, "Why are you doing all of this for us?"

"What do ya mean?"

"Letting us stay the night, giving us food, weapons... even teaching us how to shoot. It's just... very generous of you."

"Well, if y'all are right about all this, it means the fate of our entire valley is in your hands. And the other reason..." Thomas's gaze suddenly hardened. "Well, y'all already know. I owe the reptilians a lot more than just a coupla' guns after what I did to 'em."

Just as Thomas finished hitching up the cart, Marian, Arthur, and Nathara entered the barn.

"Are we all ready?" Arthur asked.

Marissa pressed a hand against the satchel hanging on her right hip. As usual, she could feel the bumpy outline of the two idol pieces beneath the fabric. Usually it brought her reassurance, but today it only made her even more anxious.

"Yes," Marissa replied, before she had time to doubt herself.

She took a moment to gaze around the dusty barn at her companions. She knew that they were just as apprehensive as she was. It seemed like every day, even every hour that they traveled, a nagging voice never stopped rattling in her head. *Hurry up. You're running out of time.*

Marissa was relieved that she'd been able to stop conflict between Canterbury and Agkistra, but there was no denying that it had slowed them down. Her worst fear was that Ezrinth would discover that Marissa and her companions had fled, and most importantly, they they'd stolen two pieces of the idol. What would happen if he caught her? Her constant reassurances that Ezrinth would never hurt her were starting to dissipate.

She may have been his long-lost daughter, but how long would he be willing to tolerate her fighting against him?

And even if they didn't run into Ezrinth, what about the royal guard? It seemed with every passing day, more and more of them were infiltrating the outer villages, pushing further and further into reptilian territory.

What if we never even make it to Testudo territory? And once we're there, what if we can't find their underground burrows? What if the Testudo turn us away, or what if Mata isn't even real?

What if-

"Marissa."

It was as if she'd been drowning, and Arthur just pulled her head above water.

"Are you alright?" he asked in his usual gentle tone. "You look a bit pale."

The spiraling what-ifs in her mind began to melt away as her thoughts drifted back to reality. She peered down at her palms and realized she was shaking.

"Y-yes, I'm fine."

No one believed her, yet no one questioned her. Nathara rubbed Marissa's shoulder, the weight of her giant scaled hand nearly causing Marissa to topple over. But Marissa appreciated her aunt's sentiment, and she could feel the color slowly returning to her face.

Nathara and Arthur were steely-eyed, with just a tinge of anxiety hidden behind their taught faces. But as the three friends stood solemnly in the dusty barn, the weight of their mission suddenly crushing them, Thomas's face had a different expression. In his eyes was a cross between longing and uncertainty. It was as if there was something he was desperate to tell them, but he couldn't bring himself to do so.

Luckily, he didn't have to.

"Thomas," Marian's voice was gentle but firm. "I know what you want."

He shook his head, "What're ya talkin' about?"

"My dear, I've known you for over a decade. Sometimes I understand you better than you understand yourself."

Thomas peered down at the ground, nudging a pebble with his shoe. Marissa knew he didn't doubt his wife, but he remained silent.

"If this is about me," Marian continued. "I'll be alright. I believe in you, and they need your help."

"Alright," Thomas replied with a hint of uncertainty in his voice. "Marissa, Arthur, Nathara... I'd like to come with y'all."

His announcement shocked Marissa, but it suddenly made a lot of sense. Part of her wanted to sneer at his piteous offering – no amount of aiding the reptilians would ever erase his past as a poacher. But a larger part of her felt a tidal wave of relief. Having an extra member of their party – especially one so skilled with guns – would be a godsend if they encountered Ezrinth or the royal guard.

And as much as Marissa still despised Thomas killing a reptilian, she knew, without a doubt, that they could trust him.

"Of course," Marissa blurted out, suddenly realized that she hadn't consulted with her companions. But it didn't seem as if she needed to – Arthur wore the same look of grateful relief as Marissa, and once things were explained to Nathara, she too agreed with the plan.

The four of them said their goodbyes to Marian, including Thomas giving his wife a long, tearful hug. Marissa noticed that Marian seemed saddened by his departure, but not afraid. Maybe being cured after years of near-death illness had given her a different perspective on life.

"Be safe," Marian waved as Thomas led the cart out of the barn, with Marissa, Arthur, and Nathara in tow. "All of you."

As they strolled solemnly down the dirt road with the cottage disappearing behind the trees, Marissa peered up at the sky. The sun was at its peak, blazing like a hot white fire above their heads. She knew that from here, it would only continue to sink in the sky; their daylight dissipating until the sun vanished completely.

And they needed to be in Testudo territory before that happened.

Chapter 14

So far, Marissa and her companions had escaped from Komodo with the idol pieces, canoed through a monitor-infested river, and bolted unarmed into an active battlefield. But despite all those encounters, the final few miles of their journey proved to be the most difficult yet.

Since the Testudo lived deep underground and few other beings knew of their whereabouts, their territory was mostly barren and uncharted. It was a relief for the group as they reached the border, as this meant that few guards were patrolling the area. But there was another, far more harrowing obstacle in their way – mud.

Up until this point, Thomas, Marissa, and Arthur had taken turns resting in the cart, with someone always walking alongside the grey horse, an older mare named

Daisy. Nathara was far too large and heavy to fit in the cart, so she scouted ahead, her serpentine body slipping through the tall grass with ease.

Arthur knew from his time as a royal herpetologist that the Testudo capital was somewhere in the middle of their territory, which meant traveling up through the southern portion of the tortoisefolks' land. Which, as it turned out, was mostly shallow marshland with no dry roads or paths in sight.

As they entered Testudo territory and the swampy ground became more and more waterlogged, the group decided that it was best for everyone to walk on foot. They couldn't risk the extra weight causing the cart to sink into the muggy dirt, and Daisy's back was already stained with sweat.

The further they traveled, the deeper the mud became, and their progress slowed to a crawl as the cart's wheels struggled to turn through the sludgy ground. Daisy's hooves were slipping, and Marissa's boots made wet squishing noises with every strained footstep.

She grumbled, exasperated by their sluggish pace. As she wrestled one of her boots from the muck, nearly yanking her bare foot out of the stuck shoe in the process, she noticed her aunt about twenty feet ahead of them. *At least she isn't having any issues.* Nathara's entire lower body was stained with mud, but she moved through it just as quickly as she did across dry ground.

"I bet this was made even worse by all the bad weather we've had lately," Arthur panted as he practically swam his way through the mud. "It really makes me wonder if the gods have something to do with all of this. Maybe Vaipera is trying to slow us down."

Marissa didn't reply, but the question continued to bounce around her head as they walked. Once they made it another long, sluggish mile with no end to the mud in sight, she decided to bring up the possibility with her aunt.

<Oh, I'm sure of it,> Nathara hissed as she slithered alongside her niece, her tail leaving a long, deep trail in the mud. <Vaipera has a fair amount of control over the weather. As the goddess of chaos, she wields one of the most powerful forces in nature – storms, particularly lightning. Us reptilians believe that bad weather is a sign that her emotions are ablaze.>

Nathara paused for a moment, her scaled face suddenly turning grim. <We can all feel it, Marissa. Us reptilians can tell when a storm is coming, and for the past week or two... we've had this odd premonition that we're about to face our largest one yet.>

<Like... a hurricane?>

Marissa only had vague memories of hurricanes - the wild, swirling storms that occasionally ravaged the valley. She remembered a bad one many years ago, late in the summertime, back when she was just a young child. It was no ordinary storm – all night long, the wind seemed to scream, and odd whacks and bumps rattle the orphanage's roof.

But being raised as a human, it never occurred to her that the forces of nature could be controlled by reptilian deities. She shuddered to think of what Vaipera would be capable of if she was summoned.

<Perhaps,> Nathara replied. <There are rumors that when our reptilian leaders were fighting over the idol pieces eight hundred years ago, a storm started brewing in the sky. We'll have to ask Mata – she'll be able to give us answers.>

If she's even real. Nathara's thoughts sent a pang of anxiety through Marissa's chest. She knew that the valley was full of mysteries, but a living Testudo being over eight hundred years old seemed far-fetched. Marissa thought about the reptilian's failed attempt at summoning Vaipera back when Mata was young, and wondered if some sort of otherworldly power had embedded itself in the Testudo's veins that day.

Marissa's thoughts were laced with frustration as the group continued trudging through the muck. It was even beginning to stain the hem of her dress, weighing it down and causing it to stick to her scaled calves. *Wherever we go,* Marissa huffed. *It's always one obstacle after another.* She reflected on their entire journey, starting from when she and Arthur first left Brennan in search of Ezrinth, and how they'd encountered nothing but hurdles. *Bandits, carts breaking down, patrolling royal guards, a river full of giant lizards, even an entire battle...*

She sighed. Maybe the gods really were trying to slow them down.

But with every roadblock the group had encountered, they always persevered. They always found a way through. And as the hours passed, and the muddy swampland began to firm up into solid, dry sand, relief washed over their tired bodies.

"Thank the gods," Thomas groaned, running his hands through his sweat-stained hair. Marissa noticed that the bottom of his trousers, all the way up his calves, were splattered with mud. Next to her, Arthur was in a similar state, pausing for a moment to crouch down and rest his hands on his knees. Even Nathara, patrolling about twenty feet ahead, was showing signs of exhaustion. Her serpentine body moved slower, and it seemed to take her a larger amount of effort than usual to slither back toward them.

"Well, we've made it," Arthur panted, standing up and wiping his forehead. "We should be somewhere in the middle of Testudo territory. The bad news is that this is the hard part – we have to find one of the entrances to their burrows."

"How hard can that be?" Thomas asked, his weary voice laced with concern. "They're big tortoises with giant shells – certainly the entrances must be huge."

"Well, yes," Arthur sighed. "But they are remarkably well-hidden. Supposedly, they're barely distinguishable from the terrain around them. I'm not sure if any human has ever found their burrows, *ever*."

"Whelp," Thomas grunted, frustration lining his face. "I guess all we can do it start lookin'."

But as Arthur and Thomas stepped past Marissa, aimlessly poking around the brush, Nim suddenly lifted his head. He'd been quiet for most of the journey, huddling around Marissa's neck as if he were scared to slip off and fall into the mucky swampland. But now he was periscoped high above her shoulders, an intense look of concentration on his face. Marissa's eyes flicked towards him, and she cocked her head.

"What's the matter, buddy?" she asked in a sweet, innocent tone. But a bubble of realization suddenly burst in her stomach. Back when they were in Canterbury, and Thomas mentioned the Testudo burrows being well-hidden, Nim had done the same thing. A sleepy snake suddenly stirring to life, radiating confidence with a warm glow in his deep onyx eyes...

Before Marissa could react, Nim bolted, unwinding himself from her neck and cascading down her body before taking off across the sandy scrubland.

"Nim!!" Marissa exclaimed, startled and panicked by his sudden disappearance. She took off across the plains, sand sticking to her still-muddy boots as she wove between the shrubby oak and pine saplings. Arthur and Thomas were distracted, still ambling through the scrubland, but Nathara's head lifted as Marissa bolted past her. A brief look of confusion flashed across her scaled face, but she quickly took off after Marissa, catching up to her within seconds.

Nim was *fast*. Too fast for a mellow, semi-arboreal python who spent most of his time napping around her neck. As Marissa chased after the slithering snake, his body forming rapid s-shapes across the lumpy sand, it was as if she were chasing a black racer. *I didn't even know pythons could move this quickly.*

But thankfully, Nim's bright yellow-and-black body made him easy to spot against the pale sand, and Marissa followed him through a winding maze of greenery, further and further from Arthur and Thomas. And once again, a single thought that was becoming truer every day crept through Marissa's mind – Nim was no ordinary snake.

<Please, buddy,> Marissa pleaded, as her panting breaths grew heavier and her sprint slowed to a weary jog. She knew that normal snakes couldn't understand reptilian speech, but she'd always had a suspicion that Nim fully understood her. Marissa finally stumbled into a walk, taking a moment to catch her breath. She was exhausted. Not just from sprinting after Nim, but from everything she'd endured over the past few weeks. It was as if all her fatigue, both physical and mental, suddenly hit her at once.

She took a moment to kneel in the sand, the fine granules sticking to the muddy hem of her dress. Nathara came to a slithering stop behind her, her bare, scaled chest also heaving from exhaustion. About a dozen feet ahead of them, Nim noticed they'd stopped, and he did the same, lifting his tiny triangular head and staring directly at them. His unblinking black eyes locked with Marissa's, and he slowly flicked his tongue, as if to ask, 'What's wrong?'

<We're just tired, buddy,> Marissa sighed. Her panting had slowed enough for her to rise to her feet, cringing as she realized her wet boots were caked in gritty sand. <It's been a long journey. We can't all curl up around someone's neck and take a nap the whole way.>

Marissa swore she saw Nim's dark eyes narrow at that statement. He then lowered his head, curling up around a clump of spindly grass. Marissa crept toward him, confused, but she could feel him trying to tell her that this spot was important.

But how? It was just a patch of grass, one that looked no different than the thousands scattered throughout the scrubland. But Nim was adamant, so she knelt next to him and placed her hand in the center of his coiled body.

The grass was long, dry, and scratchy against her bare palm. She sifted through the foliage, her fingers curling down into the roots of the scraggy plants, until she felt a hard, solid, rounded object. One that definitely wasn't natural.

She ran a finger around the rim of it, trying to decipher its purpose. It was buried so deep in the patch of the grass that she couldn't see it, but it felt like it was made of some sort of stone. Its shape was a rounded sphere on top of a narrow cylinder, similar to a door handle.

And it wouldn't budge, as if it had its own roots digging down into the earth.

"There you two are." A panting sigh of exasperation echoed behind Marissa.

She turned around, her hand still entangled in the grass and wrapped around the strange object. Arthur and Thomas were jogging towards them, their foreheads slick with beads of sweat. Nathara eyed them warily.

<Why must humans leak water out of their skin?> she huffed. <Such a crude way of cooling oneself. And it looks uncomfortable.>

Marissa shook her head, not bothering to remind her aunt that reptilians barely tolerated anything cooler than seventy degrees. She wondered if Nathara had ever even heard of snow, but pushed the question out of her mind. She had bigger concerns to deal with.

"Arthur," Marissa gestured for him to join her. As Arthur stepped forward and crouched down next to Marissa, she grabbed his wrist in her free hand and cupped his palm around the strange object.

"You feel that?" she asked, trying not to let her cheeks flush as she felt Arthur's fingers glide against hers.

Arthur nodded. "It won't budge. And-" He gave a firm tug, nearly hurting his shoulder in the process. "Pulling it upwards doesn't seem to do anything. Here, let's try this."

Arthur adjusted his stance as he crouched next to Marissa. She couldn't ignore how close he was to her, how his shirt brushed against her bare scales and how she could feel the heat radiating from the sweat-stained chest that peeked through his few undone buttons. *Stop it*, she huffed. *Focus.*

"One, two..." Arthur counted. "Three."

They both pulled together, Marissa digging her crusty boots into the sand until it nearly covered her ankles. At first, nothing seemed to happen. But Arthur was adamant, and with one final tug, the bit of earth beneath them moved.

"What the-" Marissa let go of the stony handle and peered down at the crevice that had formed in the earth. They were standing on top of a circular mound of sand, about six feet wide, that was the entrance to some sort of den.

"Did we... actually find it?" Arthur uttered the question that was rattling through everyone's minds. No one responded, but all four of them huddled around the crevice, attempting to peek down into the abyss below.

"We need to all do this together," Marissa announced, marching her way back over to the handle. "Here, everyone grab on."

Marissa, Arthur, and Thomas all managed to wrap a hand around the handle. Nathara giant scaly palms were too large to fit, so she slithered over to the crevasse and pushed from the other side.

With several great heaving tugs, the ground began to slide beneath them, like a manhole uncovering a hidden sewer. Marissa was shocked at how the previously solid ground suddenly disconnected from its surroundings, like it was a perfectly fitting puzzle piece.

Or, Marissa thought as the full entrance came into view. *There's some sort of strange magic at work here.*

All four of them stood at the edge of the giant hole in the ground. There was a several-foot drop, followed by a low, sloping path that led into a cavern of pure darkness.

Arthur crouched down, hesitantly stepping down into the hole with a single foot. When nothing happened, he planted his other foot on the ground, now chest-deep in the earth.

"It's so bizarre," he noted under his breath as he took a cautious step forward, trying to glimpse into the dark tunnel. "This seems to break every law of nature. The valley's sandy, waterlogged soil isn't meant for massive tunnels like this, and-"

<MARISSA!!>

She whipped around, panicked by Nathara's sudden screech. Her aunt was slithering backwards, pointing at the black void of the tunnel.

<Tell Arthur to get back!!>

It took a moment to register in Marissa's mind. None of them could see through the inky darkness... except for Nathara. Naga were nocturnal, and therefore had excellent night vision. *She sees something we don't.*

Marissa spun back around toward Arthur, her mouth already open and ready to shout, but it was too late. She watched her closest friend scramble backwards in terror as three giant figures stomped out of the tunnel. As the bright afternoon sun began to illuminate their figures, Marissa saw three human-sized, but very wide and stocky beings – giant heavy tortoises with thick limbs and massive, rounded shells that must've weighed several hundred pounds. Their dark, glossy eyes glowered with fury, and in all of the tortoise's giant clawed hands were loaded crossbows, pointed directly at the four intruders.

They'd found the Testudo. And they were far from happy to see them.

Chapter 15

THERE WAS A BRIEF, HEART-CLENCHING moment where Marissa and her companions stood motionless, facing off against the Testudo, both sides afraid that a sudden movement would send the other party charging forward.

With her limbs frozen in shock, Marissa used the tense moment of silence to study the three tortoisefolk. She could tell that they were all males, possibly related. Two of them looked noticeably older, with wider shells and stockier faces. One of them had a series of scars on the back of his clawed hand.

The third male was younger, with a more youthful face, still filling out and growing into his shell. Marissa realized that while his companions wore death glares on their reptilian faces, this Testudo's eyes were soft with uncertainty. Once he caught a glimpse of Nathara, who stood on level ground directly behind Arthur, his quivering crossbow began to lower.

<I remember you.> His thoughts were soft, barely a whisper.

Nathara slithered forward, which caused the two older Testudo to leer at her, pointing their crossbows directly at her chest.

<Wait, stop!>

The younger Testudo's shout caused his companions to lower their weapons and turn around, glaring at him in confusion.

<The Naga.> He pointed a claw at Nathara. <She was here less than a week ago. Wait a minute.> The Testudo attempted to peer behind Nathara. <Did you really bring- >

Marissa darted forward without hesitation; her eyes firmly locked on the youngest Testudo as her reptilian nostrils flared. Her face was bare – the dusty old scarf was tucked into her satchel, cushioning the two idol pieces. She'd been wearing it when they first left Canterbury, but after hours of trudging through the muddy swampland, she'd pulled it off her face and stowed it away. It was an unusually warm day for October, nearly eighty-five degrees outside with high humidity, and she'd decided that it wasn't worth not being able to breathe. After all, the entire time they'd been traveling through Testudo territory, they hadn't come across a single guard or reptilian.

Until now. The glow of amazement in the three Testudos' eyes as Marissa stood unwavering in front of them helped settle the swirling nerves in her stomach.

<I can't believe it,> The younger Testudo stepped forward, his dark, glossy eyes flickering around as he studied Marissa's half-Naga form. <You're real. Grandmother was right.>

Grandmother? A spark of hope jolted through Marissa's heart. *These three Testudo... could their grandmother really be...?*

<Please,> One of the older Testudo gestured toward Marissa, his urgent tone interrupting her thoughts. <You need to come with us right away.>

Marissa peered over her shoulder at her companions. Arthur was still standing behind her, while Thomas and Nathara were still on level ground above him. While Nathara understood what was going on, Thomas looked confused, and Arthur looked concerned.

<Not without them.> Marissa pointed, refusing to budge.

One of the older Testudo huffed, his overgrown beak twisting into a snarl. <You really think we're going to let two humans and a Naga into our village?>

Marissa could hear the disgust in the Testudo's thoughts as he gestured toward Arthur and Thomas. He emphasized *human* like they were the vilest creatures in the valley.

The Testudo with the scars on his hand grabbed Marissa's arm. It both frightened and startled her – his massive, clawed hand was bone-dry and leathery as it wrapped around her thin scaled bicep. She fought back a scream, anger suddenly flooding her veins.

They think they can take me by force?

They'd traveled dozens of miles and overcome multiple obstacles to make it this far. This was their end goal – but there was no way Marissa was doing it alone. She wanted to hand over the idol pieces to the only beings capable of sealing them away forever. She wanted to meet Mata and find out what significance her half-Naga heritage held. But she still knew nothing about the Testudo, and if they were this quick to lay a hand on her, she had no idea if any other villagers would turn hostile. And Marissa feared leaving her companions behind, out in the open in strange territory where they'd be sitting targets for the royal guard.

<No!> Marissa's sharp protests did little to stop the two older Testudo from restraining her. As panic pulsed through her body, she seriously considered sinking her fangs into the clawed hand currently grasping her bicep. *I doubt my venom would do much harm, just scare them off...*

But before Marissa could react, Nim was already periscoped wide above her shoulders, his body coiled in a tight s-shape, ready to strike. The sizzling fury of his hiss was enough to cause the scar-handed Testudo to drop Marissa's arm and jerk away, his frightened eyes nearly popping out of his skull.

Nim's hisses faded, and Marissa recollected herself, leering at the two older Testudo who now stared wary-eyed at her angry pet snake. The younger Testudo was several feet behind them, but instead of fear, his eyes were alight with awe.

<Look,> Marissa announced, her glare indicating that she was not willing to be intimidated by the giant tortoises. <I didn't travel all this way, dodging hostile reptilians and patrolling royal guardsmen, to be hauled off against my will and separated from my companions. It is incredibly important that I speak to Mata, but please, allow my friends entrance to your village. They are allies who want peace. They mean you no harm.>

The two older Testudo peered back up at Arthur, Thomas, and Nathara with skepticism in their eyes. Marissa sighed, realizing she couldn't blame them. After all, an outcast half-breed, a disgraced royal, a remorseful former poacher, and a rebellious Naga chieftress made for a very strange – and somewhat suspicious – traveling party. And the Testudo weren't known for welcoming outsiders.

The younger Testudo turned toward the older ones, his eyes alight with determination. <Let them in.>

The two older Testudo glared at their smaller companion, then over to Marissa, then back to the young Testudo. Their gazes were laced with uncertainty and a hint of disgust.

<Grandmother knows what she's doing.> The young Testudo insisted, his tone firm.

The scar-handed Testudo let out an exasperated sigh, as if he were mad that his young, overly optimistic companion would use Mata's opinion against them. He turned back toward Marissa, eyeing the half-Naga up and down, as if he were doubtful that she was truly worthy of meeting Mata. A faint grumble echoed from his throat, and he signaled with a swipe of his giant clawed hand for the party to follow them.

"Um..." Arthur sputtered as the two older Testudo ventured back into the darkness of the tunnel. The young Testudo hung back, peering over his shoulder as he waited for Marissa and her companions to follow them. "Does this mean we're allowed in?"

"I think so." Marissa reasoned, forcing a swallow to rid her throat of her windpipe-crushing anxiety. She turned her head toward Nathara. Her aunt nodded reassuringly, but Marissa could still see the tinge of uncertainty in the Naga's eyes.

"Wait," Thomas stepped forward, his foot slipping partway down into the tunnel. "We've still got the cart to worry about. We can't just leave it 'ere out in the open."

Crap. Marissa squeezed her eyes shut. The two older Testudo had disappeared, and the younger one was growing concerned. *How in the world are we going to persuade those gruff old tortoises to let us bring in a cart full of guns?*

RAMSEY HAD FINALLY DONE WHAT NO OTHER king – or future heir – had managed to accomplish in eight hundred years. He'd finally found the Testudo.

Even he had difficulty believing the scene before him as he and his companions hid in the forest lining the scrubland. Two humans, a Naga, and the hideous half-breed had managed to find a Testudo burrow. One that seemed to appear by magic as the earth above it slid away. And from within emerged three angry-looking tortoises, weapons loaded and ready to fire, yet they backed down in a matter of minutes.

All because of that half-reptilian girl.

As soon as she had stepped forward, the Testudo had strange expressions on their squat faces. Ramsey knew little about reptilian behavior, but it almost seemed like they were in awe. And it nearly made Ramsey scoff with disgust. Because as the girl stood there with her wretched pet snake around her neck, foolishly unwavering in front of three angry reptilians, Ramsey was able to catch a full glimpse of her features.

The king was right – she truly was an abomination. She had the body of a human – two arms and legs, ten fingers and toes, and long black hair, but partway up her limbs was an unnatural morphing of flesh into dark brown-and-black scales. Ramsey forced back a cringe as he saw her face – the lower half covered by scales with black lips and reptilian nostrils in place of a human nose. And he couldn't say for certain, but it looked like she had no external ears – just two holes in the side of her head, mostly concealed by her thick hair.

He remembered reading *Frankenstein* as a teenager in school, and the parallels shook him to the core. It was as if someone had chopped up a human and a Naga and rearranged them in the most unnatural of ways.

And the question lingered; how did she even exist? Ramsey knew that the simplest biological conclusion was that a human and Naga managed to conceive, but it was such an absurd concept that he struggled to wrap his mind around it.

Ramsey couldn't help but study the lower torsos of the three tortoisefolk guarding the entrance to the burrow.

How do they even-

"Ramsey, sir," one of the guardsmen interrupted in a tense whisper. "All preparations are ready. We will proceed upon your command."

Ramsey's curiosity about the half-reptilian's conception faded away as a small smirk crept across his face. He had much, *much* more important matters to attend to.

He peered over his shoulder. While the forest seemed innocuous from a distance, at this length Ramsey could see faint bits of glittering scales breaking up the treeline. Three hundred and seventy-nine soldiers, dressed in freshly delivered scale-mail armor, all ready to claim the tortoises' land for Brennan.

As soon that burrow closed and their nemeses were out of sight, they would begin preparations. No Testudo would escape them once the burrow inevitably reopened.

They would win. Ramsey was certain of it.

IT TOOK ANOTHER THIRTY MINUTES FOR THE whole group, plus Thomas's horse-drawn cart full of guns, to venture down the tunnel and into the capital of Testudo territory.

When the Testudo first came up to the surface, what they were initially most skeptical of was Thomas's horse. Daisy was an older mare, prone to lazing with her weight off one hoof when not being actively worked, but she still huffed and snorted and flicked her tail like every other horse Marissa had met. The creatures weren't native to the Valley of Scales, and the reptilians viewed them as giant alien beasts, approaching them with great hesitancy. The situation wasn't helped by Daisy sneezing just as the scar-handed Testudo went to touch her muzzle. The giant tortoise scowled in disgust and scurried away, wiping his snot-covered hands on the back of his shell.

Marissa grimaced. While she respected horses for their transportation abilities, her Naga half had never been fond of them.

But the tortoisefolk's reaction to Daisy paled in comparison to when Thomas opened the cases stacked in the back of the cart. One glimpse and all hell broke loose – the two Testudo lunged for Thomas, nearly wrapping their giant clawed hands around his neck until the younger Testudo intervened.

<What is the meaning of this!?> The scar-handed Testudo sputtered, panting as he was restrained by his younger brother. <We invite you and your *friends* into our home, and you dare try to smuggle in those horrid weapons!?>

<It's not smuggling if they're showing them to us, idiot!> The young Testudo released his brother's arms with a frustrated huff. As his older brother stumbled away, the young Testudo stepped toward the gun cases,

peering at the gleaming pistols inside. But unlike his brothers, he didn't explode in a range of fury. In fact, he seemed impressed.

<They're not loaded.> The young tortoise reached toward the pistols, and Thomas reluctantly allowed him to pick one up. Testudo hands were massive, shaped like clubs ending in five long saber-like claws, and the young tortoisefolk struggled to grasp the tiny gun.

<The humans, they place the little metal balls in here, don't they?> He pointed to the gun barrel.

Marissa nodded robotically, amazed that the Testudo wasn't afraid of the pistol.

<Tyrin. Peri.> The young Testudo stepped toward his brothers; the gun still hooked around one of his massive claws. He even knew to aim the gun barrel at the ground. <I know you haven't seen much of the outside world, but I have. Even deep underground in Terrapin, we're not as safe as you may think. We need every advantage we can get. And these- > He lifted up the gun. <May end up being valuable tools for us.>

Marissa smiled, remembering Thomas's speech about guns being tools. How they weren't always meant to be feared.

<Kai.> The scar-handed Testudo practically spat his little brother's name. <You better be right about this.>

<I am.> Kai grinned, marching triumphantly toward Thomas and placing the pistol back in the case. <Now let's go.>

The group, led by Kai's two gruff, reluctant older brothers, then began their long march through the tunnels. Marissa hesitated at first, not wanting to wander into the pitch-black darkness that the Testudo seemed to have no trouble with. But relief washed over her as she noticed Thomas pull two lanterns out of the cart and light them.

"Here," he handed one of the lanterns to Marissa. Her hand tingled as she clasped the thin metal handle, the hot oil sending flickers of heat toward her palm. "I came prepared."

Tyrin and Peri stayed a dozen feet ahead of everyone else, their shell-covered shoulders hunched as they muttered private conversations to one another. Marissa picked up faint whisps of their conversation, with the words 'Mata', 'outcast', and 'threat' being thrown around. But she was too far away to decipher what this meant, and she was already leading the rest of the group with Kai by her side. She couldn't creep any closer or the two tortoises would become suspicious.

<Don't worry about them.>

Kai's sudden thoughts startled Marissa. She peered over at the smiling Testudo and became painfully aware of how obvious her snooping was.

<I remember throwing our names around, but I don't believe I've formally introduced myself. I'm Kai, the youngest child of Chieftress Gala and Chieftain Alda. Those two snivelers up there.> Kai pointed a claw at the older Testudo. <Are my twin brothers, Tyrin and Peri.>

<Wow.> Marissa remarked in amazement. <So you're all the grandsons of Mata?>

<Well, yes and no,> Kai chuckled. <We're actually her great-great-great-great-grandsons, or something like that. She's eight hundred and fifty years old, after

all. But all our other grandparents have since passed, so we just call her Grandmother.>

<I can't believe she really exists. If you don't mind me asking... what has allowed her to live this long?>

Kai shrugged. <No one really knows. Some Testudo say that she's been blessed by the gods. Or it's because she's simply too stubborn to pass away. Either way, she's hasn't been chieftress for a long time. She stepped down many centuries ago and now serves as our shaman, living in her private quarters deep within our village of Terrapin. She makes few public appearances, and the Testudo generally try to keep her existence a secret from outsiders. After all, she did make a lot of reptilians very angry eight hundred years ago.>

<About that...> Marissa took a deep breath. <What exactly happened that day?>

Kai sighed. <She doesn't talk about it. I'm not in line to be chieftain, so I've only gotten parts of the story. But I do know about the idol, and how important it is that Vaipera is never summoned. My parents says that Grandmother still has nightmares about it.>

They continued their walk through the dark tunnels in a contemplative silence. Marissa was lost in thought, and Kai seemed content to let her be. Her mind swirled with questions, and anticipation burned through her veins. She had no idea what awaited at her at the end of this tunnel that seemed to stretch on forever. And she was both eager and terrified to find out.

Despite being dark and damp, the tunnels surprisingly didn't feel claustrophobic. The ceiling continued to rise for the first mile or so, until the thick layer of compacted dirt was nearly twenty feet above their heads. Marissa held her lantern up to the ceiling, its gloomy orange light casting eerie shadows across the cavernous walls. As far as she was aware, the Valley of Scales was all swampland, made up of sand and dirt with few rocks in sight. She had no idea how the Testudo had managed to build such a massive tunnel without it collapsing in on itself.

But the tunnel's size paled in comparison to what awaited them at the end of it. After walking what seemed like miles, although the disorienting darkness made it difficult to tell, the tunnel suddenly stopped. And what was beyond it made Marissa nearly drop her lantern in disbelief.

Her neck tilted upwards, her stomach plummeting in awe as she her mind absorbed the sheer scale of the village. The giant underground civilization, made up of clusters of huts built impeccably from hardened mud bricks, sprawled as far as she could see, with the ceiling towering hundreds of feet above their heads.

But what truly amazed her were the lights. All around the cavernous walls of the village were jagged cracks, streaking across the dirt like lightning strikes. Glowing brightly within each one was the unmistakable soft white glimmer of glowstone.

"I... I don't understand."

Marissa turned around, realizing that Arthur was standing behind her with the same open-mouthed, awestruck expression on his face. He seemed lost for words, but once he noticed Marissa staring at him, he shook his head and cleared his throat.

"Glowstone doesn't exist in the valley," he remarked, as if he were trying to persuade himself that what he was seeing wasn't real. "The kingdom had to go far beyond the mountains to mine it. And it's been here, in Testudo territory, this whole time?"

Kai walked up to Marissa, a smile on his face and a friendly sparkle in his eye.

<Welcome to Terrapin, the capital of Testudo territory.> He grinned, noticing the amazed expression on Marissa and Arthur's faces. <Isn't it beautiful? Within Squamata, glowstone only exists on our land. We've been the protectors of the sacred mineral for thousands of years. And trust me.> He winked. <It does a lot more than just glow.>

Marissa's amazement suddenly turned to horror that choked her throat. She realized that no matter what happened, she could not let the Testudo know that the humans were mining glowstone beyond the mountains. They would immediately throw Arthur and Thomas out of the village... *or worse.*

Marissa trusted her two human friends, and knew that they would never put the Testudo at risk. But if the rest of the kingdom eventually realized that the valuable mineral existed within the valley, it would spell disaster. And not just because the humans used glowstone as a light source.

It does a lot more than just glow. Kai's thoughts haunted her. She had no idea what sort of magic the glowstone contained, but any bit of it would be irresistible to humans. If they ever found out the Testudos' secret, they would stop at nothing to drive the tortoisefolk out and mine every last bit of the glowstone in their territory.

Marissa's eyes flicked over to Arthur and Thomas, who were both still observing the village in awe. She now realized why Tyrin and Peri were so adamant that Marissa travel to Terrapin alone. All it would take was a single human divulging their secret to put their village in peril. Her stomach twisted over itself as she imagined what would happen if the wrong human ever found this place.

At least their entrances are incredibly well hidden.

<Shall I show you around?> Kai's cheery demeanor helped disperse some of Marissa's anxiety. She smiled and nodded, her fangs gleaming under the soft light of the glowstone.

As they walked through the winding paths that snaked through the village homes, Marissa realized how much the Testudo relied on the glowing mineral. Its light gleamed through grass-woven lanterns that lined the rows of mud-brick homes. Small gardens were planted underneath sections of the cavern wall where the glowstone peaked through, which made Marissa wonder if its light allowed plants to grow underground. Even the wandering villagers, especially elders, wore fragments of it as pendants around their necks.

And one particular pair, an older male and female, strolled up to them with tall walking canes made of knotty, twisted wood, each topped with a round sphere of glowstone. As soon as Kai spotted them, he waved and began jogging in their direction.

<Kai! Tyrin! Peri!> The female shouted. <Where have you three bee- >

She froze, clearly not expecting the young Testudo to be accompanied by two humans, a Naga, and most notably, the half-breed that Mata was so determined to meet.

<You...> Was all the female Testudo could say when she saw Marissa. She stepped forward, extending a thick clublike hand as if she couldn't believe what she was seeing. Marissa noticed that her wrist was encased in layers of woven bracelets, with small stones and bits of shells jingling from them. A thin headpiece resembling a crown stretched across her forehead, and she wore multiple pendants around her neck, containing glow-stone charms carved into a variety of shapes. She was clearly someone important within the village.

Marissa's eyes widened. *This must be their mother... the chieftress...*

<I can't believe it. Mata insisted you'd come, and I'll admit I was hesitant to believe her... goes to show she is never wrong. Anyway... you may call me Gala, my dear.> The Testudo introduced herself. She gazed at Marissa with a warmth in her eyes, as if she was an old friend.

<I'm Marissa. It's a pleasure to meet all of you.>

Her mate introduced himself as Chieftain Alda, offering a firm handshake and little else. Marissa noticed that Gala shared the same warm, bubbling personality as Kai; while Tyrin and Peri's quiet, staunch demeanor mirrored their father's.

<I see you've brought friends,> Gala noted, eyeing Arthur, Thomas, and Nathara with a hint of wariness.

<They're allies who want to end this war as much as I do,> Marissa declared. <Please, they mean you no harm.>

Gala nodded understandingly. <Mata trusts you, and you trust your companions. That is good enough for me. We'll make sure they're right at home here. Now, I imagine you wish to speak with Mata?>

<Yes.> Marissa stated firmly, anticipation bubbling in her stomach. <In fact, I need to show you what I'm here to give her.>

With tense fingers, Marissa reached around to her satchel, carefully pulling out the two idol pieces and clasping them in her palms. Her scarf slipped out of the satchel, and the ribbonlike fabric cascaded to the ground. But Marissa was so anxious that she barely noticed.

Gala suddenly looked like she'd been electrocuted. Her eyes widened, dark spheres flashing wildly in panic. A clawed hand flew over Kai's open mouth. Even the sour-faced twins and their father had their brows rise in alarm.

<Don't show those here.> Gala darted forward, covering the idol pieces with her giant hands. Her head spun around, making sure that no wandering villagers took notice of them. Her initial panic began to face, and she slowly raised her palms to peek at the bits of stone, studying them with an intense gaze in her eye.

<Good gods, how in Squamata did you manage to get these here?>

Marissa sighed. <We've traveled for days, all the way across the valley, to bring these to you. We were hoping the Testudo could protect them, to prevent Vaipera from being summoned.>

Gala locked eyes with Marissa, a warm glow of amazement radiating from her gaze as her chest rose and fell in deep breaths. <I can't believe you managed to bring them here. Where did you even fi- no, I'll leave those questions to Mata. Come, we must take you to her at once. Tyrin, Peri, will you two- >

<Mother?> Kai interrupted. <Please, I'd like to take her, if possible.>

Gala's eyes flicked over to Tyrin and Peri, then back at Kai. Deep down, Marissa prayed that the chieftress would heed her youngest son's request. The twin brothers were still quiet and stone-faced, as if they didn't fully trust Marissa. She was wary of them too, and didn't want the journey to wherever Mata lived to be full of tense, awkward silence.

<Alright.> Gala replied after a moment's pause. She turned toward Tyrin and Peri. <Boys, please take care of Marissa's companions until she returns. Now, you two,> Gala turned her attention back to Marissa and Kai. <Stay safe. And thank the gods for your arrival, Marissa. Mata has been worried sick about both you and the other idol pieces.>

Marissa thanked Kai's family, wished her friends peace and safety, and told everyone that she would be back soon. But as she left, following Kai through the winding paths of the village until they were on the outskirts, she began to wonder exactly where they were going.

<Um, Kai?> she asked as they approached the far northern edge of the massive cavern. Beyond them was

nothing but bits of glowstone embedded in a dirt wall – *where else can we go from here?*

The Testudo knelt down, feeling around until he found a piece of the earthy ground that wasn't quite the same as the rest. As Kai pushed, the ground seemed to slide away without hesitation, just like when Marissa and her friends first found the village entrance.

Kai stood up, took notice of Marissa's confused face, and grinned.

<You didn't think it would be that easy to find the oldest reptilian in the valley's home, did you?> He chuckled. <Mata is beloved by our community, but she has plenty of enemies even amongst the reptilians. We keep her home well hidden – and safe.>

He stepped down into the tunnel, offering a clawed hand to help Marissa down.

<C'mon, we've got a lot of walking to do.>

Marissa took his hand, feeling the dry, leathery skin underneath her palm and the bony toughness of his giant claws scrape against her fingers. As he supported her weight while she stepped down, Marissa realized that despite the Testudo being the smallest of the reptilians, they were strong. Incredibly strong.

The pair walked onward, even deeper underground and through a much narrower tunnel. Above them, the entrance closed automatically, sliding back into place like a manhole over a sewer. As it did so, the light faded, and the choking darkness was just barely held back by the tiny glowstone lanterns along the walls.

Marissa gulped. *Good thing my snake half isn't claustrophobic.*

Chapter 16

AYS, WEEKS, AND MONTHS PASSED, AND Cassandra's already busy schedule intensified. As her sixteenth birthday approached, she found herself swept up in whirlpool of studying, exams, workouts, and combat practice. She was now in her tenth year of school at Valley Academy, which meant it was time to prepare for attending university. And Cassandra's path to higher education was more daunting than most. Not only did she need to excel at her studies, but she needed to perfect her skills to improve her chances of being accepted into Brennan University's junior royal guard.

She spent most days tired, stressed, and on the verge of a breakdown. Even if she did pass the vigorous written and physical exams, less than ten percent of each year's junior recruits were women. And as far as she was aware, no hard-of-hearing applicant had *ever* been recruited.

But her days weren't always hectic. Since she juggled so many activities, her parents had released her from many of her previous chores. As her parents aged and her father's health declined, Penelope had surprisingly offered to take over the inn. As it turns out, Cassandra's eldest sister quite enjoyed inn work when it involved balancing expense reports and not scrubbing dirty dishes.

Alice had just left for university, leaving Cassandra as the last child still living at home. Which to her, brought a discomforting sense of loneliness. She remembered how frustrated she used to be as a child, having to share a tiny bedroom with her two raucous sisters. All she wanted was peace and quiet. But now that they were gone, she missed her siblings dearly.

Sundays were Cassandra's least busy days, which usually involved hanging out with Lucy at the Thorburn Estate or taking her parents' cart to visit her brothers. She loved seeing her friends and family, but their time together was often chaotic. Both of her brothers now had families to attend to, and the Thorburn Estate was busier than ever, now home to over a dozen children.

She loved her life. Her supportive friends and family, her thriving grades at Valley Academy, and her budding future at university made it all worth it. But it was still hectic and stressful, and all that mounting anxiety in her chest needed an outlet.

And she knew that every Sunday, when she made the trip down to the waterfront and strolled into the haphazardly-repaired old shack, she'd be greeted by the Naga's scaled, smiling face.

She'd always swore that Lucy was her best friend. But the more time she spent with the Naga, and the more it began to understand sign language, she realized she may have to reclassify Lucy her best *non-human* friend.

After nearly a year of them visiting each other weekly in the shack, the Naga had an elementary fluency in sign language, able to string together simple phrases and sentences. It made every new fact she learned about it a victory. To her surprise, the creature was kind and friendly; a wonderful mystery to unravel.

The Naga was male. His parents were the leaders of the largest village in Naga territory. He was the youngest of two siblings, having an older sister who would one day be the chieftress. His favorite food was rats, but specifically the white ones. He claimed that they tasted sweeter, and laughed when Cassandra wrinkled her nose at the idea.

While the Naga was always eager to learn new signs, Cassandra wasn't always up for teaching with her busy schedule. He always looked concerned when she showed up for their weekly hangouts looking red-faced and exhausted. One day, he even brought her a bundle of fresh flowers, a combination of wild milkweed and honeysuckle, complete with a cracked vase he'd scavenged from the nearby abandoned village. Cassandra displayed them on the three-legged table in the center of the room, refusing to remove them until they were mere twigs.

It hadn't taken long for the Naga to realize that Cassandra was deaf. He found it fascinating, and explained that Naga, having no external ear openings, also had poor hearing. He claimed that he never needed it – his other senses more than made up for it. And that thought lit a spark of hope in Cassandra's heart.

If she couldn't hear, she just had to hone her other senses. The Naga seemed happy to assist, and offered to aid her with combat practice.

She was even more shocked when he brought a pair of freshly sharpened, alligator-bone daggers to the shack one afternoon. Cassandra could easily defeat any of her classmates, including the boys. But combat, even just for practice, with a seven-foot-tall Naga caused a nervous lump to form in her stomach.

But to her surprise, the Naga was both remarkably skilled and incredibly gentle. His long, slithering body was extremely agile, which made striking him a much greater challenge. He showed her various techniques unique to Naga – how to pinpoint an enemy's weaknesses, how to strike between the scales to hit the flesh that lurked underneath, and how to use deception to trick a much faster opponent.

As their practice sessions continued for nearly six months, Cassandra went from being hopelessly defeated to beating the Naga nearly half of the time. It gave her newfound confidence in her abilities, but it also scared the hell out of her. Not long after meeting the Naga, she'd rationalized her dream to join the royal guard by deciding not to enlist in the First Quadrant – those who patrolled the borders of reptilian territories. Second Quadrant didn't seem much better, as she'd still be out in the outer villages. She needed to stay within the kingdom walls, as far away from the reptilians as possible. Because she knew if she ever came face to face with one, she'd never be able to kill it.

So she decided on Third Quadrant, patrolling the kingdom streets and ensuring the safety of Brennan's citizens – mostly from petty thieves and other nefarious humans. Fourth Quadrant was the most prestigious – patrolling the palace itself, but to Cassandra it seemed boring. She wanted to serve the common folk of Brennan, not be holed up with the royal family in a snooty castle.

And she never spoke a single sign of it to the Naga. For all he knew, she just wanted to learn how to better defend herself. And he seemed very concerned about her ability to do so. A little *too* concerned.

She mustered up the courage to ask him about it one night. The sun had just slipped under the horizon, and they were both resting after an hour-long combat practice. Cassandra had performed spectacularly – which meant the Naga now had a small nick on his shoulder. She had profusely apologized, horrified that she'd injured him, but he insisted he was fine and that it would heal quickly on its own.

Even then, she made a mental reminder to bring him some orange paste the next day. But for now, he seemed content to spawl out on the floor of the shack, doodling furiously on a few pieces of scrap paper that Cassandra had swiped from her parents. Many months ago, when Cassandra brought a few ink pens to the shack, he had taken a great interest in drawing. His designs were now scattered across the walls, filling in the gaps where Cassandra and her sister's old artwork was fading away. At first his art was little more than stick figures, but since he practiced every week, his portraits were becoming more and more lifelike.

"Yes?" Ezrinth signed back at her once she caught his attention. She placed her book down on the floor next to her and took a deep breath, asking why he was so invested in her self-defense lessons.

The Naga's scaled expression softened. Something glistened his coppery eyes, beyond just the orangish glow of the oil lantern next to him. Some strange, longing emotion she had never seen him express before.

"I..." He signed slowly, with a hint of reluctance. "I don't want anything to happen to you. If my family ever finds out, I want you to be able to defend yourself from them. I don't want them to..."

His hands fell as his eyes continued to glitter in the dim light. Cassandra's throat tightened. But not because being friends with a Naga put her in danger. She'd honed her combat skills for over a decade – the Naga's kin wouldn't be able to put a scratch on her.

Instead, it was the look in his eyes that made her whole body numb. The way he stared at her as if she were the most important being in the world. One he'd protect at any cost.

It made her think back to the night they first met; when she risked her own life to save his. And how he'd returned the favor that next day. Realization made her throat sour as it occurred to her, after all these years, she'd still never asked him what caused the fight.

Now, he understood enough sign language that she could.

"The night we met," Cassandra signed. "What really happened?"

The Naga's face fell. Marissa knew it was a heavy question, one that likely had a long, complicated story behind it.

"Did you know those humans?" he asked.

"Yes."

"I'm sorry."

Cassandra nodded, "They attacked you, didn't they?"

"I was angry." The Naga's hands shook as he signed, his facial expressions fierce in the fiery orange light of the lantern. "They killed my sister's mate. I wanted revenge. But they found me first. They snuck up behind me and slashed my tail. I had no choice but to kill them. They would've killed me."

Cassandra nodded. His story was what she'd always suspected – that he wasn't a mere monster out on a killing spree. She knew how painful death was. She knew how it drove people to grief, to anger, to madness. And when the fault in that death lay with another being, she knew how tempting revenge was. She saw it in the eyes of her own community during Isaac and Curt's funeral.

"I'm so sorry."

The Naga tucked his stack of drawings away and slithered toward Cassandra. She rose to her feet, suddenly gaining full awareness of his features as he approached. How each individual scale wove together like a fabric made of polished stones. How the amber-colored dots and flecks in his coppery eyes made them look like they were on fire. How his whole demeanor, from the way he crouched down toward her to the gentleness of his foreign, serpentine features, made him look like a work of art. To most humans, the Naga were monsters. But there was no denying the beauty in his harrowing features.

To Cassandra, he was the most fascinating, enchanting being she'd ever met.

"I didn't know," he continued. "Back then... I thought all humans were monsters. Until I met you."

"It's okay," Cassandra replied. "I felt the same about the Naga. But meeting you... you're so kind. Kinder than most humans."

The Naga extended a clawed hand, pressing it against her shoulder. The scales along his palm were warm and smooth – Cassandra was tempted to admit that they felt more pleasant than human flesh. She placed her own hand, diminutive by comparison, over the Naga's as he continued tracing a line down her collarbone. His claw stopped when it met fabric – his finger now pressed against the collar of her blouse just above her breasts.

That was when everything came crashing down. Cassandra pulled away, practically throwing the Naga's arm off her chest. She stumbled backwards, wide-eyed and dazed, her stomach twisting as she confronted the newfound reality that the Naga viewed their relationship differently than she did. *We are friends, right? Best friends, always enjoying each other's company...*

But I would never...

Her frantic thoughts ceased as she looked up into his eyes. She couldn't bear the pained, defeated look on his face, as he pulled his hand back toward his chest. His scaled face was full of shame, as if he'd just made a horrible mistake.

Cassandra ran. Out of the shack and back toward the inn with blistering speed, scraping her arms on the stray branches and palm fronds as she tore through them. She needed to be alone, to process this new reality and collect her thoughts. But she mostly just needed to get away from him.

Not because she was angry. But because couldn't bear to see the pain in his eyes.

She blew through the inn doors and bolted upstairs, confusing both her mother and sister as they stood in the dining room mopping the floors. As she reached her bedroom, Cassandra heard a faint muffle carry through the hallway, which she assumed was someone shouting her name. But she didn't know if it was Penelope or Cadence - she'd lost the ability to distinguish voices a long time ago.

She flopped face first onto her bed, clenching her jaw until her face turned red. She would not cry. No matter how much Ezrinth's saddened expression haunted her, no matter how much the feeling of his claw on her chest made her stomach flip.

But in the end, those were trivial matters. As soon as she collected herself, Cassandra could always march back to the shack and apologize. She could calmly admit that she did not reciprocate his feelings, and they would move on. She knew that even if she rejected him, he would never discontinue their friendship.

But she couldn't do it.

Not because she was too disgusted. Or stubborn.

But because the truth...

The stressful, horrid, and unsettling truth...

Was that she *did* have feelings for him.

She clutched a hand to her chest, still able to feel the Naga's claw just above her cleavage. *This is insane. Delusional. Not being afraid of the Naga is one thing. Even being friends with him is understandable. But this...*

It went against everything she'd ever known. Sure, he was an intelligent being, her best friend, capable of having full-on conversations with her... so why did this feel so *wrong*?

She knew why. She was a human. He was a snake. And even if she could get past her reservations about having feelings for a reptilian, the rest of the world wouldn't. If her parents, or anyone else, ever found out about their secret friendship, the Naga would be hunted down and killed.

As for her? No one would view her the same again. Not even her own family.

Cassandra's door being thrown open was nothing more than a faint blur in her ears, but she was able to feel the vibrations through her bedframe as her mother and sister bolted into the room.

Suddenly her ears were drowning in a sea of muffled shouts. Cassandra had no idea what they were saying, but could tell by their joyous grins that they were excited about something.

"What?" Cassandra signed, tilting her head in confusion.

Cadence began a long string of excited words, her lips moving too fast for Cassandra to read them. But just as she went to ask her mother to slow down, she saw it.

A letter. And not just any letter, one wrapped in a thick envelope and sealed with purple-and-gold wax.

She knew that seal meant it was from Brennan University.

Her stomach flipped.

She'd already received her acceptance letter for admission, which was no surprise – she had excellent grades and a host of extracurricular activities. But she wasn't due to start classes until the fall, which meant she had no idea why they would send her another letter.

Unless...

Cassandra plucked the letter from her mother's hands, slowly peeling away the wax seal with shaking fingers. As soon as she opened the trifolded letter, the sight of the royal guard insignia stamped at the top of the parchment made her hands tremble even more.

Stop it. It's probably just the rejection letter that never arrived. It's probably...

In her anxious haze, the elegantly typewritten paragraph was a large black blur, her frantic mind unable to focus on the individual sentences. Her eyes scanned the letter at a rapid pace, breezing through the introductory formalities until she saw the one confirming word – *accepted.*

She'd done it. This was what she'd been preparing for her whole life. What everyone around her, even her own family, doubted she would be able to do. And deep in the back of her mind, she had believed them. How could such a wiry, small-framed woman, let alone one who was nearly deaf, be accepted into one of the most prestigious positions in the entire kingdom?

It wasn't what she'd expected. She was fully prepared to train for nearly a decade, devoting herself entirely to her dream, just to receive the rejection and walk away knowing she tried her best. Because she would've always lived with regret if she hadn't tried at all.

But I did it. I succeeded. I'm being admitted into the junior royal guard.

Cassandra repeated it over and over in her mind, anxiously awaiting the fireworks. Awaiting the moment where she would leap off the bed and join her mother and sister in their celebration, joyously praising the gods for such an achievement. But she didn't feel excited. She felt... nothing.

And as their celebration died down, Cadence and Penelope noticed. Their silent gazes fell upon Cassandra, who was still curled up in bed with her eyes locked on the letter.

She forced a heavy swallow, not knowing how to react.

"I..." she spoke, her own voice a blurred whisper in her ear. "I need a moment."

She slipped out of bed and brushed past her stunned mother and sister, racing down the stairs and bolting out the front door as her face and chest burned red.

She didn't know why she felt this way. She didn't know how she was going to explain her strange behavior to her family when she returned home. All she knew was that she needed to find him and apologize.

Somehow, at that moment, he was all she could think about.

"HELLO?" CASSANDRA SHOUTED AS SHE approached the shack. She knew that Naga couldn't hear very well, but she hoped that he could still pick up her shouts.

She paused for a moment. The sun was rapidly fading from the sky, and Cassandra cursed herself for not bringing a lamp. In the evening gloom, the shack was eerily silent. Even the long black cloth that Cassandra had used to cover the open doorframe billowed ominously in the air.

The temperature had fallen, and the air was coated in a thick blanket of humidity. Cassandra looked up, and the dim evening sky had a gloomy, greyish tinge. It was clearly going to rain at any minute.

But Cassandra didn't care if she would have to walk back in the darkness through a soaking wet thunderstorm. She had to find him.

She jogged up the rotting wooden steps and pushed the torn black cloth aside just as the first few speckles of rain dotted the peeling front deck. It looked just the same as she'd left it a few hours earlier. The Naga's drawings were scattered across the floor, and their practice swords were stacked by the front entrance. Even the oil lamp, perched on the old wobbly nightstand next to the chair she'd been reading in, was still just barely lit.

Cassandra shuddered, both from disappointment at her friend's absence and the fact that the raindrops were now seeping their way through the cracks in the roof.

She did what her and the Naga had always done when it rained - pulled a stack of damaged bowls out from under the kitchenette and placed them in the spots where the water seeped in most. The sound of splashing water – an occasional drop in some places and a slow, trickling stream in others – was calming. But it also reminded her of him. Everything about this place forever would. Even her and her sister's drawings were almost completely faded away, now replaced by the Naga's own wall art.

Speaking of art... her eyes flicked over to the Naga's drawings, splayed out like a fan in the corner of the room. *They're going to get wet if I don't move them.*

She intended to align them in a stack and place them in one of the few remaining cabinets that still had drawers. But instead, she sat cross-legged in the corner, away from the leakiest parts of the roof, and flipped her way through the Naga's drawings one by one.

He was secretive about his art, only occasionally choosing to show one of his pieces to Cassandra. She knew he'd improved significantly over the years, but she hadn't realized to what extent. As she flipped from page to page, her eyes widened in amazement as she traced over the intricate sketches. Despite having hands far too large to properly grip a pencil, he'd managed to produce artwork that rivaled that of humans.

Many of them were self-portraits, which didn't surprise Cassandra. She'd often found him gazing into the half-shattered hand mirror he'd brought back from the village, fascinated by his own features. Cassandra assumed that Naga didn't see their own reflections very often.

Each page contained several sketches – of his face, eyes, hands. But after about ten pages, she felt her heart fall into her stomach. Because there were more portraits, except this time, they were of her.

Cassandra had never thought of herself as being beautiful. She was a petite woman, who remained slender and wiry despite her years of combat training. There wasn't an ounce of fat on her, including places where she wanted it to be, such as her hips and breasts. She had always assumed she looked far too boyish to gain much attention from the opposite sex, although she'd never had much interest in men herself.

But somehow, the Naga made her look like an elegant princess. She traced her fingers over a three-quarter profile shot, where he'd given her normally frizzy hair smooth, defined waves and accentuated her cheekbones and lips. He'd drawn her from so many angles – with her back to him, leaning against a wall, even her in a combat stance, wielding a sword with a smug smile across her face.

Finally, after another dozen or so pages of sketches, she came across the very last one.

This page had just one sketch, and it took up the whole page.

It was both of them.

And...

Her whole body broke out in uncontrollable quivers, as her face flushed red and her throat struggled to swallow.

The drawing seemed so strange; a tiny human embraced by a giant, scaled snake-beast. But the Naga had managed to make it so gentle, with so much tenderness and warmth expressed in both of their eyes...

Shock turned to sickness, and Cassandra stuffed the flurry of papers into a nearby drawer. She resisted the urge to throw the last one across the room and let its fate be determined by the leaky roof.

She clutched her unsteady stomach. She couldn't be upset at him. Not when she felt the same way.

Not that any of it mattered. In a little over a week, she would be on her way to the kingdom of Brennan, ready to begin training for the royal guard. And by the end of the summer, she would begin her classes at Brennan University, and all of this would be behind her.

She stumbled out of the shack. She needed to go home. But leaving the shack, even though the Naga wasn't there, felt like betrayal.

She was due to leave for the kingdom the following Monday, one week from tomorrow. Which gave her one final Sunday with him. One final chance to say goodbye.

As she reluctantly headed home, she prayed he would show up next week. That she hadn't scared him away for good.

FROM THE OUTSIDE, CASSANDRA APPEARED CALM and composed. Throughout the week, she focused on preparing for her departure by helping her parents with the inn as much as possible. She received many congratulations and heartfelt goodbyes from friends. Some of them would be staying in the outer villages, ready to begin apprenticeships or help out with their family businesses. Others would be joining her at university – where a whole new world of experiences awaited them.

She spent as much time as possible with Lucy. Her friend had decided university wasn't for her, and instead took a tailoring apprenticeship in Augustree. Cassandra was excited for her – she'd always had a knack for sewing, and she couldn't wait to see her friend's beautiful creations. But with Cassandra being swept up in classes and junior guard training, it meant they'd be seeing a lot less of each other.

"It'll be alright," Lucy signed one afternoon while they sat on the back porch, watching the younger children squabble around the gardens. Jonas had been ill lately, and as one of the oldest children in the orphanage,

Lucy had been helping Beatrice as much as possible. Cassandra knew Lucy's presence - and help - would be sorely missed, but Jonas was always insistent that the children under their care needed to 'spread their wings and leave the nest'.

"I'll miss you," Cassandra signed back with a sad smile.

"But I'm so happy for you!" Lucy grinned enthusiastically. "University and the junior royal guard! You must be so excited!"

That was what everyone had told Cassandra all week. She'd played the part, forcing a smile, making her signs emit the enthusiasm that she was supposed to have.

But inside, the whole week, she'd been a nervous wreck.

The Naga never left her mind. He was always there, lingering even when Cassandra was busy with customers at the inn. At night, her mind ran wild with fantasies. She imagined his claws on her skin again, the feeling of his scales under her palm.

What it would be like to truly embrace him, just like in the drawing.

She'd fought the feelings off at first, but after a few nights she found herself giving in to them. What was the harm? Her fantasies were her own, locked away in the vault of her mind. No one needed to know that she was attracted to a Naga.

Besides, she was leaving in less than a week. She decided she'd make one final journey out to the shack that Sunday to say goodbye, but it would be curt and brief. Then, it would all be over. She'd likely never see him again.

As that day approached, she prayed that he would be there. As much as she wanted to throw her desires for the Naga out of her mind for good, she needed closure. He was her friend. He had been for years. She couldn't just disappear on him.

Anxiety had a chokehold on her stomach that evening as she made her final journey out to the shack. Over the years, it had come to feel like a second home. She and the Naga had patched it up as best they could, using materials from the abandoned village to make it feel more comfortable. It was their escape from the rest of the world, a place where preconceptions about monsters and villains faded away. Here, there was only peace, warmth, and understanding.

Yet Cassandra felt a deep chill wash over her as she brushed aside the black cloth covering the open door-frame. Because behind it was the answer she'd been anticipating all week – whether or not she'd be able to give a proper goodbye.

The shack was dark – the sun was rapidly setting, and the sky was damp and grey with another impending summer thunderstorm. Her heart leapt as the first thing she noticed was an old oil lamp she'd left behind. It was lit, its small, flickering flame filling her heart with warmth.

As she stepped forward and picked it up, she could feel his presence behind her. Even though she couldn't hear him coming, she'd grown accustomed to feeling of the old floorboards shifting under his weight.

She turned around, and he smiled. It was a shy, hesitant smile, as if he wasn't sure how she'd react after their last tumultuous meeting. But it was still the same black-and-brown, copper-eyed, scaled face that she'd grown fond of over the years.

The same kind, enchanting, beautiful Naga.

Cassandra never cried. Her early childhood years of bullying had forced her to choke back such emotions, and she knew that tears would be frowned upon in the royal guard. She wanted to be a hero – brave, strong, and fearless. Heroes didn't cry.

But the tears rolled down her face anyway, as she leaned forward and pressed herself against him.

His white belly scales were soft and smooth, and she could feel his chest rise and fall with every breath. She pressed an ear against him, and the rhythmic pulse of his heartbeat sent warm tingles through her stressed, sorrowful, weary body.

She knew this was insane. But she didn't care.

Once the Naga recovered from his initial shock, she could feel his shaking arms slowly wrap around her. Once they were all the way around her back, he gained confidence and further tightened their embrace.

"I'm sorry," Cassandra peered up at him, signing with a single shaky hand. "I'm so sorry."

"No, it's alright," he signed back. "I'm sorry too."

Cassandra's whole body trembled as she raised an unsteady hand to his cheek. She'd never touched his face before. His beautiful amber-colored eyes flickered in disbelief.

"I'm leaving," she continued. "Tomorrow."

His face fell in shock, as if a lightning bolt had just struck his heart.

"I'm so sorry." The tears rolling down Cassandra's face erupted into full-blown sobs. "I'm leaving for the kingdom. I'm an adult now, after all."

"As am I," The Naga replied. "My parents keep piling more duties on me. It's getting harder and harder to come out here."

"So I guess..." Cassandra choked back sobs. "This is goodbye?"

The Naga didn't answer. He lowered his head, cradling Cassandra's much smaller one under it, and tightened his grip on her. She could feel his claws press into her back, just like she'd dreamed about the entire week. She strangely found herself wanting more of it.

She placed a hand against his white-scaled chest, running it all the way down the length of his stomach. He placed a clawed hand on her collarbone.

"I love you," Cassandra was in disbelief as her free hand formed the words she'd struggled to rationalize the entire week. Yet as she said it, relief poured over her body.

"I... I love you too."

With trembling hands and a pounding heart, Cassandra wrapped her fingers around the bottom of her blouse.

Tonight was all they had. And she was determined to make it a night they both remembered.

Chapter 17

THE FURTHER THEY WANDERED DOWN THE
dimly lit tunnel, the more relieved Marissa felt
that she hadn't taken this trip with Tyrin and Peri. Not
only was the near-darkness making her dizzy, but the
ceiling was less than a foot above her head and the walls
so narrow that she couldn't fully outstretch her arms. It
wasn't a journey she wanted to make with two grumpy
Testudo that seemed to hold a grudge against her.

<1 know it's not a fun trip,> Kai remarked as he
ambled behind her, his bulky shell having about six
inches of clearance on either side of the walls. <But
it's that way for a reason, unfortunately. We make this
journey as unappealing as possible for any nefarious
beings that wish to harm my grandmother. In fact, a
lot of Testudo territory is designed that way. Besides

our magically disguised entrances, we also have a lot of false tunnels full of traps. In fact, there was this one case where...>

Marissa was only half-listening, picking up bits and pieces of Kai's chatter while the rest of her mind was distracted. As usual, her thoughts swirled with anxious questions, and the dim, suffocating air of the tunnel seemed to amplify her worries. With every step, she was getting closer to meeting Mata.

At this point, she was satisfied that the idol pieces were safe. All she had to do was hand them over to the most reclusive and well-protected reptilian in the valley, and that job was over. What really made Marissa's head swirl was wondering what Mata would say to her, because this journey wasn't just about protecting the idol pieces. Mata had specifically asked to see *her*; the half-Naga girl whose existence had remained a secret until a few weeks ago. Marissa wondered what the ancient Testudo wanted from her, and she had a creeping feeling that Mata had known about her for a long time.

Which meant that somehow, Marissa was important. But she wasn't sure if that was a good or bad thing.

<You're awfully quiet.>

Marissa realized that Kai had stopped his chattering, likely because he noticed that she wasn't paying attention.

<I...> She took a moment to collect her thoughts. <I'm just nervous, that's all.>

<Ah, of course. You really don't have to be. Grandmother is the kindest, wisest being in the whole

valley. I always enjoy my trips down here to spend time with her.>

Marissa remained quiet, which Kai seemed to interpret as Mata not being the only thing she was worried about.

<It's my brothers, isn't it?>

Kai must've noticed Marissa twitch in front of him, as Marissa could feel him chuckle.

<Don't worry about them,> he scoffed, a hint of disgust in his thoughts. <So, a little bit of backstory on me and my family. My mother Gala is the one who is Mata's descendant. She had all sisters, so she was chosen as chieftress. But Testudo are patriarchal, so my family arranged a bonding ceremony to a mate they chose – my father Alda. The problem is, they're complete opposites. My mother is much like my grandmother – enthusiastic, warm, and full of understanding and hope. My father, on the other hand, is gruff and very much stuck in his ways. He's wary of Mata's beliefs, and if he had it his way, you and your friends would've all been kicked out of here the second you found our burrow.>

Marissa sighed. <I did notice that your brothers seem to take after him.>

She felt a hint of a growl from Kai's thoughts.

<My father had molded them exactly in his image. They're twins, hatched from the same egg, and I swear they share a brain. Since they're both the oldest males, they will be co-chieftains someday. Meaning that my father has been preparing them for their future roles their entire lives. I, on the other hand, was an accident, born many years later. Since I'm not in line to be

chieftain, I am left to do as I please, as long as I don't cause trouble. Which means I spend most of my time as a courier, delivering messages and goods to the other Testudo burrows. It's a dangerous job, since it involves going above ground – there are giant glowstone deposits littered through our territory that we can't dig through. But it means that I meet a lot of other reptilians, and learn a lot from them. Unlike my brothers, whose knowledge of the world is limited to this giant, isolated cavern we call home.>

Marissa turned her head, and noticed Kai's warm, glowing smile behind her. He was so open, enthusiastic, and genuine – he gave off the same trusting aura as Nathara. He was quickly becoming one of her favorite reptilians she'd met so far, and it made her hope that once this was all over, maybe the Testudo wouldn't remain so isolated.

<And of course, when I wasn't working,> Kai continued. <I'd spend as much time with my grandmother as I could. She always told the most incredible stories. But unfortunately, the tale of when the idol pieces broke eight hundred years ago wasn't one of them.>

Marissa heard Kai's stomping footsteps stop behind her. She turned around and noticed a large wooden door on her right. It was very rotund and heavy, with decorative glowstone inlays that ignited with a fierce white aura as they approached.

<That's why,> Kai fished a silvery key out of the woven satchel slung across his shoulder. A warm grin stretched across his face as he unlocked the door. <I'm

very excited to hear the full story – now that you've finally arrived.>

THE SCENE THAT LAY BEYOND THE DOOR, AS KAI pushed it open with a loud groan, was almost too surreal for Marissa to believe.

She loved the wild beauty of the Valley of Scales – from the muddy swamplands to the primordial oak forests and even the ever-looming mountains that stretched beyond reptilian territory. But this was an entirely different kind of beauty – one that Marissa thought only existed in her childhood fantasy novels. Like the rest of Terrapin, the cavernous walls contained embedded glowstone deposits that gave off a gentle light. But this glowstone wasn't just luminous cracks in the wall – it sprawled across the cavern in intricate, lacey patterns that formed a variety of murals on the wall. And, as Marissa stepped closer, she realized that within the gently glowing stone were odd pulses and crackles, sending eerie flickers of light throughout the room.

Almost like... lightning.

Leaning forward carefully, as if she were in a dream, Marissa traced her fingers along the glowing, crackling images. Herds of tortoises marched across the scrubland, snakes slithered through tall grass, and giant alligators poked their arrow-shaped heads out of the murky swamp. Marissa's intuition told her that these images were ancient – not just by the age of the design, but also what they depicted. This was a wild, untamed Valley of Scales from hundreds, maybe even thousands of years ago. Before humans arrived and built up their massive kingdom.

Beyond the glowstone murals, the rest of the underground home gave off a cozy warmth that reminded Marissa of Sienna's cottage. The abode was arranged in a series of circular rooms, each containing colorful rugs, blankets, and chairs. A variety of patterned tapestries, each intricately woven from dyed thread, wound across the top of the walls near the ceiling. Mata's home was incredibly cluttered, and to Marissa, it was a beautiful chaos.

<Kai?> The gentle thoughts of very old Testudo trailed through Marissa's mind. <Is she here?>

Kai smiled. He took Marissa's hand in his own giant clawed one and led her into the next room.

<Yes, Grandmother. We're both here.>

Marissa wasn't sure what she was expecting. Admittedly, she had imagined Mata as an ethereal, powerful, almost god-like being, radiating ancient wisdom and energy. She wasn't quite expecting to find an extremely wrinkled and frail-looking Testudo sitting on a plush cushion, knitting what appeared to be a ridiculously long scarf. The Testudo didn't look up as they approached, but a broad smile crept across the shriveled, sagging skin that lined her face.

<I can't believe it's really you.> Mata's thoughts were soft with awe, yet her gaze was still tilted downward as she fiddled with the wooden knitting needles in her hands. <Please, have a seat, both of you.>

She pointed a long, bony claw at an empty cushion a few feet away from her. Marissa stepped forward and hesitantly took a seat, her slight frame sinking into the plush sphere as it crinkled under her bottom.

Kai did the same on another nearby cushion, sinking much further into it than Marissa did. She then realized why the Testudo used these puffy bean bags instead of chairs – to accommodate both their weight and their massive shells.

<I've been waiting for this moment a long, long time.> Mata finally stopped knitting, placing her needles and yarn aside and folding her hands in her lap. <I always wondered what you'd look like in person.>

Marissa prepared to reply, but she suddenly stopped, turning her brain off for a moment. She was confused – Mata was still looking down at her lap. Marissa wasn't even able to see her eyes – why wasn't the old Testudo looking at them? And how could she tell what Marissa looked like without even seeing her?

But unfortunately, Marissa had stopped her thoughts a bit too late. Mata could sense her confusion, and the ancient tortoise simply chuckled.

<I know you have questions, my dear.> Mata lifted her gaze, her large round eyes finally resting on Marissa. As they did, Marissa forced herself not to shiver. Normally, Testudo eyes were dark, glossy spheres, a polished-stone-like mixture of brown and black. But Mata's eyes were milky, clouded over like a foggy night sky.

Mata was blind.

<Indeed, my advanced age has robbed me of my eyesight. I lost my vision about three centuries ago. But

don't worry.> She continued. <With my powers, I don't need eyes to see.>

Mata's words made Marissa's mind start racing with questions. And apparently so did Kai's, as Marissa saw his eyes widen as he lifted himself partway out of his seat.

<Grandmother, do you- >

<I'm sorry, Kai, my dear,> Mata sighed, her exhale sounding like a deep, saddened wheeze. <I know there's still a lot I haven't told you. But please, my dear grandson, would you be willing to give Marissa and I a moment alone?>

Kai huffed, his eyes flicking over to Marissa. She noticed his steely gaze, but was too stunned that Mata already knew her name to react. But eventually, the young Testudo rose from his seat and strolled toward the doorway, muttering that he'd be waiting outside.

<Now then, my dear,> Mata turned her attention back to Marissa. <I have a lot of explaining to do.>

A slight, icy prickle ran down Marissa's arms. Because the moment Kai left, Mata's previously frail, raspy thoughts rose in volume and depth. She still sounded incredibly old, but her voice was now closer to the powerful, ancient being Marissa had once imagined.

But that wasn't Mata's only transformation. The tortoise squeezed her cloudy eyes shut, and Marissa was suddenly blinded by a burst of light. Once it faded and Marissa's sore eyes recovered from the flash, she gasped as she realized that Mata's leathery, wrinkled skin was now wrapped in the same intricate, crackling patterns as the murals on the wall.

Even her milky pupils began to pulse a soft white light, as if a storm were brewing in her eyes.

<I've never let anyone see me like this.> She sounded both shocked and saddened, studying her glowing skin as if she hadn't seen it in a long time. <Not even my own descendants. I've kept the truth wrapped up deep in my soul for eight hundred years... waiting for you to be brought into this world and find your way here.>

Mata must've noticed the wary alarm in Marissa's eyes, because the old Testudo took a deep breath, and the glowing patterns on her skin began to dim.

<I promise, I don't want to scare you, my dear. But you need to hear the truth. First and foremost, have you ever heard the story of what happened that day?>

<Yes,> Marissa replied, not needing elaboration on what 'that day' meant. <You refused to let Vaipera be summoned. This caused a disagreement between the four reptilian leaders, and while everyone was arguing, a lightning bolt suddenly came down from the sky and shattered the idol into four pieces.>

<That is correct,> Mata replied. <But there's much more to that story that only I know of. Because at the exact same moment that the lightning bolt cascaded down from the sky and shattered the idol, I felt it strike somewhere else too.>

Mata placed a hand over her chest, pointing a claw directly at her heart. As she did so, the glowing swirls on her skin began to rumble and crackle with a fierce power, their light flickering in the dim air like an evening storm.

Marissa's arms went rigid, ready to lift herself out of her seat and bolt if something went awry. She was wary of Mata's sudden power, fearing that the pulsing electricity that ran through the ancient Testudo's body. She didn't know how much control Mata had over it, and the glowing lines across her skin seemed to have a mind of their own. Even their eerie pulses and flickers resembled a racing heartbeat.

But Marissa didn't want to run. She wanted to know everything. She wanted to know what really happened eight hundred years ago, if the idol pieces would truly be safe, and most importantly, who *she* really was. Because it was becoming alarmingly clear that her half-Naga heritage wasn't just a horrid accident of nature. Her whole existence was part of something much larger, and whether good or bad, Marissa was eager to learn what it was.

<Tell me everything,> Marissa insisted, perhaps a bit too boldly. But she felt a deep connection to the strange, ancient, powerful reptilian that sat in front of her. She already knew that Mata wouldn't hide anything from her.

<Ever since that stray bit of lightning struck me,> Mata continued. <I've felt her. I know her emotions as well as my own. My dreams have turned into vivid nightmares; I see a kingdom in ruin, armies of armored serpents plowing through the swampland, and the deaths of countless humans as a massive storm rages throughout the battlefield. Every day, I fight off her hold on my mind. It's as if she's tempting me with a taste of her power, trying to persuade me to march back up that

mountain and summon her. That's why I've secluded myself down here for centuries. I'm determined to never let her win.>

Marissa gulped as the small veins of electricity began to crackle from Mata's skin, as if Vaipera's power was desperate to escape the old Testudo.

<But it's not all so mournful,> Mata's thoughts suddenly grew more hopeful. <Because sometimes, admits the storms and bloodshed, I see a single image in my mind. It's faint and hazy compared to the rest, just a brief flash like lightning, but always the same picture. I see Vaipera, in her horrid, towering, serpentine glory, her eyes raging with fury. But in front of her, like a tiny cricket confronting a giant lizard, is a young woman. I can't see her face, but she has the body of a human and the scales of a snake, with long, wild black hair and a glistening sword in one hand. She extends her other hand out toward Vaipera, and then... nothing. It's all gone.>

Marissa was numb. Even as the crackles of electricity off Mata's skin grew in length and intensity, all she could do was sit in dumbfounded silence. All of it made her nauseous. Watching that wicked serpent goddess's power torment Mata pained her, and having it be so close to her nearly made her vomit.

Vaipera knows I exist? She suddenly felt as if a thousand pairs of eyes were locked on her, as aching pulses of fear trailed down her back. *And Mata's vision... what does it mean? Does she end up being summoned despite our efforts? And me outstretching my arm... am I asking her for peace? Offering for her to surrender?*

Am I actually capable of stopping her?

<The truth is,> Marissa's thoughts shook. <I don't really know who I am. I was raised in a human orphanage my whole life and just began to discover the world a few weeks ago. I don't know what Vaipera wants with me, or if I can truly stop this war. All I know is that I want peace.> Her thoughts cracked as she nearly broke into tears. <I just want peace. And it seems impossible.>

<That's the problem,> Mata sighed. <War is easy. All it takes is a sharp sword and a bit of brute force to drive a blade through the heart of those who are different. No point in trying to understand someone that's dead.>

As Mata spoke, the crackling electricity retreated into her skin, and Marissa's nerves loosened.

<Peace, on the other hand,> Mata continued. <Is incredibly difficult. It involves putting aside one's pre-conceptions about the world and seeing things from another's point of view. Something that all intelligent beings, whether human or reptilian, struggle with.>

Marissa's heart sank as the heavy truth of Mata's thoughts weighed on her. Mata was eight hundred and fifty, the oldest being to ever exist in the valley. She had nearly a millennia's worth of knowledge, and knew more about the psyche of intelligent beings than anyone else.

<But it's not impossible.>

Marissa perked up. The simple thought was like a tiny beacon of light in the swirling darkness.

<As my mother used to say eight hundred years ago,> Mata smiled. <The most beautiful things in life are often the simplest, but are also the most difficult to obtain. And you, my dear Marissa, are one of the purest, bravest

souls to ever grace this valley. If anyone can bring peace, it's you.>

Marissa smiled, beaming at the warmth of Mata's thoughts. It was one of the kindest compliments anyone had ever given to her. And as Mata gazed warmly at Marissa, her eyes still swirling like the calm after a storm, Marissa swore that the old Testudo could see straight into her soul.

It was the look in Mata's eyes that made Marissa remember the other reason why she'd come.

<Mata- >

<I already know, my dear,> Mata's eyes dimmed. <Bring them here.>

Marissa gently scooped the idol pieces out of her satchel and placed them in Mata's outstretched claws, careful not to let stray bits of lightning shock her human skin. Mata rose from her seat, a task that took a great deal of effort for a reptilian over eight centuries old, and shuffled towards a door behind her chair.

<I want peace as much as you do,> Mata remarked as she swung the door open. Inside was a variety of knick-knacks and baskets – it was clearly a storage closet. But Marissa noticed a small box, one made from nearly transparent glowstone, that contained a small piece of rock very similar to the two Marissa had brought. Mata opened the box and placed the pieces inside, and Marissa felt a wave of relief as the heavy lid closed.

Three of the four pieces. Sealed away in one of the most secluded places in the valley.

Marissa had completed their mission.

<And trust me, peace is very much possible,> Mata closed the door and sat back down. <All because of you. You're the key to breaking down their communication barriers. I want the humans and reptilians to under-stand each other once again, the way things used to be.>

Marissa smiled and nodded, when a sudden realiza-tion shocked her heart like a lightning bolt.

<Wait.> Marissa froze. <What do you mean the way things used to b- >

Mata didn't have a chance to answer. A pounding, frantic knock shook Mata's front door, and both Marissa and Mata's heads jolted in its direction.

<One of my cardinal rules,> Mata smirked as the glowing patterns on her skin melted away. It was as if her whole body seemed to deflate, and she returned to the heavily wrinkled, frail Testudo Marissa had seen when she first arrived. <Everyone always has to knock. Can't go giving my secret away. Kai, my dear.> Mata raised her voice into the next room. <Do you and Marissa mind answering the door?>

Marissa stood up, venturing through the dimly lit, circular rooms of Mata's homes until she made her way to where Kai stood at the very wide front door. The whole time, Mata's thoughts clung to her mind. She was desperate to understand what Mata meant by 'the way things used to be'. It made her realize how little she – and the rest of the valley – knew what life was like there eight hundred years ago.

And Marissa knew she'd get her answer – as soon as they dealt with the rather irritating visitor. The entire time Marissa walked to the front door, they'd been pounding on the heavy wood as if their life depended on it.

And as Marissa and Kai answered the door, she realized it was Tyrin. He had his hands on his stocky knees, panting as if he'd just run for miles.

<Is something wrong?> Marissa asked, instinctively knowing something was.

<Marissa,> he looked up once he was able to catch his breath. <Is Mata alright?>

<Um, yes.>

Tyrin's panting slowed, and Marissa could see the alarm in his eyes.

<I need you both to come back up to Terrapin,> he stated firmly.

<Why?> Kai asked.

The thinly veiled terror in Tyrin's thoughts turned Marissa's blood to ice.

<We're under attack by humans.>

ARTHUR FELT A BUBBLE OF ANXIETY FORM IN HIS throat as soon as Marissa left.

His half-Naga companion, unmasked and with an eager smile on her face, had followed the youngest Testudo to an unknown destination to receive, what Arthur assumed, were the answers she'd needed her entire life. He knew how important meeting Mata was to her. After all, he always knew she was special. And it warmed his heart to see her starting to believe it.

But her departure meant that he, Thomas, and Nathara, who were significantly less welcomed visitors to Terrapin, were left alone with the chieftain and his family.

And Arthur couldn't understand any of them.

The Testudo were noticeably more welcoming to Nathara, if merely because they could understand her. Arthur and Thomas were left alone, standing awkwardly on the fringes of a conversation they couldn't hear. It reminded Arthur of his elementary school years – a combination of raucous behavior and social awkwardness had resulted in him being picked last for just about everything. And their current situation made that same discomforting sense of isolation boil in his stomach.

But at least Nathara has our backs, Arthur noted as he noticed the towering Naga gesture toward the two wayward humans with a smile on her face. After about ten minutes, which to Arthur seemed like an eternity, she ushered them forward and led the way on what appeared to be a more in-depth tour of Terrapin.

Arthur followed directly behind her, with Thomas hanging back as he walked next to his horse-drawn cart. The Testudo hadn't yet asked what was in the cases stacked in the rear of the cart, which filled Arthur with both relief and apprehension. The two older Testudo had nearly killed them over the contents of those cases, and the one tortoise that seemed receptive to their presence had ventured off with Marissa. Arthur had no idea how the chieftain and chieftress – or any of the other Testudo – would react to them bringing guns into Terrapin.

Although Arthur couldn't help but notice both older brothers giving him occasional wary-eyed glares as they walked. After the fourth or fifth time, Arthur took a deep breath and attempted to focus less on his companions and more on the scenery around him.

Which was incredible – the cavern ceiling stretched an impossibly high distance above their heads, perhaps even taller than the royal palace. The soft white pulse of the glowstone, being the only source of light in the cavern, gave the village an ethereal glow. Its light sparkled in the dark, glossy eyes of several Testudo juveniles as they squabbled around the gardens. They appeared to be playing a game of tag, with the young tortoises periodically popping their limbs and heads into their shells to avoid being touched.

Arthur's attention then turned to the gardens themselves, which were tended to by small clusters of older Testudo who all wore glowstone pendants. Arthur studied the variety of crops, planted in neat rows, and realized that the gardens contained food that generally wasn't grown in the valley. *Broccoli, cauliflower, cabbage...* plants that, according to Arthur's college botany classes, didn't tolerate the summer heat of the valley.

Maybe it's because it's cooler underground. Arthur paused as he watched an elderly Testudo pluck a radish out of the ground. The glowstone pendant around their neck dangled less than an inch from the radish, and Arthur swore he saw the freshly picked bulb grow larger in the tortoise's leathery palm. *Or maybe there's more to it than that.*

Arthur was so distracted by the swirling scenes around them that he nearly bumped into Nathara. He froze, shaking his head, and realized they'd halted. A quick peek around Nathara's large serpentine body made Arthur realize that something urgent had stopped them in their tracks.

Two exhausted, panting Testudo, both with crossbows strung across the backs of their shells, appeared to be frantically relaying a message to Gala, Alda, and their sons. Arthur went to tap on Nathara's shoulder when he realized the Naga's body was stiff and her eyes glistening with worry. So he pulled his arm back.

"What d'ya think is happenin'?" Thomas's whispering voice suddenly crept over Arthur's shoulder.

"I don't know," Arthur whispered back. "Let's not interrupt them. And pray that Nathara will find some way to relay all of this to us."

Beyond the conversation, Arthur noticed several more armed Testudo jogging toward one of the tunnels leading to the surface. A sickening realization crept over his body, and he could feel his stomach broil with nausea.

Someone was up there.

Nathara spun around to face her two human companions, and Arthur took a few deep gulps of air and managed settle his stomach enough to pay attention. Nathara's eyes darted back and forth between him and Thomas, indecisiveness on her face as she tried to brainstorm a way to relay her message. She made a few vague gestures with her hands, but when she realized she wasn't getting her point across, she let out a frustrated hiss and hunkered down toward the dusty ground.

Arthur was confused at first, until Nathara stuck a single claw into the dirt and drew a circle with her finger. Around the circle, she poked several dots. *A lot of dots*, Arthur gulped. And as Nathara finished her crude dirt drawing and pointed at the cavern exit a few hundred feet away, the confirmation of Arthur's greatest fear sent another wave of nausea through his stomach.

But there was still one question left. While trying to keep his hand from shaking, Arthur pointed a finger at Nathara with a questioning glance. Nathara shook her head, a solemn expression on her reptilian face, and pointed back at Arthur.

The beings that found them weren't reptilian. They were human.

Which meant Arthur knew exactly who was standing at the entrance to Terrapin.

Arthur crossed his arms to make an X shape, and that, combined with the panicked look on his face, only confused Nathara. He sighed and shook his head. Playing charades was hopeless. They were running out of time, and Arthur knew he was the only person who had a chance at stopping this.

So he bolted for the exit. Behind him, he could hear Thomas's shouts and Nathara's frantic slithering, but he never looked back.

He had to find his brother before the Testudo did.

Chapter 18

DESPITE HIS INITIAL PULSE-POUNDING sprint, Arthur realized that the journey back up to the surface was a lot longer than he remembered. After about half a mile, he slowed to a wheezing jog, then a tired walk.

It was also dark. Very dark. Arthur's anxiety rose as he realized he was surrounded by pitch-black nothingness, barely able to see the outline of his hand in front of his face. In his hurry, he'd foolishly forgotten to grab one of Thomas's lanterns, and the faint bit of light that gleamed through the tunnel's entrance was long gone.

He had no choice but to press on, one blind footstep after another, the darkness so disorienting that he wasn't even sure if he was headed in the right direction. He took a few deep breaths to slow the blood pounding in his chest and temples, and attempted to distract his frayed mind with thoughts of something other than his current situation.

And the first thing that came to mind was Marissa. He tried to imagine her standing in front of him, in that muddy yet vibrantly colored Varan dress, her face unmasked and her fangs gleaming in the soft light of the glowstone. A warm heat flushed his face, and he ached to reach out and touch her... *no, hold her. Tell her how wonderful and special and beautiful she is until she truly believes it.*

But his sweet reverie was interrupted by the bitter burn of regret as he realized what a coward he'd been over the past few days. He knew his feelings were recip-rocated – the night spent in each others' arms back in Canterbury cemented that truth. But every warm, tender moment with her was always laced with doubt. Fear. Anxiety.

All because of his family.

It was what had lurked in the back of his mind during their entire journey. When he was back in the Castella's storage room with Ramsey, it all seemed so simple – he would never stand idly by while his family destroyed the reptilians. But over the past few days, the reality of what it meant to be exiled from them had frayed his mind and haunted his nightmares. All those years with his parents and brother, all those memories... they were all snuffed out in an instant, like a candle being blown out to leave only darkness.

He knew he was a handful as a child. But his parents loved him, and he wondered if his forsaking them had caused them pain. *And Ramsey...* Arthur's throat locked up. He missed his brother. His *real* brother, not whatever spineless puppet King Gabriel had morphed him into. He knew that Ramsey's mind would never escape the king's grasp unscathed, and he feared that his relationship with his brother would never be the same again.

And standing between Arthur and his family was his love for the reptilians... and most of all, his budding feelings for Marissa. In his twenty-three years of life, he'd never had much interest in relationships, and his forced engagement to Adeline only soured his notion of love. In the world of the royals, romantic feelings were secondary to forging alliances and producing the next generation of elites. It was much easier for Arthur to lock himself away in The Menagerie and seal off his heart completely than deal with such things.

But he'd never expected this. No one, in his entire life, had made him feel the way Marissa did. He'd only known her a few weeks, but he felt an intense force pulling him toward her from the moment she bumped into him at The Menagerie. It was a spark that lit a joyous yet indescribably painful fire in his heart. One that he would never be able to put out, because he'd never met anyone like her before, and he knew he never would again.

A sudden flicker of light brought Arthur's attention back to the stifling darkness around him. He was so disoriented that he wasn't sure if it was real at first. But after a few more steps, it was unmistakable – a lopsided, half-buried oil lamp flickering less than a hundred feet away.

One that clearly belonged to a human.

Someone tried to crawl down here, Arthur hypothesized as he jogged toward the flickering light like it was his last lifeline. As he reached the wafting flame and lifted in from the dirt, he could hear the faint, muffled hum of human activity above his head.

He scoffed and brushed the dirt off the bottom of the lamp. Clearly, someone changed their mind and scurried back to the surface, abandoning the lamp in its dusty grave.

Arthur knew that the royal guard didn't find the Testudo entrance through an incredible stroke of luck – he and his companions had been followed. As the faint voices above him rose in volume and intensity, Arthur's ears picked up on the sounds of rolling cart wheels and stomping boots. And their audacity made his blood boil in his veins.

He knew he should've had a plan. He knew from every confrontation he'd ever had with his family that losing his royal-bred sense of composure would only make him look like a fool. But with anger setting his mind ablaze, he threw caution to the wind and hurled a fist into the dirt barely a foot above his head.

The low ceiling shook slightly, before sliding away. Arthur's darkness-drenched eyes were blinded by the sun, but he could clearly make out a human figure hovering over him.

And, once his burning eyes acclimated to the light, he realized that human was pointing a musket directly at his face.

"Hold your fire!!"

Arthur knew that voice. He squeezed his eyes shut so tightly that he saw red, praying that his brother's shout would prevent a bullet from being shot through his forehead.

A second silhouette appeared, this one more familiar than the first. Arthur was still bleary-eyed and disoriented, but he could clearly see Ramsey's deep hazel eyes glowering at him. It sent a sickening pang through his stomach, and he felt like a rat caught in a sewer drain.

"Get up here." Ramsey's tone was sharp. Arthur couldn't tell if it was an offer of mercy – it sounded more like an order. Ramsey didn't offer a hand or any form of assistance as Arthur struggled to crawl out of the burrow entrance. Instead, he just stood there, stiff-backed with his lips pressed in a tight line.

Arthur finished crawling out of the burrow and scrambled to his feet, trying to maintain some sense of dignity. He knew he looked like a wreck – his simple clothing was ragged and stained with dirt, and his stringy chestnut-brown hair clung to his sweaty forehead. But despite his own haggard appearance, Arthur couldn't hide his disgust at his brother's morbid regalia.

The scales glittered in the sun, each one catching bits of light and reflecting them like the facets of a perfectly cut diamond. It made Arthur's already steaming anger reach its boiling point, and it took every last bit of self-control to not charge his brother on sight.

But after a few deep breaths, he was able to calm himself enough to take in his surroundings. That was when he realized he's direly underestimated the extent of their siege. He expected Ramsey to be traveling with a few men, maybe a dozen... not hundreds. And they came prepared – bundles of pristine weapons, extensive barriers and fortifications, and even rows of spike traps that Arthur swore he could still see old bloodstains on.

Arthur turned back toward Ramsey, who still glared at him with unwavering eyes.

"What the hell is wrong with you?" Was all that Arthur could sputter in a hoarse voice.

"I could say the same." Ramsey raised an eyebrow, crossing his arms over his chest. "In fact, I've been saying it for a long time. You're delusional, Arthur, and this time you've gone way too far."

Ramsey paused for a moment, and his expression softened. His arms fell back toward his sides, and he forced a pained smile.

"But it's still not too late. Are you really going to forsake your own family for a bunch of beasts you can't understand and that villainous hybrid?"

The disgust in Ramsey's voice when mentioning Marissa sent fresh heat through Arthur's veins, but a sudden thought popped into his head. *The royal guard has no idea where the idol pieces are. They couldn't know for sure if there was one here, and they don't know that Marissa has two others...*

Which means...

Arthur gulped. They weren't here for the idol pieces. They were here for Marissa.

"Arthur, please," Ramsey stepped forward. "That half-reptilian... she's evil. She nearly killed a human. She's a threat to the kingdom, and needs to be disposed of. Please... just let us take her without a fight."

Pain seared through Arthur's face, and a burning rage caused his hands to coil into fists. Going after the idol pieces was one thing. Even evicting the Testudo from their territory was something he would expect from them. But this... this was personal. Anger dried up all remaining sense of fear. He was ready to fight his way through every soldier on this cursed battlefield if he had to.

But he would never let them take her.

"Arthur..." Ramsey's voice was gentle. Arthur could tell Ramsey was aware of the rage burning through his face. "Please... she's manipulating you."

"*ME?! I'M* the one that's being manipulated!?" Arthur exploded into a tirade. "Look at what the king has turned you into, Ramsey! This isn't you. Sure, you've always been a holier-than-thou priss, but you're not a killer. You really think you're going to be able to live with yourself if you slaughter an entire village of reptilians!?"

Ramsey paused for a moment.

"I won't have to." His expression hardened again, wearing the mask of callous indifference that Arthur feared King Gabriel had drilled into him. "Because I'll make you a deal. Hand over the half-reptilian girl, and I'll allow the Testudo time to evacuate. No one else will be harmed. How does that sound?"

It sounded inconceivable. Arthur would never sentence anyone – much less the woman he cared so deeply for – to such a certain death, no matter what the stakes. But it did give Arthur an idea.

He peered around. There were maybe three or four hundred soldiers scouring the scrublands around the burrows. They'd found both main entrances, making any sort of secret ambush nearly impossible. But the Testudo in the village below their feet outnumbered the soldiers by at least twofold. Arthur would never give up Marissa, but pretending to – at least for a little while – would buy them some time.

Time to prepare to put up a fight.

"Let me talk to her," Arthur requested. The burden of his mock betrayal, as necessary as it was, still sent stabbing pain through his chest. "Give me some time."

Ramsey was silent, but Arthur could see his brother's lower lip curl as he contemplated his request. Arthur took a deep breath, trying to look at earnest as possible and not wear his deceit on his sweat-stained face.

Ramsey held up a single finger. "You have one hour."

Arthur let go of the breath he'd been holding, letting a wave of relief cool his scorching veins.

"Just keep in mind," Ramsey continued. "You're surrounded by hundreds of soldiers, and we've already sealed off the tunnels. Don't even think about pulling any tricks."

"Of course." A lump of anxiety formed in Arthur's throat, but he quickly gulped it away. "I'll meet you back up here within the hour."

"Very well."

Before turning around to head back down the tunnel to Terrapin, Arthur took one last solemn glance at Ramsey. And he saw nothing. No expression whatsoever. His brother may as well have been replaced by a statue.

He sighed and shook his head, his shoes skidding on the soft dirt as he made his way back into the tunnel.

He couldn't worry about Ramsey. He had a much more dire situation to deal with.

MARISSA'S POUNDING HEART AND HEAVING LUNGS were exasperated by the time they made it back to Terrapin. But adrenalin kept her moving. It kept her scaled legs charging one after the other as she, Kai, and Tyrin dreaded what would await them back in the main village.

But all was still calm. Marissa noticed clusters of Testudo armed with daggers and crossbows gathering at the main tunnels, but the village itself meandered on as normal. Kai and Tyrin picked up speed as they noticed their parents waving them down near the gardens. As they got closer, Marissa saw Nathara and Thomas... but not Arthur.

<Where is he?> Marissa sputtered as she stopped in front of Nathara. The flood of adrenalin had dissipated, and Marissa nearly fell to her knees as she struggled to catch her breath. Everything burned; her arms, her legs, even her pounding head. She couldn't tell if it was exhaustion or fear... or both.

<He ran off,> Nathara huffed, shifting her glance over to the south tunnel. <It was right after he figured out that it was humans who found the burrow, not

reptilians. What in Squamata makes that boy think he could take on an entire army by himself?>

Marissa knew why. *Ramsey.* It would make sense to send Arthur's brother off to find him – the royal family probably thought Ramsey could persuade Arthur to come home. *But,* Marissa's thoughts took a sudden dark turn. *That's assuming that they want him to come home.*

Marissa knew little about the royal family, and she wasn't sure how unforgivable Arthur's actions had been in their eyes. And if they weren't looking for reconciliation, that meant Ramsey had far more sinister reasons for hunting down his brother.

It could be the idol pieces, Marissa reasoned. But she had no idea if they knew the Testudo had one, much less that Marissa had two.

The far more likely scenario...

Is that they're after me.

The sound of heaving footsteps and heavy breaths not unlike her own crept up behind her. Marissa spun around and was grateful to see Arthur standing behind her. He was an exhausted, dirty, sweaty wreck, but Marissa had to fight back the urge to engulf him in a relieved hug.

"Arthur," Marissa knelt next to him as he panted, bent over with his hands on his knees. "What happened up there?"

Arthur looked up, and his green eyes met hers. The mixture of anger, frustration, and pain swirling within them made Marissa's stomach churn.

"Tell them," Arthur wheezed in between breaths, pointing at Nathara and the Testudo. "That we're surrounded... both entrances blocked off. They must either... find a way to flee... or... put up a fight."

Marissa turned around, fear and disbelief weighing heavily on her blue eyes as she turned to face her reptilian companions. They were silent, eagerly awaiting her translation of Arthur's findings.

<We need to get out of here,> Marissa declared. <The humans have both main entrances heavily guarded... is there another tunnel to the surface somewhere?>

<Are you suggesting we flee?> Kai asked.

Marissa froze. She hadn't offered them the second option. Because in her mind, it wasn't a viable one. Not only would the Testudo inevitably lose some of their own to the humans' guns, but the tortoisefolk were staunch pacifists. Escaping seemed like the only choice.

But Kai's defiant tone told her otherwise.

<We will not abandon our home.> Gala stepped forward. <We refuse to let them drive us out of the burrow we've lived in for thousands of years.>

Kai clearly noticed Marissa's confusion, because he placed a giant palm on her petite shoulder. <I know we're seen as pacifists, Marissa. But being peaceful doesn't mean walking away from everything that's important to us. We're not ones to seek out a fight, but if left with no choice, we'll defend our home beak and claw.>

Kai's thoughts made Marissa put aside her apprehensions and think about the consequences of abandoning the burrow. The humans would seize all of Terrapin, tear it apart for its glowstone, and destroy everything that was sacred to the Testudo. Not to mention, where would they go? Leaving the burrow would make them even more vulnerable. Even if they fled, the humans would hunt them down eventually.

But the thought of fighting back still pained her. Even if they won, there would be death, something that Marissa had already seen enough of for one lifetime. She couldn't even begin to fathom losing Kai and his family, Nathara, Thomas... and especially Arthur. Just thinking of them lying lifeless and wide-eyed on the ground like the corpses in the Varan village nearly made her sink to her knees.

The only solution was to defend the burrow with such force that the humans would admit defeat before too many bodies piled up. And as Marissa peered around at the Testudo, with their tough skin and nearly impenetrable shells, she realized that they were an incredible force to be reckoned with.

<Indeed, we will.> Marissa smiled at Kai. <All of us. Together.>

Chapter 19

ONE HOUR TO PREPARE FOR WAR WASN'T nearly enough.

Terrapin was a flurry of activity, yet it was organized with militant order and structure. For being pacifists, the Testudo had an astonishing number of weapons. Daggers, spears, and crossbows were handed out from large stockpiles unearthed from within the village. Each one was intricately crafted from stone and wood and decorated with shells, teeth, and the colorful plumage of native birds. It made Marissa realize that Kai's words were true; pacifism meant not seeking out conflict, but being prepared to face it if necessary.

Kai insisted that Thomas reveal the contents of the cases in his cart, which he did with great hesitancy. Alda reacted with explosive anger, lunging at Thomas as Kai and Gala struggled to hold him back. But in his tirade, he made one thing clear – he wanted his less-than-welcome visitors gone.

That was when Kai countered with his own shouts about how foolish his father was to deny help when their village was about to be overrun. Alda calmed down, partially from being startled by Kai's sudden outburst. While the old Testudo refused to go anywhere near the guns, he reluctantly agreed for Thomas to teach his three sons how to shoot.

As they spent most of the hour practicing, shooting at targets that Thomas scratched in the cavern walls, Marissa watched with a nauseating sense of dread deep in her stomach. They only had six tiny pistols, which would be a drop of water compared to the royal guards' ocean of firearms. She wasn't sure if simple melee weapons and crossbows would be enough – she had to pray that the Testudo would still find a way to overpower the humans.

As Marissa watched, she noticed Arthur standing next to her, studying Thomas and the Testudo brothers with tense apprehension in his eyes. But Marissa could tell that this was more than just a shared worry. Something else was bothering him, and judging by how quiet he'd been since he came running back from his encounter with Ramsey, Marissa feared the worst.

Finally, with just fifteen minutes left, Marissa couldn't hold it in anymore.

"Something's wrong," she stated flatly as she turned toward Arthur, more an accusation than a question. Arthur kept watching Thomas and the Testudo, his gaze away from Marissa, but she could see a glimmer of worry in the corners of his eyes.

But he still refused to say anything.

"Arthur, tell me what's going on."

She knew that her tone was on the verge of being demanding, and in the back of her mind it pained her to do so. It seemed that the closer they became, the more Arthur pulled away. She missed the first few days they spent traveling together, two friendly, reptile-loving strangers getting to know each other, on a rocky yet grand adventure full of memories and mishaps. Before the whole valley erupted into chaos, and the emergence of *feelings* made everything so complicated.

Finally, Arthur flicked his eyes toward her, "Marissa, I can't..."

"Tell me!" Marissa cut him off. "What did Ramsey say to you up there? I know you're hiding something!"

Her reptilian nostrils flared, and she sniffled in a futile attempt to keep tears from rolling down her cheeks. Because the more Arthur denied it, the more the truth became apparent – this all had to do with her.

"They offered to let the Testudo evacuate." Arthur finally spoke after a few moments of silence, pain lacing his words. "They'd back down and let them leave."

"What did they want in exchange?" Marissa asked, because she knew it would never be that easy.

Arthur turned toward Marissa, and she could see her own barely-contained emotions reflected in his eyes.

He didn't need to reply. She already knew what they wanted.

She'd always assumed it, but now it was undeniable - she was being hunted by the royal guard. *And if they ever caught me...* they'd keep her alive for a while. Question her for information, torture her maybe... but death would be inevitable. And while the thought of being executed by the wicked reptilian-hating royal family sent ice through her veins, so did the thought of hundreds of Testudo being slaughtered trying to defend their home.

"But what if I did it?"

Arthur's brows furrowed in confusion.

"What if I gave myself up? Do you really think they'd let the Testudo live?"

Arthur was silent, his face slowly draining of color.

"They'd take me to the castle, wouldn't they? I'm sure I could find a way to escape before then. I could-"

"No, Marissa."

She froze, mouth hanging open, startled by the choking intensity in his voice.

"No. Don't be a pawn for my wretched brother. Even if I did trust his word..." He stepped closer, his eyes locked with Marissa's. "It will never end. The royal family is relentless, and they won't stop until they capture you. They want you dead, Marissa. I know I haven't always been honest with you, but I swear on every god, both human and reptilian... I will never, *ever* let them take you."

His last words were a whisper, barely holding back his anger. Overwhelmed by emotion, Marissa tossed aside her reservations about their relationship and pulled him into an embrace. It brought back all the same soul-soothing, stomach-fluttering emotions as the night before, but now Arthur gripped her far more intensely.

It nearly crushed her chest and made her arms go numb, but she only squeezed him back tighter. It was as if they both feared they'd never hold each other again.

That was when the impending tears finally slid down her cheeks. Not because of fear for Arthur, or the Testudo, or even for her own life. Instead, she cried tears of joy that someone finally cared so much about her. Her whole life, she'd felt like nothing but a burden at best, and a monster at worst. In all her years spent at the orphanage, she had a nagging feeling that Beatrice would easily discard her if not for the promise she'd made her husband on her deathbed. To hear the protective ferocity in Arthur's voice made her realize that no matter what happened, there was at least one person in the world that would stand unwavering by her side.

But as she lifted her face from Arthur's shoulder, she noticed more weapon-wielding Testudo charging toward the tunnels in neat yet hurried formations.

Their blatant yet complicated feelings for each other would once again have to wait.

And as Arthur broke their embrace, gazing deeply into her blue eyes with his hands still cupping the edges of her shoulders, his eyes reflected what Marissa already knew.

It was time.

She feared the worst, yet she refused to let it consume her mind. Arthur would survive. They all would. They would win.

They had to. Marissa couldn't fathom any other outcome.

Arthur leaned forward, and in a swift moment, brushed her thick bangs aside and placed a gentle kiss on her forehead. The feeling of his lips against her scales sent Marissa's soul reeling and electricity jolting through her veins. But before she could react, he was gone, jogging toward the lines of Testudo warriors like he was one of them.

Marissa was dumbfounded. Her head felt dizzy as her mind swirled with emotions so intense that it nearly made her nauseous. She wasn't ready for him to leave. She needed more time with him, to talk, to hug, to pour out all her suppressed emotions like a dam bursting after a storm.

But it would have to wait. Arthur, along with Thomas, Nathara, and the Testudo, had a battle to win. And Marissa, being the bounty that the guard was so determined to haul back to the palace, needed to stay hidden.

She took a deep breath, her reptilian nostrils flaring as she eyed the huts where the remaining Testudo had taken shelter.

They would win.

They had to.

ARTHUR COULDN'T SEE A THING.

The tunnel to the outside world was pitch-black, just as it was when he first went to confront Ramsey. Around him, he could hear and feel the marching Testudo who stood in formation next to him, ready to defend their home with their lives. Unlike humans, they had excellent night vision, and using a light source for the two measly humans in their party to see would only make them a bigger target.

They needed to work under the guise of darkness. But somehow, even in blinding conditions surrounded by reptilians he couldn't communicate with, he felt less anxious than when he went to confront his brother.

But he was still far from calm.

He curled his sweaty palm tighter around the gun in his left hand. Six paltry pistols were wielded by Arthur, Thomas, Nathara, Kai, Tyrin, and Peri. They stood in the second row of combatants, behind the largest and strongest of the Testudo warriors. Instead of crossbows like their comrades behind them, those on the very front lines were armed with spears. Between those and their massive shells, they would form a barrier to protect the others, and allow those with long-ranged weapons to fire through the gaps in their defenses.

When they explained it all earlier, Marissa had translated it as something called "Testudo formation", which Thomas swore was an ancient tactic used by knights in the early days of Brennan. It made Arthur wonder what sort of relationship the humans and reptilians had so many centuries ago, before the valley erupted into war.

The sound of the Testudo's heavy, stomping footfalls came to a stop, and Arthur froze in place. He didn't need to see to know where they were – he could sense the ceiling of the tunnel just a few feet above their heads.

Which meant the entrance was just ahead of them.

More shuffling sounds erupted as the Testudo took their positions. Arthur did the same, kneeling behind one of the Testudo in front of him as he struggled to load his pistol in the darkness. Those on the front lines had turned around, using their rugged shells as giant shields to protect the others.

It brought a small grin of satisfaction to Arthur's face. *Let's see you try to break through that, brother.*

As the Testudo finishing arranging themselves into position, silence settled over the band of warriors like a dampening blanket. And it allowed the voices above their heads to break through – soft, blurry shouts, muddled as if they were underwater. But Arthur could hear his name mentioned several times, and every utterance caused his racing heart to pick up speed.

Then it happened. The ground some fifty feet beyond them began to slide away, sending blinding white sunlight down into the jet-black tunnel.

Arthur could barely breathe. His heartbeat was all he could hear, as it hammered in his chest and trailed up into his eardrums until it nearly deafened him. The muffled shout was now clear – Arthur's brother was calling his name.

To Arthur's surprise, a lone figure dropped into the tunnel, just a black silhouette in the blinding sunlight. He prayed it wasn't Ramsey, but his reluctant heart knew it couldn't be anyone else.

"I thought we had a deal, brother." Ramsey's voice echoed through the tunnel.

Arthur knew that to Ramsey, he was being greeted by nothing. The band of several hundred Testudo warriors were still shielded by darkness further down the tunnel.

Arthur's heart sank as he realized that despite Ramsey's wicked behavior, he was still being true to at least one element of himself – he was upholding his deal. Arthur knew that his stubborn yet naïve brother was fully expecting Arthur to walk up and greet him like nothing was wrong.

He wasn't expecting an ambush. And no amount of anger at Ramsey's actions would prevent Arthur from fearing for his brother's life. Because right now, he was a lone, vulnerable target facing an invisible army of hundreds.

But then he stepped forward, his scale-mail armor now bathed in a ray of sunlight. And even in the silent darkness, Arthur could feel the Testudo's shock and anger spreading like a plague. The secret was out, and something about seeing their fellow reptilians' corpses used against them released a rage that Arthur didn't know the Testudo had. It was as if it had always been there, dormant but lingering like the remains of a once massive fire. Eight hundred years of living in quiet seclusion had dampened it, reducing it to mere embers. But now it was back, flames roaring with a vengeance.

Arthur squeezed his eyes shut, feeling like his galloping heart was about to burst.

Testudo, please, I beg you... don't shoot him.

"Arthur." Ramsey's voice echoed again, and Arthur's stomach lurched at his brother's plea. Ramsey took another step forward, further illuminating the scales.

Please... don't shoot...

But Arthur knew it was futile from the moment they saw Ramsey's horrid armor.

He knew that now, the Testudo wouldn't let a single soldier escape alive.

Especially this one.

The whiz of a crossbow bolt escaping its holster shot through the darkness, and Arthur watched helplessly as the bolt tore through the air, embedding itself into the edge of Ramsey's neck with a thin spray of blood.

He collapsed. Arthur fought back a muffled scream. The battle had begun.

The soldiers streamed in in like sand through an hourglass. At first it was a slow trickle, but it quickly ramped up into an avalanche that cascaded into the tunnel.

Arthur watched helplessly as Ramsey was dragged up to the surface, the bolt still protruding from his neck as blood encircled the entry wound. The cracks of gunshots and the whizzes of crossbow bolts stirred to life around him, the murderous hum of battle just like the night in Canterbury. The same flashes of fire and smoke in the darkness, the same synchronized shouts permeated by the anguished howls of the wounded.

No wonder the villagers drank themselves into a stupor that night. Arthur crouched down low, just barely able to see the battle out of one eye. The guard soldiers were still pouring in and setting up their firing lines. The few in the front who were better prepared fired off the first stream of bullets, but they bounced off the Testudo's shield-like shells with barely a scratch.

Arthur knew that their unpreparedness for an ambush was solely Ramsey's fault. Arthur was certain that his stubborn, disgustingly obedient, naive fool of a brother had expected him to march back up the tunnel and embrace his reptilian-hating family again. Ramsey had never expected Arthur to launch an ambush on his own brother.

He doesn't have the proper mentality for the royal guard, Arthur huffed as he struggled to load his gun in the hazy darkness. *Or to be king. His idealism prevents him from seeing through blatant deception.*

But through Arthur's disgusted thoughts, he was also relieved. His prayers had been somewhat answered – Ramsey was shot, but it wasn't a lethal hit, and being injured meant that he was likely being dragged off toward the apothecary tent.

Ramsey was out of the battle. Which meant Arthur didn't have to worry about eventually stumbling upon his corpse.

He shook his head, tossing his futile worries about Ramsey out of his mind. *Focus.* He poked his head around one of the front-line Testudo's shells, caught a glimpse of a musket-wielding soldier whose gun was pointed almost directly at Arthur's head, and fired.

As the puff of smoke settled, he saw a spray of blood fly out of the man's chin as his head reeled back, his neck nearly snapping from the impact. He collapsed, his half-loaded musket plopping into the dirt, and Arthur clenched his jaw to keep from retching.

He'd fired a gun dozens of times, but always at inanimate targets. As a teen, it always sent a surge of victory through his chest when he hit a metal lizard straight in the head.

Here, it felt like torture. Arthur took a few deep breaths to settle the nausea in his stomach and prepared to reload his pistol.

He didn't have time to ponder morality. In the midst of battle, it was kill or be killed.

So far, the Testudo's defenses were holding strong. Both combatants were arranged in firing lines spanning about fifty feet apart, with neither side gaining much ground. The Testudo's wall of shells were impenetrable, but the human soldiers were able to keep a consistent enough stream of firepower that driving them out of the tunnel was impossible.

As more and more soldiers filed in, Arthur swore that the synchronized gunshots got louder. The Testudo in front of him winced as a particularly well-aimed bullet scuffed the very top of his shell.

With his gun now reloaded, Arthur poked his head back out again, exposing it to the smoke-soaked air of the battlefield. Through the haze, he took aim at a soldier who dared to take a step closer to the Testudo's defenses. Arthur only managed to hit him in the upper thigh, but it was still enough to cause him to crumple into the dirt, now badly injured and vulnerable to the Testudo's stream of crossbow bolts.

Within seconds, the guard was a very dead pincushion. Arthur turned away, his stomach once again roiling at the merciless gore of battle.

As the seconds ticked like hours, Arthur continued the pattern: reload, aim, fire. Several more shots cracked through the smoky haze, each one a hit – he'd still retained his father's impeccable training. But with every shot, his anxiety deepened, the sickening burn in his stomach reminding him that this would all haunt him in his sleep that night. He'd have to live with himself after all this. After all, he was human, and so were they. And not just any humans - these were elite guard members, sworn to protect the royal family. *His* family.

But then he thought of Marissa, and protective instincts shoved his guilt deep into the back of his subconscious. Because no matter how much it pained him to end their lives, they'd drag Marissa off to have hers ended in an instant. And unlike him, they wouldn't have even a shred of remorse.

So he kept firing. The guards' side of the battlefield was now speckled with bodies, lying lifeless next to the steely-faced soldiers who were still loading their weapons. More soldiers poured from the entrance, but now their sole purpose to drag away the injured before they perished. Those still firing struggled to keep their focus, their tense faces wincing at the cries of the wounded. Arthur swore he could see nervous sweat beading across their pale faces, especially the youngest ones. Some of the recruits barely looked eighteen.

The Testudos' side was still holding, but barely. With the battle now in full force, the humans had hauled larger, higher-caliber muskets down into the tunnel. While the smaller bullets bounced harmlessly off the Testudo's shells, these more powerful muskets were starting to make an impact. The Testudo winced and stumbled with each shot, with the larger bullets scraping or sometimes even partially embedding themselves in the tortoises' shells. But despite the pain in their reptilian faces, they never faltered. They held steady, hunching closer together and grasping each others' clawed hands to reinforce their barrier.

Because the fate of their entire burrow rested in their hands. If they failed, the humans would overrun them.

Arthur took a moment to calm himself. *Breathe in through your nose, out through your mouth.* After a few meditative breaths, he felt a renewed sense of confidence. The humans' firing line was thinning as more and more injured were hauled away.

We can do this. He reassured himself, and his hammering heart started to believe it. *We can win.*

Arthur took a few moments to tuck behind the Testudo and reload his weapon when a low rumble caught his attention. He looked up, and his stomach nearly dropped out of his abdomen.

A cannon.

He swallowed, trying to force the nervous lump out of his throat. A half-dozen guards were struggling to roll the massive weapon into the tunnel, which would at least buy them some time. Arthur turned toward Thomas, and noticed that he had the same earth-shattering fear in his eyes.

The Testudo, despite the noticeable anxiety on their reptilian faces, kept firing. Two well-timed crossbow bolts knocked two of the guards to their knees, nearly causing the cannon to topple over. But they were quickly dragged away, and two new guards replaced them.

"What do we do?" Arthur heard Thomas ask, barely masking the terror in his voice.

Arthur had no answer. His mouth hung open, wordless, unable to utter a sound. It made him realize how foolish he'd been. *How did we think we would ever stand a chance against them?*

In the distance, in the blinding light of the entrance, Arthur saw a second cannon slowly being hauled into the tunnel.

It was over. The whole burrow was about to be overrun. The cannons would blow through the Testudos' barrier in an instant – and leave a massive trail of dead in its wake.

"We have to run," Arthur declared, his shaky hands struggling to slip his pistol back into its holster.

"What about them?" Thomas raised an eyebrow and gestured toward the Testudo. The tortoisefolk were still firing, desperate to pick off the humans before they finished setting up the cannon. Arthur wasn't sure if they understood the full danger of the massive weapons or were too stubborn to care. After all, they were defending their home, the only world that many of the tortoisefolk had ever known.

To them, fleeing may not have been an option.

Arthur tried to scream. "Run! Please, run!!"

He flailed his arms, doing whatever he could to get the attention of the Testudo around him. But it was no use. Not only could they not understand him, but they seemed adamant on standing their ground. The sound of a whizzing bullet cracked a bit too close to Arthur's head, and he fell to the ground, crouching behind another

Testudo. By making a racket, Arthur was only making himself a bigger target for the royal guard.

He peered back up. The cannons were now in place and being prepped to fire. The Testudo had already picked off all six of the original soldiers handling the cannon, but it didn't matter. Six more had replaced them within seconds.

Arthur clasped his hands to his head. *No. It can't be this hopeless.*

The soldiers had finished dumping a hefty load of gunpowder into the cannon, followed by a cloth wad and, finally, a cannonball the size of a large navel orange.

"Arthur, we gotta run."

Arthur turned to his right. Thomas's face was sweat-stained, sallow, and coated with dirt. His light brown eyes were grave with hopelessness and defeat.

Arthur opened his mouth to speak, and Thomas cut him off. "We ain't got time, Arthur. We have'ta go, now!"

Arthur took a step back, peering over his shoulder. A soldier had lit the fuse on top if the cannon. It's loud, sizzling hiss echoed through the tunnel.

Like an angry snake.

About to strike.

"Arthur, now!!"

He peeled his eyes away from the harrowing scene and bolted, refusing to look back. He charged full-force down the tunnel, away from the battle, all while that horrible hiss echoed through his ears.

Gods... please... no...

After a few seconds, he hurled himself into the dirt, landing on his stomach and curling his body into a ball with his hands wrapped over his head and neck.

Please...

The explosion shattered everything – the tunnel walls, Arthur's ears, and what remained of his frayed nerves. A shower of dirt and glowstone flecks sprayed Arthur's back as he curled himself into a tighter ball, waiting for his ears to stop ringing. Swarms of the Testudo fled past his curled-up body in a sea of stomping reptilian feet. He shifted his hand so that he could see out of one eye. The explosion had nearly given him a heart attack, but what scared him even more was what came after.

The silence. The silence of those who lay limp at the smoldering blast site, their limbs bent at odd angles and their shells shattered into bloody pieces. They were half-covered in dirt, as the blast had caused one of the tunnel walls to partially collapse.

Arthur had no idea if the Testudo chieftain, chieftress, and their sons were among them. The pile of bodies was so mangled that it was difficult to tell where one Testudo ended and another began. But Arthur had no time to search for them – a scaled hand yanked him upright, pulling him out of his shell-shocked trance.

It was Nathara. As Arthur peered up at the towering Naga above him, he noticed her face was streaked with blood. Yet he had no idea if it was her own.

Her other scaled hand latched onto Thomas, who like Arthur was shell-shocked and covered with debris. Arthur felt Nathara nearly yank his arm out of its socket as she slithered forward in a mad serpentine dash. Her human companions' legs struggled to keep up, but Nathara refused to slow down.

And Arthur was grateful for it. With the Testudo's defenses blown wide open, a tidal wave of armed soldiers swarmed into the tunnel. They charged for the main cavern, picking off any Testudo that got in their way with a slash of their bayonets. Arthur watched as one bold Testudo attempted to wrestle a musket out of a soldier's hands. The clever tortoise used its massive arms as shields, tucking its head into its shell each time the soldier tried to swipe at its neck.

But Arthur didn't have time to assist, or even find out who came out victorious. The tunnel was getting brighter, meaning that they were almost to Terrapin. Nathara continued to desperately drag her friends, the mysterious blood on her face dripping down her scaled brow. Arthur peered over at Thomas, who was red-faced, wheezing, and struggling to keep his feet under him. Arthur feared that if Nathara let him go, he'd collapse.

And as the dark tunnel gave way to the massive cavern and Arthur's adrenalin started to slow, he feared he would too.

But as soon as Nathara released her iron grip on his arm, he bolted. Terrapin was in absolute mayhem, with the residents' fear erupting into panic as they saw the Testudo warriors return from the front lines.

They had failed. The royal guard had pushed its way into Terrapin, and everyone would be forced to flee.

But Arthur refused to dwell on it. To him, only one thing mattered.

He had to find her before they did.

Chapter 20

ARISSA SAT IN PAINFUL SILENCE, WITH ONLY the tense breaths of her fearful Testudo companions humming in her ears. At least a dozen of them were crammed into this particular mud-brick hut, with most of them hunkered down in the corners with their limbs and heads tucked into their shells. Marissa noticed a few of them trembling.

She was crouched low, just below the only window in the hut, her body shielded by a fearfully curious Testudo that stared longingly out the window. *Waiting,* Marissa assumed. *For them to come back victorious.*

But Marissa couldn't bear to look outside. She tried her best to calm her frayed nerves, mainly by relaxing her muscles and taking deep breaths. Nim tightened his grip on her neck, and the pressure felt like a weighted blanket on her shoulders. She closed her soft blue eyes, and forced her worried mind to drift somewhere more peaceful.

Thankfully, that wasn't difficult. The sweet, intoxicating burn of Arthur's kiss still seared through her forehead. She could still feel their painful embrace, full of worry and desperation and tears. Every bone in her body ached to hold him again, but for now, at least now she knew the truth. He unabashedly, undeniably had feelings for her. That alone was enough to make her lonely, dejected heart flutter for a lifetime.

But it all came crashing down every time their current, unsettling reality crept back into her thoughts. Because right now, the man who had set her emotions on fire was on the front lines of a battle that he may not survive. *Stop it,* Marissa hissed to herself, attempting to calm the anxiety bubbling in her stomach. *Stop thinking about that. They will survive. They will win.*

For now, all they could do was wait, and it was tearing Marissa apart. Raw, cold-blooded fear had a chokehold on her stomach and was snaking its way up her throat. The minutes stretched out like hours, and she was painfully aware of every passing second. With every breath, her chest became tighter, and the aching pulse of her heartbeat became more palpable. She'd never felt such intense anxiety in her life.

Please, she begged, over and over again until her head began to pound. *Gods, please, keep them safe. Bring them back alive.*

A faint rumbling noise erupted from the north entrance, just a few hundred yards away. Up until now,

Marissa had no idea what was happening. She assumed that the battle was taking place at the entrance to the burrow, as that's where the Testudo had planned their ambush. It meant that the tunnel had been a silent, dark vacuum, giving no indication of who was winning or losing.

But that was all about to change. As the first few Testudo charged out of the tunnel, all of Marissa's paltry hopes fell to the bottom of her stomach like a rock.

It was unmistakable; they were fleeing. The humans had broken through their barriers.

They'd lost.

More and more Testudo swarmed out of the tunnel. The charging rumble of their heavy footfalls was terrifying enough, but what really sucked the air from Marissa's lungs were the noises further back in the tunnel.

Screams. Anguished, painful, grisly screams. They flooded her mind until her entire skull, from the crown of her head to the top of her temples, throbbed like a raging storm. She clasped her aching forehead with both palms, struggling to see out the single hut window as the crammed-in Testudo fled in a ruckus of stomping feet. As more Testudo emerged from the tunnel, she noticed that some had bloody wounds, which made her own blood chill in her veins.

Her reptilian nostrils flared as she took in a few heaving, anxious breaths. But she kept her focus, scanning the crowd with intense eyes. All she could see were Testudo, but she kept scanning, praying that she would find two humans and a Naga among them.

A minute passed. Still nothing. She was now alone in the hut, standing still amidst a sea of fleeing tortoise-folk. In the distance, the first few royal soldiers charged out of the tunnel.

Looking for her.

Her stomach lurched – she felt like a very exposed, vulnerable mouse in a pit full of snakes. She had to find Arthur, Thomas, and Nathara – not just to ensure their safety, but also her own. The chances of her escaping the royal guard alone were slim.

"MARISSA!!"

Her initial reaction was to duck underneath the window at lightning speed, but she quickly realized that the voice was far too familiar and full of relief to be the royal guard trying to capture her.

A few seconds later, Arthur appeared in the doorway. He was even more of a wreck than he was when he first went to confront his brother – his once pristine white shirt was torn, exposing his curly-haired chest, and his wiry glasses were bent, nearly dangling off his filthy face. But as soon as Marissa saw him, she launched herself into his arms, almost toppling him over as she fought back tears of relief.

He was alive. And seemingly uninjured. His shaking, clammy hands wrapped around her back, and for a moment she blocked out the chaos around them as she melted into his arms.

But their embrace was short-lived. Nathara and Thomas quickly appeared behind Arthur, with Thomas panting heavily and Nathara wiping blood off her face with the back of her scaled hand. Her joyous reunion with them could wait – they needed to find a way to escape.

Marissa poked her head outside, wrapping her fingers around the doorframe. At first glance, the village was chaos, with Testudo shouting and charging in all directions. A few of them even tripped over each other, with mothers carrying their hatchlings so they'd avoid being trampled. But as Marissa watched, she noticed that many of the Testudo were filing into disorderly lines being some of the huts. They jostled past each other, shells scraping as they all struggled to be next in line.

Next in line to descend into a hole barely larger than they were.

Escape routes. Marissa pulled Arthur towards her and pointed. She could tell by the tense expression on his face that he had the same concerns she did. Nathara was taller than the Testudo, but Marissa and her three human companions were much smaller and lighter than the bulky tortoises. Marissa's stomach tightened at the thought of being trampled under the Testudos' hefty frames.

But as Marissa peered around, it didn't seem like they had a choice. The royal guard now had at least a hundred soldiers scouring through Terrapin, with the booming racket of bullets continuously shaking the cavern walls. Those who fought back or managed to evade the bullets received bayonet blades to the neck. The royal guard clearly did not intend on letting any of them live.

Raw anger burned her throat as she realized why. When she was at the black market less than a week ago, there were hundreds of hides for sale. Naga, Varan, Gharian... but not a single Testudo. Now the tortoise-folk had been found after centuries of hiding, and Marissa knew that the humans had orders to scavenge every resource they could.

Including a massive supply of their bullet-resistant shells. Marissa's nostrils flared in disgust.

For a moment, fiery rage consumed her veins, and she wished she could bolt out of the hut and bite every single one of them. But she knew that would be a death sentence. Claiming the Testudos' territory and seizing their hides for armor was just a sickening coincidence. Marissa was still the true prize.

"Come on, Marissa," Arthur gently tugged her arm. She turned around, and noticed Thomas and Nathara attempting to wedge their way through a window at the back of the hut. "We have to go."

Her heartbeat galloped in her chest. She knew Arthur was right, yet she couldn't pull herself away from the grisly scene. Escaping with the others felt like abandonment for those who were falling victim to the royal guard. Whether from a bullet or a blade, Marissa noticed their deaths weren't always quick. Several limp bodies lingered outside the huts, moaning in pain and barely able to lift their heads. One of them had a massive crack at the bottom of their shell.

There would be no one to help them. There was no time.

Marissa bit her lip to keep from letting out a pained cry. There were also so many questions left unanswered.

Where were Kai and his brothers? The chieftain and chieftress?

And Mata...

Her eyes flicked over to a spot on the far side of the cavern, where Marissa knew Mata was hiding several hundred feet below them. She was likely still safe down there, tucked away in her little cottage... at least for now. *Once the royal guard seizes Terrapin, how long could she stay in hiding? Will they ever find her?*

A faint whisp of relief settled in Marissa's chest as she noticed one of the crossbow-brandishing Testudo charging toward the entrance to Mata's tunnel. As he knelt down to open the entrance, Marissa noticed a deep gouge across the side of his cheek.

Mata is going to get help. Everything will be okay.

The reassurance did little to sway Marissa's fear, but at least now she could fathom escaping without being overwhelmed with guilt. She turned back toward Arthur, who was repeatedly pleading with her to follow, when a sudden screeching hiss rattled her thoughts.

She looked up, and her stomach nearly fell out of her abdomen as she saw a royal guard member slash the crossbow-wielding Testudo across the throat. The giant tortoisefolk collapsed, a river of blood trailing from its neck, as the guard member peered down the tunnel entrance and ushered toward several of their fellow soldiers.

No. No no no. The single panicked thought rang like an alarm bell in Marissa's mind. She attempted to charge out of the hut, throwing her own safety out the window, when a sharp tug on her bicep pulled her back.

"Mata! They're after her!!" Marissa cried out in panic and pointed at the tunnel entrance as Arthur attempted to restrain her. They both watched in horror as several guard members filed into the narrow tunnel.

Marissa peered up at Arthur, and he wore the expression she'd dreaded to see – pained hopelessness for Mata combined with fear for Marissa's safety. Despite the horrid scene, Arthur refused to let go of Marissa's arm.

"Please," she uttered in a soft whisper, raising a hand to brush Arthur's dirt-stained, sweaty hair out of his face. "I have to do this."

Arthur bit his lip in distressed contemplation. They'd been through this many times before – Marissa recklessly putting her safety on the line to help someone else, and Arthur begging her not to do it. But this time, Arthur seemed to realize that there was no talking her out of this.

"I'll go with you," Arthur declared, running outside the hut and swiping a dagger from a fallen Testudo. He quickly inspected the blade before tucking it into its sheath as his waist.

As Arthur gazed off into the distance, his eyes locked on the open tunnel entrance, Marissa grabbed his hand and squeezed it tight.

"I promise I won't let go," Marissa whispered as Arthur turned toward her.

He gave her hand a final squeeze, took a deep breath, and the pair charged toward the burrows. As they ran, Marissa prayed to the reptilian gods to keep Mata safe until they arrived.

And to keep her from being captured, as she and Arthur ran straight into the hands of the enemy.

RAMSEY COULD HEAR THE COMMOTION OF BATTLE in the background, several hundred feet away from the healer's tent. The shouts and blasts were faint and muffled, but they still barraged his ears as an apothecary carefully applied orange paste to and bandaged his wound.

He hadn't even flinched when she removed the arrow. Living in the palace his whole life, he'd never received such a nasty injury before. But his mind was swamped with too many emotions to acknowledge the pain.

Several other guards sat around the tent, being treated for minor injuries. They chatted and laughed as two cannons were lowered into the tunnel, and cheers erupted across the entire field as the guards successfully broke through the tortoises' firing lines.

"Those shelled bastards never stood a chance," one of the guards, the only female in the tent, sneered. "They probably thought they had the upper hand until we lowered the cannons in there. What fools."

Fools, Ramsey huffed. No one mentioned that his brother was among them. Which was fine with Ramsey, because his breakfast began to creep back up his throat every time he thought about it. He peered over at the neighboring tent, where the more gravely wounded lay motionless in apothecary cots. There was no chatter and laughter for them. But at least they would most likely survive, unlike the bodies that were hauled out of the dark abyss and loaded into mortuary carts.

Minutes passed as more and more guards filed into the tunnel. As they did, the sounds of gunfire slowed, then stopped. Ramsey assumed it was because they were now so far underground that their musket fire could no longer be heard on the surface.

Eventually, as their victory became more decisive, guards began making their way back up the tunnel. They carried belongings that weren't theirs – Testudo jewelry, garments, and weapons that they waved around like trophies. The objects were beautiful and finely crafted, but they served little purpose to the royal guard – the soldiers simply took them because they could. Because to them, looting the bodies of those they'd defeated was fun.

"Ramsey, you genius bastard!" A high-ranking soldier with curly blonde hair, one that Ramsey recognized but couldn't remember the name of, plopped down on a bench next to him. He snapped his fingers at one of the healers, pointing to a gash on his upper bicep.

The blonde soldier ruffled Ramsey's shoulder with his non-injured arm, "You're never going to believe what they found down there. Not only did all the turtles flee, but their whole cave is full of glowstone deposits!"

"Tortoises."

"What?"

"They're tortoises, not turtles."

The soldier sneered, "Who cares? Anyway, do you realize what this means, Ramsey? We no longer have to go beyond the mountain to mine glowstone – we've claimed a massive trove of the stuff! This has to be one of the greatest accomplishments of any king in recent history! Or, well, future king in your case."

Ramsey was silent, but he still managed to force a smile and head nod.

"His Majesty is going to be thrilled. I wouldn't be surprised if he throws another banquet to celebrate your achievement. Our achievement. All of us are going to be remembered as heroes... wait, Ramsey, where are you going?"

Ramsey stumbled off toward the forest, as far away from the battle and the prattling guard as he could. His neck wasn't fully healed, and wouldn't be for another few hours, and pain throbbed through his collarbone with every footstep.

This has to be one of the greatest accomplishments of any king in recent history!

Ramsey knelt down next to a tree, clutching his aching neck.

His Majesty is going to be thrilled.

Blood leaked through the gauze and onto his fingers. He took a few deep breaths through his mouth and squeezed his eyes shut.

All of us are going to be remembered as heroes.

It was no use. He toppled over, palms against the ground, steadying his limp body as he vomited until his stomach had nothing left to give.

It didn't help. He still felt sick. He feared he'd feel sick for the rest of his life.

What have I done?

MARISSA AND ARTHUR MANAGED TO MAKE IT TO the tunnel entrance and seal it shut before any other guard members crept inside.

By their estimates, there should've been five guards already inside the tunnel. The first one was easily taken care of – Arthur pre-loaded his pistol before they descended, and a single bullet to the chest sent the guard plummeting to the ground in a pool of blood.

Marissa let out a pained yelp, covering her mouth with her hands to prevent the other guards from hearing her. She peered over at Arthur, and he gave a heavy sigh. *He's been doing this for hours*, Marissa noted as Arthur took the few seconds of silence in the tunnel to reload. His hands shook as he fumbled with the powder horn and bullets, and Marissa wished she could've been more help. Not only was she in a sealed tunnel with those who wished to capture her, but she had no weapon other than her own fangs and the agitated carpet python around her neck.

Thankfully, Arthur noticed this, and he unwound the dagger from his waist and handed it to Marissa.

"Stay behind me." he ushered Marissa back as he took the lead, his gun pointed down the tunnel and ready to fire as they inched forward.

The tunnel seemed even darker than when Marissa ventured down it with Kai. They crept further down the narrow tunnel, with Arthur having to duck his head because of his height. As they got closer to the entrance to Mata's home, they heard faint rumbles and shouts, the voices too muddled to comprehend.

Despite the danger, Arthur and Marissa were hesitant to run. They stepped forward in tense, defensive postures, Arthur's tall, thin frame shielding Marissa from any unexpected guard members. Marissa could hear his ragged breathing and see the sweat rolling down his neck, and she bit her lip in pained sympathy. She couldn't even begin to fathom the hellish nightmare he'd seen back at the entrance to Terrapin.

As they got closer, the mumbled shouts began to form into words. But just as Marissa began to process them, a booming crack erupted that caused her to instinctively duck. As the smoke settled and her teeth stopped chattering, she looked up and realized that she and Arthur were uninjured.

Arthur's hand trembled as he lowered his gun, revealing another dying soldier grasping at their bloody abdomen. Marissa swallowed to force her stomach contents back down her throat. A second guard saw his companion go down, and the burly soldier charged with a roaring shout.

Panic zapped through Marissa's veins like electricity. Arthur didn't have time to reload his gun, and the guard unsheathed a very long, sharp sword as he ran, pointing it straight at Arthur's heart. Marissa's own felt like it was about to explode out of her chest.

She had to protect him.

She lunged in front of Arthur, nearly shoving him to the ground in the process, and ducking her head low to avoid the impact of the sword. The guard's blade whizzed past her cheek just as she plunged her dagger into his stomach with all the force she could muster, letting out a panicked scream in the process. The guard screeched in pain, his sword falling from his outstretched hand and clattering to the ground at Arthur's feet.

The guard winced, sinking to his knees, but he clearly wasn't done fighting. Without taking her eyes off the guard, Marissa reached behind her and attempted to feel around for the sword.

The guard lurched forward, still on his knees, as he pulled his musket off his shoulder and pointed its bladed tip at Marissa's chest. Marissa stepped back as he got closer, but just as her palm managed to wrap around the hilt of the sword, the guard lunged forward and wrapped a thick, sweaty forearm around her neck. The sword slipped from her fingers as the guard pulled her upwards.

Arthur staggered to his feet, fury brewing in his green eyes as he grabbed the sword off the ground.

"It's alright, Arthur. No need fer rash actions." The guard uttered in a gruff voice as Marissa squirmed. Nim let out a hiss - his head was pinned against Marissa's neck, making him unable to move.

"She really worth yer life?" The guard grimaced, but Arthur refused to budge, his sword still pointed at the guard's chest. "I'll make ya a deal – let me bring the scale-faced mutt to the king, and I'll let ya live."

Panic scorched through Marissa's body as the oxygen slowly left it. As the guard's arm pressed deeper against her neck, she watched Arthur through bleary eyes. He was exhausted, barely able to stand, yet the rage in his eyes never faltered.

Marissa knew what that meant; to him, surrendering wasn't an option. Horror choked her throat as she feared that she was about to watch him be torn apart.

No... Please...

For a split second, the guard loosened his grip on Marissa's neck, and she sank her fangs into his hairy forearm.

"Gahhh!!" he screeched, jerking his bloody arm away. Releasing Marissa's arm also allowed Nim to move his head again, which he promptly used to deliver a venom-filled strike to the guard's throat.

Arthur stepped forward, hell-bent on driving his plundered sword directly through the wounded guard's chest as he writhed on the ground. But Marissa grabbed Arthur's hand and dragged him further down the tunnel – they didn't have time for petty vengeance.

Nim's venom would take care of that for them.

Marissa could see the large, rounded door that led to Mata's home. She knew there were two guards left, and there was no sign of them. *Which means they must be inside.* Her stomach twisted as she stopped in front of the door, wrapping her shaking fingers around the handle.

"Wait," Arthur whispered, grabbing his powder horn off his shoulder and kneeling down. "Let me reload, and I'll go first."

It took less than a minute for Arthur to load his pistol, yet to Marissa it felt like an eternity. She stood motionless with her eyes locked on the door, her palm beginning to sweat as she gripped the handle with enough force to turn her knuckles white.

"There," Arthur stood up. "Stay behind me."

The door crept open, revealing dark, ominous silence. The swirling murals on the wall no longer glowed, leaving behind dull, lifeless gouges in the dirt. They tried to remain quiet, but the squeaky door hinges made that difficult. Marissa winced as the slowly-opening door continued to groan behind them.

<Kai?>

Mata's voice felt even more frail than before.

<Kai? Is that you?>

Marissa's heart lurched. She had no idea if Kai was even still alive.

<No, Mata,> Marissa's thoughts shook. <It's me, Marissa.>

She and Arthur stepped forward, toward the dull light emanating from the other room. Upon entering Mata's bedroom, they realized the light was coming from an oil lamp plopped on the ground in the center of the room. One that was clearly human-made.

Arthur stepped around the room, keeping his pistol steady and ready to fire with every cautious step. Marissa's head spun wildly around as she tried to locate Mata. The oil lamp barely provided any light, leaving most of the eerie room cloaked in shadows. With hesitant fingers, Marissa plucked the lamp off the ground and held it in front of her face. But she nearly dropped it on the floor when she saw the blood trail.

Her throat burned as she clamped a hand over her mouth, desperately holding back a scream. The trail snaked behind the cushion where Mata had been knitting earlier. They found her slumped in the far corner, most of her body tucked into her shell. As Marissa's lantern illuminated her face, Mata's milky eyes glistened with pain.

<Mata!!> Marissa's knees sunk into the dirt as she placed her hands on the back of Mata's shell. The old Testudo struggled to turn over, and when she did, Marissa saw the gaping wound that cut through her plastron.

Marissa grimaced, her mind reeling at the thought of what sort of horrid weapon would be capable of gouging through the front of a Testudo's shell.

<We need to get you out of here,> Marissa declared, pulling on Mata's arm. <I know it's going to be hard, but we need to get you help.>

<Marissa... no.>

Her thoughts were barely a whisper. Marissa's face fell, her grip loosening on Mata's arm.

<I've lived a long life,> Mata continued, the life slowly draining from her thoughts. <Longer than any reptilian... to walk this valley. But I've spent so much time... in hiding... too long. I won't hide any longer.>

As Mata's thoughts pulsed into Marissa's head, so did the electricity across the Testudo's skin, its sparkling glow illuminating the entire room. Arthur's eyes went wild with astonishment, causing him to relax his tense posture and lower his pistol.

<Mata... please... no... we'll get you help...>

<There's no time,> The sparks across Mata's skin grew in brightness and intensity. <She's... she's coming

for you, Marissa. This power dies with me... I won't let her... win.>

A sudden spark shocked Marissa's hand, and she released her grip on Mata's arm.

<Go,> Mata declared, pointing a shaking claw at the tunnel behind her. <You must... stop them... leave me here...>

The tunnel... Marissa looked up. The glow of Mata's sparkling skin had illuminated the door to the closet where the three idol pieces were stored.

The door that was currently cracked open.

<I can't just leave you,> Marissa pleaded, a single tear running down her face and plopping into the dirt.

Mata took a deep, heaving breath, and her eyes began to close.

<Tell my grandsons... I love them...>

A final, crackling blast of electricity blinded Marissa, and she struggled to scramble away from the sparks. They seemed to charge after her, creeping across the ground like a horde of angry spiders.

Marissa's own anger pounded in her eardrums as she darted around the room. The sparks crawled up walls and furniture, jumping the gaps between chairs and tables. Marissa kept moving, running in erratic patterns around the room. She was desperate to escape the sparks. Desperate to escape Vaipera.

You're no goddess.

You're a monster.

And I'll never let you win.

The sparks were lightning-fast. But Marissa was faster. They slowed to a crawl before dying at her feet, just as the life dissipated from Mata's body.

Marissa took a moment to collect herself, her pained eyes still reeling from the bright burst of light. But just as she managed to refocus her vision, another loud gunshot cracked through the room.

Two guards emerged unscathed, having used the door to shield themselves from Arthur's pistol. Marissa heard Arthur curse under his breath as he holstered his gun, bracing himself with the sword he'd stolen from the earlier guard.

"I know she's in here, Arthur." One of the guards threatened in a haughty tone. "And I know you've killed off the rest of our companions. What a pathetic excuse for a royal you are."

As he spoke, a second guard took the opportunity to charge out the door and scurry past them. Marissa noticed something clasped in the guard's fists, and her stomach jolted. *The idol pieces.* Her first instinct was to charge after him, but the other guard was staring them down, with his loaded musket locked on Arthur. If she moved, he would fire. The fleeing guard, knowing this, flashed a smug grin over his shoulder as he disappeared out the door.

"Don't you dare try anything," the guard warned at his eyes locked on Marissa. He lunged forward, grasping ahold of her arm and yanking her upward. She screamed, nearly choking on her own saliva from fear. "Or I'll put a bullet through your little boyfriend's head."

Arthur panted, sweat sliding down his forehead as panic clouded his eyes. Marissa trembled, biting her lip to keep her teeth from chattering. The guard had a vice grip on her arm, with her wrist and hand beginning to go numb from the lack of blood flow. A stomach-churning fear that she'd never felt before pounded through her body, making her panicked brain feel like it was about to explode.

They were trapped. Truly, horribly, hopelessly trapped.

No... this can't be... it can't end like this...

<Don't worry, little snake. It won't.>

Marissa's shock snapped her out of her panic. She flicked her eyes in subtle movements, scanning the tunnel for the source of the sound in her head.

It wasn't Mata's thoughts. These were thoughts Marissa had never heard before. They felt stronger than most, with an almost ethereal aura as they pulsed through Marissa's mind. Yet, something about the voice seemed incredibly familiar.

<I've been trying to avoid this.> The thoughts rose again. *<But it looks like we now have no choice.>*

Marissa became even more frantic, even daring to tilt her head to locate the source of the thoughts. But there were no other reptilians in the room. Other than her, and...

Her eyes flicked to her right. A pair of glittering onyx eyes stared back at her.

<Nim? Are you... communicating with me?>

It was as if the harrowing scene in front of them slowed down, the various sounds and shouts blurring like Marissa's head was in a fishbowl. It was strangely calming, and allowed her to focus on the fact that her pet snake was suddenly far more intelligent than she'd previously believed.

<Well, sort of. You could say I'm communicating through him. We currently share a soul, you see. He generously offered for me to join him, so I could find you.>

Share a soul? Marissa's mind was reeling. *<Who... who are you?>*

<I, my dear, am the great Sauria, reptilian god of life and death. But let's put the introductions aside for now. We have much more urgent matters to attend to.> Nim's head snapped toward the guard. *<Such as getting you and your human friend out of this situation.>*

Before Marissa could make sense of what the strange deity meant, a long, slender figure sprung to life in front of the guard. As it shed its otherworldly mist and began to take shape, Marissa realized it was a massive reticulated python. It looked a lot like Tiny, the snake she'd met in Orchid; it's olive-brown skin laced with black, diamond-like patterns. But this clearly wasn't a normal snake – its coppery eyes glowed with a fierce yellow light.

And while reticulated pythons were generally mellow, passive creatures around humans, this one glowered at the guard like it was sizing it up for dinner. The guard let out a bewildered, deafening scream, dropping Marissa's arm as he struggled to aim his musket at the giant snake. Marissa scrambled behind Arthur, just in time to watch the python chomp its dog-sized jaws into the guard's shoulder and engulf him in its tree-trunk-sized coils.

"Run for it!" Arthur shouted.

Screams turned to gasps as the guard struggled for air. Despite the python's incredible strength, the guard had enough movement left in his fingers to plunge the tip of his bayonet blade into the snake's belly. It hissed sharply, recoiling as a milky ethereal substance dripped from the wound.

Its scales regrew, closing the wound within a few seconds, but it was enough time for the guard to free his musket-wielding arm. As Marissa ran past the entangled guard, desperate to escape, she felt a scorching pain slash across her calf that sent her body plummeting to the ground.

"Marissa!" Arthur yelped, kneeling down to inspect the wound. Marissa pulled her chest up so that she was propped on her elbows, not wanting to lay her eyes on what she knew was a massive gouge across the back of her leg. She could already see the thin stream of blood snaking its way across the dirt.

She closed her eyes and winced, trying not to let nausea overtake her.

Get up. You have to get up.

She pushed her body upward, but as soon as she brought her injured leg under her, agonizing pain jolted through her entire body. She collapsed, trying not to let her frustrated tears flow as Arthur desperately tried to help her.

It was no use. Any amount of weight put on Marissa's left leg would cause it to buckle. She clenched her teeth, fearing that the bayonet had slashed through far more than just her scales. She refused to look at the wound, but she could tell by Arthur's sickened expression that it was as bad as it felt.

"Come here," Arthur said, wrapping one arm underneath her knees and another across her back. He grunted as he lifted her up. She was a petite woman, barely five foot two and rail-thin from years of undernourishment, but she knew she was still a lot of weight to carry.

Arthur took a deep breath and started to run. His pace was more of a shuffling jog with Marissa in his arms, but it was still enough to get them out of the tunnel and away from the coiled guard. Marissa winced as the gasping screams echoed into the next room.

Then, another booming explosion. The gunshot caused some of the dirt on the cavern walls to crumble down like a rain shower. Marissa's heart lurched as Arthur froze, his muscles tensing as if something pained him. Marissa assumed the bullet missed, ricocheting across the room somewhere, as Arthur quickly shook off his nerves and continued running.

And running. And running, his breaths heaving and his legs less steady with every step. By the time they made it back into Terrapin, Marissa could feel his hands shaking. She grimaced, her heart aching to see him so exhausted. She tucked her head underneath his neck and placed a hand on the torn collar of his shirt.

I'm sorry... I know it's a lot carrying me all this way...

But reaching the main cavern and seeing both the piles of dead Testudo and the hordes of wretched guards scouring around the pillaged grounds sent super-human rage through Arthur. Marissa felt him pick up speed, weaving between mud-brick huts in a mad dash to reach the tunnel up to the surface. Before anyone spotted them.

Thankfully, Terrapin was still chaos, and Arthur and Marissa were able to slip away to the northern entrance. From here, they'd have to travel hundreds of feet through pitch-black tunnels – and pray that they didn't run into anyone in the process.

Just before the last bit of light vanished, Arthur took a moment to breathe and shift Marissa's weight in his arms. It was then that Marissa realized that the arm cradling her legs was soaked in blood. It dripped down his arms and left a thin, spotty trail in the dirt behind them.

They descended into the dark tunnel. Nausea made Marissa's stomach wobble again, and she took a few gasping breaths to clear the impending sickness from her throat. But fighting off her urge to vomit wasn't enough to make her feel better. Blood loss was making her whole body numb, and she was barely able to keep her head up.

"Hold on, Marissa," Arthur whispered in a soothing yet worried tone as her pale face sank into his arms. The disorienting darkness, combined with the fatigue and nausea, made Marissa nearly delirious. She lost all sense of orientation and time, and as she eventually found herself washed in the blinding daylight of the surface, she had no idea if they'd been traveling for minutes or hours.

Arthur led them into the woods, his pace barely a stumble as he set Marissa down at the base of a large pine tree. Her head hung limply from her neck as the world spun around her. She was on the verge of unconsciousness, but through her bleary, half-open eyes, all she could see was red.

Arthur was covered in blood. It was smeared across both of his hands and stained the upper half of his trousers. Her weary eyes trailed up to his face, and she could see the fear in his eyes. Fear for her.

But there was also something else. Pain. Not just pain for Marissa's severely injured state, but his own pain. Something was hurting him.

Her eyes flicked down to his torso, as he laid a shaking hand over his right hip. A gaping hole tore through his shirt, surrounded by oozing blood that clearly wasn't Marissa's.

The bullet didn't miss.

"Arthur..." Marissa's voice was barely a whimper. Her fading consciousness smothered her panic. *He ran... all that way... with a bullet wound through him...*

Her pained lips barely parted as she whispered, "Why?"

Arthur clutched his bleeding hip, his head hanging low. His dirty hair contained red streaks from touching it with his bloody hands.

"I promised," his voice quivered. "I promised... I'd never let them take you."

He collapsed in the dirt, just as Marissa's last bit of strength gave out.

Together, they drifted back into the darkness.

Chapter 21

*E*ZRINTH HAD MADE IT.

A triumphant grin snaked its way across his scaled face as soon as the first bits of swampland peeked through the thick tangle of trees. He took a deep breath, puffing his chest as he batted palm fronds out of the way. Dirt turned to mud, which turned to dark, still water that wove between marshy patches of grass and stretched all the way across the horizon. Ezrinth knew that the swampland eventually drained out into the ocean, where the two ecosystems met and the water turned brackish.

That was where they'd find them.

Rathi finally caught up, his slow, silent pants barely masking how hard he was breathing. Varan weren't aquatic creatures, and while they were adept at skittering across mounds of dry soil, swampland was a different story. Ezrinth sighed, trying his best not to appear frustrated.

And the other races insist feet are superior, he huffed, swishing his tail for emphasis.

The other Varan quickly shuffled in behind Rathi, who wore a confused expression on his narrow lizard face.

<What are we waiti- >

<Hush,> Ezrinth hissed, pointing a clawed finger at the water. <Don't you see him?>

<Him? I don't see- >

Rathi's thoughts were interrupted by a shudder as the shallow water in front of them began to boil. Ezrinth's grin deepened. He was familiar enough with Gharian to know exactly how to spot them – a single bumpy snout and pair of bulbous eyes lurking above the water.

The snout and eyes moved, making the Varan flinch. The massive alligator rose like a titan from the water, his heavy, lumbering form sending small waves crashing against the swamp grass. Gharian were the largest of the reptilians, standing nine to ten feet tall and weighing up to half a ton. Their snouts alone were several feet long, equipped with dinosaur-like teeth that jutted from their upper jaws even with their mouths closed. Their leathery bodies were incredibly stocky, covered in bony armor-like scutes that could resist bullets. A slash of their long claws could rip open flesh, and a swipe of their hefty tails could break bones.

Even Ezrinth was in awe of the Gharian's presence.

<Ezrinth.> Its thoughts were deep and guttural, echoing its eerily imposing presence. They were truly ancient beings, emanating a primordial terror not contained by the other reptilian races. As Ezrinth gazed at the Gharian, he swore it was like looking into the eyes of a god.

<We've been expecting you.> He continued, gesturing with a gigantic clawed hand. <I'm Caine, chieftain of the Gharian. Come with me.>

It sounded more like an order than a request.

Ezrinth slithered forward, and as he did so, Caine submerged his hefty body back into the water with a thumping splash. Only a snout and pair of eyes emerged, the dark water swishing from side to side as the Gharian swam toward the horizon.

Ezrinth followed, a tingling sensation creeping down his long spine as the water engulfed his scales. He loved that feeling. Naga were aquatic snakes, and he felt just as comfortable in the water as he did on land.

The same couldn't be said for Rathi and the Varan. They huddled on the shoreline, hesitant to step a foot in the water, which caused Ezrinth to let out an audible hiss.

<You fools. It's *water.* It's not going to kill you. Let's go.>

None of them budged.

<Good gods... *please* tell me you all know how to swim.>

Silence.

<They'll be fine.> Caine's gravelly thoughts interjected, although he didn't turn around or stop swimming.

<The water barely goes past three feet deep. Now let's get a move on. We're losing daylight, and from my understanding, the lizardfolk cannot see well in the dark.>

The Varan waded cautiously into the water, wincing every time a slight ripple or splash touched their spotted scales. Ezrinth sneered. It reminded him of nervous Naga hatchlings learning how to swim. He lowered his serpentine body, submerging himself until only his head and arms remained above water, and slithered his way through the swampland.

With the Varan's reluctant pace, it was a painfully slow journey to Crocodilia, the capital of Gharian territory. Ezrinth struggled to balance keeping up with Caine's smooth, speedy pace and not letting the Varan lag too far behind.

Even after a mile of traveling, Ezrinth wasn't sure how close they were to Crocodilia. The water was getting deeper, and the swamp grass clusters more sparse. The water was more open, with little land in sight. Which meant they were getting closer to the ocean.

Ezirinth dove his head under the water, propelling off the mucky bottom with his tail, and surfaced a few seconds later. He smacked his scaled mouth – he tasted a faint hint of salt. *Yes, definitely close to the ocean.*

He was disappointed that they wouldn't be traveling all the way out to the coast. It was always an awe-inspiring sight, with the roiling waves licking the coarse white sands under a soft blue sky. It was a perfect place to bask in the sun, even if the water was a bit too salty for his liking. The Scaled Sea was bordered almost exclusively by Gharian territory, meaning that Ezrinth rarely got to see the ocean. But he knew that it was better that way – with the amount of damage the humans had caused over the last few decades, the most beautiful part of the valley was best guarded by the largest and most formidable of the reptilian races.

Finally, after wading forward a few hundred feet, Caine came to a stop in front of a long, narrow sandbar that cut through the brackish water like a knife. He surfaced, once again causing a torrent of waves to emanate from his massive body. He lumbered forward a few steps onto the gritty sand and shook himself off.

Ezrinth surfaced and did the same, although he noticed that far less water came off his much slenderer body. The Varan managed to kick up a rowdy mess of waves as they squabbled for shore, somehow managing to be much louder than Caine despite being half his size. Ezrinth shook his head.

So much for being subtle. He prayed that no lurking human guards managed to crawl their way this deep into reptilian territory.

On the other side of the sandbar, two more cumbersome giants emerged from the water. Ezrinth and the Varan were now met with three massive Gharian, their bodies so much taller that they had to gaze downward when addressing them.

Even Ezrinth fought back a shudder.

<Do you have it?> Caine turned toward his companions.

One of the Gharian nodded, reaching into a clamshell satchel slung around its hefty body and pulling out a small object. It was concealed by the alligator's closed palm, but Ezrinth knew from the flash of grey stone that it was the third idol piece.

His heart leapt as he tried his best to maintain his composure and not resemble a giddy hatchling about to receive a toy.

<I imagine you're here to commence our agreement.> Caine addressed Ezrinth and the Varan. <But unfortunately, before I can give you what you came for, there is some news I must share with you.>

Ezrinth's heart, which was previously buzzing with excitement, came crashing down in an instant.

<I'm not sure if you're aware, but Crocodilia does some exchanges with a Testudo village to the south.>

Ezrinth was aware. While the reptilian races were typically solitary from one another, some villages that lay near the borders of their territories engaged in trading. In this case, Crocodilia was far to the west, only a few miles from Testudo territory.

<Several of my scouts returned this afternoon with some goods – and news. Apparently, the village they'd traded with received word from the south that Terrapin was attacked and overrun by humans.>

Ezrinth's jaw fell. The news was incredibly shocking – no human had ever managed to find the tortoisefolks' burrows. It made him guess that Caine wasn't done relaying the bad news – there was far more to the story than just an attack.

<And, apparently... your daughter was spotted there.>

Silence. It took several seconds for Ezrinth's brain to process the news, his eyes glazing over as he stared lifelessly off into the distance and realized what a fool he'd been. He hadn't wanted to risk her safety by bringing her along to Crocodilia, and he'd figured she'd be safer back in the Varan village. But he had ignored the fact that his daughter was yet to trust him, rebelling against his attempts to help her... and he had left her alone in the less-than-capable hands of Rathi's timid mate.

And that human boy... he exhaled rage through his scaled nostrils. *She fled with him.* It was inevitable – he never should've caved to Marissa's pleas to let the human stay. He should've banished that wretched creature while he still had a chance.

But regardless of how she ended up in Testudo territory, Ezrinth's new priority was finding her. The idol pieces, summoning Vaipera... none of it was as important as Marissa. Without her, the entire mission meant nothing.

He needed answers.

<Was she- >

<Yes, according to my sources, your daughter survived and escaped with the others. The remaining Terrapin villagers were taken in by Apalone, near the southern Testudo border. As she was reportedly injured during the escape, I imagine she's still there recovering.>

<Then we'll go there,> Ezrinth replied, noticing that his declaration made the Varan uneasy. His eyes flicked toward Rathi, <And before you and your fellow lizards object, I know the risks. I know that Testudo aren't kind to outsiders.>

<Well yes, and- >

<And I don't care,> Ezrinth hissed. <Nothing will stop me from finding my daughter and making sure she's safe. Wouldn't you do the same?>

Rathi's head lowered, and a pang of regret scorched through Ezrinth's chest. *That may have been a bit harsh.*

Ezrinth sighed, <My apologies. That was callous of me.>

<No.> Rathi raised his eyes to meet Ezrinth's. <You are absolutely right. I know exactly how you feel. We'll find her, Ezrinth. I won't let you lose her again.>

<I'll come too,> Caine announced, much to everyone's surprise. He let out a chuckle at their reaction, his exposed teeth glinting in the setting sun. <But my prerogative is ensuring the safety of the idol pieces. I need to ensure that the Testudo's piece is still in their possession. And if your daughter fled Komodo, she may have taken the other two pieces with her.>

He's right. The thought jolted through his mind like a lightning bolt. *She probably did.* But despite his lingering anger at his daughter betraying him, he realized the situation was perfect. He could find Marissa, make amends, and possibly get ahold of all four idol pieces by the day's end.

And once he did, the only missing piece of the puzzle was his estranged mate, lost somewhere in the crypt-like maze of the human kingdom.

It's not just for me, Ezrinth reasoned, lost in his own thoughts as Caine and the Varan discussed their plans for the journey ahead. *It's for Marissa too. She deserves to meet her mother. She deserves a true family.*

I just have to hope that Marissa recovers quickly from her injuries, Ezrinth prayed as he, Caine, and the Varan began the journey south through the swamplands, toward Testudo territory.

He refused to acknowledge any flaws in his plan, or that it may not come to fruition. He would finally summon Vaipera and wipe out the humans, but most importantly, he would win his mate and daughter back.

MARISSA WAS RELIEVED TO FIND SHE'D AWOKEN in a cot in a Testudo burrow. It was a different one than Terrapin, much smaller and less elegantly designed, but it was still much preferable to being locked up in the back of a royal guard caravan.

She blinked a few times, reassuring herself that she was awake, and this wasn't some strange dream. As her mind stirred to life, she became aware of the layers of bandaging wrapped around her right leg. Strangely, it didn't hurt anymore, but Marissa didn't know if that was a positive sign.

The first thing she noticed was Nim, who was curled around a small bedpost at her feet. His shiny black eyes were wide open, but Marissa assumed that his coiled-up form, still as a statue, was fast asleep. Not a single ethereal thought emanated from him. At the moment, he looked like a perfectly normal, not-possessed-by-a-reptilian-god carpet python.

Her mind flashed back to Mata's home, with the massive reticulated python materializing out of nowhere and bleeding ethereal goop every time it was stabbed by the guard it viciously coiled. Nim's, or rather - *Sauria's* - thoughts still drifted through her mind. But the memories of the encounter were faint and hazy, and Marissa had a hard time believing they'd ever happened at all.

For all I know, I was hallucinating. From fear, and anxiety, and... blood loss.

But the guard was already coiled when he slashed me... And it would explain why Nim is venomous...

Ugh, forget it. I'm worry about it later.

She squeezed her eyes shut, brushing the thoughts away. Nausea and fatigue took over, still muddling her consciousness. Lifting any part of her body was out of the question, but she managed to sluggishly roll her head to one side. Arthur was in a cot next to her, fast asleep with his face pointed away from hers and his hand resting on his bare stomach. He was shirtless, most likely due to the amount of bandaging it took to cover his bullet wound.

With his bare torso exposed, Marissa realized just how hard the past few days had been on him. Odd scrapes and bruises trickled down his ribcage, ending in a thin, bloody line that cut through his belly button. Marissa remembered the first time she saw him bare-chested in the stream, right after she was stabbed by Thomas. He'd always been thin, his tall frame wrapped in lean muscle with the tiniest bit of softness around his stomach. But now, he was withering away, his stomach sunken in and his muscles protruding in an unhealthy manner. He looked pale, dehydrated, and most importantly, exhausted.

Marissa managed to muster up the strength to extend a shaking hand in his direction, but it fell limply to her side long before it reached the cot. Another wave of nausea roiled her stomach, and she turned her head back up to face the ceiling, taking deep breaths and praying that the urge to vomit would pass.

Not that there's much left in my stomach.

<Oh, thank Chelon, you're awake.>

Marissa felt too ill to move her head again, but she could hear the stomping footsteps of a female Testudo lumbering towards her. As the tortoise hovered over Marissa's battered body, Marissa noticed that the jewelry she wore was different than those back at Terrapin, and she had markings on her face that looked like they were made with a white, chalky substance.

Marissa forced a smile, assuming the Testudo was a friendly face, but her mind was too fatigued for conversation.

The Testudo seemed to sense this. <Don't worry, my dear. You're safe. You're in Apalone, a few miles north of Terrapin. It's a good thing some of the evacuees found you two. You were collapsed just a few hundred feet from the front lines.>

Marissa nodded, forcing a swallow. This confirmed her suspicions – the residents of Terrapin had fled and were taken in by another, smaller Testudo village. But how many survived? And where were Nathara and Thomas?

As if the Testudo could read her closed-off thoughts, she continued. "The refugees were accompanied by a human and a Naga. Sadly we can't understand the human, but the Naga kept asking about you two. They're both fine, by the way – being patched up in another ward by some other healers. We've had to convert nearly half of our wards into apothecaries for all of you.>

Marissa's body was beginning to shake off the post-traumatic exhaustion, and she forced herself to sit upright. She could now see the bandages wrapped around her lower calf, as well as the various nicks and cuts along the scales that lined her knees and thighs. Arthur may have been in rough shape, but she wasn't much better off.

<I know it's hard, but try to relax, my dear.> The Testudo continued. <I need you to rest for at least another few hours before you try putting weight on that leg. We're running short on orange paste, but I've put enough on there for your wound to close within a day or so.>

Orange paste. Marissa peered over at Arthur's cot and realized he had some rubbed into his gunshot wound as well. It already looked like it was healing.

The Testudo healer checked Marissa's wound, offered her some water, and then left to attend to other, more gravely injured patients. With a bit of her energy restored, Marissa peered around the room. She was in a small, hollowed-out dome, surrounded by dirt walls that rose about ten feet high. Based on her conversation with the Testudo healer, Marissa assumed that this village, unlike Terrapin, was made up of a series of chambers, instead of a massive open cavern.

Her heart ached every time her eyes flicked back over to Arthur, but with time she knew that he too would heal. And like him, she needed rest. Despite the harrowing events of the day before weighing on her chest like a rock, she forced herself to empty her mind and close her eyes. She could worry about the aftermath of losing Terrapin to the humans later – she was severely injured, and fretting would only slow her recovery.

She managed to get in about fifteen minutes of sleep before a loud wailing sound woke her. She jolted upright, her blood souring as she feared that the agonizing cries were coming from Arthur. But he was still asleep, in the exact same position he'd been in when she first awoke.

The cries were coming from further down the tunnels. And they were getting closer.

Marissa squeezed her eyes shut, wincing as the wails rattled her eardrums. Whatever Testudo was making these sounds was in absolute agony. Whether from physical or mental pain, Marissa had no idea, but she could tell that the refugee was being brought into this ward.

A few seconds later, two Testudo emerged from the exit tunnel, both wearing the same garments and white chalky face paint as the healer from earlier. They stood on either side of a badly injured refugee, holding the edges of his shell like he was on was a stretcher. Marissa's breath slowed as she saw the blood staining the patient's arm and chest. One his right hand, two of his claws were replaced by bloody stumps.

Multiple sections of his body, including the two missing claws, were heavily bandaged and tainted orange from the orange paste. As she watched him be hauled into a cot on the other side of Arthur, Marissa realized that his cries weren't from physical pain. His pain was mental – anguish at losing his home and possibly those he cared about.

As the healers finished laying him in the cot and left the ward, the injured Testudo turned his head and locked eyes with Marissa. She knew those eyes.

She couldn't believe it. Kai had survived the battle.

And he wasn't happy to see her. As soon as Kai realized who was occupying the two cots next to him, his eyes flashed with rage.

<You...> he hissed, struggling to point a shaking claw at Marissa. She gulped, feeling her throat go numb.

<Kai...> Her thoughts were soft. <You're alive. I'm so happy to see yo- >

<Don't you dare!> he growled. <They're all dead because of you! Mother, Father, my brothers... all gone. I'm the only one that survived. I should've listened to my father and my brothers. I insisted that you be let in here... and you led those wretched humans straight to us! This is all your fault!!>

A hot shiver ran down Marissa's spine. She could feel Kai's pain aching in her body as if it were own. His words sent raw guilt seeping through her veins and stole the breath from her lungs, as if her ribcage was being crushed.

What if... he's right? If we'd never showed up, the royal guard would've never found their burrow...

421

Kai broke down into tears again, and Marissa trembled as she fought back the urge to cry too. Her heart ached for Kai... but nothing she could say would soothe him. In the brief moments she'd gotten to know him, she appreciated his cheery, open-minded nature. With time, she could've easily considered him a friend.

But the old Kai was gone. In his place was a badly injured, anguished shell of his former self. Marissa hadn't grown up with a family, so she didn't understand what it meant to lose one. But she understood how it felt to be completely and utterly alone, and all the heart-wrenching emotions that accompanied it. She feared that Kai would never be the same again.

And that he would, for the rest of his life, view Marissa as the monster that took his family away.

She turned away from the sobbing Testudo, burying her face in the pillow beneath her head, and cried silent, painful tears that burned her cheeks as they dissolved into the thin cloth.

Gods... why... why did this have to happen?

MARISSA ASKED THAT SAME QUESTION IN HER head, over and over for hours, as Kai's anguished cries continued to echo through the ward. He eventually erupted into another tirade, even trying to step out of the cot and get ahold of Marissa, who was still unable to stand. But thankfully, upon hearing the commotion, two more healers appeared and escorted Kai to another ward.

She took a deep breath, her ears still ringing from his cries. She turned over, praying that the mourning, injured Testudo would eventually be able to relax enough to get some sleep. She prayed that it would allow his mind some sort of respite, but she knew that was likely far from true. From her experience, grief turned the mind into a monstrous mess, plagued with nightmares and restlessness that compounded the mourner's fatigue. Grief was a cage that would imprison his mind for a long, long time, even while asleep.

Even though she'd slept for hours, her body still felt weary. She sat upright again and examined her bandaged leg. *Still working.* She managed to lift it a few inches, and while it did hurt, it was more of a dull ache that a stabbing pain. She took a deep breath, deciding to be brave. But just as she went to slide off the cot and put weight on her injured leg, she heard a groan and the sound of blankets rustling behind her.

She spun around, and despite her injury, she nearly shot out of her bed.

"Arthur!!"

He was awake, but still groggy. He groaned again, struggling to raise his hands to his face and rub his bleary eyes. Marissa perched herself on the very edge of his cot, gently placing a hand on the triangular patch of hair on his chest.

"Marissa..." his voice was soft and hoarse. He slowly extended a hand toward her face, and Marissa took it in hers and pressed it against her scaled cheek. Arthur grimaced, his eyes glazed over with pain.

"Marissa... you're alright..."

"I am. It's okay, Arthur," she squeezed the hand against her cheek harder, and Arthur pressed his fingertips against her scales, stroking them as if he questioned her being real.

"I kept having nightmares..." he croaked, his eyes still distant, not quite anchored in reality. "That they captured you... they pulled you away from me... there was nothing I could do..."

"It's okay, it's okay," Marissa continued to whisper in soothing tones, pressing her other hand deeper against his chest. "I'm here. You're safe. We're safe."

"Marissa," Arthur's voice cracked, his gaze finally locking with hers. "My Marissa."

"Yes," Marissa nuzzled her cheek into his hand, her heavy heart lifting at his words. "I'm here. I'm yours."

"Mine," Arthur repeated, although his words quickly turned into a rasping cough. He took a few moments to catch his breath, and continued, "I'm so sorry. They came so close to capturing you... I swear on my life, I'll never let it happen again. I know I've struggled to say it... but Marissa... you mean so much to me. More than finding peace, more than ending this war... I want you. I need you. And I promise, from now on, I will fight for you."

"You always have, Arthur," Marissa smiled, her overwhelming emotions clinging to the corners of her eyes. "From the moment I met you, you were always there for me. But it's okay to be afraid. It's okay to be cautious. I know you miss your family, and I don't want you to be-"

"No," Arthur growled through clenched teeth as he struggled to lift his head. "It's true, I was struggling with being exiled. But that was before. After what Ramsey did, after what my whole family did... pardon my language, but... fuck them. All of them. It's a lot easier for me to sever ties with my family now that they've shown what wretched monsters they are. Gods, all those slain Testudo... their lifeless eyes..."

"Arthur..." Marissa gulped, taking both hands and cupping them around Arthur's neck, below his jaw. "There's something I need to tell you."

"What is it?"

Marissa's expression grew grim as she gestured toward the cot next to Arthur. "Kai survived the attack. He was just here a few minutes ago."

Arthur's eyebrows shot up. "Good gods, I can't believe it. He was on the front lines with me when the cannon hit, and..." his voice trailed off.

"The rest of his family didn't make it," Marissa sighed. "And he blames it on me. And deep down... I know he's right."

"Marissa..."

"He is! I'm the monster that led the royal guard right to them. This... all of this... is my fault..."

Her throat quivered, and she squeezed her eyes shut, fearing that more tears would escape. Arthur sat upright a few inches, straining as he went, and placed his hands on her shoulders, slowly sliding them down her back.

"You are not a monster," Arthur proclaimed in a firm tone, pulling Marissa toward him until their faces were just inches from each other. "You are a miracle."

Marissa didn't have time to react. Before her mind could process what was happening, Arthur's lips were already pressed against hers. It felt strange for a moment, but as Arthur's grip on her back tightened, a surge of emotions crashed over her like a tidal wave. Her cheeks, chest, and other less familiar areas were on fire. Yet it was the most exhilarating feeling she'd ever experienced, soothing and scorching at the same time.

In that moment, reality slipped away. All of her heaviest emotions, all of the fear and anxiety weighing down her mind, seemed to pour out of her, dissipating into the air. All she could focus, all she needed, was this moment. She was determined to make it last as long as possible.

But she knew it had to end. They had Thomas and Nathara to find, idol pieces to hunt down, and a whole valley to save. Not to mention every second that Marissa spent hovering over Arthur, with his hands wrapped around her back and her stomach pressed against his bare chest, the more she felt an all-consuming urge to go further. But that was unknown territory to both of them, and it wasn't something they could figure out while they were refugees in a Testudo burrow on the brink of war.

After what seemed like an eternity, although it was likely only a few seconds, Arthur gently pulled away. He pressed his forehead against hers, blushing but overjoyed as his lips radiated a warm smile.

For now, the kiss was enough. Arthur placed a hand over Marissa's jet-black hair and pulled her head against his chest. Marissa giggled, the heat of his skin warming her cheek as his chest hair ticked her nose. His affection, although still foreign and terrifying, was also incredibly intoxicating. She swore it was the happiest she'd felt in her entire life.

But she knew her joy was fleeting. Kai, devastated and gravely injured, was still grief-stricken in one of the nearby wards, blaming Marissa for the loss of his family. Marissa was yet to find Nathara and Thomas, but she knew that outside their small abode, the burrow was littered with hundreds of survivors, many of whom were just as badly injured as they were. And they were the lucky ones – there were still hundreds more lifeless bodies left behind in Terrapin, those that would never have a chance to recover.

A shudder trailed down Marissa's spine, and Arthur squeezed her tighter.

"It's alright," Arthur whispered, now the one doing the reassuring. "You're okay."

But Marissa knew she wasn't. She feared she never would be again.

IT TOOK SEVERAL HOURS FOR THE TESTUDO healer to come back in and check on them. Marissa imagined she and the other healers were incredibly busy, with their abode suddenly being overwhelmed with refugees. She realized it was incredibly generous of them to suddenly take in hundreds of injured Testudo from a different village. Perhaps their pacifistic ways extended to always helping those in need.

Arthur tried to stand, but Marissa didn't want him to put too much strain on his injured hip. The orange paste was working, and the previously coin-sized gash was now smaller than a blueberry. But it was still open and oozing, so Marissa forced him to sit down.

She was stuck in her bed as well, unable to do more than hobble a few steps on her injured leg. As much as she wanted to find Nathara and Thomas, she feared that collapsing in the middle of the tunnel was worse than waiting for the healer to return.

With nothing else to do, she and Arthur laid in bed and talked. Aimlessly, endlessly, about everything from their childhoods to their favorite foods to their hopes for the future. As they chatted, Marissa felt a similar warmth in her stomach to when Arthur kissed her, but less intense. This feeling was less of a raging fire and more of a cozy blanket, warm and comforting even on the coldest of days. It made Marissa realize how much she still had to learn about Arthur, and how eager she was to be with him. A quiet, comfortable life together, spending their days tending to The Menagerie, still felt like a distant dream. But Marissa clung to it like it was her last fraying thread of hope.

Eventually, as Arthur was enchanting Marissa with his tales of reptilian research expeditions deep within the swampland, the Testudo healer shuffled into the ward.

She looked exhausted – Marissa swore that the creases that lined her reptilian eyes were more sunken-in than before. But she forced a warm, tired smile as she examined Marissa's healing leg and Arthur's now nearly-closed bullet wound.

<It looks like you two should be fine to walk at this point,> The Testudo told Marissa. <You ought to find that aunt of yours and your human friend. Your aunt especially has been a mess. She keeps trying to slither away in search of you, but we managed to convince her to rest. She had quite the nasty gash on her head. Thankfully, it's almost healed.>

<Thank you,> Marissa replied as she slid out of the cot. Her sore legs felt unsteady under her weight, but as she took a few steps forward, she realized that she no longer felt like she was going to collapse. <Where are they?>

<They're down the left tunnel, second ward on the right.>

Marissa speed-walked down the tunnel as quickly as she could on her half-mended leg. Arthur strolled next to her, offering an arm every time Marissa's calf began its throbbing complaints. He tried to get her to slow down, but after two reminders, it became clear it was no use. Marissa was eager to see them.

Nathara shot upright the second Marissa stepped into the ward. Her eyes had been locked on the tunnel entrance when Marissa and Arthur entered, as if she'd been spending the last few hours keeping an eye out for them. Her slithering coils trailed behind her as she jolted forward and engulfed Marissa in a hefty yet gentle hug.

<Gods, I was so worried about you.> Nathara's thoughts carried a heavy dose of anxiety, which was unusual for the tough-as-scales Naga. She was so tall that she had to bend down and lower her arms just to wrap them around Marissa's head.

Marissa felt a gentle, blooming warmth in her heart. Nathara's scales were cool and smooth to the touch; it was comforting to feel the embrace of another reptilian. Especially one that was family.

Family. She grinned, burying her face in the crook of Nathara's arm. With her absent mother and wicked father, Nathara was the closest thing to a parent she'd ever had.

Nathara raised her head and looked up, locking eyes with Arthur. She seemed confused by his current state – shirtless with bandages wrapped around his hips – but she shook her head and smiled.

<I was worried about both of you,> Nathara continued, peering back down at Marissa. <I take it you're healing well?>

<Yes.> Marissa knelt down, examining her calf. The fresh bandaging was no longer oozing with blood, meaning that her wound was nearly fully closed. Unfortunately, orange paste wasn't a miracle cure, and she'd still have a nasty scar and some missing scales. But it was much preferred over letting her body do its own healing, as it was far too slow at that job.

A pair of filthy boots appeared in front of her, and she craned her neck upward to see Thomas hovering over her, his overgrown mustache curling over his smiling lips.

"Thomas!" she exclaimed, standing up just as he leaned in for a hug.

"I was worried about y'all too," Thomas noted, pulling away and ruffling Marissa's dark hair. His gaze shifted past Marissa, and he raised an eyebrow at Arthur. "How did'ya manage to get a bullet wound *after* we left the tunnel, pal?"

Arthur gave a half chuckle, "Let's have a seat. We have a lot of explaining to do."

Marissa was deep underground, unable to see the sky, but a strange feeling in her gut told her that it was late, well past midnight. *Call it reptilian intuition.* But despite the group's worn-out state, they stayed up well into the early morning, munching on their rationed meals and discussing the aftermath of the battle.

Marissa hated it. She hated reliving those hours spent crammed in a mud-brick hut, hiding from soldiers hell-bent on capturing her while having no idea if the people she cared most about in the world were still alive. Watching Mata die in front of her; both her and Arthur being gravely injured by a guard.

Learning that Kai was the only surviving member of his family.

Nathara gasped upon hearing the news, raising a scaled hand to cover her gaping mouth. Thomas just sighed and shook his head, remarking that Kai was lucky to be alive. Marissa assumed he thought that every Testudo that was on the front lines when the cannon hit had died.

He was right. Kai was lucky to be alive. But with the amount of pain, both physical and mental, that he was in, Marissa wondered if that was a good thing.

"Well," Thomas continued, shrugging off his dirty jacket and nestling it under his head like a pillow as he laid down. "I dunno what it is, but even after hours of sleep I'm still exhausted."

"It's late," Marissa replied. "And it's because we're all injured."

With Thomas's jacket off and his bare white undershirt exposed, Marissa could see the cuts and bruises crisscrossed down his arms and trailing across his shoulders. He didn't have a massive injury like the rest of them, but he was still just as scraped up.

<We should all rest until morning,> Nathara remarked, slithering into the corner and coiling her body into a tight spiral. Marissa chuckled as her aunt laid down, using her own coils as a pillow for her head.

<Good night, Marissa.>

Marissa peered around the room. The ward was mostly bare, with two thin cots and a few other simple pieces of furniture. With Thomas and Nathara lying on the dirt floor, both beds were empty.

Marissa opened her mouth to protest, but Thomas quickly interrupted her, "Yer aunt's a snake, and I'm not nursing a major wound. Y'all need the beds more than we do."

A major wound that's almost healed. Marissa stared down at her calf. But she was still too sore to walk more than a few dozen feet, which would be an issue when the next day came.

The next day, Marissa thought as she crawled into one of the cots. She had no idea what the next day would bring. She had no idea where they went from here.

Her mind flashed back to the guard fleeing with the idol pieces, and she sighed. She hadn't thought about it much until now. They had been so close to safety, so close to ending all of this... but at least the pieces weren't in reptilian hands. The humans would likely lock the pieces away in their palace, deep within the kingdom and far away from Ezrinth and his cronies. The idol pieces were safe... for now.

But as Marissa closed her eyes, she knew that safety wouldn't last.

It never did.

MARISSA COULDN'T SLEEP.

She wasn't sure if it was because she'd spent the past few hours resting in a hospital bed and was no longer tired, or if the haunting nightmares of the previous day were keeping her shell-shocked mind awake. But either way, she found herself staring empty-eyed up at the cavern ceiling long after everyone else had fallen asleep.

At one point, when she assumed it was early morning, she decided to give up on sleep. She was sick of tossing and turning in her cot, her legs restless and her mind racing. So she sat upright in her bed, running her fingers through her long black hair and peering over at the carpet python coiled around her bedpost. He was still as a statue again, but this time, Marissa could tell he was wide awake.

<*I suppose it's time we talked.*>

<Seriously?> Marissa nearly huffed her thoughts. <You've been silent this entire time, to the point that I believed I was imagining things, and *now* you want to talk?>

<*I wanted you to get some rest.*> Nim raised his head slightly, flicking his tongue. <*But you seem to have had enough of it, since it's 4 o'clock in the morning and you're wide awake.*>

The last thought sent a chill through Marissa's mind. They were deep underground, with no hint of daylight – or a clock - anywhere in the entire village. Yet he knew exactly what time it was.

She really was talking to something from beyond the mortal realm.

<*I heard that.*> The voice grumbled. <*I summoned a giant python from the lands of Reptilia to save you, and you still don't believe you're conversing with a god?*>

Marissa froze, her blood curdling. *Seriously? He can read my thoughts? Has he been doing that the whole time?*

Marissa sighed, letting out a full, gaping-mouthed yawn that exposed her fangs. <Sorry. It's just a lot to process. And I still have a lot of questions.>

<*Go on, then. We have plenty of time.*>

<Um, okay,> Marissa rubbed her head, deep in thought. <Well, let's start with the obvious questions - why is a reptilian god possessing my pet snake, and why did you wait until I was about to *die* to reveal yourself?>

<Well, to answer that question, let's go back to the beginning. When it became clear to me that a certain reptilian was plotting to summon Vaipera, I knew I had to act. I had the exact same fear as you; that thousands of beings, both human and reptilian, would die in the process. And being the god of life and death, I have issues with so many poor souls being thrust into my proverbial claws at once. So I left Reptilia, floating around as a spirit, undetectable to those around me. But in order to stay in this realm for longer than a few hours, I needed to bind myself to something more... mortal. While drifting through the valley, I came across a stack of crates. Inside one of them was a beautiful carpet python, part of a shipment of reptiles headed right for the human kingdom. Where I knew I would, inevitably, run into you.>

<But I still don't understand,> Marissa lowered her head, trying to process all the information Sauria was throwing at her. <Why *me*?>

<You know why. You heard it from Mata herself. You're the key to ending all of this.>

<But *how*!? I can barely fire a gun or swing a sword – how am I suddenly the chosen one that must bring down a goddess?>

<We need to work on your self-confidence.> Sauria huffed. <And you're looking at it all wrong. Yes, in order for there to be peace in the valley, Vaipera must be stopped. But you forget what happens after that problem is gone. Do you really expect the humans and reptilians to make amends when they can't even communicate with each other?>

<Um... no?>

<Exactly. Your birth was no accident. You are the one who will bridge the communication gap between the two worlds. With time, you will settle conflicts, negotiate agreements, and tear the old barriers down. You, my dear Marissa, are a born leader. You are the granddaughter of a chieftain and chieftress, a royal descendant of the Naga throne, a reptilian princess. You must not be so hard on yourself.>

Sauria's words caused Marissa's head to spin like a top. *Leader? Royal? Princess?* These were titles that Marissa couldn't fathom associating with herself. Her entire life, she'd assumed she little more than a mistake. Outcast, abandoned, homeless... the lowest of the low in society, unable to even show her full face to the world.

Has it really been just a few weeks since I was back in the orphanage storehouse, hiding from the world? So much had happened since then; it felt like a lifetime ago.

<Well, let's move on to my next question,> Marissa continued, once her overwhelmed mind stopped reeling. <I always knew you were no ordinary snake. But a *god?* Why didn't you say something before?>

Nim's head lowered again. *<Well, there are a few reasons. First, and I am reluctant to admit this, but... I'm not exactly supposed to be here right now.>*

<Wait, what?>

<It's forbidden to jump the barrier between the mortal and immortal worlds, and the other gods were not willing to bend the rules to stop Vaipera. Bastards – I swear they're on her side. But I don't actually need their permission to cross over. See, my position as god of life and death already gives me that ability. That's how I collect the souls who have passed and bring them to Reptilia to be reborn.>

Marissa sighed. *So not only is my pet snake possessed by a god, but that god is a fugitive. Great.*

<So you just... came here and never went back up?>

<*Um... yes, exactly.*> Sauria's previously booming, ethereal voice now contained a hint of hesitation, as if he shouldn't be freely relaying this information. <*I can be summoned with a portal written in ancient reptilian – they're located in every temple, and it's a common practice in funerals to activate them. There was one for a Varan girl who was poached by humans a few weeks ago, and I simply... stayed here.*>

<Um, alright then,> Marissa replied warily, realizing that this put yet another target on her back. <And what're the other reasons?>

<*Well, keeping hidden until now protected not only my safety, but yours. I've been able to keep you safe in subtle ways, such as using my venom, but yesterday's battle required more... elaborate means of protection.*>

<Speaking of which...> Marissa interjected. <How in the world did you summon a giant snake in the first place?>

<*That's the thing – I am not a full-fledged god, more of a glorified public servant that happens to be immortal. What you humans would call a 'grim reaper' of sorts. So, my powers are limited. The reticulated python wasn't something I created – it was the spirit of a recently deceased snake brought back into the mortal world. That, along with my venom, are the extent of my abilities.*>

Bringing back snakes from the dead... It made Marissa wonder about the consequences of Sauria's absence. There were likely dozens, maybe even hundreds, of reptilian souls lingering in Reptilia, unable to pass on to their next lives until he returned.

And Sauria was bringing them back as familiars to guard her. It seemed kind of morbid.

<It's not morbid,> Sauria scowled. <The snakes are honored to fight for you. After all, the fate of the whole valley rests in your hands.>

Marissa cringed as she realized Sauria was once again reading her mind, but she hadn't thought of it that way. The newfound realization that she was far more than just a rejected mistake of nature was still difficult to grasp.

<But back to my original point,> Sauria continued. <Every time I use my powers, not only does it drain my fragile spirit form, but it carries enormous risks for you. If someone comes after you and sees a giant snake pop out of nowhere, they're going to assume you caused it. They'll assume they're your powers. The royal family already views you as dangerous, Marissa. We don't want to feed into that lie any more than we must.>

A cold shudder tingled Marissa's shoulders. Sauria was right. The guard that they encountered in Mata's home was likely suffocated by the python's massive coils. But before he died, Marissa knew what the last thought on his mind was.

That the strange-looking half-snake in front of him was a monster, one who wielded dangerous magic.

As much as she detested killing, Marissa was grateful for his death. If he'd escaped... gods knew the consequences. He'd run right back to the palace and tell the king that the half-Naga girl was far more dangerous than they'd anticipated. Putting an even bigger bounty on her head.

A sudden wave of nausea rippled Marissa's stomach, and she lurched over, cluching her abdomen and gagging into her elbow.

Gods... I really am in deep trouble...

<*Marissa, relax. You should lie back down. Deep breaths.*>

Nim rose to attention, slithering off the bedpost and hugging the edge of Marissa's hip with his long body.

<How?> Marissa asked in a pained, weary tone as she rested her head back on her pillow. <How am I supposed to relax after you've told me all this?>

<*I know it's hard.*> Sympathy laced Sauria's thoughts as his tone softened. <*But you can't hide from the truth just because it's frightening. Rest for a few minutes, until your stomach settles.*>

Marissa nodded, laying the back of her forearm against her head. *Deep breaths, in and out.*

The nausea slowly faded, but the knot in the pit of her stomach didn't. She peered over at the cot against the opposite wall. Seeing Arthur's dark, sleeping form made her heart flutter, but it also caused the anxious knot to tighten.

Right now, she needed his comfort. She longed for his touch, his skin against her scales, now that he was finally *hers*. But for how long? How would they overcome the ever-growing pile of obstacles in front of them?

A sharp thud interrupted Marissa's thoughts, as the door swung open so fast it shook the little dirt room.

She bolted upright in her cot, her nervous stomach protesting her body's sudden movement. It was the healer from the day before, except her previously calm, gentle demeanor was gone. Instead, her eyes were wild with panic.

<What's going on?> Marissa asked. Around her, Arthur, Nathara, and Thomas were beginning to stir, awoken by the sudden slam of the door. She saw confusion in their bleary eyes as they struggled to process what was going on.

<Thank the gods.> The healer gave a weary sigh. <Marissa, whatever you and your friends do; do not make a sound, and do not leave this room. I'm going to lock it when I leave.>

<Why?> Uneasiness snaked up Marissa's throat.

The healer stepped back, peering to her left and right as if to make sure no one was listening.

<Your father is here.>

Chapter 22

ASSANDRA LEFT HER HOME THE NEXT morning with a heavy rucksack and an even heavier heart.

She'd packed as few belongings as possible, yet she still struggled to sling the bag over her shoulder. It contained a several sets of clothes, toiletries, and a few of her favorite books. She sighed as her eyes scanned over her still mostly-full bookcase, as well as her jewelry box and desk full of stationary sets. She didn't want to bring anything too sentimental – homesickness had no place in a dorm full of staunch royal guard recruits.

Despite her sadness at leaving most of her belongings behind, excitement and adrenalin overshadowed most of her worries. At least, until she opened the bottom drawer of her desk, making sure she hadn't left any essentials behind.

The drawer contained a small bouquet of dried flowers wrapped in baling twine. She gently fingered the brittle petals. They were mostly milkweed and honeysuckle – native flowers that grew in the fields between Live Oak and the surrounding forest. Where the Naga had picked them for her, many years earlier. The cracked vase that once held them had been left behind in the shack. She'd never see it again. She'd never see *him* again.

Her stomach twisted as she slammed the drawer shut with a blunt wooden *thud* and stomped out of the room.

She was ready to leave.

William was confused by her sullen behavior on the very long cart ride to Brennan. But he didn't say anything – Cassandra assumed he'd chalked it up to nerves. Which wasn't entirely false. She *was* nervous. Incredibly nervous. Some of was excitement – after all, this was her chance to finally chase her dreams in the beautiful, majestic kingdom of Brennan, far away from her sleepy hometown.

But most of that excitement was overshadowed by fear. After all, she was a deaf woman joining one of the most elite groups in all of Brennan. She worried that she'd have to work twice as hard to prove herself. That no matter how athletic or cunning she was, that it wouldn't be enough. No amount of skill would make up for the fact that she couldn't hear orders on a battlefield, or that an enemy could sneak up behind her and she'd never know until it was too late.

And lastly, amidst the excitement and fear, was the sadness. She pulled a scrapbook out of her rucksack and flipped it open, tracing her fingers over the signatures littered across the pages. Some of her classmates merely signed their names, others wrote sweet words of encouragement and wished her best of luck with university. And of course, there was Lucy's letter, which took up nearly an entire page. She clenched her jaw, forcing back tears as she read the final sentence.

Remember, I believe in you. Always. Even when the rest of the world doesn't.

But at least she would see Lucy again. Not until the end of the summer, when her apprenticeship began, and Cassandra could travel over to Augustree to visit. It wouldn't be the same as spending every day together in school, but at least it wasn't a permanent goodbye.

Him, on the other hand...

Her throat quivered as she huffed, cursing her eyes for daring to produce such a watery display of cowardice. Last night was the end. A strange, intoxicating, beautiful end. It was also sheer insanity, an act that would make her a social pariah if anyone found out. But Cassandra was content that no one ever would. Last night was between her and the Naga, and it would stay that way forever.

She pressed a hand against her chest. She could still feel his claws there, pressing into her flesh, so gentle yet forceful at the same time. Her heart fluttered in her chest, sending warm pulses down her torso.

She regretted nothing.

"So," William tapped her on the shoulder. "Are you excited?"

Cassandra gulped. In the distance, she could see the wall surrounding the kingdom beginning to peek between the trees.

It was such a simple, yet complicated question. She felt a lot of things at the moment, and while one of them was excitement, it was just a single thread in an incredibly tangled web of emotions.

But of course, she couldn't explain any of it to him. Even without the scandalous truth of her night with the Naga, she didn't want her father to know how terrified she was. Or how much she dreaded the homesickness that she knew would creep over her in the coming weeks.

"Yes," she signed back, a heavy, forced smile on her face.

William didn't say anything else for the rest of the cart ride. Which was a relief for Cassandra, because all she could focus on was the clip-clop of their gelding's hooves and how they synced with her ever-loudening heartbeat.

They came to a rolling stop at the gates, which stretched several stories high and loomed ominously over them.

This was it. Everything she'd been working towards was finally happening.

Yet she knew it was going to be the hardest eight weeks of her life.

CASSANDRA HAD ACED HER ENTRANCE EXAMS, both physical and mental. She was in peak physical shape, her wiry body wrapped in layers of lean muscle. Yet she still felt dwarfed amongst the other recruits. They were mostly men, well over six feet tall, with forearms much larger than her scrawny biceps and hands twice the size of hers. She clasped her hands behind her back during orientation so no one could tell they were shaking.

On and on their staff sergeant went about how they were the chosen ones – only the most elite fighters were allowed to enroll in bootcamp. It lit a spark of hope in Cassandra's heart, one that was quickly extinguished when the sergeant declared that they still had a long road ahead of them. The only way to get into the junior royal guard was to pass the bootcamp, and after four years of university, they'd be able to apply for the *real* royal guard. All that the junior guard gave them was a chance. They'd still have to prove themselves after graduation.

The speech then morphed into a solemn yet vicious tirade about how danger was always lurking at the edge of their borders. That the monstrous reptilians would always be a threat, always looking to reclaim bits of the humans' territory. No matter what rank they were or quadrant they were in, the rule was the same – if you see a reptilian, kill it on sight.

Cassandra knew it was impolite to leave the university great hall in the middle of a speech, but she found herself bolting to the bathroom anyways.

She managed to fight back the urge to vomit, steadying herself against the toilet seat while she took deep, gasping breaths to settle the nausea in her stomach.

I can't do this. I can't do this.

No, she clasped her frustrated hands against her skull. *Stop it. You can do this. You have to.*

The speech was merely the beginning of what Cassandra had correctly predicted would be the most difficult eight weeks of her life. She'd been training for years, and had built up an impressive amount of strength and stamina. But she only ever trained for an hour or two at a time, and that was always supplemented by plenty of food, water, and rest.

At bootcamp, Cassandra was subjected to grueling eight-hour days, with only a brief lunch break for her to catch her breath. Despite having access to the university's dining hall, the recruits were fed prepackaged rations. *Get used to them,* their sergeant would say. *It's all you'll be able to eat if we're ever sent out to battle.*

By the end of the first month, Cassandra was bruised, exhausted, and both physically and mentally fatigued. On top of the grueling workouts, she'd been ostracized by most of her comrades. The men, who made up over ninety percent of the recruits, immediately snubbed her as a scrawny wimp that wouldn't make it through the first week. After surviving four of them, she'd managed to impress a few of her comrades, but they still gave her a wide berth at mealtime and made snide faces behind her back. Even the female recruits, being few and far between, still rejected her. She was the smallest and weakest of them all, and the women, already disfavored because of their gender, didn't want to be associated with her.

She may have survived the first month, Cassandra managed to lip-read the conversation of several men in the dining hall, just a few feet from her. *But she sure as hell won't survive the second.*

She hunkered down, refusing to look their way and pretending to be engrossed by her porridge. Her size already made her an easy target, and her lack of hearing only made it worse. They acted like it was exasperating to communicate with her, and not a single recruit was interested in learning sign language. They all repeated what she'd always feared – that her hearing loss made her incredibly vulnerable.

She hated how they gossiped right in front of her, as if she weren't even there. But many of them didn't know that she could lip-read, and she'd occasionally catch fragments of their conversations. It made her angry, but it also made her more determined.

Even if she didn't always believe in herself, she'd always had an urge to prove those who doubted her wrong. She would do this. She would survive the second month – hell, she'd survive all four years. And then she'd join the real royal guard with a proud but smug smile on her face.

But she quickly realized that the second month would be even more difficult than the first. A major factor was that they were now sparring directly against each other. While the fights were heavily regulated, a few of the recruits didn't mind playing dirty if it meant shoving Cassandra's face into the ground. They'd get a scolding from the sergeant for breaking the rules, but no amount of punishment seemed to deter them. Cassandra couldn't speak up for fear of looking weak, and she knew that in a way, her comrades were right. Enemies didn't play by the rules on the battlefield, and they would show her - a short, scrawny girl who couldn't hear - absolutely no mercy.

The worst part was that after nearly six weeks, her body showed signs of giving out. She was sore and covered in bruises, but most alarmingly she couldn't stop getting sick after fights. She'd dart away, trying to find the quietest restroom in the emptiest building where her comrades wouldn't hear her vomit. Food was difficult to keep down, and after a while she gave up on eating altogether. All she could stomach was the hardtack from her rations, which wasn't nearly enough calories for a recruit in a grueling bootcamp.

It all came to a head just a few days before the bootcamp ended. She went into sparring practice that day feeling weak and exhausted, but also hopeful. She'd survived this long – just a few more days and she would officially be inducted into the junior royal guard. Classes would start soon, and her training would drop to only a few days a week.

The light at the end of the tunnel was finally in sight. She could do this.

But by noon, the fact that her head was hovering over a latrine in the College of Sciences building said otherwise.

She clasped a hand to her aching head as she stepped out of the restroom. There was no denying it – this wasn't just stress. She was sick, and she decided that if a quick apothecary visit was needed to get through the next few days, then so be it.

She just needed to be as secretive about it as possible.

"You're pregnant."

The diagnosis was so unexpected that it didn't register with Cassandra at first. Granted, she had to lip-read the apothecary's words, so maybe she misunderstood something. *No, that can't be right. I expected a cold, or the flu, or some sort of stomach illness... what other words are mouthed similar to pregnant?*

Just her mind uttering the word *pregnant* sent a cold chill down her spine. It was impossible. She was barely eighteen years old, a college freshman. Marriage and starting a family were still many years down the road. She barely ever interacted with men her age, much less being intimate with them.

When she saw the apothecary write her diagnosis in his notes, it was unmistakable; even in his scraggly healer's handwriting. *Pregnant. So I did read his lips correctly.*

"This must be some sort of mistake," Cassandra's voice shook as the apothecary looked up from his notes. Her thinly veiled panic combined with the fact that she couldn't hear her own voice made her heartbeat pound in her ears.

"No mistake," the apothecary shook his head. She'd asked him to speak slowly and clearly, and make sure she had a full view of his face. He clearly hadn't had many deaf patients before, and raised an eyebrow when she mentioned that she was currently in bootcamp for the junior royal guard. If it wasn't for her overwhelming sickness and anxiety, she would've scowled at him for doubting her. "You are definitely pregnant. About eight weeks."

Eight weeks? Cassandra turned back the calendar in her mind. That would put the conception at the beginning of June, shortly after school let out, and...

No. No no no no.

It wasn't him.

There's no way.

That's impossible.

But there was no one else. It couldn't have been anyone else.

An explosion of nausea broiled her stomach, and Cassandra bolted for the nearest trash bin. She emptied what little food she'd eaten into the wooden basket, gasping for breath as cold sweat stained her forehead.

No. No. Please. Not this.

The apothecary stepped forward, offering a sympathetic pat on the shoulder.

How could this even happen?

"It's called morning sickness," he explained once Cassandra had collected herself enough to read his lips. "It will go away after a month or two."

Cassandra's hands balled into fists as her gaze fell to the ground, struggling to swallow as her mind processed her new reality. She hated the way the apothecary looked at her – as if he assumed she'd been fooling around with her male cadets. Thankfully, she'd slipped away to an off-campus apothecary, as she didn't want to risk her diagnosis putting her future in jeopardy. She was fully expecting to be diagnosed with a minor illness, sent home with a potion, and force herself to struggle through the last few days of bootcamp.

But this would derail everything. She pressed a shaking hand against her stomach – right now, it was flat as a board, even a bit concave from her recent lack of meals. But eventually her condition would show, and there was no way the guard would allow a deaf *and* pregnant woman to join their ranks.

Hell, she wasn't even sure if she'd be able to attend her classes. Not if this sickness was going to continue for a month or two. How long would she even be pregnant? She knew that normal human pregnancies lasted about nine months, what about this... half-Naga one?

She cringed at the thought. *Half-Naga. Half-reptilian. This shouldn't even be possible, for gods' sake!*

But the most horrid question of all remained – what would the baby even look like when it was born? What unholy monstrosity would the combined genes of a human and Naga produce?

Cassandra's racing thoughts were interrupted by a knock at the door. She couldn't hear it, but she could feel the vibrations along the floor and see the apothecary bolt upright from his seat.

She buried her face in her palms, wiping damp strands of brown hair away from her forehead. Her body felt freezing and on fire at the same time, and she alternated between sweating profusely and having that sweat feel like ice against her skin. She was too stressed, sick, and lost in her own thoughts to pay much attention to their visitor.

Until, between the gaps in her fingers, she caught a glimpse of purple and gold.

Her heart plummeted out of her chest.

It was the staff sergeant.

THE GOOD NEWS WAS THAT HE WASN'T THERE TO scold her for sneaking off campus. In fact, he didn't even seem concerned that she was at an apothecary looking like she hadn't eaten or slept in days.

The true reason why he'd gone searching for her was far more dire. Her already exasperated stomach clenched even more when she saw the torn-open letter in his hands. Communication with family members was usually forbidden during bootcamp, to help prevent distraction and homesickness. Which meant that this letter was no friendly correspondence – something was wrong at home.

Just two days earlier, the sergeant explained, her father had a heart attack.

The sergeant quickly followed the devastating news up with the fact that her father was still alive and recovering, although he was currently bedbound. But between Cassandra's lack of hearing causing communication issues and the fact that she was already ill and in shock, Cassandra felt like she was about to have a heart attack herself.

Her face burned with both pain and embarrassment as her squad captain pulled her crumpled body off the floor. She couldn't stand. She couldn't breathe. Her life was becoming a series of nightmares, piling up like a stack of heavy books and crushing her underneath them.

She was relieved that the staff sergeant was sympathetic and not as callous as some of her other comrades. Once she was able to stand on steady legs and get her breathing under control, all she could focus on was getting home as soon as possible.

Thankfully, she was granted formal leave from both the junior guard and school. Senior guard leadership agreed to let her take her final assessments when she returned, and she could catch up on classes once her father had recovered.

For the entire journey back to Live Oak, the pregnancy almost entirely slipped from her mind. She feared she'd descend into lunacy if she allowed it to. She needed to focus on her father, handling one disaster at a time.

The seconds ticked like hours as she ventured home, desperate to see her father. The sergeant had said he was alive and recovering, but she needed to see it herself. To hear him greet her and stroke her hair like he always did, even if he couldn't rise from his own bed.

Thankfully, as soon as she arrived home and rushed upstairs, that was exactly what he did.

She pulled away, shaking as tears pooled in the corners of her eyes. She'd bolted to her parents' bedroom and darted into his outstretched arms so quickly that she hadn't been able to assess his current condition.

He wasn't the same strong, resilient, healthy parent she'd left nearly eight weeks earlier. She'd felt it in his arms when he hugged her – his grasp was frail and tender. She gazed into his eyes – they were the only thing she recognized about him. His skin had an odd bluish tint, and his once plump, hearty face was gaunt and pale. The veins that wove underneath his skin were more visible, and even his hairline was thinning. His condition reminded Cassandra of visiting her grand-parents when she was a child, the ones that passed away when she was ten.

Cadence, as well as Cassandra's four other siblings, hugged the outer perimeter of the room, watching with bowed heads and wrought hands. She was the last to arrive. And according to them, William had been unwell for some time. They'd kept his illness a secret from her, wanting her to focus on making it through bootcamp. But this time, they had to write. Because they feared that if they didn't, she wouldn't have a chance to say goodbye.

"No," Cassandra spoke, her voice choked with tears. "That's not going to happen. You're going to recover. Promise me that. Please."

She wiped her tears away, her gaze locked with her father's. She saw a lot of emotions in his eyes – love, sadness, fear. But they didn't contain the same warmth they used to. The constant parental reassurance that everything would be fine.

He gave her a shaky kiss on the forehead. She knew he couldn't promise her anything. Because this time, he didn't know what would happen next. None of them did.

As much as the entire family was desperate for his recovery, they had to prepare for the worst. Which meant learning how to manage the inn without him. The apothecary wanted him on full bedrest until his condition improved, and Cassandra's older brothers had families and jobs to attend to. They visited when they could, but most days, managing the inn was left to Cassandra, her mother, and her two older sisters.

Keeping up with the daily management of the inn was no issue for them. The three sisters had worked there all throughout their teen years, and immediately resumed their previous routine of serving customers and scrubbing dirty dishes. Cadence managed the cooks and the bartender, while also balancing expenses for the inn.

This worked for a while. But not only was the inn busier than ever, but the building was nearly fifty years old and starting to fall apart. William was the one who usually managed repairs of the inn, and without his help, the girls struggled to patch holes in the roof and replace molding floorboards in the dining room.

It ended up being mainly Cassandra's job. She may have been small-framed and weak compared to the other junior guard recruits, but compared to her mother and sisters she was all grit and muscle. But endless wood-working and carpentry duties were taxing on Cassandra, who was still suffering grief for her father's health... and morning sickness.

But the pregnancy that she so desperately tried to shove out of her mind was proving to be a mystery. After six months, not only was she barely showing, but her bouts of vomiting still hadn't ceased. It occurred to her that she had no idea now long Naga pregnancies lasted, or how long *this* one would last. She imagined that her body was horribly confused, trying to build something resembling a baby out of both human and Naga DNA.

Do Nagas even get pregnant? Or do they lay eggs?

Am I going to lay an egg?

It didn't help that most of her horrid worries occurred when she was hunched over the latrine in the inn's outhouse. She'd told her mother and sisters that her illness was nerves, but she had no idea how long that lie would last. Eventually, the bizarre baby growing inside her would be impossible to hide.

In the months that followed, her stomach finally started to show. It was subtle at first, like bloating after a large meal, but eventually she grew so rotund that the only way to hide her condition was loose clothing. Her mother and sister found it odd that she chose to scrub the floorboards while wearing baggy, flowy dresses, but they were too caught up in other worries to remark on it.

Her father had recovered – at least as well as he ever could. He was no longer bed-bound, but he'd lost a lot of weight, and needed a cane to walk. His pale, sallow, skeletal appearance remained, causing Cassandra to mourn every time she caught sight of him. His warm, loving smile had never changed, but his appearance was a shell of the father she'd grown up with. He had always been so strong, so resilient... his illness had thrust him into old age far too soon.

William took over managing finances, but his brittle body couldn't do any physical labor. That was still Cassandra's job, and as her pregnancy progressed, it became harder to keep up with maintaining the inn. Her mother worried that Cassandra was overworking herself, and after a few hours would often usher her upstairs with a glass of water and a cool rag for her forehead. But Cassandra couldn't help but notice the frustrated glare in Penelope's eyes every time Cassandra went upstairs.

And one night, in mid-spring, Cassandra's worst fears were realized. She was changing into her nightgown when Penelope burst into her room. She saw her sister mutter an apology, which quickly morphed into a scream when she took notice of Cassandra's bare, rotund stomach.

Her mother nearly fainted, and she feared her father would have another heart attack. They were all exhausted from working a busy Saturday at the inn, but Cassandra's family still managed to corral her downstairs and question her nearly the entire night.

They were flabbergasted at how it happened. They assumed she'd been fooling around with someone in Live Oak, and her mother and sister spent nearly an hour speculating over who it could be. As nerve-wracking as the interrogation was, Cassandra was relieved that they assumed it was some dalliance with a local boy. She could handle the shame of being an 18-year-old girl having a baby out of wedlock.

What she couldn't handle was anyone finding out the truth.

Despite her family's theories, they never managed to uncover the paternity of her mysterious child. Spring morphed into summer, and Cassandra's stomach continued to grow. By the end of August, her belly was round as a balloon and covered in discolored, claw-like stretch marks. Cassandra groaned about her massive size, but Cadence assured her that it was normal. *After all,* she chuckled. *I've done it five times.*

With normal babies, Cassandra grumbled one evening as she waddled towards the outhouse and plopped down on the toilet. She had to pee. She *always* had to pee. She also got frequent headaches, felt dizzy when outside in the heat, and hated the smell of burning firewood. Again, her mother assured her this was all normal.

What *was* abnormal was the length of her pregnancy. It had been well over a year, and she had no idea when the hybrid creature would suddenly decide to pop out of her. By mid-September, she concluded that her stomach couldn't possibly get any larger. This baby needed to come out, *now*.

But where? Generally, babies with birthed at home with assistance from a midwife, but Cassandra couldn't risk anyone helping her. She had no idea what this child would look like, but she knew it would have features that would immediately distinguish it as not-fully-human. So instead, she went to the library and scoured every book on childbirth that she could find. But there weren't many, and she knew that no amount of reading was going to prepare her for this.

At some point, she would have to give birth to this mutant baby completely alone.

One late September evening, Cassandra felt sicker than usual. Her mother, convinced that she was due any day, had excused her from most duties around the inn. She'd spent most of the afternoon in bed, although as the hours whittled away, she became more and more restless. She needed to check and see how things were going with the dinner shift.

She clutched the railing as she jostled down the steps one at a time, wrapping her other hand around her massive, swollen stomach. She kept her gaze downward, focusing on not tripping, when another pair of feet stepped in front of her and came to a halt.

Cassandra looked up. Penelope's arms were crossed, and her eyebrows narrowed.

"You're supposed to be upstairs," she stated flatly.

Cassandra sighed. She wasn't in the mood to talk. She preferred to sign, which Penelope knew little of, and her sister had a habit of talking too fast for her to lip-read. She tried to brush past Penelope, who shifted her body to block her path.

"Go. Upstairs."

"No. I'm fine," Cassandra muttered, again trying to push past her sister. "I just want to-"

"Want to what?"

Cassandra didn't understand the fury in her sister's eyes. She knew that Penelope was stressed from managing much of the inn on her own, and that Cassandra's pregnancy caused her to be a burden. But that fury had been lingering in her eyes for months, and Cassandra decided that she needed to confront it.

"What is your problem?"

Those words were a like a lit fuse. Penelope exploded into a tirade, one too fast and with too much movement for Cassandra to comprehend fully. But she understood enough; her sister was mad at her. Not just for her pregnancy, but for the fact that she'd done so when she had the brightest future out of all of them. A future brighter than her sister's.

"You could've gone back to the guard by now if you hadn't been sleeping around!"

Cassandra's throat locked up, tears threatening to spill from her eyes. Going back to the guard was never an option – her hybrid child had already been conceived by the time she stepped foot on campus. Her family assumed the conception had occurred last winter, when in reality, it was happened far earlier. With her best friend, the one she still held feelings for, the one that she hadn't seen in over a year.

The one who wasn't even human.

And now her own sister, one of the people she trusted most in the world, viewed her as a disappointment and a failure.

Cassandra felt a tap on her shoulder.

"Are you even listening to me?"

Penelope's shrill words set off Cassandra's own fuse. *No. Of course I'm not. Because you, and everyone else in this family, act like I'm a burden because I'm deaf. You don't bother to slow down, or speak clearly, or learn even the smallest bit of sign language. And you act like I'm the problem.*

But as the furious thoughts scorched through her mind, she refused to say them aloud. Shouting back at her sister would only fan the flames, and she didn't feel like having to speak when she couldn't even hear her own voice.

Instead, Cassandra slowly signed a curse so horrid that she'd never be willing to speak it aloud. Penelope didn't understand what she was trying to say, but Cassandra's flared nostrils and narrowed eyes made her take a step back in horror.

"It's okay Cassie, calm do-"

To hell I'll calm down. Cassandra tore past her sister, nearly knocking her over in the process, and jogged down the stairs and out the door. As she ran into the murky forest, framed by a rapidly setting sun, she left a trail of angry tears behind her.

It was as if every mounting frustration from the past year suddenly exploded inside her aching head. Her father's illness, leaving the royal guard... but most importantly, feeling like a burden because she was pregnant with a horrid mutant baby that she didn't want.

Her swollen stomach only allowed her to run so far, and it bounced painfully with every stride. She eventually came to a stop and leaned against a tree. She could see her and the Naga's shack in the distance, and her heart lurched. She wondered if he still visited the little run-down abode. She wondered if he was doing alright.

She wondered if he still thought about her.

A scorching cramp in her lower belly sent her crumpling to the ground, her face grimacing as waves of pain coursed through her body. Running through a forest while being heavily pregnant was a bad idea.

A few minutes later, she experienced another cramp. Except this time, it was lower, near her pelvis. She balled her hands into fists and clutched the surrounding grass, squeezing it until her knuckles turned white.

Gods, I've never felt pain like this before.

Wait...

They weren't cramps. They were contractions. Cassandra had read about them in her childbirth books.

The baby was coming out.

Chapter 23

*E*ZRINTH SLITHERED THROUGH THE LABY-
rinth of Testudo tunnels with ease. As a snake,
tight spaces comforted him, bringing a sense of safety
and warmth similar to being in the water. He brushed
past the concerned Testudo, with Caine and his band of
Varan companions marching behind him, and ignored
the stares that tortoisefolk burned into his brain.

He wasn't welcome here. But he didn't care.

Because they were so preoccupied with the hundreds
of Terrapin refugees that Apalone had taken in, there
were no guards at the entrance to the village. One of the
Testudo from the village Caine and the Gharian traded
with happily showed them where the entrance was
located, which was surprising to Ezrinth. He knew that
the southernmost Testudo were less opposed to war than

those in the capital, but perhaps the extent of the humans' destruction had eroded their pacifism even further.

And within Apalone, it had clearly eroded their ability to resist Ezrinth's presence. He'd seen battle before, but the sight of the overcrowded tunnels full of bandaged, bleeding, and exhausted refugees made his heart sink. But the sadness was quickly quashed by simmering rage. His top priority may have been reuniting with his mate and daughter, but his quest to destroy the human kingdom was for the sake of all reptilians, so they would never feel this sort of pain again.

Ezrinth was so lost in thought that he nearly bumped into a Testudo blocking his path. He shook his head, snapping back to reality, and peered down. It was a female, possibly a healer based on her garments, and she appeared to have no intentions of moving. Her arms were crossed in front of her plastron, and as soon as Ezrinth attempted to slither past her, she blocked his path with her massive shell.

<May I help you?> Ezrinth raised a scaled eyebrow, trying to mask the irritation in his thoughts.

<I could ask the same of you,> The Testudo hissed. <My name is Reeve – I'm the chief healer in Apalone. And you seem to think that you and your fellow reptilians can march in here unannounced and do what you please. I think otherwise.>

Ezrinth's eyes flashed with anger, but his rational mind quickly kicked in - arguing would only get him kicked out of the village. He took a deep breath, forced a tight-lipped smile, and softened his glowering gaze.

<My apologies.> He gave a long, slow tongue flick. <How inconsiderate of me. My name is Ezrinth, son of the Na- >

<I know exactly who you are.>

He froze, straining to keep his smile. He pressed his lips tighter together and continued, <Anyway, I'm here looking for my daughter, the half-Naga girl. Her name is Marissa, and I was told that she was brought here after Terrapin was attacked.>

<I don't know who- >

<And before you lie to me,> Ezrinth hissed, flicking his tongue again. <I can smell her scent on you. Where is she?>

Reeve paused for a moment, <She left.>

Ezrinth's slitted pupils dilated as he studied her, trying to read her expression. She could've been lying, but it was entirely possible that Marissa had left. *If she had access to healers, her injury may have fully healed by now. And there's no other reason for her to stay here.*

<Very well.> Ezrinth nodded. <Do you have any idea where she was headed?>

<She didn't say.>

Ezrinth held his breath. With every bit of conversation, his illusion of calm was growing more and more frayed. This Testudo was just as stoic and tight-lipped as he was, and she was clearly unwilling to spill more information.

He peered around the room. It was circular, about ten feet in diameter, with the ceilings giving little headroom to an eight-foot-tall Naga. The walls were lined with refugees, most of them nursing bandaged wounds, their expressions somewhere between shell-shocked and bored. There were far too many of them to each have their own cot – most of the healers tended to their wounds as they sat slumped against the walls.

There was little furniture – just some baskets and carts full of earthy-smelling herbs and rapidly depleting vials of orange paste. But clinging to the bedpost of one of the few cots in the room, a serpentine figure suddenly disappeared from view, slithering into a dark corner of the room.

What in Squamata is a snake doing in Testudo territory?

He continued to stare dumbfounded at the cot, startling when the snake's head emerged from the shadowy underside of the bed. There wasn't enough light for Ezrinth to make out its features, other than a smooth, glittering pair of black eyes. The way it glared at Ezrinth made him uneasy, as if it were intelligent enough to understand their full conversation. If he were more paranoid, he'd swear it was spying on him.

Wait a minute...

A sudden marching sound snapped Ezrinth's attention back on Reeve. She was now flanked by two crossbow-wielding Testudo guards, and they did not look pleased to see Ezrinth and his band of interlopers.

He gulped. As desperately as he needed to find Marissa, he did not want to start a fight with the tortoises. After all, he still needed the idol piece from them, and his ability to be hailed as sovereign by his fellow reptilians would be severely hampered by bloodshed.

Speaking of the idol piece...

<Alright, alright.> Ezrinth held up his clawed hands in a gesture of peace. <I believe you. Marissa isn't here.

But if you don't mind, I just have one more request while I'm here...>

<I know all about your little mission, *snake*,> Reeve growled. <Did you really think we'd just hand the idol piece over? Let you cause even more destruction? I suggest you leave, *now*, before myself and my guards lose our patie- >

<It's not here.>

Reeve froze mid-thought as shock coursed through Ezrinth's veins. The female Testudo turned around, and one of the guard's gave her a steely gaze.

<The humans stole it from Terrapin,> the guard continued. <They most likely brought it back to their kingdom. Supposedly there's a massive fortress in the middle of the wretched place where the chieftain and his family live. I bet it's locked away in there.>

Ezrinth was so shocked that he couldn't think. Reeve looked like her head was about to burst into flames.

<Radian!> She screeched. <Why would you- >

<Wake up, Reeve!> The Testudo hissed. <You really want to sit here and play peacekeeper right now? You've seen what the humans did to our kin at Terrapin, and I sure as hell don't want it to happen here. I'm tired of hiding.> The Testudo gazed up at Ezrinth. <I say we let the Naga take down those humans for good.>

To both Ezrinth and Reeve's shock, the other Testudo guard seemed to agree.

Reeve was left completely and utterly speechless. Ezrinth's stomach turned as he watched the healer's anger turn to fear. And realization. And finally, horror.

<Let's go.> Ezrinth turned toward Caine and the Varan. Not only was he desperate to reclaim the idol piece from the humans, but he wanted to leave Apalone while Reeve was still lost for words and unable to stop him.

<Um, Ezrinth.> Rathi piped up. <What exactly is the plan here?>

<Simple,> Ezrinth replied as he slithered away from Reeve and the guards, his companions reluctantly following. <We break into the humans' kingdom and get the idol piece back.>

<But Ezrinth, that's *impossible*. How are we going to sneak our way through?>

<I have ideas.>

<And what about your daughter?>

That question made Ezrinth freeze. He was skeptical, but he had to admit that the scent of Marissa that lingered on Reeve's skin was very faint. It was probable that she was telling the truth. Besides, if he tore through the rest of the village searching for her, it would cause chaos. He hated the dozens of uneasy stares from the tortoises that still lingered in his mind.

<We'll find her,> Ezrinth replied, trying to hide the uncertainty creeping through his mind. He flicked his tongue again. <But right now, I want those idol pieces out of human hands before they start experimenting on them. Or worse.>

Ezrinth knew the idol pieces were supposedly indestructible, but he had no idea how many beings had tested that theory in the past eight hundred years. He certainly didn't want to let the humans find out.

This had to be their top priority. For now, he needed to reassure himself that wherever Marissa was, that she was safe. And as much as he hated that puny human that she fawned over, Ezrinth hoped he was at least keeping her alive.

<Let's go,> Ezrinth hissed, abruptly slithering away from Reeve and the Testudo guards. <We don't have much time. We need to get to the kingdom by nightfall, so we can complete this mission in the dark.>

Ezrinth knew this mission was insanity, meaning they needed to use every advantage they had. *And my largest one,* Ezrinth grinned as his slitted pupils flared. *Is that Naga are nocturnal. Perfect time to take out those night-blinded human bastards.*

MARISSA SWORE SHE HELD HER BREATH THE entire time Nim was gone. It was her idea, and thankfully Sauria seemed to agree with it. A snake slithering around tortoise territory was mildly suspicious, but not nearly as much as a half-Naga trying to hide in the shadows and spy on her wretched father.

She was practically hovering over the door with anticipation as it cracked open. Her body tensed for a moment, concerned that it may have been Ezrinth himself ready to snatch her, but relief trickled down her spine as a long, slender figure slithered innocuously through the door.

Nim returned to his usual position coiled up on one of the bedposts. As he did so, Marissa wondered how much control Nim truly had over his own body. And if Sauria's possession of the snake was truly consensual. But she had to admit, Nim seemed calm and attentive, his glossy eyes reflecting the dim light of the glowstone sconces as he flicked his tongue.

Marissa had explained everything to her companions while Nim was gone. She decided it was time – she wouldn't be able to hold Sauria's secret much longer. And Arthur was already incredibly suspicious; after all, he was present when Sauria summoned a giant python out of nowhere.

But Nim was gone for less than ten minutes, which wasn't nearly enough time for Marissa to answer their barrage of questions. And there were still a lot of questions she still didn't know the answer to. She hoped that she'd have more opportunity to learn about Sauria – and herself – over the coming days. Marissa was the only one who could hear him, as Sauria's communication method was clearly different than that between normal reptilians. Which meant that their conversations would be entirely private.

Which is a good thing, Marissa grumbled. *Considering that he can read my thoughts.*

<Alrighty then.> Nathara slithered toward the bedpost, fists on her hips as she glowered at the snake. <Since you are apparently possessed by a god, little one, I want to know exactly what you saw out there.>

Nim stared at her blankly, flicking his tongue.

Nathara turned toward Marissa, one scaly brow ridge lifted in suspicion, but Marissa simply shook her head and brushed past her aunt.

<Let me talk to him,> Marissa insisted, scooping Nim off the bedpost and wrapping him around her neck.

<*I like her,*> Sauria noted, gesturing toward Marissa. <*Gentle-hearted, yet tough as scales. Typical of Naga females.*>

Marissa chuckled, wondering if those traits also applied to half-Naga.

<*Have a seat, Marissa. I'll explain everything.*>

Marissa did, and she gazed into Nim's black eyes as Sauria explained his encounter with Ezrinth. As she listened, clinging to every detail, she realized that to her companions, she was merely having a very intense staring contest with her pet snake. Yet they seemed to believe her insistence that Nim was possessed by a minor reptilian god. They hovered in a semicircle around her, eager for her report.

Once Sauria was finished, Marissa sighed, trying to find the thoughts to condense everything into just a few sentences.

<Alright,> Marissa peered up at Nathara. <Sauria says that Ezrinth believed the healer that I wasn't here. The good news is that he left.>

Nathara let out a sigh of relief, that to Marissa seemed premature.

<But,> Marissa continued. <The bad news is that one of the guards admitted that the humans stole the last idol piece. I don't know if Ezrinth is aware that we have the other two, but he and his companions plan on storming the palace tonight.>

<What!?> Nathara exclaimed. <Has my brother lost his mind!?>

While Nathara continued fretting over Ezrinth's insane plan, Marissa relayed the same information to Arthur and Thomas. Their reactions weren't that far off from Nathara's.

And Marissa could tell by the looks on their faces that they knew what was coming next.

She placed her fingertips against her temples and dug deep into her mind, determined to relay her next sentence to all three of them simultaneously.

It hurt, but thankfully she didn't need many words. <"We're going to stop them.">

It was as if a gunshot echoed through the room. All three of them stopped worriedly prattling and stared wide-eyed at Marissa.

"I know that look," she glared at Arthur. "It's the same one you gave me when I wanted to infiltrate the black market. But just like last time, I have a plan."

Arthur sighed, rubbing the back of his neck with his palm, "You did have a plan. And thankfully, it was one that didn't result in our demise. You know I believe in you, Marissa, and I want to stop this as much as you do. But the black market, even the Castella's party... it all pales in comparison to this. Sneaking into the palace is hands-down the most insane thing we could do right now. We're risking our lives. *Your* life."

Arthur's voice shook with his last sentence, and so did Marissa's chest. Arthur was a kind, gentle, caring human being, and like Marissa, he wasn't afraid of standing up for what he believed in. But Marissa had to admit that while she dove headfirst into these insane missions, he had a healthy dose of cautiousness.

Not to mention, he feared for her safety. Because now she was his. Really, truly his. Heat flushed her cheeks as she remembered their passionate kiss the night before.

"Well, before we make a decision," Marissa continued. "Let me tell you the plan."

"Alright, I want to hear it."

"Just a fair warning, you're probably going to hate it."

Arthur raised an eyebrow. "All the more reason that I want to hear it. Now what's the plan?"

"I HATE IT," ARTHUR grumbled ten minutes later.

"I figured," Marissa retorted, raising an eyebrow. "But you have to admit, it's a good plan."

"It's our only choice," Arthur sighed. "Otherwise, getting past the palace doors is going to be impossible. But I still hate it."

Marissa nodded, a sad frown drifting across her face. She knew that Arthur always feared for her safety. She feared for his as well – the sight of him the night before, knelt in front of her, covered in blood with a bullet wound through his hip, would forever haunt her memories. It drowned her heart in guilt that he carried her all that way while being so badly injured. *If he died trying to save me...* she bit her lip. She didn't want to think about it.

But wherever they went, whatever they did, the stakes were always higher for Marissa. She was no longer just a lonely drifter hiding her face behind a scarf. She a fugitive; public enemy number one for the royal family. *All those soldiers outside Terrapin, hundreds of men and women...* they were all there for her. She remembered Sauria's words earlier that morning, as explained her importance in this whole charade. *A leader, a royal, a princess...* the only one in the whole valley capable of communicating with both humans and reptilians. Her existence was the key to peace – something that the royal family was vehemently against.

A mask wasn't enough anymore. Nothing was.

Marissa stepped toward Arthur, trying to express her warm affection for him through just her gaze. While she wasn't willing to fully embrace him in front of Nathara and Thomas, there was no point in hiding it. They knew. They'd known this whole time.

"I'm going to survive this," Marissa insisted, trying to make her own mind believe it. "Just like I did at the black market, and at the Castella's party. Everything will be fine."

Arthur nodded, the worry on his face barely masked by his acknowledgment that Marissa was right. They had to make this plan work. Letting the idol pieces fall back into Ezrinth's hands wasn't an option.

Marissa explained everything a second time to Nathara, who disliked the plan just as much as Arthur did. Maybe even more so, because she wouldn't be present at the palace when it unfolded.

<There's no way for a giant Naga to sneak through the palace without arising suspicion,> Marissa explained.

Nathara raised a scaled eyebrow, <Do you question my stealth skills, niece?>

<No, not at all,> Marissa shook her head at her aunt's teasing. <But the palace halls are a very different place than the forests of Squamata. This mission must be done by me, and me alone.>

Nathara nodded in agreement. She had the same gentle, concerned glow in her eyes as Arthur. Her whole life, Marissa had always been at risk – her existence alone was a death sentence. But to now have people who cared about her, feared for her... it made it even more heart-wrenching. And worth it - if she succeeded.

All three of them shifted their gazes to Thomas. He was alone on one of the cots, tracing his fingers across the woven pattern of the blankets. He'd been silent this entire time, and Marissa knew that he likely wouldn't join them. He'd experienced enough hell at the front lines in Terrapin, and he had a wife to return home to.

Which was why it sent shock through Marissa's veins when he uttered, "I'm in too."

"But Thomas-"

"I know what yer thinkin'," he cut Marissa off. "I bet ya didn't even expect me to dive in this far. I do have Marian on my mind, but she's all better now, and headin' home to my wife ain't gonna be much good if that giant snake goddess gets summoned and destroys us all. I'm in this until the end."

Marissa didn't know what to say. She was surprised to find tears welling in the corners of her eyes.

She brushed them away, cursing her frail emotional state, and did the only thing that felt right – she gave Thomas a hug.

He wrapped his large, hairy arms around her back and chuckled, embracing her like she imagined a father would to their child. She realized; he *was* the closest thing she'd ever had to a father. He was the first one to make her confront her feelings for Arthur. He lent her his horse when she needed to get to Copperton. He had insisted that she had it in her to fire a gun when she was too afraid. The amount of times he'd helped them, encouraged them, supported them, all while risking his own safety, were innumerable.

The gruff, alcoholic poacher who she once tried to kill for murdering a reptilian was now one of her closest friends. It all seemed surreal.

Marissa broke the embrace after a few seconds, her whole body buzzing with happiness.

And fear. But for now, she shoved that emotion aside.

"We need to get going," Marissa declared. "Ezrinth and the others plan on breaking into the palace tonight, and it's a full days journey to get there."

"Sounds good," Arthur nodded. "Let's just see if we-"

The door cracked open, sending a loud squeak through the domed room.

Marissa turned around, expecting it to be the healer from earlier.

It wasn't. To her surprise, it was Kai.

He held his right arm close to his chest, his two missing claws still raw, red stumps. But they would grow back with time, and the rest of his body seemed to be healed. He smiled, which Marissa could tell was painful for him to do.

<I came here to apologize,> he sighed. <This wasn't your fault, Marissa. And I don't regret bringing you into Terrapin, or having you meet Mata. And I appreciate everything you and your friends did trying to protect us.>

<No, it's okay,> Marissa could feel her heart sinking. <You don't have to apologize. You have every right to be upset after... what happened.>

It was incredibly difficult to look at Kai as he stood in the doorway. Despite his attempts at cheerfulness, a mournful mask still hung over his face. He looked exhausted despite his many hours of rest, and the past few days seemed to have aged him several decades.

<You should go lie back down,> Marissa insisted. <Have the healers check on your- >

<No. I'm fine – my wounds have healed. And I heard everything you said to Nathara through the door. About your plan. And I want to come with you.>

<Kai...>

<I'm serious. My mother and her ancestors fought for peace in this valley for eight hundred years. Grandmother sacrificed her life for it. I won't fail them now. Please, let me help you.>

Marissa turned toward the others. Nathara was the only one who understood, but she gave a firm nod.

<He can come with me,> Nathara concluded. <We'll wait for the rest of you in the forest just past the southern kingdom gates.>

Marissa nodded. It did make her feel better to know that Nathara wouldn't be waiting for them alone.

She explained everything to Arthur and Thomas, who were in unanimous agreement.

"Alright," Marissa took a deep breath, curling her fingers around the satchel that hung near her hips. As always, she could feel the bumpy outline of the idol pieces, reassuring her that they still had a chance.

"Let's do this."

Chapter 24

*E*ZRINTH WAS CONVINCED SHE WAS NEVER coming back.

It had been over a year, and he still hadn't seen her. For all he knew, she was off in the human kingdom, starting her adult life among her own kind. He was a relic of her past, something she would toss out of her mind and forget about.

Yet, he still returned. Every chance he had, he'd sneak his way back into the shack. He spent quiet afternoons swimming in the shallows, continuing his sketches until he ran out of paper, and admiring the beautiful sunsets out the open doorway. It was his place of peace. Yet without her, it always felt horribly empty.

He assumed she was gone forever, and he'd made his peace with it. He'd always have sweet, innocent, beautiful memories of her, and less innocent ones of their final night together.

That's why when she burst through the cloth-covered doorway one late September evening, he thought he was imaging things. He bolted upright from the wooden chair that his coiling body was draped around, ready to joyously embrace her... until she collapsed.

A deep, low groan of pain radiated from her crumpled form, and Ezrinth quickly gathered her in his arms and set her down on the bed in the far corner of the room. It was nothing but a rusted bedframe with a bare, paper-thin mattress, but he figured it was better than laying her down on the floor.

She groaned again, her pale fists clutching her pelvis. As Ezrinth set her down, he suddenly noticed her incredibly swollen, rotund stomach.

Is she... gravid?

Ezrinth knew little about gestation, whether human or reptilian. He knew it was a slow, painful, messy process, as his mother often helped with more complicated births back in their village. He had no idea if human birth was similar, but her screams were like those he'd heard from the shaman's hut when he was a child.

He was bewildered. *Why did she suddenly show up over a year later, ready to give birth? Where has she been all this time? And who sired the child?*

His scales ran cold at the thought of her taking a human mate. Despite her long absence, he'd struggled to comprehend that she was no longer his. That she never truly was, and never would be. Deep down, all he wanted was to take her as his mate, to build a life with her, whether in this decrepit shack or elsewhere in the valley. But he knew it was impossible; all their relationship would ever be was forbidden.

He pushed the thoughts out of his mind, and tried to focus on the present. His beloved was here, now, desperately in need of help. He could focus on the rest later.

He tried to sign to her, asking what was going on, but she was in too much pain to focus. Her hands were still balled into strained fists, the blue-tinged veins across her arms bulging with pain. He placed his open palm over her fist, scales against flesh, and through the pain she forced a weary smile.

Tears laced the corners of her eyes, both from the pain and from her happiness at seeing him. She raised a shaking hand, and signed slowly.

"Thank the gods you're here."

She sat upright, bracing herself against Ezrinth's chest, her breaths shallow and her forehead stained with sweat. Ezrinth craned his neck past her and watched as the last sliver of sunlight disappeared below the horizon through the doorway.

He didn't know what to expect with the birth, other than that it would be a very long night.

For the first few hours, she alternated between lying down and pacing throughout the shack, clutching her swollen stomach. Every ten minutes or so, she'd be crippled by waves of pain, ones that would nearly make her fall to her knees. In those moments, she clung to Ezrinth as he wrapped his body around hers. He rubbed her back and scalp delicately with his claws, wincing every time she cried out. He hated seeing her in so much pain.

As the hours passed, her contractions became closer and closer together. She was no longer able to stand, so Ezrinth sat with her on the flimsy mattress, allowing her to squeeze his hand until it nearly lost blood flow. Even if he didn't know what he was doing, he knew that she needed support. So he did whatever he could to make her comfortable.

Suddenly, everything changed. She became incredibly restless, preferring to sit upright rather than lie down. The pair spoke when she wasn't in too much pain, and she finally relented that Ezrinth needed to take off her underwear and check the progress of her labor.

Ezrinth did so with utmost hesitancy. He had no idea what sort of blood, tissue, or other fluids to expect. But what he was not expecting was the sight of the baby's head nearly all the way out, pushed even further by a sudden contraction.

It was time. Daylight was seeping through the open doorway. Ezrinth was exhausted from being up all night, and he couldn't even begin to imagine how she was feeling. He knelt in front of her, his eyes wary and hesitant, but she gave him a pained smile that told him that everything would be alright.

It all happened incredibly fast. A few pushes, and the screaming newborn plopped into Ezrinth's arms. He could barely breathe from shock.

I've done it. The baby is here. And healthy. And...

No...

It can't be...

Ezrinth had been so focused on helping her that the parentage of the baby had slipped his mind. *But this... this shouldn't be possible...*

But it was. As he traced the mottled black-and-brown scales that lined the baby's torso, limbs, and lower face, he broke into a grin when he realized how similar they were to his own.

It was a girl. A daughter.

His daughter.

Their daughter.

EZRINTH'S MATE SLEPT THROUGH MOST OF THE morning and afternoon, tucked into his coils and using them as a pillow. She awoke several times, attempting to feed the baby, but the crying half-Naga infant had little interest in nursing. She did, however, dig into a mouse that Ezrinth caught scurrying across the wobbly shack floors.

Which was a relief for Ezrinth, because his mate needed rest. It had taken her a while to finish passing the afterbirth, and her abdomen was still swollen. She was pale, exhausted, and covered in dried sweat, but to him she'd never looked more beautiful. He resisted the urge to trace a clawed finger across her cheek for fear of waking her.

But this moment of newfound beauty and peace wouldn't last. Ezrinth knew that it was only a matter of time before they came looking for her. Naga hearing was poor, but he remained alert, studying the air for vibrations and flicking his tongue to pick up on any foreign scents. He had to keep his mate hidden – and protect his newborn daughter. *Gods know what the humans would do to her if they found her.*

Or even what my own family would do. The weight of their precarious situation came crashing down on Ezrinth like a boulder. At some point, they would have to face the reality that a human and Naga pair, much less one with a hybrid child, would never be accepted by either society.

A sudden stir against Ezrinth's scales caused him to turn his attention back to his mate. She shifted her head, her vibrant blue eyes flickering open and greeting his copper-colored ones with a warm, loving glow. Ezrinth smiled, his gaze radiating tender happiness as he adjusted his coiled body to pull her closer to him. Her attention turned to her sleeping newborn, contentedly nestled in Ezrinth's arms.

"Did she eat?" she signed weakly.

"A rat," Ezrinth responded. "Not much, but at least she's content to sleep for now."

"What are we going to do?"

Ezrinth's heart sank. It was a massive, complicated, impossible question, one that he'd pondered all day while his mate slept. He had a few ideas, but they were all far from ideal. He knew that whatever happened, he needed to keep all three of them safe – and together.

"We'll run away," Ezrinth responded. "We'll disappear into the swamplands and build a new life, away from everyone else. Together, with our daughter."

Ezrinth knew it wasn't an ideal plan, but he was still surprised by the horror on his mate's face. Her gaze flicked downwards, away from him, as her mind retreated deep in thought.

Panic zapped through Ezrinth's veins. To him, this was their only option. They had to stay hidden. They had to protect their child. But most importantly, they had to stay together.

But as Ezrinth watched his mate struggle with a decision, he wondered if that was what *she* wanted. He wondered what her plan had been with this child, and if she had ever intended on keeping the newborn at all.

"I can't."

Ezrinth's face fell. He held a hand up, ready to beg her to reconsider, when she cut him off.

"We can't live like that," she continued. "We have homes, families, lives outside of this shack. We can't just abandon them. I... I can't abandon them."

"But..." Ezrinth struggled to string his signs together. "What are we supposed to do?"

Because even if we do part ways and resume our normal lives... Ezrinth peered down at the sleeping infant cradled in his right arm. A hybrid child, one with the body of a human and the scales of a snake. One that in theory, shouldn't even exist.

But she did. And she needed them.

A faint shout permeated the hazy afternoon air. Ezrinth bolted upright, his gaze fixated on the front door. He flicked his tongue in long, slow movements, trying to pick up on a hint of human scent.

He could smell his mate, but there a trace was a second, unfamiliar human lurking in the distance.

Wait, no... several humans.

Ezrinth's mate had picked up on his alarm, and she was now struggling to stand. Ezrinth helped her get her weight under her feet, and she plucked the newborn from his arms.

"You need to go," she signed with her free hand. "Now."

"I won't leave yo-"

"No. Please go. If they find you, they'll kill you."

Ezrinth peered down at the infant. "But what about her?"

His mate hesitated for a moment, "I know a place for her. Where she'll be safe. Don't worry about us."

"But wh-"

The shouts were getting louder. And multiplying. Ezrinth figured they couldn't be more than a few hundred feet from the shack, which meant they had probably spotted the old structure and were headed right toward it.

"Go!" she signed furiously. Ezrinth was hurt by her tense demeanor, but he knew that it was because of fear. Fear for his life.

She was right. He had to flee.

He bolted out the rear entrance of the hut in a fury of slithering coils, diving into the water just as his mate scrambled off the porch and into the forest. He couldn't hear any cries coming from the newborn, and he prayed that it would stay that way. Whatever safe haven she was headed to, Ezrinth prayed with every scale on his body that she'd make it there.

It was all he could do. A mob of angry humans had congregated on the docks, and as Ezrinth surfaced and took a breath, he saw them pointing and screaming at him. He scowled, hissing in disgust as he dove back under the water.

But the swampland surrounding the shack was shallow, and Ezrinth's serpentine form was still clearly visible below the water. Unfortunately, the water-logged terrain didn't slow the humans down, and they immediately waded into the shallows in a ruckus of splashing boots.

Ezrinth kept swimming, only occasionally lifting the tip of his nose out of the water to take a breath. The sun was setting, which Ezrinth hoped would give his nocturnal self an advantage. Yet no matter how fast he swam, the mob was always just a few dozen feet away, their dark figures illuminated by the orange glow of freshly lit oil lamps.

He gulped as he raised his coppery eyes above the water's surface. In front of him was a thin stretch of shoreline – a peninsula covered in sparse trees. He'd have to cross it to return to the safety of the water – and make it back to Nerodia in one piece.

He scrambled into the thin brush, which barely concealed his towering, serpentine figure. A thin, sandy patch snaked its way through the foliage, but Ezrinth chose to avoid it, relying on what little coverage he could get from the trees. The rapidly fading sunlight was making it difficult for the humans to keep up, and their voices were now just faint rumbles in the distance.

Somehow, he had to lose them. He had to disappear.

<Ezrinth?>

He spun around. A middle-aged, well-adorned female Naga stood in the center of the sandy path, with a bow slung across her back and a dagger clutched in her right hand.

It was his mother, Chumana.

<Ezzy? What are you doing out here? What is going o- >

Her thoughts snapped off as soon as she heard the shouts of the humans in the distance, her orange eyes suddenly flaring like embers. She rushed in front of her smaller son, readying the dagger in her palm.

<Mother, wait- >

<We'll discuss this later. Quick, go back to the village and get your father and sister. I'll hold them off until you return.>

Ezrinth hesitated. His mother was their leader; chieftress of the Naga, the strongest warrior they had. Humans were generally no match for her, but Ezrinth still feared leaving her at the mercy of a whole mob of them.

<Go!> she hissed once she realized Ezrinth was still standing behind her.

She's right. Ezrinth reassured himself as he slithered away. The humans were now close enough that he could hear them rustling through the trees. *She'll be fine on her own.*

Chumana's hisses echoed through the darkening brush. Ezrinth could hear screams and gasps as her dagger, claws, and fangs tore their way through several of the humans.

What's most important is that I get her hel...

A sudden gunshot cracked through the air, following by a long, serpentine shriek. Ezrinth's blood froze in his veins.

No. It had to have missed.

He heard a faint thud, then nothing. Human chatter slowly filled the silence, and their footsteps resumed. Right towards him.

No. No no no no...

His whole body was paralyzed. *How is this happening? Why isn't she still fighting them? She can't be...*

He swayed as if he were able to collapse. He took a few gasping breaths, his chest heaving as if he'd been holding his breath for an eternity. Every second he stood still allowed the humans to catch up with him. To find him. To kill him.

Yet he couldn't move.

Another crack exploded behind him, followed by a metallic whiz across the bushes in the distance. Ezrinth spun around, his eyes flashing with horror. The long, metallic barrel of a gun was pointed directly at his face.

They'd missed. But now that they were this close, that mistake was unlikely to happen again.

He hissed, loud and shrill, fury contorting his face as he did his best to intimidate the humans. He hated them. He hated all of them.

He lunged forward, diving into the water just as another bullet skidded across the surface.

He'd make them pay for this. *For killing my mother, for making my mate run away...*

From tearing me and my daughter apart.

As he swam through the inky abyss, now nearly black from the lack of sunlight, something broke deep inside him. It was as if his heart had turned into limestone, cold and hard but ready to shatter if it took another hit.

This was his worst nightmare. And he knew he'd never be the same again.

MONTHS PASSED, AND EZRINTH DRIFTED between abandoned huts and homemade shelters, clinging to the fringes of the village he'd once called home.

He knew the aftermath of that night would be dreadful. He knew that the sight of his normally proud, regal father, crumpled over his mother's corpse and drowning in mournful screeches, would be the worst feeling he'd ever experienced. He expected all of it – the pain, the disappointment, the flash of betrayal in his father's eyes. He knew he would be interrogated about where he'd been and how this could've happened. All while he stood still as a statue, one so brittle that it could crack at any moment.

What he hadn't expected, and what hurt the most, was being banished.

Ezrinth peered out the window of the makeshift shelter he'd resided in for the past week. News had spread quickly about the chieftain's son's exile, and with it rumors and false accusations swirled like the wind howling outside. At first, he'd spent his time clinging to the fringes of the village, sleeping on old, unoccupied huts on the outskirts of Nerodia. But within a week or two, he'd always be discovered and forced to move elsewhere. He was now so far outside the village that he could no longer see the clusters of huts in the distance.

A storm was brewing, which was unusual for a December in the valley. Thin, branching veins of lightning flashed a stark white against the black sky, their light illuminating the ember-colored flecks in Ezrinth's eyes. As a child, he'd always thought storms were beautiful. But that was back when he was in his own home, tucked into a cozy hammock, surrounded by warmth with a sturdy roof over his head. Out here, storms meant that water would be seeping into his scraggly hut all night.

He hated rain. It felt like nowadays, he hated everything.

But he especially hated humans. Not only had they pulled her away from his mate, but now his daughter as well. He was still in shock at her existence, of the fact that he was a father. Since the moment he held her in arms, catching her as she was born, something changed within him. Suddenly, there was a life in the world that mattered more than his own.

He had to find her.

But over the next several months, he had no luck. Not only was there an entire valley to search, but a Naga lurking through human territory was a massive target. On his few futile attempts to leave Naga territory and search for her, he'd been swung at with a dagger, chased with a lit torch, and shot at several times.

Eventually, it threw him into a pit of despair. He was still mourning the loss of his mate, of her choosing the human world over him and their daughter. And now he feared he would never find his child. A cold shudder ran down his spine as he wondered if she was even still alive.

He couldn't find her.

Or at least... not alone.

But who would he ask for help? He was an outcast, a pariah amongst the Naga. There were always the other reptilians, but why would they help him? What would they gain from it?

He spent the next few years pondering that question. Plan after plan crumbled into dust, and Ezrinth grew into a depressed, angry, bitter husk of the Naga he once was. The isolation had taken a toll on his mental state, and that, combined with his all-consuming desire to find his mate and child, caused him to consider more drastic measures.

Thoughts of finding the idol had always lurked in the back of his mind. At first, it had seemed like an impossible plan – how could he possibly convince all four reptilian races, especially the Testudo, that they needed to finally summon the goddess? Not to mention, how would he get the idol in the first place? It was sealed in a half-buried temple, covered in a thick, impenetrable layer of limestone. It was a grave for the wretched artifact, built so that it would never be uncovered.

But over the years, the already tense relationship between the humans and the reptilians had worsened. Border disputes increased, the humans developed more advanced weapons, and the horrid practice of poaching continued to rise. Even in his isolation, he could feel the anger brewing amongst the reptilians. Something needed to be done.

Everything changed one afternoon, almost eighteen years after his mate and daughter's disappearance. Ezrinth was tidying up his shack; a hodgepodge creation built with materials from both the nearby forest and long-abandoned, waterlogged Naga huts on the outskirts of Nerodia. It wasn't pretty from the outside, but the years he'd managed to turn into a sturdy, permanent abode. He was in a remote part of the swampland, just barely able to see the peninsula of his former village as a speck on the watery horizon. All alone, an isolated outcast, but that barely bothered him anymore. After nearly two decades, it was just a normal part of life.

This part of Naga territory was generally very quiet, with few hunters or travelers in sight. Which was why it alarmed Ezrinth when he heard a series of booming rumbles in the distance, on the shoreline in the opposite direction of Nerodia.

That's... where the temple is.

He hurriedly gathered up his weapons – an old dagger and bow that he'd swiped from the abandoned huts – and slithered off to investigate.

By the time he got there, whatever had been causing the disturbance was gone. The temple was still as always, a silent limestone titan sunken into the watery swampland. Only the occasional trill of the forest geckos providing any source of sound.

Ezrinth's eyes narrowed. It was as if he's been imagining things.

At least, until he rounded the corner of the submerged temple.

The sight of it rattled his stomach. A giant hole was blown open in the side of the temple. The limestone around the edges was cracked and jagged, making it look like an angry, screaming mouth. As Ezrinth moved closer, wading through the shallow water, he noticed several large chunks of the temple settled in the mucky sand. He picked one up, a palm-sized piece in the shape of a lopsided diamond, and hurled it towards the open swampland. It splashed in the water several dozen feet away with a gurgling *thunk*.

A wicked grin crept across his face. He didn't bother to question how this had happened. This was his opportunity, and he was going to take it.

It was almost too easy. Within an hour, he had the damp, muddy idol piece in his claws. He spent some time surveying it back at his shelter, amazed that such a simple piece of rock once caused so much chaos in the valley. *But now,* Ezrinth grinned. *It's time to take advantage of the gift Vaipera gave us.*

But this was only a piece of the idol – he needed all four to summon the goddess. The other three pieces were hidden away in the other three reptilian territories, which left Ezrinth with the burning question: who should he approach next?

The Gharian were all the way across the valley, and the pacifist Testudo were out of the question. Which left Ezrinth with the option of approaching the Varan. It seemed like a feasible plan; he knew that the chieftain, Rathi, hated humans almost as much as Ezrinth did. Since the Varan lived in the driest parts of the valley, many human villages bordered their territory, which had resulted in increased border disputes and poaching. It seemed like the perfect opportunity to persuade them.

He was able to make it to Varan territory within a day, eager to speak with Rathi, show him the idol piece, and discuss plans for obtaining the others and ending the human's reign for good. Yet once he reached Komodo, he never even made it past the guards. Naga weren't allowed in Varan territory, and Ezrinth couldn't risk showing them the idol piece for fear that it would be taken away. Which meant that his vague pleas of "I need to speak with the chieftain" fell on deaf ears.

Being barred entry and unwilling to fight his way through the guards, Ezrinth dejectedly returned to his shabby home outside Nerodia. There, he sat for days, scheming any possible way to make this plan work. He needed to summon the goddess. He had to. He spent so much time gazing at the idol piece that it began appearing in his dreams. It was all he could think about, and he feared that his already unsteady mental state was now bordering on insanity.

But one morning, when Ezrinth felt so frustrated by his failure that he was tempted to hurl the piece of rock into the reeds and forget all about his wretched plan, he heard a sudden knock on his hut.

It nearly caused him to leap out of his scales. In all eighteen years of being an outcast, he'd never once had a visitor.

<Yes?> Ezrinth barely poked his head out, concerned it was some angry Naga that had come to skewer him.

To his surprise, it wasn't a Naga. It was two Varan guards; the same ones he'd encountered in Komodo just a few weeks earlier.

<You're Ezrinth, son of chieftain Orami, yes?>

Ezrinth nodded, scowling at the mention of his father's name.

<You're to come with us immediately.>

What? Ezrinth was confused. But as he flicked his copper eyes up and down the lizardfolk's bodies, he noticed that they didn't seem hostile. Or upset. In fact, they seemed almost eager. They were happy to see him.

<Um...> Ezrinth stepped out of the hut, attempting to hide his confused tone. <May I ask why?>

The slightest hint of a grin appeared across one of the Varan's scaled faces.

<Rathi wishes to speak with you.>

Chapter 25

*A*FTER TRAVELING ALL THE WAY ACROSS THE valley to meet Mata and the Testudo, Marissa was relieved that it would be less than a day's journey back to the kingdom. She wasn't used to walking for hours at a time, and even though the deceased guard's boots were comfortable and well-crafted, she could still feel raw, damp blisters forming between her toes.

She huffed as she watched Nathara slither ahead, jealous that her Naga aunt's scales still looked immaculate after days of trudging through the forest. Marissa, on the other hand, was a wreck – her long black hair was stringy and gritty, and her fingernails were nearly black from the amount of dirt caked under them. Her beautiful Varan dress was destroyed – its once vibrant rainbow stripes were now a muddled mess of browns, and the torn-up sleeves was as ragged as her hair. Not to mention the splotchy bloodstain that hovered just above the hem, right where the dress touched her freshly scarred calf.

But at least I still have clothes, she noted as she eyed Arthur walking next to her. His ruined shirt had been a lost cause, and within the kingdom walls, he'd be less suspicious bare-chested than wearing a blood-stained shirt with a bullet hole through it.

Though not by much. They needed new clothes.

Although, Marissa turned her head, concealing a sly grin. *I certainly don't mind the view.*

She couldn't help but admire his slender yet muscular frame, even with its newfound array of scars and freshly healed bullet wound. They walked side-by-side, their bodies just inches from each other, although Marissa didn't dare try to hold his hand. Not with Thomas directly in front of them, perched atop Daisy and whistling folk tunes like he always did. The cart too badly damaged to bring to Brennan, so the group was forced to leave it behind. Thankfully, Thomas wasn't too bothered that his parents' mode of transportation would likely be pulled apart for firewood.

"I'm just glad to be alive," he had said back in Apalone.

Marissa nudged slightly closer to Arthur. Her attraction to him was intoxicating – and painfully obvious. She couldn't help but fantasize about kissing him again, holding him, *feeling* him. Wondering what lurked beyond what little clothing he had left. It was like a fever dream – consuming her thoughts with raw, burning emotions that tingled her skin and made her entire abdomen flutter. Even the exhaustion of their journey didn't bother her anymore – her steps felt lightweight and airy, as if she were walking on a cloud. She wondered where these sudden feelings had been all her life, and what they all meant. What mysteries of affection and romance she still had left to unravel.

As they walked, Marissa loosened the tension in her left arm, and heat prickled her neck as her fingertips brushed against his. Arthur's gaze was shifted downward, his green eyes scanning the dense forest floor for any stray vines or roots. But a warm grin radiated across his face, his cheeks flushing the slightest shade of red.

<Alright.> Nathara stopped suddenly, her tail forming a winding s-shape in the dirt. <The road splits up ahead. This is where Kai and I must leave you.>

Marissa nodded. She, Arthur, and Thomas would be entering the kingdom alone. Nathara and Kai, being too large, imposing, and obviously reptilian to be creeping through Brennan, would meet them just past the southern gates once they completed their mission.

We better complete this mission, Marissa gulped, forcing her anxiety back down her throat. She didn't want to think about what would happen if they didn't.

Nathara turned toward the silent Testudo behind her. <You, ready, Kai?>

He nodded, still rubbing the jagged stumps where his missing claws used to be.

Marissa watched for a few moments as they departed, a slithering snake and a stomping tortoise disappearing through the woven abyss of jungle. She knew Testudo were the slowest of the reptilians, and she hoped that Nathara wouldn't snap at Kai if he couldn't keep up.

But as their silhouettes faded away, Marissa was relieved to notice that Nathara had significantly slowed her pace. She slithered right next to Kai, not leaving his side.

"Well," Thomas sighed as he pulled Daisy to a halt. "It's ain't much further to the kingdom gates. How're y'all feeling?"

"Tired," Arthur raised a hand behind his head and rubbed his sore back. "And desperately in need of a shirt."

"Well, I've got good news for ya," Thomas raised an eyebrow. "Just before the western gates is a large shippin' warehouse. Giant carts come in carryin' supplies from beyond the borders for processin'. I worked there as a teenager, and I know exactly where they hide their extra shirts and breeches."

The thought of sneaking into yet another forbidden building made Marissa cringe, but she was incredibly tempted by the thought of wearing fresh, clean clothes. Even if they covered Marissa's face once they entered the kingdom, her ruined, bloodstained dress would raise immediate suspicion.

"Sounds good," Arthur nodded. "We need to blend in as much as possible. There's another thing we'll need to swipe from there too, if Thomas can find it."

"What?" Marissa asked.

Arthur gave a long, heaving sigh, "Rope. We'll need to bind your hands behind your back."

Marissa gulped, her face draining of color as the grim reality of their plan sank in.

"Or, at least, make it *look* like your hands are bound," Arthur reassured her, clearly noticing her sickened expression. "I know some knot tricks from my time spent fishing with my father."

He placed a hand on her shoulder, rubbing her dark scales underneath his thumb, "It will be all right. I promise."

Now he's the one having to reassure me. Marissa sighed and nodded.

"I know. Everything will be all right."

"It will be," Arthur grinned at her. The affection that glittered in his forest-green eyes allowed Marissa to smile despite her fears.

Everything will be all right.

Maybe if I repeat that to myself a thousand times, she thought to herself as they kept walking. *Then it might actually happen.*

A SMUG GRIN TWISTED ITS WAY ACROSS EZRINTH'S scaled face as the cart came to a halt in front of the palace.

The sun had finally disappeared under the horizon, giving them enough darkness to slip through the human kingdom undetected. It involved a few tricks, including stealing a shipping caravan and giving Rathi impromptu driving lessons while he hid his reptilian body under a cloak, but they'd made it.

While Rathi was up front, directing the bewildered horses through the kingdom, Ezrinth and Caine were stowed away inside the caravan. Unlike the passenger carts, these vehicles were fully enclosed, shaped like a giant wooden box on wheels. Inside, Ezrinth and Caine were surrounded by damp, claustrophobic darkness, which made Ezrinth feel right at home but rattled Caine's nerves. Their only source of light was the gaps between the wooden slats, which Ezrinth had had his slitted eyes peeking out of for the past hour.

Coming across the lot of shipping caravans was a stroke of incredible luck. The compound, which was made up of plain-clothed workers scrabbling between carts and buildings, was located just outside the kingdom gates. While the caravans full of shipped goods were heavily guarded, the empty ones on the back of the property were not. The trio of reptilians came across only a single guard on their mission to steal one of the empty caravans, and one bite from Ezrinth's venom-filled fangs sent him running.

But now, this was it. They'd made it all the way through the kingdom undetected. While traveling through the maze-like streets, they weren't exactly sure where the palace was. But once they came across it, it was impossible to miss – a colossal structure of spiraling limestone towers topped with earth-toned tile roofs. Ezrinth couldn't help but let his mouth hang open in awe when it came into view through the wooden slats of the caravan. As much as he hated the humans, he was impressed by what they were able to achieve.

But remember, Ezrinth reminded himself as Rathi opened the caravan and the Naga slithered into the shadows. *It's what makes them all the more dangerous.*

As Ezrinth slid around the perimeter of the palace, his eyes narrowed. Purple-and-gold-adorned guards stood stiff as wooden posts next to every entrance. They were so lifelessly still that it almost gave Ezrinth a false sense of security. Right now, their eyes were locked straight ahead, but he knew one wrong move would send them bolting after him.

He was playing an incredibly dangerous game. *But,* he noted as he lowered his serpentine body, preparing to dash forward. *I'm a Naga. We're reptilians of the shadows, able to slink through the darkness without a sound. A few pompous human guards don't stand a chance.*

A*ND, ULTIMATELY, THEY DIDN'T.*

Like the lone guard at the shipment grounds, a single bite sent them fleeing in panic. Ezrinth had to admit, at first they put up a decent fight – but his long, slender snake body was able to easily dodge the guard's bayonet strikes. Once Ezrinth's fangs delivered a potent dose of venom to the guard's neck, the panicked human attempted to scramble towards the rear palace entrance that he'd been stationed at. But Caine blocked his path, his massive crocodilian body nearly as wide as the door frame.

The guard fell, blood dripping from his neck and splattering the ground. Ezrinth slithered toward the man, pulling a dagger from a sheath against his waist and pointing it in the guard's face.

<If you're going to run.> Ezrinth growled, his slitted eyes narrowing. <Run off into the city streets. This palace is mine.>

The guard couldn't understand him, but he seemed to get the message, as he quickly scrambled to his feet and fled through the palace gardens.

Ezrinth gave a triumphant hiss before shoving the dagger back into its sheath.

<I don't understand,> Caine stomped toward Ezrinth, his heavy body rumbling with every footstep. <Why didn't you kill him?>

<And where would we hide the body, genius?> Ezrinth raised a scaled eyebrow.

Caine was skeptical, but Ezrinth's explanation seemed to be enough to silence him. While leaving a trail of bodies behind them *was* a bad idea, there was another reason why Ezrinth didn't want any murders on his hands. A reason that terrified him.

In all his travels, in all the time he'd spent on his quest to summon Vaipera, he was yet to kill a human. He'd bitten a few, but he's never stayed around to deliver the finishing blow. He was yet to see one dead. Now was his chance. But the entire time he'd been staring down the bitten, helpless guard, with a dagger pointed inches from his face, a foreign, disgusting emotion snaked through his mind. *Pity.* When he glowered at the human, studying its strange features... all he could think about was *her.* The way she used to smile at him, the way her blue eyes sparkled, the way her soft, peachy skin felt under his scaled palms. The way both his and her features were reflected in Marissa, their daughter, a beautiful accident of nature.

All those features. All those human features.

He couldn't bring himself to kill the guard. And he hated it.

<Caine.> He turned his attention back toward the Gharian. <It may be best for you to stay out here. Keep an eye on Rathi and the caravan, and take care of any guards that get suspicious.>

<You're going in there *alone*?> Caine huffed, his deep thoughts booming in Ezrinth's skull.

<Well, yes. The less of us, the better. And please don't take this the wrong way, but you're quite... *big.*>

Caine stared down at his wide midsection and massive, stomping clawed feet, and groaned.

<Fine. You're right. You'd better come out with the idol piece, snake, and *be* in one piece.>

<Oh, I will be.> Ezrinth flashed a sly grin, trying to hide his nerves. <I won't be long.>

He reached for the ornate metal door handle, took a deep breath, and pulled.

He was greeted by darkness on the other side. This entrance, being discreet and tucked away in the back of the palace, led to a spiral staircase. And there were no guards, or any other humans, in sight.

Perfect, Ezrinth dove inside, closing the door slowly behind him so it didn't make too much noise.

He was alone. Which meant he could do this heist *his* way. Scour the palace, find the idol piece, and try to bite down as few guards as possible while doing so.

He was glad Caine had agreed to stay behind. Gharian were masters of stealth in the water, but on land a heavy, bumbling ten-foot reptilian was a liability. Not to mention, they were known for making a gruesome mess when it came to dealing with their enemies. Having evolved from snakes, Naga were far more subtle about it.

There will be plenty of time for bloodshed later, Ezrinth reasoned. *When Vaipera is finally summoned.*

Chapter 26

MARISSA WAS SILENT THE ENTIRE CARRIAGE ride through Brennan. Partially because she didn't want to draw attention to herself, but mostly because there was a dusty scarf wrapped tightly across the lower half of her face. That, along with her hands tied behind her back in a false knot, severely limited her communication abilities. Not that she wanted to say much. Their carriage driver was right behind her, and they needed to make this convincing.

She was the one that insisted on being bound once they stepped through the kingdom gates. Being spotted walking jovially through the cobblestone streets with Arthur would arise suspicion if they came across a guardsman. And once they arrived in the kingdom, Marissa realized they were *everywhere*. Foot soldiers were perched suspiciously on every street corner, and trios of mounted cavalry wove between the passenger carriages. Marissa was afraid to look any of them in the eye.

Once they rented a carriage, Arthur sat facing her against the opposite wall, his lips pressed in a thin line. His royal upbringing allowed him to maintain a steady mask of stoicism, but Marissa could feel the fear and sympathy radiating from his tense body like a furnace. His expression was hardened, but his eyes seemed to plead, *I'm sorry I have to do this to you.*

With her hands and lower face bound, all she had were her bright blue eyes to reassure him that everything would be all right. After all, this was her plan. She was the one that suggested he play the part of a callous traitor.

Yet as she sat across from him, her body just a few feet from his but his heart feeling miles away, she desperately wanted to hug him. No, *hug* wasn't the right word. She wanted to *embrace* him, wrap her arms around him and squeeze all her affections into him. Reassure him that they would be fine, that they would survive this. All of this. That someday the valley would no longer be tearing itself apart, and they could embrace the new world together. Without fear.

But to do so, she'd have to believe it herself first.

The palace was now visible through the large side windows of the carriage. Marissa resisted the urge to scratch her nose, keeping her wrists pinned together under the false knot, and shook her head to readjust the scarf over her face. It didn't budge. Normally, Marissa wrapped her scarf around her lower face and neck, tight enough to not slip but loose enough to be comfortable. But this time, Arthur had tied her scarf in a firm knot at the base of her skull. It was tight, itchy, and uncomfortable, but it made the capture look more believable. And she didn't want to risk the guards pulling it off her when they arrived at the palace.

Because below the knot, the last few skeins of cloth were draped around her neck, covering an essential part of the plan.

Nim.

"Alright, here we are," the driver shouted as the carriage came to a stomping halt just outside the palace.

Marissa went to stand up, but she noticed Arthur didn't. Instead, he jerked his head in both directions, searching for onlookers, before lunging forward and wrapping her in his arms.

"I'm sorry," he whispered as he pressed a kiss against her scarf-covered cheek. "I'm just..."

"Scared." Marissa finished his sentence. "I am too. But I'm going to be okay."

"You promise?"

Marissa could hear Arthur's voice quiver.

"Y-yes, of course. I promise."

Arthur pulled his head back, admiring Marissa with watery eyes as he cupped her jawline in his hand. The way he looked at her sent a soothing warmth through her bones, but it also steeped them in fear. Because she knew that gaze – it was the gaze of a man who feared the worst. A man who feared he'd never see his beloved again.

"C'mon, I ain't got all day." The driver's gruff voice echoed from outside the carriage, and the pair instantly jerked away from each other.

Arthur scrambled backwards into his seat. He took a deep breath, and in an instant, the worried tenderness was wiped from his face. His expression was now hard and stoic, an impenetrable mask of deception. As much as she missed his smile, it offered her solace that Arthur was so skilled at playing the part. A lifetime with the royal family allowed him to change his emotions on the fly, blending into social situations as swiftly as a chameleon changing colors.

Arthur offered little more than a firm nod to the driver as he stepped out of the vehicle, his hand firmly wrapped around Marissa's bound wrists. She could tell that he was trying to be gentle, but his grip couldn't be too light or the row of guards eyeing them by the front entrance would become suspicious.

She did her best to act like a resistant captive, keeping her head down and brows furrowed. She wanted to look angry. And she *was* angry; angry that the humans destroyed Terrapin, angry that her wretched father had started this whole disaster, and angry that she now had to risk her life sneaking through a massive palace to find a lousy piece of rock.

Her reptilian nostrils flared. *Excellent,* she thought. *Channel that rage. Play the part.*

Marissa found it surprisingly easy. Maybe *too* easy, because as soon as the massive front doors opened to reveal Ramsey standing in the foyer, she had to fight back the urge to rip off her bindings and sink her fangs into him.

Her eyes flicked up at Arthur for a moment, amazed at how well he managed to maintain his emotionless mask. But she knew that deep down, there was a raging storm brewing behind those stony green eyes. He was just as pissed at Ramsey as she was.

"It's a pleasure to see you, Arthur." Ramsey's tone was warm and sincere, but to Marissa it sounded like claws scraping against metal.

"Likewise," Arthur replied curtly. He stood behind Marissa with his hands still clasped around her bound wrists. She forced back a shudder, wishing she could see Arthur's face.

"I'm glad you've come to your senses," Ramsey stepped forward, along with the two guards behind him. "Truly, I am."

"Of course." Arthur's replies were sharp and blunt.

"Well, then, if you don't mind stepping aside."

Marissa's body tensed as Arthur's hands slipped away, fearing it may be last time she experienced his touch. She took a deep breath, reminding herself it was all a ruse, a trick, and that she would retrieve the idol piece and escape without a scratch.

But as the guards stepped forward and grabbed her bony shoulders, it all felt horrifyingly real. To them, she was a prisoner being led to her execution.

One of the guards reached for her scarf, and she resisted the urge to hiss at him. Beneath the part wrapped around her neck, she could feel Nim's coiled muscles tense.

"I would advise against removing that scarf," Arthur interrupted. "She's pissed, and she's venomous. You don't want those fangs sinking into your arm."

Thankfully, the guard heeded Arthur's warning and pulled his hand away, eyeing Marissa with repulsion. She sneered.

Arthur wasn't wrong. Once their plan went into motion, she had no reservations about biting down any guards that got in her way. She had to use every defense at her disposal, and even though her venom wasn't lethal, the guards wouldn't know that. They would still panic and scurry away in search of antivenom.

The guard's grip on her shoulders tightened as they began to lead her away.

"Thank you again, Arthur." Ramsey turned back to his brother. "In fact... why don't you come in for a while? Father just put on some tea, and we still have some of your... *nicer* clothes upstairs."

Dread numbed Marissa's veins. She knew that this confirmed her and Arthur's worst fears. His family was willing to welcome him back... as long as he severed his ties with the half-Naga girl. *She* was what was keeping him from his family. It was her or them.

Her heart broke for Arthur, but she prayed that he wouldn't betray her now. *I'm so sorry Arthur, I don't want you to have to choose...*

"I appreciate the offer." Marissa heard Arthur reply as she was led around the corner. "But I have matters to attend to elsewhere."

"Ah, of course," Ramsey answered courteously, but Marissa could hear the deflation in his voice. "Well, I'll see you later, then."

The guards led Marissa down the hall and away from the front entrance before she could hear Arthur's reply.

This was it. Arthur was gone. It was just her. Alone.

The walk down the winding maze of hallways was eerily silent, with only the sharp clacking of the guard's boots against marble providing any noise. She couldn't help but admire the intricate halls of the palace – she'd never been inside it before, and the sparkling ceilings were even taller than the ones as the Castellas' estate. The doors that lined the halls were made of dark wood, intricately carved and incredibly heavy. As they passed one that was cracked open, Marissa heard a joyous squeal and caught a glimpse of several well-dressed women gathered around a table, sipping wine and playing some sort of card game.

After what seemed like an eternity of walking, they descended a spiral staircase. As they reached the bottom, Marissa's stomach lurched as she realized the scene around her was far less regal and welcoming. The polished marble walls were replaced with cold, rugged stone, and the gentle glimmer of glowstone was nowhere to be found. One of the guards fetched an old oil lamp and some matches out of a shabby cabinet. Its light was an eerie shade of orange, the same glow Marissa had been accustomed to her entire life in the storehouse. But here, it barely fought back the shadows. She couldn't see more than a few feet in front of her face, meaning that she was walking into a black, sightless abyss, one that never seemed to end.

The moans and shouts didn't start until after a few minutes of walking. They rattled Marissa to the core – haggard prisoners banging on the cell doors and shouting obscenities at the guards, trying their best to elicit a response. While some of them were simply angry, others seemed to have lost their mental faculties entirely, howling strings of incomprehensible words into the gloomy halls of the prison.

But not all the prisoners were intent on making as much noise as possible. Several of them, noticeably less pale and dingy than the rest, were silent. They glowered at Marissa as she passed, slumped against the prison walls with their arms crossed. *They are likely newer prisoners*, Marissa assumed. *Ones whose sanity is still intact.*

Thankfully, the prison cell that the guards led Marissa to was empty, if much smaller than the rest. They practically tossed her inside, causing her to stumble to the ground. Without free hands to catch herself, her face ended up colliding with the hard stone floor.

Behind her, a metallic rattle of keys signaled the locking of her cell, and the guards strode away, sneering and muttering words like "monster" and "ugly".

"Bastards," Marissa hissed, biting her lips to check for blood. She didn't taste any, but that didn't rule out the possibility of her having some nasty bruises later. She sat up and turned around, locking her eyes on the two chattering guards as they disappeared down the hall.

She waited until she could no longer hear their footsteps, and let out a smug grin. Because this was the end of their victory. Up until now, she'd been an unwilling prisoner, being mocked as a monster and thrown in a horrid cell awaiting her execution. She'd been exactly what the king, and the rest of the royal palace, wanted her to be.

But now, she released her hold on the knot, exactly as Arthur had instructed her to do, and the rope coils fell harmlessly to the floor. *That all ends. It's my turn to be victorious.*

<That's it, little snake.> She felt Nim writing with anticipation beneath her scarf. *<Now, do me a favor and get this putrid cloth off me. It still smells like smoke.>*

<Certainly.> Marissa fumbled with the knot, gently cursing Arthur for tying it so tight. Within a few minutes, her lower face was free, the chilly prison air feeling surprisingly refreshing against her bare cheek scales.

In an instant, Nim slithered off her neck and slid his slender body through the narrow bars of the cell door. Marissa couldn't help but grin. Thankfully, her cell was far away from the rest, possibly used for more dangerous or notorious prisoners. She didn't want the others to notice her escaping.

But as Nim fiddled with the lock, his thin tail prodding around inside the keyhole, Marissa realized freedom might take a bit longer than she expected.

<Don't give me that look.> Sauria growled as Nim's black eyes flashed up at Marissa. *<It's been a while since I've done this, and this little python's flimsy tail isn't exactly the best lockpick.>*

<I think Nim might've taken offense to that.> Marissa noted as her pet snake continued fumbling with the lock.

<*Serpentine bodies come with a whole host of advantages, little snake, such as slipping right through the bars of this metal cage. Something your bumbling human form can't seem to manage.*>

Nim's tail flicked upward, and with a final click the cell door creaked open.

<Alright, fine, I'm sorry.> Marissa stepped outside the cell, scooping up Nim and gently tapping him on the nose with her finger. She could practically feel Sauria's spirit flinch.

<*I didn't appreciate that.*>

<But your little snake face is so cute.> A sly grin slipped across Marissa's lips as she wrapped Nim back around her neck and covered him with her scarf. <And Nim likes being petted. It's his body, after all.>

Sauria groaned. <*Just get us out of here.*>

<Right.> Marissa peered down the hall. As she began to jog into the shadowy abyss, she heard a raucous mixture of shouts and banging. She cringed as she darted past the other prisoners, mentally apologizing for not being able to help them. She wondered if they truly were wretched criminals... or if they were just poor, misunderstood souls caught in a terrible situation like she was.

But as much as she empathized with them, there was no time to stay and ponder. The guards could come back at any minute, and Marissa needed to be out of the foul prison and upstairs before that happened. She quickened her pace to a run, her boots squeaking against the gritty stone floor as she bolted through the darkness towards the exit.

SINCE IT WAS LATE AT NIGHT, THE HALLS WERE quiet. Marissa managed to slip her way through the first floor while only dodging a few wandering guards.

Marissa shuddered as she returned to the foyer, the open floor plan and towering ceilings making her feel incredibly exposed. She hugged the wall behind the grand staircase and squeezed her eyes shut, trying to use Arthur's instructions to draw a map in her mind.

"If he brings you to the prison, once you escape, you'll be on the far eastern side of the palace. The halls are a maze, but whatever you do, keep heading west until you reach the main kitchen. Just to the right of it is the servant's stairwell."

She peered around the corner, keeping a sharp eye and ear out for any wandering guards. Once she was satisfied there were none, she darted to the left, down yet another maze of hallways until she heard sizzling sounds behind a large double door.

She crept closer, and the scent hit her like a tidal wave – some sort of stew made with fresh herbs and spices that were intoxicating to Marissa's reptilian nose. Her stomach rumbled. She hadn't eaten all day, and the scent of food was overpowering. She couldn't help but creep closer, just to get closer to the tantalizing-

<Foolish little snake. Are you trying to get yourself killed?>

Marissa jolted backwards, muttering a sheepish apology to the python around her neck.

<*You mortals are such slaves to your ravenous stomachs. I can assure you, if the guards catch a glimpse of you scurrying around the palace, you won't be getting another meal for a very long time.*>

<Yeah yeah, I get it.> Marissa muttered as she opened a small, plain door next to the kitchen entrance. She winced at the condition of the stairs – well-worn and grubby with the few bits of remaining paint peeling off like snake shed. The third stair up from the bottom was broken, with a hole in the middle large enough for a foot to easily get stuck.

<*What a lovely tripping hazard for the servants.*> Sauria snorted, as Nim glowered at the stairwell with disdain. <*Shows how much the royals value them.*>

Marissa placed one boot on the first step, and it gave an ominous squeak. She sighed, took a deep breath, and dove up them as quickly as possible, hoping that her speed would counteract all the noise she was making.

She didn't stop until she reached the third floor, where Arthur told her the king's private archives were located.

"It's like a vault in there, with a giant lock only he has the key to. It holds some of the palace's most secretive and valuable treasures, and no one outside the royal family knows about it. So naturally, it's the most likely place for him to hide the idol piece."

And, according to Arthur, it was just down the hall and to the left from the servant's stairwell. A nervous, shocked smile crept onto Marissa's face. She couldn't believe she'd made it this far – or how easy it had been.

Just down the hall, to the left, and...

"What in the-"

Marissa whipped around. Which she immediately realized was a mistake, because as soon as the servant saw her reptilian face, he let out a bloodcurdling scream. Marissa lunged on him in an instant, clamping a hand over his mouth to muffle the incriminating noise.

"I'm sorry," Marissa locked eyes with him, and he stopped screaming. Yet the panic in his wild gaze remained. Marissa could tell by the tenseness of his body below hers that if she let him go, he'd run.

"I'm so, so sorry," Marissa kept apologizing as she pulled the rope from the pocket of her breeches and tied his hands behind his back. Nim wrapped his slender body around the man's mouth to keep it closed, which Marissa noticed made the panic on his face reach near hysteria.

Marissa then wrapped the scarf around his head, muffling another tirade of screams, before gently dragging the man into a supply closet and locking the door.

<I feel so guilty.> Marissa sighed as she walked away with Nim around her neck.

<*Don't. You did what you had to do to survive. And if a guard catches you, surviving might involve more... extreme measures.*>

Marissa gulped. She was lucky it was just a servant. Not only did she want to get through this mission alive, but she hated the idea of having to sink her fangs into any more humans.

She took a deep breath, steadying her rattled nerves, and kept walking.

Down the hall, to the left, she repeated to herself. *Down the hall, and...*

Wait?

Which left?

She froze, realizing she was an intersection of two hallways. In front of her were three possible routes – left, right, and straight ahead. Yet she swore she could see two more left turns further down the hall, directly in front of her.

Arthur wasn't kidding. This place really is a maze.

She decided to take the first left, pressing a palm against her aching head. Her already anxious mind struggled to keep a mental map, and all the hallways looked the same. Even the doorways were all oddly identical, with only a handful marked with placards detailing what was inside.

Chapel, family quarters, yet another kitchen... good gods, where is it?

She stopped at the end of the hall, in front of a lavishly decorated yet nameless door. There was no placard identifying what it was, yet it had a peculiar feature that none of the other doors had – an elaborate filigree lock, made of heavy brass and nearly the size of the door handle.

She gently pressed her fingers against the dark wood and pressed inward. The door, to her amazement, crept open, revealing a thin sliver of the nearly pitch-black room.

It was unlocked.

Marissa squinted, and she swore that she could spy rows of bookshelves arranged like a library.

This must be the ar...

"HEY!!"

Marissa tilted her head, just barely enough for the corner of her eye to spot the two guards. They had rounded the corner at the far end of the hall, and they looked both bewildered at her escape and furious at her attempts to access such an off-limits area.

As soon as they took a step forward, she bolted. Her arms and legs flew at a wild pace, not knowing where she was going or what her plan of escape would be. All she knew was that she had to get as far away from them as possible.

But she still needed to get inside the archives. She needed that idol piece. Without it, their entire mission would be for nothing.

<*Make a broad loop around the entire third floor,*> Sauria instructed, Nim's body squeezing her neck as he hung on for dear life. <*Zigzag through the halls. Throw them off your trail.*>

<I'll get lost!>

<*No, you won't. Don't forget, little snake, I am a god, and I have the memory of one. Now, turn down that corridor. I'll lead you back to the archives once we lose them.*>

Hallway after hallway, turn after turn, all of rushing past her eyes in a blur of glossy floors and glittering lights. So much opulence, yet it all looked the same. So gaudy. So sterile.

Marissa didn't dare look back, but she could hear the guards' footsteps growing fainter in her reptilian ears.

Once she couldn't hear them at all, she pressed her body against the wall and took massive, gulping breaths, her chest heaving with every inhale.

<No time to rest, little snake. Those guards will be back with reinforcements. You need to go to the archives, grab the idol piece, and run for it.>

Marissa took one final breath, her chest sore and her heart hammering from her exertion, before slipping back down the hallway.

<Okay, now go right, down that hall, to the left.>

Sure enough, Sauria knew his way back to the archives. And luckily for her, the guards were in such a rush that they never locked the door. It was still cracked open, just as she'd left it.

<Alright,> Marissa sighed. <Here we go. It better be in here.>

<I'm sure it will be. I trust Arthur's judgment. After all, what better place to store such an item?>

Marissa looked left and right, making sure there was no sign of the guards, before opening the heavy wooden door and disappearing through the dark entryway.

Chapter 27

RAMSEY COULDN'T WAIT ANY LONGER.
The feeling nagged him, clawing at the back of his skull, ever since he returned to the palace. It haunted him every day, while he sat empty-eyed in a room full of royal cabinet members listening to debates he couldn't bring himself to care about. At night it kept him from sleeping. He paced his apartment in the darkness, both exhausted and wide awake at the same time. It was like a fever dream, consuming his thoughts and causing his brain to twist itself in knots with theories.

King Gabriel told him that all was well. That he'd gone beyond all expectations by claiming the Testudo capital for the humans. The fact that the half-reptilian girl escaped seemed trivial, and the king reassured Ramsey that everything was being taken care of. *You need rest,* he insisted. *Go on, spend some time with your family. Especially your wife. After all, you're expecting a future heir soon.*

It should've been a relief. It should've brought him pride to know that he'd pulled off such a massive accomplishment, and solace to know that he could finally rest and spend time within the comfy confines of the castle.

But rest evaded him, and he no longer felt any comfort within the stiff palace walls. Despite the king's reassurances, he knew something was wrong. Something was being hidden from him.

It started during the cabinet meetings, when during an unusually long, drawn-out lecture, it suddenly occurred to Ramsey that he shouldn't be here. He was the future ruler of Brennan. He should've been meeting with higher-ups of the royal guard – the sergeants, the captains, the general. Why wasn't he apart of the king's discussions in the war room? And it made him wonder; was he truly being prepped for his future role, or was he just a glorified errand boy?

That night when he went to bed, his brother's words once again taunted his insomnia-riddled mind.

Look at what the king has turned you into, Ramsey!

He'd told himself dozens of times that it wasn't true. Arthur was the one being manipulated. The half-reptilian girl was the real villain at work.

That was his truth. It had to be.

Because if it wasn't, Ramsey knew his whole reality would come crashing down on top of him.

But that accusation wasn't what haunted him the most. It was the single, brief sentence that came immediately after.

This isn't you.

And it begged the question; what *was* he? He, Ramsey Brennan, was a model child, prim and proper, one that earned the right to be bestowed the throne. He was a royal heir. The future king of Brennan.

But that was all recent. Before, he was just Ramsey, a distant royal struggling to find his place in the world, one with two loving parents, a beautiful wife, and a stubborn yet kind-hearted sibling. He and Arthur were so different, always pulling each other in the opposite direction in an endless tug-of-war. But they were brothers. Family. And deep down, Ramsey knew that Arthur knew him better than anyone else. He knew who he *really* was, not just the perfect façade that hid behind.

And that was how Ramsey found himself standing in front of the archives that night.

He knew that the real truth, the answers he so desperately needed, were hidden somewhere within the palace.

And this place was the most likely culprit.

Normally, no one was allowed inside except the king, at least without explicit permission. But said king had left the key behind in the throne room after a particularly long meeting, and no one questioned Ramsey waltzing in and snatching it up. *After all,* he told himself. *I'm heir to the throne. As future king of Brennan, I have every right to visit the archives.*

At least, that was what he repeated to himself as his shaky hands fiddled with the massive lock, keeping his eyes peeled for any roaming guards.

The door opened with a loud groan, further rattling Ramsey's paranoia. Beyond him was a very dark room, one where he could just barely make out the silhouettes of shelves. Bookshelves. Rows and rows of them.

He gently pressed the door shut behind him, and several glowstone wall sconces flashed to life. Ramsey found himself underwhelmed – for such a secretive trove of knowledge, it was awfully cramped and messy. The shelves were overflowing with books; ancient tomes that were crammed into tight rows and stacked in haphazard towers on the floor. A desk in the far corner of the room was piled high with paperwork and rolled-up scrolls. It looked more like an eccentric professor's attic than a proper royal archive.

But it didn't matter. Regardless of the current state of the room, Ramsey hoped it contained the answers he was looking for.

He dove in, combing through pile after pile of books, scrolls, and letters. But he quickly realized that he was woefully underprepared. This room was crammed full of the entire history of their kingdom – finding the information he needed would take hours, if not days.

He rolled up his sleeve and examined his watch. Nine o'clock. The king was known for retiring to bed early on weeknights, which meant that Ramsey could likely stay in the archives the whole night undisturbed. He gulped, and his eyes flicked toward the door. Outside, the halls were eerily silent. *Hopefully they will stay that way.*

Ramsey could feel the fatigue after the first hour, his mind tied up in knots and his eyes tired from reading so many lines of ancient, scraggly handwriting. He skimmed book after book, scroll after scroll, digging through the banalities of ancient politics in hopes of finding something relevant. Something secret. Something that the king wouldn't want others to know about.

He slumped into the far corner, plucking a random hardcover off one of the piles next to him. He took a deep breath, ready to dive into what he assumed was yet another dead-end. But as soon as he saw the title of his book, his heart skipped a beat.

Across the brittle, leathery cover, in gold text that was beginning to peel, was printed: *On the Nature of Reptilians, Volume I.*

Ramsey's eyes widened. In all the texts he'd read so far, there were very few mentions of the reptilians. Which was unsurprising, as much of the kingdom preferred to pretend that the beasts didn't exist at all. This was the first book he's come across in the entire archives that was explicitly about the creatures.

And based on the book's condition, it was very, *very* old. The spine fell apart as soon as Ramsey opened the book, and a slew of loose, yellowed pages spilled into his lap.

Everything was hand-written, which meant that this book predated the kingdom's invention of the printing press. But what made it seem even older was its bizarre vocabulary – a more primitive form of the kingdom's modern tongue, with strange spellings and odd phrases that weren't used in the current era. Ramsey had difficulty deciphering it all, which forced his already tired brain into overdrive.

But he understood the basics. This was a field journal, likely created by a researcher from many centuries ago, outlining the basic facets of reptilian life. As Ramsey combed through the brittle pages, tracing his fingers over the splotchy handwriting and crude sketches, he realized there was far more to reptilian society than he'd initially thought.

They lived in huge villages, with complex family structures, customs, and ceremonies. They had knowledge of basic tools and weapons, but Ramsey even found some sketches of crossbows and a primitive cannon. There were capitals, a head village for each territory, made up of an entire city's worth of intricately thatched huts.

It was all intriguing. And fascinating. And - Ramsey hated to admit - beautiful.

But while it was all an eye-opening glimpse into reptilian life, there was no truly profound information. Nothing that shook Ramsey to his core.

That was, until he reached the very last pages of the book.

His mouth fell open in disbelief. He ran his fingers across the sketches, pressing against the ink as if he truly couldn't believe what he was seeing.

An alphabet. Words. Complex sentence structures. It was a dictionary, all made up of hand signals.

A sign language.

The reptilians *could* communicate.

Or at least, they could eight hundred years ago.

He sat upright, the disheveled book resting in his lap. All his life, throughout his entire schooling years and time spent in the palace, he'd been taught that reptilians were incapable of speech. After all, they had no vocal cords, and to Ramsey's knowledge, no human had ever been able to communicate with them. A lot of humans believed the reptilians weren't even intelligent enough for such things.

He tore through the yellowed pages, eager for more information. The sign language had been developed by both humans and reptilians, to bridge a gap between their worlds. Eight hundred years ago, the humans and reptilians had gotten along. They had built an entire society, living, working, and trading amongst each other. At one point, the humans and reptilians had been truly at peace.

The other books in the same stack unlocked more clues, including the real reason why the humans arrived in the Valley of Scales. They weren't ambitious pioneers in search of resources like his academic textbooks claimed. At least, not entirely. The truth was, the humans had been forced out of their original homeland – by dragons.

The few hundred survivors traveled for weeks, through freezing, mountainous hellscapes until they came to the Valley of Scales. It was an oasis; a warm, tropical swampland with pleasant weather and an abundance of natural resources. It seemed like the best place for the refugees to settle – that was, until they were discovered by the natives.

While some of the reptilians were wary of the new-comers, overall their society welcomed the humans with open arms. They took a great interest in the humans' more advanced technology, and the reptilians were happy to show the humans how to hunt and farm in the swamplands. Over time, they built a joint community, both human and reptilian, communicating with each other using sign language.

But just a few decades after the humans settled in the valley, tension began to brew. Not all humans were grateful for the reptilians' generosity. To them, scales were scales, and the reptilians were just as monstrous as the dragons that had destroyed their previous home. The disgruntlement continued to spread, until a small yet vocal minority of humans declared that they wanted the whole valley to themselves.

Hence... the start of the first war... eight hundred years ago.

Even though the conflict had ended in an unsteady truce, with the humans and reptilians now living in separate societies, Ramsey realized that the kingdom had been determined to erase as much of their peaceful past as possible. Their former society crumpled into ruin, their shared sign language was forgotten, and humans and reptilians became sworn enemies, once again unable to communicate with each other.

It made Ramsey realize how much of a barrier communication truly was. Without their shared language, it made it easy for the kingdom to demonize the reptilians. They could make up whatever lies they wanted about the creatures being murderous, unintelligible beasts, and no human would ever be able to speak with them to find out the truth.

But that was where it ended. At least, with that pile of books. Ramsey reached the end of the stack, pressing his fingers against the dusty wood floor where the books once lay. He couldn't stop here. He needed to know more.

His eyes darted over to the cluttered desk.

His throat quivered. Sorting through archived books was one thing. Rummaging through the king's personal correspondences was entirely another. It was something that could get him into serious trouble and permanently damage his relationship with the ruler of Brennan.

His fear was strong. But his insatiable desire to know the truth, the whole truth, was even stronger.

Despite being alone in a silent room, Ramsey tip-toed between the cluttered shelves at a snail's place. Paranoia prickled up his neck, settling his scalp on fire and causing his temples to break out in a cold sweat. He kept his breathing low and steady, a sharp contrast to the rapid hammering of his anxious heart.

He would do this.

He *needed* to do this.

At first, his clammy fingers could barely unravel the parchment. But as he combed through the letters, his eyes flicking from word to word, he slowly lost track of how much noise he was making. He dug through them at blistering speed, the sound of fluttering paper like the flapping of bird wings in the vacant room.

The books had been a shock; one that had him questioning everything he knew about the reptilians.

But these letters had him questioning something far worse.

His own family.

Five letters in, he laid the parchment flat against the table, taking a moment to steady his wobbly head and pull his spiraling thoughts together.

His suspicions were right; he'd been lied to. While King Gabriel sequestered Ramsey in trivial cabinet meetings, he was secretly meeting with a select few higher-ups in the royal guard. They were the only ones who knew the king's true plans for the war.

The truth was that the temple in Naga territory had been found over a year ago. The king and his confidantes already knew what was inside; a piece of a mythical idol capable of destroying the entire human kingdom. The solution seemed simple; if they snatched the idol piece and hid it within the palace walls, they would be safe. The reptilians would be unable to summon the goddess if the idol was incomplete.

But that wasn't enough for the king. Ever since his son's death, he had made it his mission to leave behind a legacy. He wanted to be remembered at the king that finally exterminated the reptilian scourge that lurked at their borders. And for that happened, there needed to be war. Not just any war, but a war instigated by their own enemy.

They spent months brainstorming how to do it. Somehow, they had to bait the reptilians into finding the idol. Once they possessed it, it would be easy to cry foul. They could claim that the reptilians were hell-bent on destroying them all, and the idol piece in their possession would be incriminating evidence.

While making expeditions out to the temple, King Gabriel's secret task force came across a lone Naga living in an abandoned shack, way outside the village borders. Likely some sort of outcast, ostracized from his kind. One that they assumed had a lot of pent-up frustration and anger lurking within it.

They decided that the Naga was the perfect target. Once everything was in place, the guardsmen laid the trap; blowing open the side of the temple with dynamite. Then, they left, waiting for the Naga to wander inside on its own.

Ramsey's mission to find the temple had been a farce; an elaborate trick to help sway both him and the rest of the royal guard off the king's trail. The tablet was fake. Everyone, from the researchers to the royal guard to Ramsey himself, had been deceived.

Ramsey clenched his teeth, his jawbone burning all the way up his temples. He was never truly the perfect heir, the next king of Brennan. He was just a pawn in King Gabriel's elaborate scheme.

People *died* on the mission to the Naga temple. He'd been up endless nights wrestling with survivor's guilt, tormented by the memory of his companions' empty-eyed stares. But to the king, it was all trivial. Those guard members weren't human to him; they were just disposable set pieces for his wretched play.

Ramsey shuddered. *They were all disposable.*

Once this is all over...

He struggled to swallow. *Am I disposable too?*

His heaving breaths rattled his eardrums as panic gripped his chest. He braced a palm on the antique desk, the last of the letters fluttering off the table as he staggered.

Good gods, I can't breathe. I can't think. Is this... a panic attack?

His eyes flicked over to the desk. Now that it was almost empty, with most of the papers sprawled across the floor, he could see an object previously hidden under all the letters.

He grabbed the shade of the glowstone lamp on the table, pointing it in the direction of the object.

It was a stone tablet, not unlike the one King Gabriel had tricked him with.

But as soon as the soft white glow illuminated its features, he had a horrible, sinking feeling that this one wasn't fake.

Because the scene it depicted was one the king would never want anyone to see. A massive serpent, many stories tall with scales made of rugged crystal, towered above the forest with storm clouds brewing near its head.

Ramsey knew it was likely the diety that the reptilians were trying to summon. But that wasn't the part that concerned him.

It was what the snake was being confronted by – a tiny figure, one with long black hair and a sword in her hand. One with the body of a human and the scales of a snake.

That can't be-

The door swung open, and Ramsey shot up like a spooked cat. As he did so, the remainder of the rolled parchments on the desk fluttered to the floor.

He spun around. He'd expected guards, or in his worst nightmares, the king himself.

What he didn't expect was the silhouette of a woman, a young, petite one, with long dark hair and thick bangs that rested just above her eyelids.

Who is sh-

She stepped closer. Under the soft aura of the glow-stone, Ramsey could see the dark scales glittering across her skin. Ones that matched the tablet drawing perfectly.

Her.

It was at that moment that she spotted him. She froze, wild-eyed with panic, her muscles tensed as if she were ready to bolt.

"No, wait!" Ramsey stepped forward, accidentally crushing a piece of parchment under his boot. "I'm not going to hurt yo-"

The door burst open again. And this time, it *was* guards. Two of them. And Ramsey knew that they weren't there for him.

In fact, they seemed delighted to see him, even if he was lurking around a place he shouldn't have been in.

"Ramsey." One of the grinned, a bit of gold flashing at the back of his mouth. "Excellent work. Thank you for finding her. The little mongrel must've escaped."

"Oh, uh..."

Cold, damp horror flooded his face. He had no idea what to do. He felt like he was being torn in half.

The half-reptilian girl locked her eyes on him, her bright blue irises pleading with the faintest bit of hope.

I... I...

"Y-yes, indeed I have found her. And I appreciate you two arriving to finish up the job."

Pain and betrayal welled in her eyes, but not shock. Ramsey knew that she must've expected this. He huffed. *Why would I ever defend such a monster?*

Yet, as the guards took a step towards her, it occurred to Ramsey that to her, *he* was the monster.

She brushed her long hair aside, revealing a slender, vibrantly colored snake coiled around her neck. She took several steps backwards, her wretched pet poised to strike, as the guards attempted to reason with her.

"You're just making this more difficult for yourself." One of them taunted. "You're wanted by the royal family, little monster. Enemy number one. You honestly think you're going to make it out of this palace alive? Out of this *war* alive?"

She stood her ground, but Ramsey could see the panic rising to the surface, welling up on her face and making her eyes water. One of the guards extended a hand, and the snake struck in an instant, just barely missing the guard's pointer finger.

The tension snapped like a spring. The guards dove after her, chasing her over piles of books and shelves until the already messy archives became a total disaster. The girl flung giant hardcovers over her shoulder, occasionally smacking a guard in the face in an almost comical fashion.

He had to admit, she was fast. It was going to be difficult to catch her.

And he was merely standing there like a fool.

Despite her speed, the archives were only so large, with no other entrances or exits for her to slip out of. Within a few minutes, the guards had her backed in a corner.

It seemed like it was all over; that there was no escape for her. But Ramsey studied her face intently as the guards crept towards her, realizing by the glint in her eye that she wasn't done yet. That she had some sort of trick up her sleeve.

He'd expected her to pull a dagger from her breeches, or toss some sort of poison vial in their faces. But what did happen made Ramsey fall backwards, stunned and in disbelief over what he was seeing.

They materialized out of nowhere. Giant, lumbering pythons, their necks held high over the guards' cowering frames. Two of them, at least fifteen feet long, and ready to strike.

A wicked grin crept across the reptilian girl's face.

We've sorely underestimated her.

The pythons had both guards coiled in an instant. One of them was consumed by the python's massive, writhing scales, his screams turning into sputters while his outstretched arm turned a sickly shade of red. Ramsey flinched in horror.

But the second guard wasn't so unfortunate. He'd had his sword in his right hand upon being coiled, and with the last bit of flexibility in his arm, he was able to plunge the blade into the python's pale belly. A misty blue substance, one that reminded Ramsey of stardust, exploded out of the snake's torn flesh. The wound quickly closed back up, but it gave the guard enough time to scramble out of the pythons' coils.

Good gods, Ramsey shuddered at the snakes' rapid healing abilities. *Those are no normal snakes. What sort of otherworldly beasts did she summon?*

A loud, shrieking hiss erupted across the room, burning Ramsey's ears like an exploding tea kettle. The freed guard had slashed his sword across the python's neck, decapitating it. More stardust poured out of its body, but it did not regenerate its head. Instead, the now empty snakeskin crumpled to the ground, slowly dissipating into a fine blue mist.

With the second snake distracted by its prey, the guard was also able to decapitate it. Another shriek further tortured Ramsey's already-ringing eardrums, and as the python dissolved, it released the second limp guardsmen from its coils.

The guard had killed both snakes. But it was too late for his comrade, who lay crumpled and lifeless on the ground, his oxygen-starved body marbled in sickening shades of red and purple.

The reptilian girl looked worried, but she still wasn't done. This time, a different snake spawned, some sort of massive storm-colored cobra with a white belly. It was the largest one Ramsey had ever seen, and it looked just as murderous as the first two snakes.

Being a venomous species, this one's strategy wasn't to coil, but bite. It was lightning-fast, with spring-like reflexes and a tremendous strike range. The guard staggered backwards, able to just barely dodge the cobra's fangs, but it was clear he was struggling.

It was a tense, exhausting standoff. The guard was able to stay out of the cobra's strike range, but the snake was far too fast for him to deliver the killing blow. He was losing momentum, his reflexes muddled by fatigue, while the snake showed no signs of slowing down. It was clear that eventually, the cobra would win.

And the half-reptilian girl would get away.

Ramsey swallowed, his anxious throat feeling like it was full of marbles. He raised a cautious hand and plucked a razor-sharp letter opener from one of the bookshelves next to him. Ramsey was currently facing the guard, which meant he was also staring directly at the cobra's back.

The snake didn't see him.

It didn't know he was there.

Ramsey screamed, throwing all of his weight into the blade as he tore it across the air and through the cobra's flesh. Another shriek, another round of tinnitus in Ramsey's ears, and it was over. Three snakes down, and based on the look of fear in the girl's face, there were no more left to be summoned.

Her luck had run out.

The guard, panting and sweat-stained, let out a hearty laugh.

"You're full of surprises, Ramsey." The guard cackled as he stood up, brushing the sweat off his forehead as he stomped toward the defenseless reptilian girl. "I appreciate you saving my life. One day, I'll be proud to serve you as our king."

He clutched a fist around the girl's scaled bicep and yanked her forward. Her exhausted-looking pet snake attempted to strike, but the guard deflected it with his blade. The snake went to strike a second time, but this time the guard swung his blade at the little python's neck, determined to have it meet the same fate as the others.

The guard missed. But just barely. And to survive the blow, the snake was forced to scramble off the reptilian girl's neck. It flung itself to the floor and attempted to climb into one of the empty bookcases for refuge, but the guard laughed and kicked the snake across the room with his boot.

It was over. No more tricks, no more battles, no more giant mythical snakes. The girl had been captured.

"Do you need assistance bringing her back down to the prison?" Ramsey offered.

The guard chuckled as he brushed past Ramsey. The girl's arms were pinned behind her back, and as she passed, Ramsey noticed the same faint glimmer of betrayal in her eyes.

He knew she likely remembered his words from earlier.

I'm not going to hurt you.

What a wretched lie that had been.

"Oh, she isn't going back to the prison," the guard grinned, seeming to take enjoyment in squeezing the girl's wrists as tight as possible. "This time, she's headed right to the throne room. The king is waiting for her."

Chapter 28

ASSANDRA TRIED TO FORGET.

Thanks to both her superb academic record and her excellent performance in her initial attempt at boot camp, she was re-admitted to both Brennan University and the junior royal guard that spring. She poured her full attention into her training and studies, nearly working herself to the bone for the following four years until she graduated at the top of her class. Not only had she obtained nearly perfect marks, but she'd been offered her desired position in the royal guard; Third Quadrant. She would be patrolling the city streets, keeping Brennan's citizens safe without having to encounter the reptilians.

Even with her studies behind her, Cassandra continued to devote her full attention to her career. She threw herself into her work, taking on as many assignments as possible and often not returning to her apartment until long after the sun went down.

Her whole life revolved around the royal guard. And Cassandra wanted it that way.

Because during the day, when she was busy, she was distracted. She hated having free time because it allowed her mind to wander. Wander to places it shouldn't go back to.

But she still had to sleep. And as she sat still in the darkness of her bedroom each night, every painful memory came rushing back like a tidal wave. They'd keep her awake for hours, her body sickeningly numb in the pitch-black silence, as the weight of her actions crushed her chest like limestone bricks.

Sometimes she wouldn't sleep at all. Other times she'd allow herself to slip away, to drift back into the Naga's soft, scaled embace, only to awaken panting and covered in cold sweat. She could still hear the baby's cries, the sound permeating her ears until they screeched with tinnitus. Her dreams always brought her back to that night; the last night she saw him.

The last night she saw *her*. Her daughter. The daughter that shouldn't exist.

But she did. And her whereabouts never ceased to linger in the back of Cassandra's mind. She was still out there, somewhere. Growing older. *Three, four, five years old... good gods, she'd be a kindergartener by now.*

Cassandra always assumed she was still alive. Despite her own reservations about the child, she he refused to entertain the possibility of anything else.

The years passed. Slowly, steadily, as indisputably as existence itself. Her performance in the royal guard had been nothing short of extraordinary. Being a deaf, female guard had its drawbacks in boot camp, but out in the real world, she learned how to use her differences to her advantage.

As a woman, Cassandra was always much smaller and slighter than her male companions. But she was incredibly fit and nimble, with a great deal of stamina. And her petite frame was useful in certain situations; such as when a fellow guardsmen needed to lift her up to reach a second-story window in a pinch, or when crawling through a tight hole in a pile of rubble to reach a child on the other side.

She even found perks in her hearing loss. People often assumed that she couldn't hear sounds at all; when in reality they were just severely muddled. She couldn't decipher conversations or hear high-pitched tones, but she found herself especially sensitive to rumbles and vibrations. In addition, few people knew that she could lip-read, which was helpful when she needed to understand conversations that weren't meant for her ears. Over the years, she became a master at appearing to be oblivious; when in reality she was always picking up bits and pieces of information.

With her excellent performance came a slew of congratulations, promotions, and even a few awards. She accepted them with a beaming smile and glistening enthusiasm, but inside she always felt hollow. Because no matter how well she performed, no matter how many of her dreams she accomplished, she'd still have to return to her empty apartment at night. She'd still have to face the daunting task of lying awake with a mind full of cursed memories.

She could never forget. No matter how hard she tried.

But she pressed on, forging a life without the Naga and her hybrid daughter. Keeping herself as busy as possible was her coping mechanism. And for nearly fifteen years, it worked.

Then, the ultimate promotion came. After a decade and a half of loyal service to the royal guard, she was to be brought before His Majesty himself. And he had an offer for her; to be the official King's Guard, keeping watch in the throne room while he oversaw his day-to-day duties. It was the most prestigious position in the royal guard; one that came with many perks, including a luxurious apartment within the palace walls.

Yet the thought of accepting the position filled her with absolute dread. She loved her job, despite her tumultuous past lurking at the back of her mind. She enjoyed the fresh air and humidity-soaked skies atop the backs of the guard's loyal horses. She had a mental map of every cobblestone-lined street in the kingdom, and knew almost every business, church, and factory by name. She belonged out there, interacting with Brennan's citizens and keeping them safe. Not playing bodyguard for an already well-protected royal.

But she knew didn't have a choice. To refuse such an offer would be an incredible dishonor. In the royal guard, reputation was everything, and she couldn't risk toppling over everything she'd built over the past fifteen years.

So, she accepted. And as she expected, she hated it. Sure, the apartment was beautiful, her family was incredibly proud, and her working days were a lot shorter and less hectic. But it was also quiet and uneventful, which gave Cassandra's mind plenty of time to wander. She'd spend hours drowning in her gut-wrenching memories, not even attempting to lip-read while the king was attending his meetings. Now she felt the Naga's embrace more than ever, and the pain of losing her daughter was ripped open like old scar tissue.

For the next three years, they were all she could think about.

They were even on her mind that night, when the king announced that her sudden presence was needed in the throne room. Cassandra sighed, tossing aside her silken sheets and fetching a clean uniform out of her gold-trimmed wardrobe.

Since it was this late, she knew it was probably some half-mad prisoner being dragged up for an interrogation. *Or,* her throat tightened as she fitted her blunderbuss into its holster. *It might even be an execution.*

She hated executions. Because she was the one that had to put the poor souls out of their misery.

The halls were silent. Cassandra noticed that they seemed more ominous than usual, implying that some sort of invisible terror lurked in the dark halls. She paused for a moment upon reaching her usual spot in the throne room, mentally preparing herself for whatever events would unfold that night.

It wasn't long before the doors opened. Cassandra expected the guard to be dragging some haggard old figure, bound in shackles, one whose mind had melted away in the tormenting confines of the prison.

She could hear the usual metallic jingle of prison chains. But the prisoner wasn't what she'd expected. It was a small, frail woman, one with long black hair curtained in front of her slumped-over face. She wore worker's breeches, a loose white blouse, and a pair of royal-guard-rationed boots. Cassandra couldn't see her face, but she looked very young, likely still in her teens.

Cassandra stood as still as possible, trying not to cringe, but she could still feel the veins in her neck throbbing. The guard seemed to take great pleasure in throwing the prisoner to the ground, which clearly caused the young woman pain.

King Gabriel must've asked the prisoner to show him her face, because the girl slowly craned her neck upwards.

Revealing pale skin.

Vibrant blue eyes.

And...

Those dark marks on her cheeks and neck...

Are those....

No...

It can't be... she can't be...

Standing just a few dozen feet in front of Cassandra, a prisoner at the king's mercy, was her long-lost, half-reptilian daughter.

And it made her heart nearly fall out of her chest.

MARISSA CLENCHED HER JAW TO KEEP FROM shaking. No matter what, she refused to show even the slightest hint of fear. She wouldn't give him that sick satisfaction.

She'd never seen the king before, nor did she have any idea what he looked like. To her, he'd been nothing more than a name, a mythical being hidden away in a tower of opulence and horror. He was her worst nightmare, the one who sent his minions crawling through every corner of the valley, making sure that nowhere was safe for her. And now, she was bound and chained before him, his beady brown eyes regarding her with a mix of morbid fascination and disgust.

He was a sharp-faced man, one with immaculate grooming and a thin, well-oiled mustache that accentuated his narrow mouth. Marissa supposed he'd be considered handsome to the rest of the kingdom; but to her, his appearance was a smug, repulsive façade of corruption and rot. His tight, curled smile reminded Marissa that he wasn't merely disgusted by her appearance. That he actively enjoyed watching her suffer.

"What's the matter?" his deep voice taunted, sickly sweet and full of venom at the same time. He brushed his cape aside and reached into the pocket of his trousers, fishing around for something inside. Marissa's stomach twisted as she caught a flash of grey stone in his closed palm.

"Were you looking for this?"

King Gabriel held the idol piece less than a foot from Marissa's face, clutching it between his thumb and index finger and waving it in a taunting manner. He then set it on a small glass-mosaic table next to the throne. "You really thought it was in the archives, didn't you? I suppose I can't blame you, it is a logical place to look. But I had a feeling some nefarious reptilian would try to steal it. And I was right. Well... *half*-right."

A biting, chilly trickle seeped through Marissa's veins, making them feel like they were full of ice. The idol piece was never in the archives. The mission was doomed all along.

And now it was just feet away from her, so close yet so completely unobtainable.

"What a horrid freak of nature you are." The king raised a narrow, arched eyebrow. "An unnatural mix of scales and flesh. It's like your body couldn't figure out how to put you together. You really are a monster, aren't you?"

Marissa jaw clenched even tighter, until she could feel her molars gritting against one another. She shouldn't give him the satisfaction of a response. But between his blatant insults and his smug grin, she couldn't help but defend herself.

"Appearances aren't what make us monsters," Marissa hissed, shifting her shoulders to adjust the uncomfortable chains digging into her wrists. "It's our actions."

His laugh, dark and haughty, made Marissa's stomach churn.

"Is that an attempt to insult me?" He seemed sickeningly amused. "Very well. I won't rattle your nerves with further comments. But I do want to remind you that my statement isn't my mere opinion. It's what every human in Brennan would think of you if you were to reveal yourself."

More cold ice poured through Marissa's veins. She could feel her temples beginning to throb. In the far corner, beyond King Gabriel's oversized throne, she noticed a small female guard hugging the back wall. Royal guards, especially those stationed around the palace, usually wore stony, expressionless masks. But this guard looked terrified. Fear glistened like crystals in her surprisingly blue eyes, and her body was unusually tense, as if she could barely keep still.

She's probably disgusted by me, Marissa sighed. *The king is right. I truly am a monster in the human's eyes.*

"But... it doesn't have to be that way."

Marissa snapped her attention back to the king. His leering, pompous attitude had faded, revealing a softness that Marissa refused to believe was sincerity.

"You proved yourself quite... skilled in otherworldly magic during your confrontation in the archives." The king grinned. "Despite your peculiar appearance, we could use someone with your talents. Tell me, where did you obtain such powers?"

This time, Marissa refused to speak. She glowered at him, reptilian nostrils flaring, her steely façade faltering as she began to realize what the king was asking of her.

"No? Won't give your secret away?" The king leaned back in his throne. "Very well, I won't pry. But like I said before, we could use your abilities. You are part human, after all, and were raised in our society. Therefore, I have a proposition for you. I'd like for you to become an official member of the royal guard. Together, with your powers, we will rid this world of the reptilians once and for all."

Marissa was now beginning to visibly shake.

"What? You don't like that plan?" The king planted a finger on his chin. "May I remind you what they're capable of? What they intend to do to us humans if we don't stop them?"

The worst part, the part that truly set her nerves ablaze, was that the king's words were true. The reptilians were trying to summon a goddess to destroy the humans. They weren't blameless in this war either. But from the day Ezrinth showed her the idol pieces, begging her to join his cause, she'd sworn she wouldn't take sides. And she still never would.

"I also must remind you of what it means if you accept my offer. You will be a hero; a respected member of human society regardless of your heritage. I will see to it that you receive your own lodgings within the kingdom, and plenty of coin to sustain a comfortable lifestyle. And most importantly, you'll no longer be the monster the humans believe you to be."

Marissa's lungs ached as she struggled to control her breathing. Part of her wanted to tear off her chains and throttle the king senseless. But another part of her, the abandoned, outcast, tortured part, was enticed. She tried to fight it, shoving the feelings into the deepest recesses of her mind. But they were still there. Tangible. Unavoidable.

"Oh, and I forgot one last thing." The king continued. "I'm aware of your little plot to sneak into the castle with the aid of my cousin's youngest son. It's a shame that he didn't have the change of heart I had hoped for."

Sweat stained Marissa's forehead, threatening to spill down her temples at any moment.

No...

Don't you dare bring him up...

"You obviously care for him. And it's clear that Arthur values you as well. I'm sure it would be much easier for you two to be together if you had a place in human society, wouldn't it?"

Marissa trembled with both disgust and anger, her paper-thin emotions threatening to spill from her eyes.

You monster. You vile, horrible, wretched monster.

"Should I take your silence as a no?" The king learned forward in his throne, propping a chin on his fist. "Or do you need time to think? To come to your senses?" He chuckled with morbid amusement. "Go on, ponder my request. But remember, I don't have all night."

It like the ground was sinking beneath her. Or maybe it was a warning that she was about to faint. Either way, she wavered with fear and sickness, anxiety and worry, every possible negative emotion tearing her fragile nerves apart. She knew that she would never, ever side with the king. But a tiny, hopeful flicker in her brain tempted her with the possibilities. Being accepted in the society that had branded her an outcast her entire life. Even more than just being accepted, being their *hero*.

And Arthur...

Her mind flipped back to the day she spent with him, tending to The Menagerie before the Castellas' party. The peace, the calm, the laughter and jokes. Arthur filling her head with all the reptile knowledge she could devour. Her sharing the less painful pieces of her life story. All she wanted was to return back to that day. For all of her days to be as peaceful as that one was.

But it would never happen. Because even if she accepted the king's offer, Arthur would never forgive her.

But most importantly, she could never forgive herself.

She knew what the consequences were of saying no. There was no refusal. There was no walking away from this. It was betray the reptilians, or be executed.

Marissa couldn't fathom dying. This wasn't how it was supposed to end.

But it was. And she had to swallow her fears and accept it. She would never align herself with the king.

There was no point in living if she couldn't live with herself.

Her lips could barely move, but she still managed to utter the word, harsh and full of hatred.

"No."

The king nodded, slightly disappointed but unsurprised.

"Very well." He extended his right hand and snapped his fingers. The female guard behind the throne took a step forward.

King Gabriel turned to face her. "Cassandra, do the honors, please."

No amount of deep breaths, no amount of calm thoughts, could quell the full-body trembles that consumed Marissa's slight frame. She watched the female guard step towards her, so slowly that Marissa could barely tell if she was moving. Marissa's vision was blurred with tears, but she refused to let them fall. She wouldn't let her last moments be spent crying.

Instead, she closed her eyes, hugging her chain-bound arms and legs together so that she was nearly curled up in a ball. She let her imagination take her back to The Menagerie. Back to the tanks full of curious snakes. Back to Arthur's cheery laugh as he dusted his collection of knickknacks behind the counter. Back to the only place where she ever felt like she belonged. The only place that felt like some semblance of home.

Back again to Arthur. His smile, the warm gaze behind his thin-framed glasses, how handsome he looked in his tailcoat jacket the day she first bumped into him. How much they'd bonded over the past several weeks, kindred spirits with a shared love of the reptilians.

Those brilliant forest-green eyes.

She would miss everything about him. All of it.

But what pained her most was how she always promised him, no matter what insane, dangerous plan she's concocted, that she'd always come out of it alive.

This time, she wouldn't. She'd made a promise she couldn't keep.

The guard was now just a few feet away from Marissa. She pulled out a small blunderbuss and began the painstaking process of loading it. Marissa shuddered at the sight of the musket ball, the black piece of metal that would soon be her end.

Arthur...

I'm so sorry...

I wish we had... more time...

Marissa couldn't stop shaking. Yet as she looked up, she realized that the guard – Cassandra - was too. The dark, circular abyss of the musket barrel hovered in unsteady circles before Marissa's eyes.

She wondered if the guard had performed an execution before.

She's just doing her job. Marissa sighed. *She doesn't know me, or what my life has been like, or what I'm trying to do. She's just as lost in this twisted world as I am.*

All that was left now was to wait for the inevitable.

"Close your eyes," Cassandra whispered. Marissa noticed that her voice sounded different than most.

She nodded, and did so. She certainly wasn't going to watch as the bullet penetrated her skull.

Seconds passed. Marissa's chest pounded so ferociously that she feared she may die of a heart attack instead.

Finally, the valley-shattering echo of a gunshot.

Marissa expected pain. Or maybe for her mind to blip out of existence entirely.

But with her eyes closed, she realized that she was still alive. And unhurt.

She was too afraid to open her eyes.

Until she heard a gasping sputter. One that wasn't her own.

She looked up, and immediately clamped a hand over her mouth, determined to muffle her screams. But she could hardly believe that what she was seeing in front of her was real.

Cassandra was no longer facing Marissa. She was facing the king.

The great Gabriel III, King of Brennan, mortal enemy of the reptilians, was slumped over in his crimson-stained throne. A gaping hole in his chest, roughly the size of a musket ball, poured profuse amounts of blood.

I... I... don't... understand...

Cassandra turned back toward Marissa, a fearful but joyous smile on her face. A face that was suddenly overrun with tears.

But why?

Marissa was so stunned that she couldn't move. Even as the guard crouched next to her, digging a key out of her uniform pocket and removing Marissa's shackles, she remained frozen in place. Only the guard's gentle fingers on her scaled chin broke her out of her shocked trance.

Cassandra's face was beaming, yet silent tears flowed like rain down her cheeks. It was a face that bared strong similarities to Marissa's own, from the pale skin to the upturned nose to her large, rounded eyes.

Eyes that were an incredibly bright shade of blue. Between Marissa and Cassandra were two identical pairs, as clear as a cloudless sky, locked intensely on one another.

"Who are you?" Marissa mouthed; her words barely audible.

She already had a suspicion of who the woman was. There could only be one human in the entire valley would be willing to do what she just did. No one else would assassinate a king just to save a monstrous hybrid's life.

"I..." The guard rubbed the side of Marissa's cheek with the back of her hand. "I..."

"You're my mother, aren't you?"

Cassandra gave an enthusiastic nod, more tears cascading from the corners of her eyes.

Marissa didn't know how to react. Whether she wanted to throw her arms around her, ask her a million questions, or take a step back just to absorb the reality of the situation.

My mother. What're the chances? I found her. I can't believe I found he-

The throne room door burst open, and they both nearly jumped out of their skin. Marissa's posture loosened upon realizing it was just Ramsey, but she immediately tensed up again when Ramsey's jaw gaped open.

The two women were silent and still as statues, not daring to move as Ramsey paced toward the king's throne, his face deep in shock and contemplation. Marissa knew from their encounter at the archives that his loyalty was beginning to crack, but she had no idea how he would react to the sovereign's brutal killing.

After a few moments, Ramsey's gaze snapped toward Marissa.

"I did it," Cassandra proclaimed, raising a protective arm in front of Marissa and gesturing toward the blunderbuss on her hip.

This only caused the confusion on Ramsey's face to deepen. His eyes flicked between the two women, his mouth still hanging open but devoid of words.

Eventually, Ramsey managed to collect himself and snap his slack-jawed mouth shut. But he still didn't say a word. Instead, he marched right up to the throne, stepping gingerly across the now sizable pool of blood, and plucked the idol piece from the mosaic-glass table.

Initially, Marissa's stomach sank, but to her surprise, Ramsey immediately walked up to her and pressed the piece of rock into her palm.

"If you go out the back door of the throne room, to your right will be a spiral staircase," he whispered in a low tone. "Go down the staircase, and at the bottom is a small hallway that leads to a back door. Go out the door and you'll be in the palace gardens. Security is scarce this time of night, so it's your best chance of escape. I'll distract the guards."

Now Marissa was the one that was slack-jawed, unable to formulate a response to Ramsey's surprising words.

"What? Stop staring at me like that," he growled, waving them both toward the back door of the throne room. "Now go!"

Ramsey was right; Marissa didn't have time to do anything other than sputter a quick "thank you" and run for it. She and Cassandra locked hands, pulling one another along as they bolted through the back door and scrambled down the hall, determined not to lose each other.

Marissa turned to her right. Sure enough, she could see the very top of a staircase at the end of the hall. But just as she went to run towards it, a sudden sputter of whispers in her head made her jolt.

But it wasn't a guard. These words weren't being spoken aloud.

As they got closer, she realized that they were the muttering of a very frustrated reptilian, uttered in between heaving pants of exhaustion.

<Curse this slow... serpent... body... I miss having legs...>

Marissa whipped around. A familiar black-and-yellow creature was frantically slithering down the hallway.

<Nim!> Marissa exclaimed, bolting toward her beloved pet and scooping his winding body up in her arms. She couldn't help but chuckle at his slow pace. Carpet pythons were arboreal creatures, with bodies built for climbing through dense foliage. Despite Sauria's best efforts, Nim's ground speed was at a snail's pace.

Marissa rubbed the top of Nim's head, smiling as she wound him around her neck like a scarf. She was about to ask how he managed to slip out of the archives and find her, but then she remembered Nim escaping his tank and appearing in the bushes the night of the Castellas' party. She figured it was difficult to contain a god, even one stuck in a mortal snake body.

<You're alive,> Sauria exhaled in relief, still out of breath from slithering down the hallway. <I was so worried about you. It took me a while to regain my strength

after summoning all those snakes...> Nim raised his head, his onyx eyes staring directly at Cassandra. *<Er... why is a royal guard member following us?>*

<I'll explain later.> Marissa grabbed Cassandra's hand as they both ran toward the staircase. <Right now, we need to get out of here.>

The spiral staircase was tight and narrow, causing Marissa to nearly trip over her own feet as she jogged down the corkscrew steps two at a time. They reached the bottom, and a small hallway led to a discreet side door. Out the small window above the handle, Marissa could see the starry night sky. And most importantly, there wasn't a single guard in sight.

Ramsey hadn't been deceiving them. This wasn't a trick.

Alright, just go down the hallway and out into the palace gardens.

This will be easy, she reassured herself, desperate to calm her racing mind.

Piece of cake.

Except it wasn't. Marissa and Cassandra only managed to take a few steps forward before the squeaking of boot soles on the marbled floors echoed behind them.

Marissa cringed as the guards began to shout. She'd never checked behind them, beyond the exposed staircase. Two guards had been stationed at the opposite end of the hall, and they were now bolting right towards them.

Marissa felt her arm lurch as Cassandra pulled her forward, desperate to reach the door before the guards reached them. But just a few feet from their escape, the door swung open.

Two more guards, stationed out in the gardens, had heard the commotion.

Now both exits were blocked.

The familiar stomach-dropping sensation of dread returned to Marissa's abdomen. The feeling of no escape. The feeling of impending doom.

Her temples throbbed as her mind scrambled to come up with a plan. Any plan.

<GET THE HELL AWAY FROM MY DAUGHTER!!>

The thought was a sudden roar in Marissa's mind, one so achingly strong that nearly caused her brain to bounce around her skull. It threw off her sense of concentration, but it also immediately filled her with relief.

She knew those thoughts.

Ezrinth came barreling down the hallway, weapons brandished and copper eyes flashing with the ferocity of a torrential storm. Two of the guards struggled to load their weapons, while the other two didn't even bother and scrambled away. If either gun fired, it would be a death sentence for Ezrinth. But he reached both guards and plunged blades through their ribcages long before they were even able to load their gunpowder.

Ezrinth knelt down, picked up both blunderbusses, and studied them with a mischievous cackle.

<I thought I'd find you here.> He smiled at Marissa. Except this time, his smile wasn't laced with venom like it normally was. It was a true, genuine, loving smile, and despite everything, it nearly made Marissa want to throw her arms around him.

<C'mon.> Ezrinth gestured towards the door. <Let's get out of he- >

Cassandra stepped out from behind the staircase, and Ezrinth's entire face dropped in an instant. Cassandra's did too, the pair staring at each other in absolute disbelief and awe. The type of expression only ever worn by people who used to be close, yet who hadn't seen each other in a long time. Years. Decades.

Yup. Marissa peered back at Cassandra. *She's definitely my mother.*

But Marissa had to pry their attention back to their current situation. Her parents were both lost in a trance, likely reliving a million old memories at once, but this was no time for a family reunion. They needed to flee before more guards arrived.

Before the rest of the palace realized what had happened.

Before they realized that the king had been murdered by his own guard.

Marissa pulled Cassandra forward, and Ezrinth quickly snapped out of his dazed stupor and followed. Just as the three of them exited out the back door, another guard appeared at the end of the hallway. Ezrinth hissed in disgust and slammed the door shut just as the guard began to shout.

"We don't have much time," Marissa turned to Cassandra. "We need to-"

<You need to fully face her when speaking to her.>

Marissa looked up at Ezrinth, confused.

<And speak clearly,> Ezrinth continued. He pointed at his own nonexistent ear openings. <She's deaf.>

<Oh.> Marissa peered back over at her mother, who smiled innocently. Not only did Marissa find it incredible that a deaf woman was a member of the royal guard, but her mind began to spiral with theories about how her parents had met. How they had communicated.

<Don't deaf people speak with their hands?> Marissa asked.

<Yes. It's called sign language,> Ezrinth replied curtly, his slitted eyes scanning for more guards. <But we don't have time for chatter. My companions should be arriving shortly with the cart.>

<Your companions?> Marissa's eyes narrowed, confused.

<Yes. I came here with the Varan and Gharian chieftains.>

<Wait, how?>

Marissa couldn't fathom how three massive reptilians had managed to slip into the kingdom, let alone make it to the palace, without getting bullets through their chests.

<We stole a shipping cart.>

A shipping cart?

It was like a glowstone snapped to life in Marissa's mind.

<I know how we're all getting out of here,> she announced.

It was a bewildering scene once Rathi, Caine, Arthur, and Thomas arrived. Thomas and Arthur were overjoyed upon realizing that Marissa was alive and uninjured, and significantly less overjoyed once they realized that they were now teaming up with three reptilians and an ex-royal guard member.

"Ezrinth saved my life." Marissa declared firmly. "And right now, if we all get into the shipping cart, they'll be saving *our* lives."

All of them, human and reptilian alike, piled into the back of the cart while Thomas took the reins. Daisy had been hitched up, with the old draft gelding previously pulling the cart now gallivanting around the palace gardens.

Marissa took a moment to study Arthur's face as they settled into the boxy wooden interior, before the door closed and consumed them all in darkness. His brows were furrowed in confusion, but his vibrant green eyes glistened with affection. Joy. Relief.

"I'm just happy you made it," Arthur whispered as the last of their party settled into the cart. As the door closed and moonlight vanished, she felt his hand brush against her hip, pulling her up against him. His lips grazed her ear. "I was so worried about you."

Marissa gave a faint chuckle. "I told you my plan would work."

"Well, not quite yet," Arthur sighed as the shipping cart lurched forward. Despite Daisy speeding up to a trot, the cart seemed to lag. With three humans and three reptilians inside, it was clearly over its weight limit.

Arthur cringed as the faint shouts of guards began to echo around them.

"We still need to get the hell out of this kingdom."

Chapter 29

*T*HE GROUP SAT IN THE BACK OF THE RAUCOUS shipping cart for what seemed like an eternity; their perception of time and space distorted by the darkness. Marissa focused on the clattering sound of Daisy's hooves as she alternated between a trot and a canter, moving far faster than what was safe for a cart so large.

But Marissa knew that Thomas had no choice. She couldn't see him, and with the cart fully enclosed, no one had any way of communicating with him. But she could tell by the frequent jerks and lurches of the cart that he was bolting down every side street possible, weaving in and out of the roads in a maze while trying to lose the guards.

Marissa could hear the guards too. Their horse's hooves alternated between being nearly out of earshot and so close that it made her nervous hands clammy with sweat.

She was just as restless as the cart was. Unable to stand in such a confined and unstable space, she crawled her way to the back of the cart and peered out of the gaps between the wooden boards.

Six guards, all on horseback, were galloping madly towards them. They wove between traffic in a manner that would have any other citizen arrested, and nearly ran over a few pedestrians trying to cross the street.

Good gods. She knew she'd heard a lot of hoofbeats, but she hadn't expected so many pursuers.

I mean... She gulped. *We did kill the king.*

She had to know how Thomas was doing. Ambling her way between a tangle of arms, legs, and tails, she tried to scramble towards the front of the cart.

That was, until a familiar hand clasped her wrist.

"Marissa," Arthur whispered sharply. "Relax. You can't keep scrambling around the cart. It's already unstable enough."

Marissa chewed her bottom lip. Arthur was right. She was already bracing herself every time Thomas rounded a corner, terrified that the rickety cart would topple onto its side and go flying across the cobblestone.

And they would all be trapped inside the cart. Which was already shaped suspiciously like a casket.

"Alright," Marissa muttered, settling back in next to Arthur. She focused on keeping her body still, even though her nerves were far from it. She hated having to stay put, unable to do anything other than wait. She hated feeling so helpless.

"It's okay," Arthur whispered in her ear. Marissa assumed he could feel how tense she was. "We're going to make it."

"How do you know that?"

"You know how you always promise me that you'll survive your crazy schemes?" Arthur asked. "And you ask me to trust you?"

"Um, yes."

"Well now, I'm asking you to trust me. Trust that we'll get through this alive."

In the darkness of the cart, he pulled Marissa's hips towards him until she was nearly in his lap. His firm arms enclosed her in warmth and comfort, and most importantly, kept her from scurrying off again.

"After all," Arthur continued, his lips inches from her ear. "We've made it this far. *You've* made it this far."

She sighed, pressing a palm against the wall as Thomas made another harrowing turn. There was nothing she could do. *Other than stay calm,* she pressed her head into Arthur's chest as he slid his arm across her back, her body enveloped by his. *As calm as possible.*

And considering how soothing Arthur's embrace was, maybe that wouldn't be too difficult.

THE THRONE ROOM WAS CHAOS.

A flurry of guards, apothecaries, and horrified members of the royal family scrambled in a mad swarm around the king. The guards scoured the crime scene, examining every corner of the room, while apothecaries desperately poured vial after vial down the king's languid throat.

Ramsey stood off to the side, unable to move, unable to think. But he knew their efforts was all futile. The king was dead. That had been fact since the moment the bullet penetrated his chest. And the culprits had escaped, much to the guard's fury and chagrin.

No one knew of Ramsey's betrayal. That he helped the half-reptilian girl and the guard member get away.

No one knew that Ramsey had handed over the idol piece.

He still couldn't figure out why the guard did it. The instant he walked in the room and saw the king in a pool of blood, he'd naturally assumed it was the half-reptilian girl. She was unchained, after all, and could've used the threat of her venom-filled fangs to obtain the guard's gun.

But just as those conclusions raced through his mind, right before he could assign blame, the guard took full responsibility. She even seemed to *protect* the half-reptilian girl.

Maybe the snake girl has other powers. Maybe she can mind-control people to do her bidding... Maybe...

No. Ramsey huffed to himself. *Stop it.*

He knew he needed to stop racing to conclusions. Always placing blame on the half-reptilian girl, always assuming she was the enemy. The villain. The source of all their troubles. When he'd found substantial evidence in the archives to prove that she wasn't.

Somehow, the guard knew her. They had some sort of connection, some sort of past together. Ramsey knew that the odds seemed ludicrous, but it was the only reasonable explanation. In addition, the guard still had the gun in her hand when Ramsey barged in, and other than the massive blood pool around the throne, there was no sign of a struggle.

He shook his head, pulling himself back to reality. There was still a sense of frantic, desperate madness swirling in those around him. After all, King Gabriel was the ruler of Brennan. His subjects were determined to save him, even though he was already long gone.

Ramsey had expected to feel shock, or grief, or some other mournful emotion. But instead, he felt nothing. The past several weeks, it had felt like his heart was being carved out from the inside, leaving nothing behind except an empty shell. A shell now unable to dredge up an ounce of sympathy for the dead king.

But his emotions weren't gone completely. It took a moment for Ramsey to realize what the nauseating feeling was, and it made his hollowed heart sink.

Relief.

He hated it. That emotion betrayed everything he was, everything he'd been brought up to be. Not mourning the king's death was betraying his own family.

But he felt it all the same. And deep in the back of his mind, beyond all the niceties and pretenses, was the truth. His entire life, even before he was chosen to be the future heir, he'd never been very fond of the king. He'd looked up to him, idolized him, but that was because society told him to. He was the ruler of their kingdom.

As a child, he remembered feeling both awe at his presence and boredom at his long, droning speeches. As he grew into a teenager and actually began listening in on those speeches, he thought that King Gabriel came off as smug and pompous. That intuition remained in adulthood, where Ramsey maintained the highest respect for the sovereign while ignoring his own underlying feelings of disgust.

Arthur was right. This wasn't him. Or at least, it wasn't him a few weeks ago, before King Gabriel dragged him into this nightmare. Now he was in too deep, drowning in a sea of bloodshed and regret.

Ramsey's eyes flicked over to the mosaic-glass end table. The table he'd plucked the idol piece from before handing it to the half-reptilian girl. Telling her to run while he distracted the guards.

Slowly, without disturbing the frantic swarm around him, Ramsey stepped out of the room.

Maybe it isn't too late.

He walked aimlessly, lost in thought about how to handle his hideously tangled situation, eventually ending up outside the palace grounds. He sat on a wooden bench in front of some rose bushes, observing the silent silhouettes of the Everwind factories underneath the midnight sky.

The factories.

The Castella's factory.

He stood up, curling his hands into fists with his fingernails digging into his palms. He knew he could never take back what he'd done. He knew he was far beyond forgiveness. He knew that his brother would hate him for the rest of his life.

He accepted those things. He didn't expect or want forgiveness, especially from his brother.

Nothing he could do would set things right.

But I can still do this, Ramsey thought as he dug through the gardening shed, pulling out a pack of matches and several bottles of kerosene. There were rows of lamps hanging from hooks in the far corner, but Ramsey left them behind. He didn't need them.

I can do this for their sake.

Ramsey still had the king's keyring, and thankfully the smallest key pried open the lock to the Castellas' factory. It was eerily dark and silent, with Ramsey barely able to make out the black silhouettes of forges and anvils. He crept around them, a blind rat in a maze, before arriving in the rear courtyard.

Sure enough, the building used to house the scale-mail armor was the same as it was before.

It was still made of wood.

Before beginning his task, Ramsey took a moment to stand before the hundreds of armor sets within the building. He knelt to the ground, whispering a prayer for them, hoping that the reptilian gods would hear his human thoughts.

I don't ask for forgiveness. I've committed horrible crimes against the reptilians, and I deserve every bit of hatred that I encounter for the rest of my life. But please let me do this for you. Let me at least put your souls to rest.

Ramsey took one last look at the hundreds of silent corpses, their beautiful scales just barely picking up the glow of the moonlight.

I just regret that I must do this here, and not in your homeland where you belong.

He opened the first kerosene bottle, spraying it all over the wooden floors.

Then the second.

Then the third.

As he lit the first match, he hoped it would be enough.

May you all forever rest in peace.

It took a while for the flames to spread, but as they crept up the walls and to the ceiling, soon the entire building was engulfed in an arch of fire. The heat permeated the air, leaving it parched and smelling of ash and burnt leather. The hides slowly melted under the intense temperatures, wilting off their stands and falling into the burning flames.

Ramsey stood just a few dozen feet outside the building. He knew he needed to leave. He needed to flee before someone caught him. But he didn't. He stood there until the building collapsed into a pile of burning planks, burying the cremated hides within.

He was determined to stay and watch, until the Castella's horrid achievement was nothing more than a pile of charred ash.

Besides, he reasoned. *King Gabriel is dead. He named me as his heir.*

Which means... I'm the king now.

The final few beams of the ceiling crumbled into the flames. Ramsey scrambled backwards to avoid the resulting shower of embers, a triumphant grin on his face.

And kings do what they please.

Once he was satisfied that the hides were burned, that there was no salvaging any of it, he left. He took off in the dark, chilly, humid night, only stopping once he got back to the palace. The Castella's factory was still visible from the gardens, way off in the distance on the Everwind border. Except now, looming behind it, was a massive, storm-colored pillar of smoke.

He entered the palace, and exited ten minutes later with the one thing he needed to bring with him.

The tablet. The one with the snake goddess and the half-reptilian girl.

With his artifact acquired, he snuck into the royal stables, swiped one of his favorite horses, and took off at a hard canter into the city streets. The tablet was tucked away, hidden in a saddlebag on the horse's flank.

He wouldn't stop until he found them.

Chapter 30

MARISSA'S HEART LEAPT WHEN SHE HEARD A familiar metallic groan.

They'd arrived at the southern gates. And they were opening. Letting them through.

She knew she needed to stay quiet, but she couldn't help but emit an excited yelp at the sound. Arthur squeezed her tighter, his relief melding into hers, their embrace a silent rejoice at their narrow victory. They'd escaped. Their treacherous, impossible mission was a success.

The clip-clopping horde of guards had hushed a while ago, but Marissa had still held her breath the entire journey through Alistar. She knew they could come popping back up at any moment, rounding some hidden corner and sending Thomas on a mad maze run to lose them again.

She knew that their escape wasn't truly a success until they reached the southern gates. Until they left the kingdom.

The hard clacking of hooves on cobblestone was replaced with soft thumps. The road beneath them had turned to sandy dirt.

Once they were well into the forest, with Brennan long behind them, the silent tension erupted into cheers. Hugs, human and reptilian alike, were shared throughout the entire group. Marissa embraced both of her parents, scales against flesh, tears gathering in the corners of her eyes.

They'd made it.

Now all that was left to do was find Nathara and Kai.

That task wasn't difficult. Their large, overburdened cart was quite noisy, and through the gaps Marissa could see the silhouette of a Naga and Testudo pop out of the forest.

The cart rolled out to a stop. Marissa practically leapt out of the cart, relieved to breathe in the vibrant, moonlit sky and stretched her cramped legs. She could still feel the final idol piece in her trouser pocket, pressed reassuringly against her scaled thigh.

She peered around. Their party had grown to eight members; three humans, four reptilians, and her - the one in-between.

And between them were all four idol pieces. Thomas still had the satchel with the first two slung over his shoulder. She had the third one in her pocket.

And Ezrinth...

...is currently being coiled by Nathara. Great.

<Alright, brother,> Nathara growled. <Hand it over.>

Ezrinth grimaced, struggling against his larger sister's serpentine body. Nathara wasn't coiled tightly enough to injure him, but she still had an iron grip. There would be no slipping away for the Naga who started their entire situation.

<l... l...> Ezrinth gritted his fangs, clearly struggling to breathe.

<Nathara,> Marissa scolded. <Loosen up a bit. Let him speak.>

Marissa's aunt gave an exasperated sigh, allowing just enough give in her coils for Ezrinth to free his chest and a single arm.

He extended that arm toward Marissa, uncurling his fist. Inside, surprisingly, was the idol piece.

<Take it.> His thoughts were strained but firm.

Marissa was so surprised that it took her a moment to react. As she plucked the idol piece from his palm, studying it clasped in her fingers, Nathara released her grip on her brother. Marissa and Nathara both stared at Ezrinth in shock, clearly not expecting him to simply hand over the idol piece. At least, not without a fight.

They continued to stare as Ezrinth picked himself up off the ground, shaking himself off and taking a few deep breaths. He noticed them gawking at him and scowled.

<l assume you're expecting an explanation?> he hissed.

Marissa and Nathara nodded.

<Alright,> Ezrinth stretched, still recovering from his sister's iron grip. <During our harrowing little journey in that cart, I had some time to think. And I've realized... summoning the goddess isn't really what I want. I don't really want to destroy the humans. All I ever really wanted was my family back. My mate. My daughter. And...> he smiled at Marissa, then at Cassandra. <Now I have them.>

Marissa's eyes grew wide. Nathara was completely dumbfounded, unable to sputter a response.

It does all make sense. Marissa thought. *The entire purpose of destroying the humans was always to get me and my mother back.*

Marissa peered over at Cassandra. She looked distressed and exhausted, her mind clearly still wrestling with the reality that she'd killed the king. But as Cassandra noticed her daughter's eyes on her, a wide, beaming grin still broke onto her face. A smile. Despite everything.

<I agree with Ezrinth.>

Everyone spun around to face Rathi. He stepped forward, his giant clawed feet leaving tracks in the soft sand. His hands were folded in front of him, and his long, narrow face was pointed at the ground.

<I was wrong,> the Varan continued, his pale amber eyes glossy with remorse. <Revenge truly is foolish. I could destroy every human in the valley, and it still wouldn't bring my daughter back. It would just make me as monstrous as those who killed her.>

A hot, bitter splash of anxiety trickled up Marissa's scales like acid. Just a few feet away, Thomas stood still, watching Marissa and the reptilians engage in a conversation he couldn't understand.

Thomas. Mikara's killer. Marissa's friend.

Anxiety morphed into guilt, until Marissa's whole face was on fire. But she remained silent.

<And you?> Nathara raised a scaled brow ridge at Caine.

The alligatorfolk lumbered towards them. Marissa was amazed at his massive size, as she'd never seen a Gharian before. The Naga and Varan were tall but slim, the Testudo wide and stocky but barely above human height. The Gharian had both height and bulk, with Caine's colossal figure dwarfing the rest of their reptilian companions.

Yet, for such a gigantic creature, his posture and facial expressions were just as solemn as Rathi's.

<I saw the destruction at the human village in the north,> Caine sighed. <When we attacked them. The fire, the screams, the blood... I don't want to go through that again. Not on such a massive scale.>

Everyone then turned toward Kai, but no one said a word. It was as if uttering a single thought would further deepen his grief. The forlorn Testudo had suffered more than any of them, yet he still forced a smile on his face. It was a pained, mournful expression, one of politeness without a shred of genuine happiness behind it. Guilt had Marissa's throat in a chokehold, and she struggled to keep her chest from shaking. She couldn't even look Kai in the eye.

Like the rest of them, he was silent. It was probably still too painful to speak. Marissa hadn't heard him utter a thought since they left Testudo territory.

But after a few minutes, he nodded. The smile had already faded from his face, and his eyes never left the ground. But he agreed with them.

<Well, it's great and all that you feel remorse,> Nathara sighed, a hint of disdain in her thoughts. <But it's not that easy. You three- > She pointed at Ezrinth, Caine, and Rathi. <-especially my brother, have created a gigantic mess of a situation. The whole valley knows about the idol now. Even if you don't summon the goddess, some other disgruntled reptilian will. What are we even supposed to do with those damn bits of rock?>

Nathara pointed a claw at Marissa, who sighed and took the other two idol pieces from Thomas. All four pieces, together for the first time in eight hundred years.

The fate of the entire valley. Everything they'd been fighting for. It all rested in her hands. Even though the pieces were small and light, Marissa's arms seemed to strain under their weight. The burden of it all was an invisible force, tied to these four pieces of stone, crushing her whole body until she couldn't breathe.

She hated it. It took a tremendous amount of willpower to not hurl the stones into the nearby stream. To throw this whole mess behind her and move on.

But it would never be that simple. The idol pieces were indestructible, meaning that they would always exist somewhere in the valley. They could bury the stones underground, toss them into the deepest part of the ocean, or lock them in the most secure tomb in all of Squamata. But eventually, whether it be in a week or a thousand years, the idol pieces would be found. And the whole war would be doomed to repeat itself, over and over again.

They had to be destroyed. It was the only way to end this.

And the truth was, they weren't completely indestructible.

There was still one being that could.

<We go to the top of Mount Krait and ask Vaipera to destroy them,> Marissa declared.

<Marissa,> Nathara gave an exasperated sigh. Marissa could see the frustration mounting on her aunt's face. <We've already discussed this. You can't- >

<Not us alone,> Marissa continued. <Look, I know persuading Vaipera to destroy them seems impossible. But the whole reason why she wants to be summoned is because she cares about the reptilians, right?>

Nathara nodded hesitantly.

<So maybe she'll listen. Not just to us, but to a much larger group of reptilians. Hundreds. We'll go back to Agkistra and gather the Naga – they're on our side. Rathi and Caine – I bet you can persuade Komodo and Crocodilia. If we have enough reptilians pleading our case, it'll make our argument much more powerful. It'll make it look like this is the true will of the reptilians – that we want to learn to live with the humans in peace. That genocide isn't the answer.>

Marissa and her reptilian companions were silent, but she noticed that their expressions had softened. As if her idea wasn't so absurd after all. Nathara still looked skeptical, but the flash of frustration in her eyes was gone; replaced by a hint of intrigue.

<Let's rest on it,> Ezrinth announced, breaking the contemplative silence. <It's well into the early hours of the morning, and we need sleep. I see a clearing past those trees.> He pointed off in the distance, beyond the main road. <We can set up camp.>

Marissa nodded. Ezrinth's suggestion seemed like the best course of action. Now that they were no longer in imminent danger, the adrenalin had dissipated from Marissa's body, leaving behind a sluggish fatigue that seemed to seep into her bones. She was so tired that even her head felt heavy atop her neck.

As the group stepped into the woods, crisp branches and leaves crunching underfoot, Arthur and Thomas caught up to Marissa.

"So... what happened?" They asked in unison.

Marissa let out a soft chuckle, "We're setting up camp. And while we do... I have a lot to explain to you two."

IT WAS AN ODD SIGHT; A MISFIT GROUP OF HUMANS and reptilians huddled around a campfire as the black sky hung heavy above them. Despite not having any bedrolls, Thomas almost immediately fell asleep, his distinctive snores eliciting a few chuckles from the group.

Marissa noticed that Ezrinth kept a sharp eye on him, gazing him up and down as if studying a research specimen. Another trickle of anxiety crept up her neck as she wondered if he recognized Thomas. He did look quite different than he did a few weeks ago. He'd lost weight, looking gaunter and paler than before, with his now-wiry body covered in dirt and scrapes. He was also no longer clean-shaven, with his bushy auburn mustache now accompanied by a rapidly growing beard. Yet he was the same man Ezrinth had bitten and almost killed back in Copperton. Back when it all started.

But she could tell that Ezrinth wasn't certain of who he was. Or at least, even if he did, he didn't say anything about it. He remained silent, his eyes burning as the campfire's reflection danced in his copper irises, until Cassandra took him by the hand and pulled him towards the woods.

Clearly they wanted to talk. Alone.

Marissa smiled. After eighteen years, she knew they had a lot of catching up to do.

And Ezrinth wasn't the only one being pulled away. Arthur placed a hand on Marissa's elbow as she stood on the edge of the campfire, just barely able to feel its warmth.

"Want to help me gather more firewood?" he asked.

Marissa eyed the heaping stack that Nathara had gathered earlier. They had plenty, but she knew that wasn't the real reason why Arthur wanted to slip away.

A beaming grin across Marissa's face gave Arthur his answer. He smiled back, offering her his hand. She took it, enjoying the feeling of her fingers laced through his. The feeling of how much larger his palm was, his fingers long and slender yet callused and covered in dirt. His grip was firm yet gentle at the same time, a reminder of both his heartfelt affection and his fierce protectiveness.

Marissa knew nothing of relationships or romance. But even with her inexperience, she knew how special Arthur was, a hidden gem amidst a sea of limestone buildings and judgmental humans. He was quick-witted and clever, full of passion and enthusiasm. He shared her interests, whether it be reading, caring for his snakes, or even just admiring the beauty of the swampland they called home. She enjoyed every minute of his company, and always craved more of it. More of him.

But what made Arthur truly exceptional was how steadfast his beliefs were. How he was willing to fight for them even when faced with tremendous obstacles, such as his family's constant disapproval. Whether it be his friends, the reptilians... or her.

They walked silently the forest, with Marissa's chilly fingers absorbing Arthur's warmth as she gazed up at the glittering stars that peeked through the forest canopy. The sky was now a less severe shade of midnight, hinting at the impending morning sunrise. Marissa nuzzled into Arthur's shoulder, enjoying the comforting warmth of his skin. In turn, he made Marissa's heart leap by wrapping a lean, muscled arm around her shoulder.

Eventually, amidst the tangle of tree trunks, palm fronds, and snagging vines, they came across a clearing. In the middle was a strange object, one definitely not of nature. As they crept closer, they realized it was an old wrought-iron bench, one covered in snaking vines. To their left was an old swing set, also consumed by foliage.

This place had clearly been abandoned for a long time, and was slowly being reclaimed by the forest.

The swing set was too rusted and vine-choked for use, so they settled into the bench. Marissa twitched as the vines brushed against her bare, scaled arms.

"What is this place?" she asked as Arthur sat down. He shrugged, once again slinging an arm over her shoulder.

"Who knows? It's probably some long-forgotten park, or maybe it was part of an abandoned village. We've been in this valley for eight hundred years, which is plenty of time for humans to ditch old, bygone places. I'd say it's been rotting away here for at least a few decades."

Marissa let out a soft sigh. It was almost amusing, how everything was destined to fade away with time. Fallen leaves crumbled into dust, waves eroded sand and rock, and all living beings eventually turned to bones. Everything had a beginning and an end.

Except for these stupid idol pieces. Marissa fished them out of her satchel, once again cupping them in her palms. She hated them. Yet she couldn't stop thinking about them.

"I know you're frustrated," Arthur sympathized, running his hand along her upper back. "But there's nothing we can do until morning. Can we just... forget about all this until then? Just be at peace, and focus on forest and the stars? And maybe... us?"

Arthur nuzzled closer, a pleading smile on his face. Marissa grinned back, immediately shoving the idol pieces back in her satchel. She pressed her lips on his in an instant, before he had time to react, stealing a kiss in the blink of an eye.

As she broke away, she took a moment to study his face. To really see him, from every little birthmark and scar on his skin to the faint chestnut-colored stubble prickling across his cheeks.

"You're scratchy," she rubbed the side of his face. It had felt like sandpaper when she kissed him.

"Oh, am I?" Arthur grinned deviously, grabbing Marissa's arms and pressing his cheeks against hers.

Marissa laughed, wild and joyous, her voice echoing through the black forest. Arthur was much stronger than she was, and he had her completely restrained. Which was somehow... thrilling. He continued to scrape his beard stubble across her cheek scales, eventually switching to planting kisses along her collarbone and neck.

She knew that the more she played along, the more she returned his affections... the more impossible it would be to stop. Her attraction to him had always lingered, a faint ember glowing in her heart. But now it was a raging fire, one that consumed her whole body, threatening to reduce her to ash if she didn't reciprocate his desire.

Thankfully, she didn't need to restrain herself. Arthur did for her, his face flushed red with a mixture of desire and guilt.

"We... should stop," Marissa uttered faintly, and Arthur burst out laughing.

"Agreed. There's not enough privacy out here. We can't have our companions hearing us. Mainly... you." The mischievous grin returned. "Besides, we do need to talk first, before we let our emotional fervor take over."

Marissa drew in closer, pressing a cheek against his chest. Arthur responded by wrapping his arms around her, engulfing her in a sea of affection and warmth. She felt safe. Protected.

"I'm so glad you made it out of the palace," his tone suddenly turned grim. "The truth is, I've been terrified every time we leap into a dangerous situation. I can't lose you. Because never, in a million years, will I find anyone in this valley as special as you."

Marissa smiled, a deep blush turning the skin above her scales crimson.

"But I know you have to do it," Arthur continued. "You're like me in that way. You fight for what you believe in. You fight for a better life not only for yourself, but for others. A better world. That's what I want too."

"I have to," Marissa replied. "Finding peace is the only way that I can truly belong in this valley. It's the only way I can live a normal life. It means everything to me, and it's worth the risk."

"And I will continue to fight alongside you the whole way. I'll do everything I can to keep you safe."

"*Both* of us safe," Marissa pointed a finger at his chest. "I can't lose you either."

"You won't," Arthur pressed a gentle kiss onto her forehead.

Marissa closed her eyes, nestling her head under Arthur's chin, studying the thumping rhythm of his heartbeat. It was like a metronome, warm and familiar, one that cleared her mind of all its distractions. It allowed her to set aside her fears and anxieties, tossing them in a box in the back of her mind. Those concerns were for tomorrow.

Tonight, all she wanted to think about was him. Because during their entire journey, with all the weary days spent trudging through the forest, she longed to be at home. The issue was, she didn't know where home was anymore. She'd been kicked out of the orphanage, forced to sleep on the streets, and now The Menagerie was gone. She'd always assumed that she had no home to return to.

But that night, she realized that home wasn't a place, but a feeling. It was the feeling she had when being around Arthur. It was a feeling of comfort, of security, of peace in an unsteady world. He was her rock, amidst the tumultuous storm. *He* was her home.

<It truly is,> Marissa smiled, the side of her dark lips pressed against Arthur's chest.

Off in the distance, another sight further filled her heart with warmth. Through a tense tangle of foliage, Marissa was able to see Ezrinth and Cassandra sitting on a fallen log a few dozen feet away. They communicated in sign language, with Cassandra's hand motions being fluid and rapid while Ezrinth struggled to keep up. Marissa assumed he hadn't used the language much after they separated. But Cassandra was eager to help him when he struggled, and as Ezrinth slowly regained his skills, their conversations grew longer and more animated.

Marissa couldn't understand what they were saying, but she didn't need to. The smiles on their faces told her enough.

Her parents, together after eighteen years apart, mending their long-lost relationship.

"It's a beautiful sight," Arthur remarked. Marissa realized he was also staring at her parents.

Marissa chuckled, "I agree. It's nice to see them together again."

Nim lifted his head, his flicking tongue grazing the side of Arthur's cheek. Arthur laughed and tapped the top of Nim's head with his finger.

<I like him,> Sauria remarked. Marissa's face flushed, embarrassed by her god-possessed-pet-snake being privy to her private conversation with Arthur.

<He's perfect for you. And don't take that comment lightly - I've seen thousands of couples in my existence, and none as well-matched as you two. The snake girl and the snake keeper. It's fate.>

She continued listening to Arthur's heartbeat, feeling his ribcage rise and fall with every breath. Together, they were the most beautiful, calming sounds she'd ever heard.

<I like him too. In fact... I think it's more than that. I think... I'm falling in love with him.>

Epilogue

EVERYONE WAS ASLEEP, NESTLED AROUND THE fire in a loose circle, using their arms as pillows in the absence of bedrolls. It was an uncomfortable way to rest; with cold dirt underneath their bodies and a chilly breeze crawling under their skin. Arthur kept tossing and turning, and Marissa was noticeably shivering. No one would sleep well tonight.

But for Kai, who had offered to stand watch the entire night, there would be no rest at all. Despite not needing a bed, being perfectly at home in his own shell, sleep still eluded him. After what had happened, he feared he'd never sleep again.

The past few days didn't seem real. Kai had slogged through them, his thoughts clouded and his judgment impaired, as if as if his mind had died alongside his family that day. At least, that was what it seemed like to him. He felt like a living corpse.

In his few moments of clarity, he'd asked himself the same unresolvable questions, over and over again. *How am I supposed to live now? How am I supposed to move on from this? What am I going to do?*

Sometimes, he'd turn to his usual tactic when he felt stressed - slipping away into daydreams. But even those were tainted now. He couldn't think about his mother's calming thoughts, his brothers' games when they were young, his grandmother's dozens of stories, without inevitably remembering what he'd lost.

He still couldn't process it. He'd just seen them a few days ago – how could they possibly be gone forever? Was he just supposed to press on, continue with his life, with everything he'd ever known just memories doomed to fade with time?

That was the part that scared him the most. Forgetting. Forgetting their thoughts, their facial expressions, their mannerisms and quips. Everything that made up his family. His village. His entire life.

Gone.

He'd been stuck in such a dark pit, in such a thick, hazy cloud of grief, that he hadn't allowed himself to feel anything. But now, in the stillness of night with only a crackling campfire for company, it bubbled up from deep within him like vomit.

Anger. Hatred. So much of it that it seeped into every nerve, making his bones burn with uncontrollable rage. He curled his club-like hands into fists, desperate to calm the tension threatening to boil over like a teapot. But all that did was remind him of his missing claws, those two bloody stumps, and he could feel the veins in his neck start to bulge.

The humans couldn't get away with this. Those atrocious guards shouldn't get to march into Terrapin, destroy his entire village, and go back home to their families without a care. They didn't get to return to their normal lives after they ruined his. They deserved to suffer, just as he and the rest of the Testudo had.

But what could he do? He was one reptilian, a single being in a valley occupied by tens of thousands. How would he avenge his family?

His eyes flicked over to Marissa, who was still shivering in her sleep.

Slung over her shoulder, tucked against her chest, was the satchel.

The idol pieces.

He wrung his hands, overwhelmed by the weight of the decision. Just a few days ago, he'd been a sworn pacifist, just like the rest of his family. He'd spent his days holed up in his cozy underground village, peacefully oblivious to the world above him. He'd religiously followed his mother and grandmother's teachings, accepting them as truth, protecting the sanctity of their ways with his whole self.

But those days were gone. That Kai was gone. He was now outside Testudo territory for the first time in his life. His family was dead. What his mother and grandmother believed in didn't matter anymore.

And Kai was starting to think that maybe – just maybe – they were wrong. That peace wasn't the solution.

Peace was what got his village destroyed.

Peace was what killed his family.

Peace, he growled as he crept toward Marissa, snatching the idol pieces out of her satchel. *Is impossible.*

His hands trembled as he cupped the idol pieces within them, as if the bits of rock gave off some other-worldly power. He couldn't help but break into a maniacal, satisfied grin. It was the first smile, the first bit of happiness, he'd felt since that day.

He would do this. He would destroy the kingdom. He would secure a safe future for all reptilians, free of the humans' ever-looming threat.

He would avenge his family.

As he slipped away, wandering south with the idol pieces tucked into his shell, he turned back and gave his former traveling party a final glance.

Especially Marissa. Who was still asleep, the now empty satchel still tucked against her.

He scowled.

What complete and utter fools you all are.

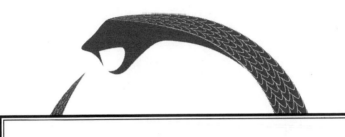

Marissa's journey will conclude
in Book Three of *The Valley of Scales Saga*,
Strength of Scales.
Available in 2025.

Acknowledgments

ADMITTEDLY I DIDN'T HAVE ACKNOWLEDG-ments in my first book, *Daughter of Serpents*. But a lot has changed since then. It's been a major roller coaster, from having surgery less than a week after the book launch, to stocking my book in stores, to hosting my first ever book event. I've met a lot of wonderful people, received some amazing reviews on my book, and found a community of fellow authors to exchange stories with. I learned that writing a book is only the beginning of an author's journey, and I have a lot of people to thank for their help with this series.

Since its publication in August 2023, I've managed to stock *Daughter of Serpents* in many bookstores in Central and South Florida. But the first place to ever accept copies of my book was my own hometown shop,

Spellbound Bookstore. Since then, I've made many return trips to drop off more copies, and my I had my first book signing event with them in February of 2024. Sarai and Stacy, thank you so much for the opportunities you've given me. I appreciate you both.

And of course, I need to thank my husband, Robert. He's always been my go-to beta reader, and as a fantasy novel enthusiast himself, he always gives me both wonderful praise and helpful constructive criticism. I love you very much.

Heart of Venom introduces a new character, Cassandra, who is hard of hearing. It is incredibly important to me that characters be portrayed as accurately as possible, so I owe a huge thank you to Candice for being my sensitivity reader (and fellow snake lover!). I really appreciate your help, and your review was so sweet and meaningful. I can't wait to send you a physical copy and have you see this!

And lastly, while it may be a bit odd to give a shoutout to my pet snakes, I'm going to do it anyways. Niv, Java, Mochi, Onyx, and Miso, you are my beautiful little reptilian inspirations. I love being known as the 'crazy snake lady', and your interactions with my friends and family have shown them that snakes are not the monsters the world believes them to be. I'm so glad you fill my home office as my serpentine muses.

About the Reptilians

Naga: The Naga are snakefolk native to Squamata. Long and slender, with serpent bodies and scaly arms, they can reach 18-20 feet long and stand up to 8 feet tall. The Naga draw inspiration from several semiaquatic snakes, including the venomous Florida cottonmouth (*Agkistrodon conanti*) and the similar-looking but non-venomous banded water snake (*Nerodia fasciata*). Their name comes from the mythical serpentine creatures depicted in Hinduism.

Varan: The Varan are lizardfolk native to Squamata. Wiry-bodied with thin faces, they have long teeth, a trail of dorsal spines, and are 12-14 feet long, and stand 6-7 feet tall. The varan draw inspiration from monitor lizards, specifically the Ackie monitor (*Varanus acanthurus*).

Their name comes from *varanus*, the genus containing monitor lizards.

Gharian: The Gharian are gatorfolk native to Squamata. Heavy-bodied with tough bullet-resistant skin, they are the largest of the reptilians, reaching up to 20-22 feet long and standing 9-10 feet tall. The Gharian draw inspiration from crocodilians, specifically the American alligator (*Alligator mississippiensis*), despite their name coming from gharials, another species of crocodilian.

Testudo: The Testudo are tortoisefolk native to Squamata. Sturdy creatures with heavy, almost impenetrable shells, they are the smallest of the reptilians, standing 5-6 feet tall. The Testudo draw inspiration from tortoises, specifically the gopher tortoise (*Gopherus polyphemus*), which, like the Testudo, are known for digging underground burrows. Their name comes from the Latin word for tortoise, which is also a genus of tortoises found in the Mediterranean.

Book Club Questions

1. Although Ezrinth is Marissa's father, she doesn't agree with his plans to destroy the humans. Have you ever had a family member or friend whose actions you didn't agree with? How would that affect your feelings towards them?

2. Arthur has trouble confronting his feelings for Marissa due to being disowned by his family. Have you ever had difficulty confessing feelings to someone? Were there obstacles that got in the way of your relationship with them?

3. Cassandra wants to join the royal guard, but faces difficulties due to being a woman and being hard of hearing. Have you ever had trouble accomplishing

your dreams because of something outside of your control?

4. Marissa frequently places herself in dangerous situations, and she tells Arthur it's because finding peace is the only way for her to live a normal life. Do you agree with this? If you were an outcast, how far would you be willing to go to find a place in society?

5. How did you feel about Cassandra killing the king to protect Marissa? Would you do the same in her situation? How do you think King Gabriel's death will affect the rest of the story?

6. Now that Cassandra and Ezrinth have reunited, do you think they will rekindle their relationship? How will 18 years apart, with everything that's happened since then, affect how they view each other?

7. Did the epilogue surprise you? Did you have suspicions that Kai may not agree with the others? How do you thinks the others will react when they discover what he did?

About the Author

ŞYDNEY WILDER IS A YOUNG ADULT FANTASY author whose inspiration comes from a lifetime of writing, gaming, and caring for reptiles. She has spent many years immersing herself in fantasy worlds through video games, Magic: The Gathering, and Dungeons & Dragons. Growing up in Florida, her love of reptiles, especially snakes, began at an early age. Her first pet reptile was a bearded dragon, and her collection has since grown to include five snakes. Her favorite reptile species are carpet pythons and tuataras. When not writing, she loves bike rides, playing board games with friends, and attending geek conventions. She currently works as a web developer in Central Florida, living with her loving husband and menagerie of pets, both scaled and furred.